ANYONE IS POSSIBLE

ANYONE IS POSSIBLE

Contemporary Short Fiction

edited by
Kate Gale
and Mark E. Cull

Red Hen Press

1997

Cover art by Marsha Effron Barron

Book design by Mark E. Cull

Our sincere thanks to the following readers for their contributions : Mona Houghton, Marlene Joyce Pearson and Helen Saltman.

First Edition, January 1997
Second Printing, July 1997

ISBN 1-888996-01-3
Library of Congress Catalog Card Number 96-72329

Red Hen Press
Valentine Publishing Group
P.O. Box 902582
Palmdale, California 93590-2582

ACKNOWLEDGMENTS

"Torch Street" by Frederick Barthelme. Copyright © 1996 by Frederick Barthelme. Reprinted by permission of the author.

"Flood Show" by Charles Baxter. First published in *The Atlantic*. Copyright © 1995 by Charles Baxter. Reprinted by permission of the author.

"Humpty Dumpty" by Kika Bomer. Copyright © 1996 by Kika Bomer.

"Sing a Song o' Sixpence" by Kika Bomer. Copyright © 1996 by Kika Bomer.

"The Further Adventures of Tom, Huck and Jim" by Greg Boyd. First published in *Artful Dodge*. Copyright © 1994 by Greg Boyd. Reprinted by permission of the author.

"The Bellydancer" by Stephen Dixon. Copyright © 1996 by Stephen Dixon.

"It's for You" by Leonard Gray. Copyright © 1996 by Leonard E. Gray.

"Waltz: The Secret Diary of an Underling at the Department of Water and Power" by Jordan Jones and Randall Forsyth. First published in *Fiction International*. Copyright © 1996 by Jordan Jones.

"Hens, Cows, Canoes" by Nancy Krusoe. Copyright © 1996 by Nancy Krusoe.

"Anyone is Possible" by Micah Perks. First published in *The Louisville Review*. Copyright © 1996 by Micah Perks. Reprinted by permission of the author.

"The Black Sun Rises" by Leslie Stahlhut. First published in *Bakunin*. Copyright © 1992 by Leslie Stahlhut. Reprinted by permission of the author.

"Family Fishing - Fairhaven Style" by Brad Wethern. Copyright © 1994 by Brad Wethern.

"Heroes" by Tina Wiatrak. Copyright © 1996 by Tina Wiatrak.

"Pocket" by Mark Wisniewski. First published in *Kansas Quarterly*. Copyright © 1990 by Mark Wisniewski. Reprinted by permission of the author.

Contents

Preface — *xi*

Stephen Dixon | *The Belly Dancer* — *1*

Helen Saltman | *The Palm* — *9*

Mark F. Cull | *The Red Notebook* — *20*

Doug Lawson | *The Particular Lechery of Jacob* — *29*

Rochelle Natt | *Elements* — *32*

Leslie Stahlhut | *The Black Sun Rises* — *34*

Jordan Jones & Randall Forsyth | *Waltz: The Secret Diary of an Underling at the Department of Water and Power* — *40*

Kika Bomer | *Sing a Song o' Sixpence* — *43*

Kika Bomer | *Humpty Dumpty* — *44*

Lance Olsen | *Cybermorphic Beat-Up Get-Down Subterranean Homesick Reality-Sandwich Blues* — *46*

Joe Malone	*Now, Now* — 50
Mark Blickley	*Dear Miss* — 57
Kate Gale	*Steve as Altar Boy* — 60
Marlene Joyce Pearson	*The Story of the Fish and the Man Who Took Her from the Sea* — 65
Cameron Fase	*Some Kind of Smorgasbord* — 71
Travis Hodgkins	*75 MPH* — 75
Robert Reid	*Thaddeus* — 87
Fernand Roqueplan	*The Monarch of Hatred* — 91
Greg Boyd	*The Further Adventures of Tom, Huck and Jim* — 106
Richard Grayson	*Moon Over Moldova* — 120
Leonard Gray	*It's for You* — 132
Nancy Krusoe	*Hens, Cows, Canoes* — 138
Gary D. Wilson	*Promises to Keep* — 144
Gary John Percesepe	*Chase* — 160

Charles Baxter | *Flood Show* — *169*

Nora Ruth Roberts | *Adagio in Black and White* — *180*

Mary Hazzard | *Playing Dead* — *183*

John Domini | *Minimum Bid* — *189*

Brad Wethern | *Family Fishing - Fairhaven Style* — *200*

Frederick Barthelme | *Torch Street* — *211*

Micah Perks | *Anyone Is Possible* — *217*

Mark Wisniewski | *Pocket* — *225*

Arin Hailey | *The Dead Fly on the Dashboard* — *237*

Tina Wiatrak | *Heroes* — *246*

Mona Houghton | *The Woman Who Lives in the Avocado Grove* — *252*

Contributors' Notes — *259*

Preface

The story of prehistoric man is mostly gathered from clues in the shape of a skull, a pelvis, the outline of a palm on rock. This collection, or the idea for it, seems at times murky and indefinable as well; indeed, several times during the collecting and editing, we asked each other who thought of this? and insisted, I know it wasn't me.

Perhaps it's better that way, not understanding why you began a project, but knowing that at some point, you are caught by it. Much of the history of human beings seems like a vague collection of stories sifted together, changing shape depending on who collects the stories, who writes them.

In pre-Columbian America, priests climbed the steps of temples, now buried deep in jungle, to observe the night sky. What they found there often led to war with a neighbor or perhaps an arranged marriage. Little remains of the literature from this period; however, if works such as the *Popol Vuh* are of any indication, the Maya loved a good tale.

Some hundreds of years later, Europeans put an end to this random nonsense of temple climbing. Enlightened thought was on its way, and on a certain day when the stars were just so, one man argued before some of the most learned men of Western civilization that the world was not flat as scholars had taught for centuries, that boats full of people would not simply pitch off the edge into a pit of monsters, that the world was round, curved like the body of a female.

Science ordered the universe for us, and it came; the world changed shape. It was round, the map took shape, the lines of the world were laid out in latitudes and longitudes. The inner workings of the human body became clearer to doctors who argued the benefits of leeches and hysterectomies. We have Shakespeare and Cervantes. We can see for ourselves that writers of the Renaissance obsessed over the same circumstance of life we do today. Relationships have not improved.

Now, the last century of the millennium, enlightened thought is on its way again. Women in the western world begin to take on their own power. We are told that all races on the planet are in some sense, "free," and racial equality seems a little closer to reality than ever before. Just now, so close to millennium, so close to understanding what it means to be fully human, to understand each story as a cry for freedom, for glory, for the reality of human existence, we find ourselves climbing the steps of temples all over the planet, hoping to find some pattern in the stars. We are as confused as ever.

We looked for stories that felt themselves cascading into the next century, and we found an increasing sense of edginess, of fragmentation. The world, the universe is tipping again, off balance, perhaps eternally off balance. This collection of stories ripples with desire, carried along the chasm of hard strung need, along the chasm of a fault line, which we as human beings are forever unable to bridge. These stories are edgy, alive, full of the questions that shake us as humans. Who will I be today? What will I do? Is the universe right side up or upside down?

On the ceiling of the Sistine Chapel, man reaches out to touch the fingers of God, that eternal gesture, that holy gesture for prayer, for understanding, touch me, God, tell me who I am, let me understand what it is to be fully human, and yet, fully God. Those fingers never touch God's hands. The fingers of God are forever out of reach. Would answers be better, or do unanswered questions make the best stories? We ask you.

ANYONE IS POSSIBLE

Stephen
Dixon

The Bellydancer

HE'S ON A SHIP four days out of Bremerhaven on its way to Quebec. He'd been in Europe for seven months, was supposed to have returned to New York in late August and it was now November, had delayed college a semester and didn't know if he'd ever go back to school. Had worked in Koln for three months, learned to speak German, had known lots of women, taken to wearing turtleneck jerseys and a beret after he saw a book cover with Thomas Mann in one, was a pre-med student, got interested in literature and painting and religious history on the trip and carried two to three books with him everywhere, always one in German or French, though he wasn't good in either, now wanted to be a novelist or playwright.

Meets an Austrian woman on the ship who's fifteen years older than he. She saw him on the deck softly reading Heine to himself and said she finds it strange seeing a grown man doing that with this poet, as he, Schiller and Goethe were the three she was forced to read that way in early school. Tall, long black hair, very blue eyes, very white skin, full figure, small waist, or seemed so because of her tight wide belt, embroidered headband, huge hoop earrings, clanky silver bracelets on both arms, peasant skirt that swept the floor, lots of dark lipstick. Her husband's an army officer in Montreal and she was returning from Vienna where she'd visited her family. "I'm not Austrian anymore, but full Canadian with all your North American rights, though always, I insist, Viennese, so please don't call me anything different." He commented on her bracelets and she said she was once a bellydancer, still bellydances at very expensive restaurants and weddings in Canada if her family's short of money that month: "For something like this I am still great in demand." They drank a little in the saloon that night, when he tried touching her fingers she said "Don't get so close; people will begin thinking and some can know my husband or his general." Later she took him to the ship's stern to show him silver dollars in the water. He knew what they were, a college girl had shown him them on the ship going over, but pretended he was seeing them for the first time so he could be alone with her there. "Fantastic, never saw anything like it, I can see why they're called that." She let him kiss her lightly, said, "That was friendly and sweet, you're a nice boy," then grabbed his face and kissed him hard and made growling sounds and pulled his hair back till he screamed and she said "Excuse me, I can get that way, my own very human failing of which I apologize." When he tried to go further, hand on her breast through her

1

sweater, she said, "Behave yourself like that nice boy I said; with someone your age I always must instruct," and he asked what she meant and she said "What I said; don't be childlike too in not understanding when you're nearly a man. Tonight let's us just shake hands, and perhaps that's for all nights and no more little kisses, but that's what we have to do to stay away from trouble."

They walk around the deck the next night, she takes his hand and says "I like you, you're a nice boy again, so if you're willing I want to show you a very special box in my cabin." "What's in it?" and she says "Mysteries, beauties, tantalizing priceless objects, nothing shabby or cheap, or perhaps these things only to me and to connoisseurs who know their worth. I don't open it to anyone but my husband whenever he's in a very dark mood and wants to be released, and to exceptionally special and generous friends, and then for them only rare times." "What time's that?" and she says "Maybe you'll see, and it could also be you won't. From now to then it's all up to you and what you do and say. But at the last moment, if it strikes me and even if it's from nothing you have done, I can keep it locked or only open it a peek, and then without your seeing anything but dark inside, snap it shut for good. Do you know what I'm saying now?" and he says "Sure, and I'll do what you say."

She shares the cabin with a Danish woman who's out gambling with the ship's officers, she says, and won't return till late if at all: "I think she's a hired slut." They sit on her bunk; she says "Turn around and shut your eyes closed and never open them till I command," and he does, thinking she's going to strip for him, for she gets up and he hears clothes rustling; then after saying several times "Keep, your eyes closed, they must keep closed or I won't open what I have for you," she sits beside him and says "All right, now!" and she's still dressed and holding a box in her lap. It looks old, is made of carved painted wood and shaped like a steamer trunk the size of a shoebox. She leans over and opens it with a miniature trunk key on a chain around her neck and it's filled with what seems like a lot of cheap costume jewelry. She searches inside and pulls out a yellow and blue translucent necklace that look like glass and sparkles when she holds it up. "This one King Farouk presented to me by hand after I danced for him. And I want you to know it was only for my dancing, not for my love. Bellydancers in the Middle East are different from those kind of girls, like the Danish slut in the bed I sleep beside. You know who Farouk is?" and he says "A great man, of course, maybe three hundred blubbery pounds of greatness," and she says "You're too sarcastic and I think confusing him with the Aga Khan. Farouk was cultured and loved the art of bellydancing, and it is an art, only an imbecile could say it isn't without knowing more, and he didn't sit on scales and weigh himself in jewels. That one I never danced for, since it perhaps wasn't anything he was interested in." "Farouk was a fat hideous monster who was also a self-serving pawn of the English till his people dumped him, though for something better I'm not sure," and she says "This shows you know nothing, a hundred-percent proof. He had rare paintings, loved music, and would pay my plane fare back and forth from Austria and reside me in the top Cairo hotel, just to have me dance one evening for him and his court. He said I was the best—to me, to my face, the very best and ancient men in

The Bellydancer

his court agreed with him, ones who had seen the art of bellydancing before I was born," and he says "Sure they agreed; how could they not?" and she says "What does that mean? More sarcasm?" and he says "No, I'm saying they were very old, so they knew." "I also danced for the great sheiks and leaders of Arabia and many of the smaller sheikdom there. That was when I lived in Alexandria and Greece and learned to perfect my dancing and received most of this," dropping the necklace into the box and sifting through the jewelry again. "It is all very beautiful and no doubt valuable; you should keep it with the purser," and she says "They all steal. Here, only you and I know I have it, so if it's stolen we know who did it." "Me? Never. But show me a step or two, if it's possible in this cramped space. I want to learn more about it," and she says "Maybe I will, but only if you prove you're not just an ignorant immature boy." "How do I prove it?" and she says "For one, by not asking me how." "That seems like something you picked up in your dancing; clever sayings that put something off," and she says "You're clever yourself at times and bordering on the handsome, a combination I could easily adore," and she kisses her middle finger and puts it to his lips. "This for now," she says and he moves his face nearer to hers, if she kissed him hard once she'll do it again, he thinks, and it seems he'll have to push the seduction a little and she's making him so goddamn hot, and puts an arm around her and she says "What gives now? Watch out, my funny man, and more for the jewels. They are precious, even the box is precious, and some can break," and pushes him off the bunk to the floor. "Haven't you heard? Good things come to those who wait, and even then they may not arrive," and he says "I've heard that, except the ending, but okay, I won't push—not your way at least," and she says "Now you talk in riddles. And come, get off the floor, you look like a dog," and he sits beside her and says "I meant pushing with the hands. Nor the other way, urging myself on you romantically, though it's certainly what I'd want, the romance—you wouldn't?" and she says "That kind of talk should only be between lovers and we aren't that yet and may never be. Time will tell, time will tell," and he says "You're right. If you're interested you'll tell me, agreed?" and she says "Now at this point I can see where Europe has sharpened and civilized you, as you told me yesterday, but only in spurts. You need to travel there more. And now that you're in a soft mood it means I can go past mere love and sex and friends' playfulness and tell your fortune. Would you like me for that?" and he says "I don't know if I could believe in it," and she says sulkily "Then I won't; without your faith, I'd only rummage over your palm," and he says "No, please, do, I'm very interested, and you're probably an expert at it." She closes the box— "I am. But you're a liar, though I like it"—takes his hand and traces it with her finger, tells him he'll marry early, have a good wife, fine children, then a second good wife, young and beautiful and wealthy as the first. "The first won't die but she will disappear and everyone will wonder why and even accuse you but no one will find out, and the mystery will never be solved. The law will permit you to remarry after two years to let the new wife help you with your babies." He'll do well in his profession. He has a romantic and artistic turn to his nature but also one that will make barrels of money, so much so he won't need his wives'. He'll be well educated, travel the world twice, marry a third time— "Did I mention that before?" and he says "No, just two," and she says "Perhaps because the first two are real marriages, the second one running off with someone like your brother—do you have one?" and he says "Yes, older," and she says "Then you have to watch out for him, but it could also be a best friend. And then, soon after, while you're broken down in sorrow—and this is why I must have said you only marry twice. You settle down with a young woman so young she is not even legal for you and you must live elsewhere and out of wedlock. I think it says here," jabbing the center of his palm, "she is first someone you teach like your student and then pretend to take in as an adopted daughter, and have two more children." "How many all together with the three women?" and she counts on his hand "Four . . . five . . . six, which is a lot for today," and he says "And their sex? . . . how are they divided up male and female?" and she says "It's difficult to distinguish those markings here. But soon after your final child, and while all never leave home from you, it says . . ." and suddenly she looks alarmed, drops his hand and says "No more, I don't want to go on," and he asks why and she says "Please don't ask," and he says "What, my lifeline?" and she says "I won't go into it further . . . please, it's much better you leave the cabin now, I'm sleepy," and he says "What, did it say something about making love to bellydancers? Is that what scared you?" and she says "Don't be an idiot. What I saw was very serious. I don't want you to know and no matter how often you ask I won't tell you. It would only tear at you, and what I saw can't be prevented, so it would be of no use for me to say," and he says "Is it about someone other than myself? For with two wives and a young lover and six kids and a good profession and art and wealth and lots of travel in my life and I hope some wisdom—is there any?" and she rubs the cuff of his hand and examines it and says "Yes, there's some of that here and another place," and he says "Then no matter how early I'm cut off—thirty, thirty-five—at least I've lived," and she says "Then do so without the knowledge I found here. I know from experience that this is what has to be. I shouldn't have played around with your fortune. I should never read it with people I know and like, for if I find something that's terrible I can't hide it with my face," and shoves him to the door. "Tomorrow, at breakfast, if I'm awake," and kisses his lips—"That's for putting up with me"—he tries kissing her some more and touching her breast and she slaps his hand away and opens the door and laughs: "See, I'm already feeling better," and with her head motions him to leave.

They take walks together around the ship, kiss on the deck if it's warm enough out there, play Chinese checkers in the saloon, in her cabin, which she takes him to see her wardrobe and jewelry box again, she says "You once said I was fat; well, see that I'm not," though he doesn't remember ever saying anything about it, and she stands straight and places his hands on her breasts through the blouse and says "Hard, yes, not fat; no part of me is except what all in my family were born with, my derriere," and when he tries unbuttoning her blouse she grabs his hand and bites it and laughs and says "You'd get much worse if you had gone farther without my noticing it," and he thinks "What's she going to do, bite me again, slap my face?" and says "Sorry," and takes her hand and kisses it and moves it to his crotch and she says "No, not now, and perhaps not later. I'm sure you'll want me to say it's hard like my chest, and I'm not saying—that day will never come for this, but only maybe." "When?" and she says "I'll write down your address in New York and if I go there I'm sure I'll see you. It's not that I don't want to myself sometimes. You're a nice boy. But then I'd have to tell my husband and I don't want to hurt him. You can understand that. But if I do feel a thrashing craving with you the next two days, then we'll do something at the most convenient place feasible, if there's one, okay?" and he thinks she's warming, up to him; he really feels there's a good chance she'll do it; she was earnest then and her kisses have become more frequent and passionate and longer, not just mashing her mouth into his and pulling his hair back till it hurts, but going "whew!" after, "that was nice, I was overcome," and she did let him touch her breasts, big full ones—soft; he doesn't know what she's talking about "hard." He'd like to just pounce on her on her bunk and try to force her, pull all her bottom clothes off quickly and start rubbing and kissing, but she'd scream bloody-murder and probably punch him and do serious biting and then order him out and avoid him the rest of the trip, though he doesn't think she'd report him. No, go slow, be a little puppy, that's the way she wants it done, at her own pace, and the last night probably—a goodbye gift, she might call it. And then she won't exchange addresses. She'll say something like "We did what overcame us but shouldn't have, but I won't apologize. If we meet again then we meet—it's all written before as to what happens—and perhaps we can continue then, but only perhaps."

At the captain's dinner the last night, everyone can sit where he wants and he sits beside her at her table and out of desperation whispers into her ear "Really, I'm, in love with you, deep down to the deepest part of me, it's not just sex but it's about that too. You look beautiful tonight, but you're always beautiful. Please let's make love later, the stars say so," and she says "Oh, do they? You are tapped into them today? I've had my influence; I feel good about that. Well, we'll see, my young friend, we'll see, because I too think you look handsome tonight," and he whispers "You mean there's hope? I'm only asking. I won't pout or anything, and I'll be totally understanding if you end up by saying no," and she takes his hand out from under the table, brings it to her mouth and kisses it and says "Yes, I would be encouraged," and someone at the table says "Oh my goodness," and she says "We are only special shipmate friends, nothing more to us."

There's a passenger variety show after dinner, drinks still compliments of the captain, and people say to her "Bellydance, please, bellydance for us," and she says "no" and they start chanting "Bellydance, bellydance, please, please," and she says "All right, but I'm out of practice; and the air temperature isn't right for it, so perhaps only for a short while," and goes below and returns in costume and makeup and bellydances to a record she also brought up. Her breasts are larger than he thought or remembers feeling that night, legs longer and slim, while he thought they'd be pudgy; she shows a slightly bloated belly though—it moves, he supposes, the way it's supposed to in such a dance and maybe it's supposed to be that shape, and her buttocks and hips wiggle in what he thinks would be the right ways too, but what does

5

he know? It all looks authentic, but sometimes it seems she's about to fall. Maybe she drank too much, but at dinner she said she'll only have one glass of wine, "don't let me have a second. Scold me if I even try to; on evenings like this where the sentiment runs so much, one can see oneself getting carried away." Maybe she has a bottle in her cabin. She's less attractive to him dancing. In fact she looks ridiculous, her face sort of stupid and at times grotesque, and too many of her steps are just plain clumsy, and her belly's ugly. She's no bellydancer, she's a fake. She's Austrian, that he can tell by her accent, and maybe married to a Canadian soldier, but that's all. If she bellydances in Canada, it's in cheap bars or at costume parties when everyone's loaded, or something like that. The passengers applaud her loudly, surround her after, want to inspect the jewelry she's wearing, feel the material of her clothes. "This anklet came from a very rich Lebanese I can't tell you how many years ago," she says. "King Farouk, who many people look down upon, and perhaps there's some truth to it, but he would have given me this brooch after I danced, he said, if I didn't already own an exact one. Who would have thought such valuable things could be mass produced." She looks at him through the crowd and smiles demurely and then closes her eyes and her smile widens and he thinks so, it's going to happen, whether he wants to or not. Good, he's going to take complete advantage of her after all these dry days and give it to her like she's never got in her life, and if she thinks he's too rough or just a flop, who cares? —Tomorrow they'll be so rushed and busy with packing and customs and getting off the ship, he doubts he'll ever see her. Anyway, it's been weeks and he suddenly can't wait, his last a bad-tempered whore in Hamburg who wouldn't even take her stockings and blouse off.

He'd put his name on the variety show list as "singer," and when his name's called he gets up on the little stage and says he's going to sing the "never-walk-alone song from *Carousel*, the only one I know the words to." The pianist, who's also a steward, doesn't know the music to it, so he says "I won't be at my best then, which is never that good, but I'll try to do a semi-decent job as an unaccompanied solo. Well, violins and cellos do it—think of Bach—so why not voices? But please, anybody wants to join in and even drown me out, do." A couple of people laugh. He thought he was a tenor but he can't get above certain notes. So he stops partway through and says "Excuse me, mind if I start again but as a baritone? I think this song was originally for a contralto—deep—so maybe it's better sung at that range. Anyway, my voice must have changed while I was in Europe—you didn't know I was so young," and the same two or three people laugh. The pianist says "Sure, if you feel you have to go on, but we do have a big lineup still to follow and it's getting kind of late," and he says "So, I actually won't. I'm making myself into a first-class ass. Better, if you can't sing, to be voiceless without Portholes, right?" and several people say "Huh?" and nobody laughs and he says "Sorry, but I'm not much of a comedian either," and steps down.

They walk on the deck after. He says "I was really stupid tonight, wasn't I, and you were so great," and she says "You were quite charming and hilarious; I laughed a great deal. But you liked my dancing? I looked at you once while I was in the middle of a difficult step and you didn't seem pleased. I broke a serious rule of mine tonight and danced for people who aren't special or paying me at expensive celebrations, except for you, my dear," and clutched his hand and nuzzled into his upper arm and he says "Thank you, and I can see what you mean about it being an art form." She's still in costume, they kiss and then kiss hard and she let's him keep his hand on her breast when he puts it there and he says "Tonight, right? We'll do something at least," and she says "Truly, and without exaggeration, I want to—what better time and setting, and the night's mild for once—but I don't think we should when too many people could be watching. You've a bunkmate, I have one, we should plan for it in a simple but sweet hotel room," and he says "Where, Quebec? Won't it be expensive and isn't your husband meeting you?" and she says "I'll pay, if you don't mind, and he'll only meet me at the train terminal in Montreal. But I'm to call him to say the ship got into Quebec, and for that I can be a half-day late."

They meet after customs, "To save on the expense," she says, "can we take a tram to the hotel?" They check in as husband and wife—It's not what I want to do, to fabricate," she says, "but it's the law," and they go to their room. He says "Would you get peeved very much if we do it right away—at least start? I've been wanting to with you all nine days," and she says "Let's have a big drink first—I'm nervous. I haven't done this from my husband for many years," and he says, "But drinks will jack up the expenses," and she says "Just wait," and opens her valise and brings out a bottle of Pernod. They drink, kiss, he feels her breasts, she touches his penis through the pants and then jerks her hand away. "It scares me, it feels so powerful and big," and he says "Nonsense, nonsense, I'm normal." She says "Now this is what we'll do, and I insist if we're to go through with it. First I wash up thoroughly and alone. Then you go into the bathroom and take a long shower and clean every part of you, inside and out; every hole there is below the neck, but many times. I want you smelling of so much soap that I would think I'm at a perfume counter in Paris," and he says "Okay, that's easy enough."

She goes into the bathroom—he hears water running, the toilet flushing several times—then she comes out in her clothes. He undressed while she was in there, is sitting naked on the bed and she says "What are you doing? Be a gentleman; put on your clothes," and turns around and he says "But I'm going right in there to shower," and she says "Do what I say," and he puts his pants on and says "Okay, you can look," and she says "Did you put everything on? Undershorts, slacks, shirt, socks, shoes? I want it to begin at the beginning and slowly, not just quick without preparations and for your contentment only," and he says "Oh God, this is something; funny, but all right," and takes the pants off and then dresses completely and she turns around and he says "There, see?" and goes into the bathroom, takes a long shower, washes his anus and penis several times, gets into every hole with a washrag and soap, rubs his ankles down with the washrag, shampoos, makes sure his ears are clean, even the tips of his nostrils are clean, all the cracks and folds and places he wouldn't normally take so much time at. He turns the shower off, dries and yells out "Okay, I'm finished. What should I do now, come out nude or just in my briefs or fully or semi-fully clothed? I'm so clean I think any used clothing I'd wear would soil me," and she doesn't say anything. "Bet she's left," he thinks, and says "I'm coming, out, Lisabeta, no clothes, so let me know," and opens the door and she and her things are gone. She left a note: "My darling. It would have been exciting but never have worked. Not only would I have had to tell my husband who I love, but he would have hurt me and I think come to kill you. I decided: all that for one short day's fun? Besides, I checked in my own ways, while you were under the shower, and everything said it was the wrong time. Maybe we will meet another day. I can't say that I hope so. I embrace you."

He thinks: "The hotel bill; she pay it?" He calls the front desk and says, "Did my wife pay the hotel bill? I just want to know so I don't have to bother about seeing to it later," and the clerk says "No, sir. In fact, I saw your wife leave with much luggage." "Yes, she had to go home early, I'm staying the night," and he doesn't know how he's going to get his bag and books out of the hotel without someone seeing him. He calls the desk again and says "What do we owe you?" and the clerk gives the price in American dollars and he figures it's about the same or even less than what his things are worth, and he goes downstairs, says to the clerk "Something just came up, I remembered, and I have to leave too. Can we get a break on the room because we only used it an hour or two?" and the clerk says "Sir, what are you saying?" and he pays, decides to take a train because he doesn't have enough money now for a plane and walks the two miles to the station.

Helen
Saltman

The Palm

The palm at the end of the mind,
Beyond the last thought, rises . . .
                                        —Wallace Stevens

1
Alpine and Bunker Hill

MY SISTER IRENE likes to read in bed, the bed I share with her and the candle is on the small table by the narrow bed. My father shouts upstairs, "Is the light out?" My sister yells, "Yes," and creates a light under the sheets to read by, of what I can't remember because I am too young. I admire her reading and lying to our father—I will never lie, be able to, to lie to my father.

The next day Irene washes the laundry on the big stove in the kitchen while Grandmother Reva watches—I move through the kitchen to the back porch which has been enclosed to make a bathroom. The toilet is high and I'm afraid to pull the chain after I get down, in the air, the box, the water will fall and Irene who is so tall and thin does it for me. She will tell me all the terrible things about our family, but not yet, not until I am thirteen.

When I am five, I go to kindergarten down Alpine Street to the school I don't remember because my mother is dying, that is why we are back again with my father's mother and father. They take me from school from paper and tambourine to climb the big steps at County General Hospital—the name I remember—up the elevator through the green pasty halls to the room where my mother lies. My mother holds my hand but does not kiss me, does not hold me. "Be a good girl Boo Boo"—she kisses my hand. My mother's mother, my Gramma Anna, tells me it is I who will take good care of my father now. Gramma Anna will forget me and call me Miriam, my mother's name. *Anna will never see my children, although I don't know that now.*

Because I have no mother I cannot go to school; when I return I cannot go to first grade, but must hit the tambourine harder and color pictures. When I return to Grandmother Reva's, I smooth a place in the dirt and press my back against the rough trunk of the Palm tree fingering the small, hollow seeds.

Dorado and Maria are in the back by the side of the house; their family comes to cook and make tortillas and I wander over to join them. "Pobrecita, mi pobrecita, conme, venga aca." But my sister Maisie stops me as I try to climb down from the low stone wall that separates the houses. I move to the hedge at the front of the house and climb through on the hard dirt to lie against a stem pulling a loquat from the pocket of my dress; I squeeze out the large smooth seeds and stuff the fruit in my mouth, the sweet juice, the tough skin and raspy, furry end. I pick up a gold ring I find on the ground and put it on my finger, but it won't stay and rolls on the dirt.

When I show it to my father, he is pleased. It is worth something and I must leave it with him. He puts it on the high dresser in grandmother's room. When he is gone, I return to the room to see my prize. I pull the chair over and pick up the ring from the flowers sewn on the cloth on the dresser. I put it on my finger.

I am hiding and my father is looking for the ring. My sister Irene sees me and goes into the house. I am sitting in the dark under the back porch which is our bathroom leaning my head against the cold metal pipe. I play with the palm seeds in my pocket. My sister Irene will tell my father where I am and he will beat me as he does her. But he comes and lifts me from my dark place and carries me into the house.

"Where is the ring you found?" he asks.

"I put it on my finger."

"Why did you take it? I told you what a smart girl you were to find it." My father is trying to coax me into telling, but I only say, "I am married." I know that I have done a bad thing, that food must be bought—but I am married and this is my ring. I don't get a beating. Not now, not ever. The beatings are only for skinny Irene. Not for my sister Maisie, soft and quiet, who has disappeared as if she were never here to lead me silently from Dorado and Maria's. *She will marry a rich man and have many children and divorce him and not see me. But first she will run away from home twice.*

My mother is dead and my father has no work and he beats my sister Irene but not me. Irene reads to me at night and tells me how mean our Grandmother is to her but never to me, never. *I will not remember this grandmother. I must look in a book to know her name.* She also beats my sister while petting me. *She will die soon and I will even forget what she looked like.*

My father has found some work in San Pedro and is happy. He jokes that we should stand by the toilet looking for green bottle flies to capture—for the prize—a cash prize—*the Examiner* will pay—green bottle flies, green. I stand by the toilet most of the day with a large mason jar and lid. My sister Irene laughs at me, even my grandmother who never smiles seems to smile now. I will get money for my father.

2

The Tailor Shop on Beaudry

My sister Irene combs my hair and takes my hand in hers. Under her arm is a bag with my sweater and dresses and a doll that I sleep with whose name has been lost with the past—we walk down the steps, Irene stops to pick a loquat; she offers it to me and I put in my dress pocket.

The Palm

We head down the hill past Alpine school to Temple street and the large hill with the big hospital. We walk to Gramma Anna's and Grampa Sam's Tailor shop. It smells of steam and sweat and cigars. Grampa Sam is a tall man who never kisses me because he always has a cigar in his mouth. Anna takes me behind the curtain to the back of the store where they live and sits me on the bed with the bag of clothes Irene has carried for me. "Good Bye Boo Boo. I'll see you soon," she says and walks out the back door to the alley. "Be a good girl."

I won't see my sister again until I am thirteen and she can tell me stories about her family and our family. She will run away and be punished. She will be raped by a truck driver and will have a long scar on her arm from the glass of the window when she jumps free of the truck on Interstate 90. She will limp and be put in a convent school for two years. I will never run away.

My Gramma hugs me and gives me sweet tea. I am sitting on a steel double bed, another just like it is next to me. Calendars with pretty girls cover the walls and cheap ceramic animals sit on the doilies on the table with a very large radio. A hot plate is on the sink in the corner and an ice box sits on a worn Persian rug that covers only part of the cement floor. Racks of clothes line the curtain, like a wall that separates this room with the tailor shop. *I will remember the framed pictures by Maxwell Parish forty years later when I write this and when I understand for the first time that Gramma Anna was ironic when she spoke of the great important family that my father was from: "the Feinbaums," she says, "very important, fine name, not everyone can have a name like them."*

All day long I sort buttons and thread for Grampa and turn out the pockets on the people's clothes. If I find money, I give it to my Grampa. My Gramma Anna worked in a cigarette factory in Poland when she was nine. She tells me, "You are lucky. Your mother was an angel that God wanted in heaven. Her cousin Sophie adored her and went to live near her in New York." This is my mother's legacy still. This is all I have of her except for what Irene will tell me. I play outside on the street by the gutter, my Grampa taps on the window with his scissors to call me in. I hear Gramma Anna crying at night and I shut out the sound with my fists.

The sun is shining and I can't go to school. Gramma asks me to help her. She has caught a rat in a trap in the tailor shop. But I know the trap was under my bed in the back of the shop where we sleep. She gives me a knife and tells me to kill it. "Not here," she says.

I pick up the knife and the trap with the rat who is moving and I look out the front window of the shop at the sunny street to find a place. I say "I *will* do it for *you*." I am a good girl and I carry it out into the sunlight across the street. I lean on the cement wall and cut off its head with the dull small knife. It is hard work and I am very hot and tired. I carry the dead rat back to the shop through the back door from the alley and place it on the table. I will never kill anything again. Of course, I can't keep this vow and once many years later I pour hot water on a spider and I do kill snails in the garden but not for anyone in particular.

3
Echo Park

I do not know why Gramma Anna cannot keep me, but I do not care. My father takes me to live with him in Echo Park where I feed the ducks, but we do not stay very long.

4
Hancock Park

He takes me to Aunt Rose who lives on the edge of the La Brea Tar Pits in an apartment house that looks like an ocean liner. Her children are successful. My father sends me to live with her, to cross the tarry field to Hancock Park School and make tug boats out of scrap wood. I watch the jack rabbits, their white fur spotted with the tar that oozes on the bottom of my brown shoes. If Aunt Rose finds out I have crossed the fields, she will tell my father and he will come for me.

I hide next door with Ralphie who cannot play; he will bleed, the father tells me. And I stare at the gray blanket covering him on the sofa, and I can't tell where it ends and his arms begin, and I don't see IT. It is hidden in the palms of his hands under the blanket. I tell him stories since I am too young to read. "Begin, begin," He begs me. I tell him of the children on the block who have never seen him. They all play cowboys and Indians. I am the Indian. Ralphie's father tells me to leave. It is too exciting for him. I cannot leave; I cannot leave him.

5
Aunt Tillie's on Kingsley Drive

He brings me to Aunt Tillie's, the mother of two young boys and a baby. Uncle Ray is Grampa Sam's son. My father pays them money to keep me, and I have a cot in the dining room of their one bedroom duplex which I share with large spiders. Big spiders. "Big spiders" I scream in the middle of the night climbing out of my bed into Tillie's and Ray's. Wet, always wet. They teach me to write with my right hand and feed me bacon sandwiches. I rock the baby and change his diaper and sleep with a light on *Until I Am Thirty* and have my picture taken on the piano stool—moon face. When I leave, Tillie says I refused to comb my hair.

6

Cochran across from Page's Military Academy

I am living two lives at once for I am also living in an upstairs apartment with my father and my sister Maisie. Maybe this happens before I am sent to Aunt Tillie's. We have a Christmas tree and presents. My sister Maisie is sixteen and runs away. She says to me, "Bye Boo Boo. Remember me." I walk to school down Olympic Boulevard past La Brea and come home to sit on the floor and eat raw onions.

I don't have a key and cannot get in. The woman on the corner reads me stories. I think I am seven. She sends me home when it is dark and I wait leaning against the outer door—for my father. When he doesn't come back, I go outside and pee in the bushes. The neighbors begin to scream at me. Their son who is seventeen takes me behind the garage and holds me close. I don't care if his hand is under my dress.

7

A Rooming House on South Rampart

It is Christmas again and my sister Maisie has called our father and I am to visit her at six o'clock one morning. I am to wait in the dining room of a big house for her to come down to get me. I think she is rich but it is just a boarding house with many girls who can't live with their fathers. I wait. I go up the stairs and open a blue door. A young woman sits up in bed and stares at me and I close it. I wait on the steps and hear the bells from the church chime ten. The door opens. She is ironing in her slip. Her roommates give me some cereal and milk. They have the radio on: ". . . in a small cafe, the park across the way, the children's wishing well . . ." We say goodbye. When I am twenty-five she will see me once more and then disappear.

8

The Convent in Eagle Rock

My father sends me to live with Uncle Paul and Aunt Sally and the twins and to go to convent school and listen to the nuns who tell me I have killed Christ and who make me walk and walk and walk until my feet are all blistered. And my cousin (I can't remember her name) tells me we will always be friends. My uncle plays the guitar, is very handsome and looks like John Payne. He laughs and has converted because he married his wife. I can't stay because I haven't converted, because I am nothing.

9
Pismo Beach

The road curves along Ocean Street and the houses sit at the highway. We have two rooms on top of the Coca Cola bottling plant. My favorite song is "The Lady in Red." My friend Renee is hit by a car when she tries to come across the street to play with me. She died. We liked the song and I used to play it for her on the record player. The lady next door teaches me to sew, and I put the needle through my hand when I sit down on the sofa because I forgot to put it away and it is my fault. I like to go out to feed the chickens. Mrs. Petters teaches me to wring their necks, pluck them shiny pink, and clean them for cooking. When it's Easter I hunt for eggs with the other children at the big house and wear white shoes and whirl a baton. *I have no inner life until I am thirty.*

10
The New House

My father has told me he will keep me forever with him.

11
Larkspur Lane

I will scrub the oak floors on my hands and knees and swear eternal devotion to my stepmother queen charming if she will be mine. I stare at the poplars and watch them change forms, change forms. I rake the leaves and burn them in the incinerator in the back of the garage by the sweet honeysuckle where I will sneak a cigarette when I am twenty. I will wash the clothes and clean the toilets and stop wetting the bed and make the beds and sweep the floors and make the dinner if she will be mine, be mine.

12
Whittier Boulevard by the Cemeteries

My sister "skinny" Irene is "here from the dead" with bruises intact, wraps my head in braids. She takes me to visit my mother's grave. "She looks like an angel in porcelain on stone." It is already summer evening and when we walk back to the bus station in the dim light, a man stops and speaks Spanish to her. I look at the pavement. When I ask her what he says, she tells me, "He thinks you look just like the Virgin Mary. It is a compliment."

She plies me with dark stories of family betrayal, of fathers and mothers, of uncles and husbands. I believe her because she is thin and pregnant and hates me. I tell her I am already an adult, I am thirteen, and her stories are for nothing. She coughs. I do not understand and tell her I am hungry. She buys me a hot dog and takes me home.

13

Lark Ellen Circle

A woman is murdered at the top of the circle; the gardener did it, and I go to look at the house where the gardener murdered the woman on Lark Ellen Circle. I see nothing. Past the house, the bean fields have been ploughed under and the radio blasts incessantly. Cars drive by honking their horns. I get back on my bike and ride home. At night I know I hear the Japanese planes overhead coming to bomb our house and I am sad the dog sleeps outside.

14

Canfield Avenue

Estelle, my dark friend with the curly hair, hides vegetables under my bed. As a result, my stepmother won't speak to her. We all laugh. Her twin brother and sister, three, by the chain link fence, expose themselves to the children. Estelle will be Mary Magdalene in the Christmas play, I will be the Virgin Mary. When we graduate, our faces are glued to stick bodies, pipe cleaners spotted white. We can't recognize ourselves. Sephardic, she had escaped to California and twin maple beds. The airplanes dropped me like a bomb through the screen to my room.

15

The Tennis Courts on La Cienega

Poor Uncle George ugly and trembling presses his left hand on my right breast. His first wife has died and his second makes him take off his shoes before he comes in the house. When he puts his salamander tongue deep in my mouth, I hide under the bed, then under the rug. Now I tremble while sitting at lunch counters. He will prosper in Real Estate and remarry. His daughter will win a scholarship to Stanford. I will stop wearing my brown sweater.

16
Beverly Hills

Cousin Madeleine's husband the minister won't look at me.

17
Preuss Road

Bobbie sits like a fish out of water in her heated bed, in her heated room, inhaling the summer through an aerosol bottle. Her stepfather chases her around the small room; she will not tell me if he has caught her. Sometimes she visits her father. She has contempt for his love. Her mother and grandmother keep a clean house, bake cakes and cookies, serve white divinity ten years old, accuse young children of stealing and larceny. They shop for Christmas all year.

18
Berkeley

Cousin Eddie mixes drinks in a huge beaker and birds die trying to fly through his living room. I have a martini at Vanessi's and wear a grey dress. I would stay with Cousin Eddie in Berkeley with his wife and six children, but he does not know who I am.

19
The Circle at Night

A cripple stands at the corner begging. I do not know her and offer three cents. She decides that is plenty and hobbles off. I shall dream of pink chickens and tweezers and knives and visit my mother the by light of the moon. Soon we shall be together.

20
La Paloma Court, Venice Beach

My Gramma Anna meets me at the Blue bus stop, takes me home to her musty house near the beach on La Paloma and cooks me lamb chops in a glass frying pan, like

Cinderella. She watches me in my bath and warns me "Never, down there, to let boys touch you." Can I tell her she is too late and it doesn't matter? She calls me Miriam, saves string, and takes off her jewelry for visitors. I want to tell her my name and reach for the truth of my mother, but she just says, "Your mother, an angel in heaven, should never have children"; and "America is a wonderful place," how much she "loves it," how her husband had "fallen off a ladder in New York," and how she had to put "two of her children in the orphan's home" and how "they still won't see or talk to her."

21
Ocean Park

We walk on the pier hand in hand. I throw a ball at a target and walk away. "Boo Boo," she says, "eat something instead, it ain't good, money to throw away." She buys me three big shrimp for nineteen cents and I eat them carefully, one by one as we watch the mechanical lady laughing, shaking her sides, on the entrance roof: "ha ha hahaha, ha ha hahaha," the mechanical voice on the fun house roof says. She looks like my Gramma with dyed red hair, and a straight round line from shoulder to knee. I laugh at Gramma shaking, and finish the hot, greasy shrimp.

"Let me in, Let me in," I beg her.

She gives me a quarter to see the funny shapes and get lost. I leave the two of them laughing outside as I go through the narrow door. The mirrors tell me my fortune in distortions. First, my feet, then my head; soon I can't find my way, all the images of me coming along through a dozen doorways that I cannot choose. My Gramma's voice, patience thin, calls me, "Miriam, You should *Now* come back."

22
God Bless America

Each morning I wake to the smell of cigars and weak coffee; each evening to lamb chops at six. At eight we salute Kate Smith, "adorably healthy," Gramma tells me, who sings patriotically to me, "God Bless America . . ." My Gramma adores her: "an angel just like your mother." Who will you like to be like? she sings to me. I think of myself, forty years later, as I fathom the moment, that I would be a murderer, kill my grandmother with a word. "No, that's not me, I shall tell her, that's not me."

23
The Art Lesson

I am sitting in the hot musty room, on the campus, charcoal held against a piece of paper, a line or perspective to make tangible on this paper. The teacher places a garland of flowers and ribbons on my head and I become a part of the room where twenty students carelessly place my life on paper. Carefree flowers, ribbons flowing, celebration, but I do not smile for them. The flowers are not my soul which I hide deeper than the scalp or bone. The palm at the edge of me, grows still, as still as I appear for you. An artist, without name or features captures the future: the lines on the forehead, a pull at the mouth, a window opening from the eye looking back. White pain, pressed with fine black lines, on thick white paper.

24
The Palm

I look for the palm at Pismo beach—thirty feet above the freeway on the house where we played "The Lady in Red." It tells me to stop to read the lines on its outstretched fingers. It happened there or here, it says to me mysteriously. It promises an offering of nasturtium blossoms the color of loquats, of sweet dates. Next time when I drive this way, I shall drive the car off the freeway and turn right to the two-story white washed building, park right in front; open the car door and feel my uneven feet on the gravel sidewalk.

I expect the door is red like the lines in the palm. It will open if I knock and a woman will smile and offer to tell me about lost wedding rings and bitter seeds. I shall say, "No thank you." In my mind the palm disappears—it leaves the air, the sign beneath it stays—it says "PALMISTRY," and I see that the cars travel both ways on 101, and that the birds fly through the pink condominiums whose windows mirror the sea.

If I enter, the room will be clean and square white with billowing curtains. She will motion me to a spare orange couch and tell me she'll be back in a moment. I see a sign above the window—"all offerings give or take by the door." When she returns, wiping her hands on a yellow towel, she tells me, "You've come for a reading?" I nod yes, my head says yes. She sits before me, eyes closed and reaches for both hands, palms open, memories peeled, one by one, like a deck of cards. Her voice, a dirge, melts into my brain. "Imagination uses memory," she says. I feel the pain of the needle as she touches my finger and the skin on my hands feel shiny pink and exposed. Dry pit and sweet burst of loquat, a garland of flowers for my hair, a thin line holding it together.

She places my palms together, and we stand. I hear my voice ask, "The sign on

The Palm

the freeway? The palm?" "It's been here as long as I can remember," she tells me. I stop by the door, look into the box and leave a bill; she is watching me and I turn to look at her, her hair in braids wrapped around her young face, flowered blouse billowing like the curtains. I see her dark legs below her shorts and the sandals on her feet. She stares at me as I take a small coin from the offering and go out the door. "Hello, Elizabeth," she says to me.

| Mark E. Cull | *The Red Notebook* |

OLD ORCHARD ROAD runs parallel to Main Street, beginning just behind the closed dairy, breaking for the drainage wash and then running the rest of the way to the other side of the freight yard just east of town.

It is the first week of kindergarten. José and Molly follow Cherry Avenue until it meets Old Orchard. This is the section of the road which passes just behind their school. They are only a block away from their normal path and José tells Molly that they will probably not be late. Nobody will know where they had been anyway.

It is with an odd sort of pride that José carefully steps through the charred remains of his grandfather's home. The fire had been the town's big event of the summer. All the volunteers were called in, but the house had long since burned to the ground by the time they arrived. The better half of the town watched as the house blazed away for nearly an hour. It was later discovered that the old man never made it out of bed. José lowers his voice while retelling this particular fact. Molly covers her eyes and begs him to stop. She does not want to hear another word. Molly has already heard far too many of the horrible details from her older sister. José begins to describe how his grandfather's body had been found. It is at this that Molly begins to scream wildly, and then runs toward the street with still covered eyes. In the distance a dilapidated rust-red pickup truck backfires as it lurches down Old Orchard. José dashes after Molly, grabbing her dress sleeve as she steps onto the cracked sidewalk.

"Stop or we'll get in trouble," he says pulling her to a stop.

"What trouble?" she asks uncovering her eyes. "You're saying stuff I don't want to hear."

"You'll get runned over and we'll be late to school. That's what trouble," José eyes the old truck as it slowly rolls by. Molly stares after its large black tires and then gives José a shove.

"You're stupid to go in the street José, my sister told me to only walk on the yellow line when cars *stop*."

"You're stupid, you're gonna get runned over," José points after the truck thinking how he should just hit her in the arm. He decides not to since she is a girl, and his father might find out. Instead, he grabs her by the hair and pulls her off the sidewalk. Molly shoves him again.

"You're stupid to always play in the street. *You're* gonna be runned over. You're the trouble," she says, stepping back onto the sidewalk. Molly starts to walk toward school. José jumps over a crack in the sidewalk and lands on the narrow curbing next to the street.

"My brothers and I never get hit. Watch!" he shouts.

Molly looks back to see José performing a high wire act along the curb's edge. Turning back around she sees another car driving onto Old Orchard from Cherry Avenue.

"Car!" she shouts and looks back again to see José immediately dropping his outstretched arms and stepping back onto the sidewalk.

The advancing car seems to be moving far too quickly for such a narrow street. It is the sort of white convertible her sister calls a "sports" car. Molly looks into the car to see if its driver is someone she knows. Seemingly there is nobody behind the steering wheel as the car veers sharply from the center of the road toward the sidewalk just ahead of her. Before hitting the curbing, a woman's head appears from the passenger side. The car immediately rights itself. Molly recognizes their kindergarten teacher, Miss Conejo.

The woman smiles and waves to Molly as her car rushes along the street. At this, Molly smiles to herself and skips cheerfully for a few paces. She is shocked by the screech of braking tires and spins about in time to see Miss Conejo's car swerve directly into the sidewalk and do a perfect somersault into the middle of the burned out lot a short distance behind. The upside down wheels of the little white car spin madly for a moment as the engine roars. After a few moments, the engine fails and the rear tires jerk to a halt while the wheels in front continue to spin without change. From the middle of the street, José stares with his mouth wide open

"Now we *are* in trouble!" Molly cries as José cautiously steps back onto the curbing. Staring at the still spinning wheels, she feels incapable of deciding between running the rest of the way to school before getting into still more trouble or staying to take a closer at Miss Conejo's upturned car.

Molly and José stare in awe at the spinning wheels for nearly a minute. After the wheels slow and then finally come to a stop, José finds he is able to look around. The street is empty. Running to the upside down car, he attempts to open Miss Conejo's door. His brothers had told him that this was the sort of thing a gentlemen does. José tilts his head sharply to one side in hopes that the proper perspective might be helpful. The door is obviously stuck.

As José makes a variety of unsuccessful attempts to open Miss Conejo's door, Molly slowly paces around the car in a wide arc being careful to not get any closer than she already is. Stepping around the remains of a yellowed shattered commode, Molly's eyes are drawn to a bit of dark red coming out from under the car's passenger side door. Stepping closer, Molly recognizes the red notebook their teacher took attendance in the day before. Kneeling on the blackened ground, she tries to pull the half-exposed notebook from under the car. It is clamped tightly between the white car door and a black pile of loose ash, refusing to move when pulled by the young girl. Molly wriggles the notebook from side to side for a few moments and then manages to pull it free.

Wrapping her small arms tightly around the now charcoal black and red notebook, Molly springs away from the car and runs as quickly as she can toward school. Nearing Cherry Avenue, she can hear the sound of José's feet close behind.

Unlike the well known one room schoolhouse, the town's only school is relatively modern in design, and has enough students that from kindergarten through twelfth, every grade has its own classroom. Like many of the larger schools, the kindergartners are separated from the rest of the children. The small ones' classroom and playground are isolated from the rest of the school by a chain link fence. They have their own street entrance in addition to an interior gate that opens near the main office. The town is small enough that is has not learned the sort of cynicism that closes windows at night or puts locks on gates.

Just as many young children run through the kindergarten's open street side gate as walk. A few of these runners have oddly imbalanced systems fueled by artificially sweetened meals. Some dash about so wildly that when Molly and José arrive breathless nearly five minutes before the school bell rings, they are barely noticed.

Once inside the gate, Molly skips over to the playhouse, next to the large sandbox, where her friends meet before the morning bell rings. José runs directly for the jungle gym.

When the bell rings, the children quickly form a line beginning just outside of the yellow arc painted on the ground near the classroom door. Since he and Molly walk together, José stood just behind Molly and her friends for the first few days of school. This morning he stands closer to the back of the line with the children who shove into each other laughing.

After a few minutes pass and Miss Conejo fails to appear from the classroom, even the children near the head of the line begin pushing each other. Molly looks for José and then dashes toward the back of the line once she sees him.

"Open the door," she whispers into his ear. José's eyes become wide as he shakes his head *No*. When his head finally stops shaking, Molly pushes him hard enough to make him trip as he steps backward. While the other children laugh at this, Molly runs past the head of the line and pulls the classroom door open. Molly disappears into the dark room, and in a few moments lights flicker on.

The kindergartners file into class, seating themselves at their tables in groups of four as they had been taught the first day of school. Not all of the lights in the classroom had been turned on. At the front of the class, the bank of bulbs near the large green chalkboard are still unlit. A bulb near the door flickers without rhythm, unable to turn completely on. The children sitting at the table under it laugh as they try to blink their eyes in time with its flickering. The children with tables nearest the chalkboard begin to wonder where the teacher is. Someone close to the coat room shouts that it must be Saturday.

Within minutes the children seated beneath the flickering bulb begin to dance on top of their table. The shouting child near the coat room swings from the flag pole mounted on the wall. Those nearest the chalkboard begin to cry. A few of the seated children remain relatively quiet as they gape at the classroom sights.

Though they do not sit at the same table, Molly and José's seats are quite close to one another since they are at adjoining tables.

"Don't say nothing," Molly tells José as she gets out of her seat. Taking a mat from one of the storage boxes under the window, she unfolds it in the area where the students normally take their afternoon nap, and lies down. With both arms wrapped around the red notebook, Molly closes her eyes and instantly begins to make quiet little snoring sounds. José unfolds a mat next to Molly and closes his eyes also. Soon the rest of the children are pulling out mats.

It is difficult to say how much time passes between the closing of the last pair of eyes and when Molly quietly sits up to examine the sleeping classroom. Walking quietly to Miss Conejo's desk, she sits down and opens the red notebook. She studies its pages intently, though she cannot read. After examining the notebook for nearly a minute, Molly closes it and removes a dictionary from the shelf next to the desk. This she sets on top of the closed notebook.

Leaving the teacher's desk, Molly walks around the classroom looking at each of the tables and then to the empty mat lying next to José. She folds up the mat, returns it to its storage box and then pushes open the classroom's playground door. Smiling to the sunlight, Molly skips away into the warm playground.

Some minutes pass and the classroom door opens. Molly pulls it as hard as she can, and before it closes all of the way, she pushes a flat of strawberries through the doorway. The closing door bumps into Molly from behind, pushing her back into the classroom. Once inside she picks up the flat, which is almost too large for her to carry, and walks the strawberries to the front of the classroom. Molly sets them on the floor just below the chalkboard.

Returning to the teacher's desk, Molly opens the dictionary and studies the small print inside. Flipping through several pages, she is unable to find any illustrations that might help her determine what story she has open before her. Closing the book, Molly examines its blank cloth cover and then notices a small embossed bird on the book's spine. As though this were enough, she reopens the volume. While moving her small fingers up and down the pages, she proceeds to recite out loud Andersen's "The A-B-C Book" word for word from memory. At home, next to her bed, Molly has a small illustrated volume of such stories she sleeps with. As she recites this tale, the other children wake, put away the mats and return to their tables. There is snickering from somewhere near the coat room as Molly recites the last line.

"Quiet!" Molly shouts, looking around the classroom attempting to locate the heckler. When her eyes come to José, she smiles and points to the strawberries on the floor.

"Excuse me, but who died and made you teacher?" asks a voice near the coat room. Molly guesses this to be the heckler.

"Nobody, that's whose dying!" José shouts, jumping out of his chair.

"Let's have more story time!" says a child from José's table.

"First everybody gets a snack," Molly announces, walking toward the flat of strawberries. The children rush to the front of the room and quickly grab up the strawberries. A few try filling their pockets. Many of the smaller students return to their tables weeping and empty-handed. One child with two berries, shares with one of the empty-handed children.

Molly climbs onto the top of the teacher's desk and stamps her feet until everyone is looking at her. "Miss Conejo isn't here 'cause she crashed up her car."

José is suddenly wide eyed. "She's just late! Her car didn't get smashed up!" he screams jumping out of his seat again.

"She's not late. She got *killed* maybe," Molly adds, waving her arms in the air. José runs up to Molly and pulls her off the desk.

"You're gonna get me in trouble," José says, shaking her with tears in his eyes. "We wasn't supposed to go over there!" Molly knows that José is afraid of his father.

"Sit down or you'll have trouble for reals," Molly says pushing him back toward his table. The class has fallen silent and waits for José to sit down.

"Me and José was walking to school and Miss Conejo was driving very, very slow and she got crashed into by a another car. She was on the cherry street by the big church by our house and a sunlight from the church's big window made her not see the other car. She got smashed over and went upside down and . . . and she got squished with *blood*."

"It was by our house!" José shouts from his seat.

"She gave me her teacher book," Molly says, holding the red notebook over her head, "and told me I'm supposed to make sure everybody's in school. Don't tell nobody Miss Conejo gave me this, or she'll get some troubles. We'll all get big trouble."

"You said she might be dead," says the voice from the coat room vicinity.

"She did got killed," Molly says, nodding her head.

The children nearest the chalkboard begin discussing how they already miss the teacher and wonder how they will continue school without her.

"We can all take turns being teacher!" yells a child, jumping up and down under the flag.

As the level of noise from discussion increases, the children beneath the flickering bulb climb back onto the table and resume their dance. Seeing this, the child jumping about under the flag runs to the light switches and pushes up the last one. The bulb near the door stops flickering as the final bank of bulbs at the front of the room light up.

As the dancers return to their seats, the school bell rings. Some of the children begin to shout that it must be time for recess.

"We had a big nap time today," Molly announces, standing in front of the big green chalkboard, "so that's the bell that says it's time to go home."

This announcement is met with a loud hurrah and rush for the door. Within minutes the kindergarten yard empties as the children run and skip through the street side gate.

In the kindergarten's playground there are two sandboxes. The smaller of the two is situated in the playground's far corner next to the chain link fence separating the kindergartners from the rest of the school. The large sandbox is perhaps twice its size and is located between the playhouse and jungle gym. This sandbox attracts many of the small children, while it is the smaller sandbox where the quiet children usually spend their recesses. Today, the day after Miss Conejo's accident, there are only two children in the small sandbox during recess; Craig and his brother Jeffery.

Close to the small sandbox, in the main school yard, are the big kid's swings. The older children's morning break coincides with the kindergartners' only recess of their brief school day. Often, the children on the swings will make fun of the kindergartners closest to the fence, calling them such things as cry babies or monkeys in a zoo. Craig and Jeffery rarely get upset by such name calling. They continue to play, not allowing the older children's taunts to interfere with the construction of their most recent city. This morning however, Nick, a child they know from their neighborhood, calls the two boys over to the fence.

"Hey Jeffy, my brother says you guys got no teacher in there," Nick says poking a stick through the fence into the sand.

"Stop it, you're messing up our road!" Craig shouts, grabbing the stick out of the boy's hand.

"I ain't mess'n up nothin'!" he says, standing up. "So you monkeys got nobody to clean yer cage, huh?"

"Miss Conejo got killed by a car crash," Jeffery says as Craig pushes the stick back through to Nick's side of the fence, "so we get to be our own teachers now."

"You kids are full of it," Nick says crossing his arms. "I saw Miss Conejo talkin' to Mr. Reynolds this morning."

Rather than respond to this last remark, the brothers return to their construction site in the sand. Craig imitates a combustion engine as he pushes a rusted yellow tractor through a pit that should soon be breaking through to China.

"You're stupid liars!" Nick says, throwing the stick at the fence. He stares at the boys for a moment and then runs off toward the other side of the playground.

Jeffery watches Nick dash away and then disappear into a crowd of children. Once he is out of sight, Jeffery borrows Craig's tractor to repair the damaged road bordering the fence.

The two boys become so involved with their system of roads and fancy gates that they do not hear the bell ring. They continue to play while all of the other children return to class.

In the school's main playground, a few of the more troublesome children often continue to play until they are certain that it is even time for the pioneers, as they like to call themselves, to return to class. Today, the last of these *pioneers* are a couple of older boys on the swings. They do not sit quietly in an attempt to avoid being noticed, but swing wildly in high arcs that almost make them do mid-air flips. Finally, as the classroom doors begin to close, they leap from their swings and approach the fence next to the small sandbox. At first neither of these two boys say a word as they study the handiwork of the two young brothers. Nearly a minute passes when the older of the two clears his throat in order to get Craig and Jeffery's attention.

"Nice castle guys, but you better get inside before your teacher catches you out here."

Jeffery looks up from the sand and stares at the empty playground. Craig continues to make little rumbling noises as he pushes up more sand out of the growing pit.

"We won't get into trouble. Molly's teacher today," Jeffery says turning his smiling face toward the two older boys.

"Oh yeah, somebody said you kids are alone in there," the older boy says. Jeffery stands up to speak with the older boys.

"Who's Molly?" the older boy's companion asks.

"Molly sat at the white table," Craig says without looking up, "but she's in charge of us today."

The older boy motions Jeffery to come closer. Looking secretively from side to side he tilts his head forward as though to whisper. As Jeffery leans against the fence, the older boy hooks a finger on the collar of his shirt.

"If you kids are lying," he whispers to Jeffery, "Mr. Reynolds is gonna expel you or somethin'."

Standing up, Craig brushes the sand off his hands and runs off toward the kindergarten classroom as the older boy holds Jeffery against the fence. A few moments later Craig reappears followed by Molly, who is carrying the red notebook.

"Let go a him," Molly says nearing the fence. "He's missing story time."

"Oh yeah?" the older boys says releasing Jeffery. "He says you kids got no teacher in there."

"No, I'm teacher today," Molly says, leaning into the fence next to the older boy. She sticks out her tongue and then adds sharply "Jeffy gets to be teacher *next* time."

"Do you kids know what kind of trouble you're gonna get when Miss Conejo finds out you're out here after recess?" the older boy says giving Molly a light push. Molly opens the notebook and pulls out a pencil from its cover pocket.

"What's your guys' names?" she asks with the pencil poised, ready to take notes.

"I'm Tommy and he's Matt," the older boy says, trying to peer into Molly's notebook. "Whatcha doin'?"

"Writing your names in the book," Molly says, smiling, "'cause you're being bad."

"No way!" Tommy says, "let's see."

Molly tilts the notebook so Tommy can take a look. Although her attempt at writing his name was not very good, he observes the notebook indeed contains much of the same paperwork as his own teacher's notebook.

"Today's Friday," he comments, examining the blank role sheet. "You guys are gonna get caught with that blank paper."

"No we're not," Molly says, smiling, "Craig took the tendance paper to the office lady this morning. My sister Lisa told me she'll tell me when it's Fridays."

"You kids are somethin'," Tommy says. "If you guys have no real teacher, the principal's gonna make you go home."

"We been our own teacher for a long time," Jeffery says.

"Oh yeah?" Tommy says, eyeing the notebook, "then let me see you guys make the principal do somethin' right now."

"Like what?" Jeffery asks.

"Ask Mr. Reynolds to give you a movie to watch."

"Oh," Molly says, flipping through the papers in the notebook, "which paper is that?"

Matt pokes his finger through the fence, "I think it's that one," he says pointing to a small yellow slip.

"I don't know any movies," Molly says, looking at the slip.

"I do," Tommy says, holding out his hand. "Gimme the pencil."

Molly passes Tommy a yellow slip and the pencil. After filling out the top part of the slip, he pushes it back through the fence along with the pencil.

"All you gotta do now's sign it!" he laughs.

Molly looks at the slip for a moment before writing her name on its backside in large crooked letters. She hands the slip to Craig, who immediately dashes off toward the school's office.

"Let's go Jeffy," Molly says, turning around.

"Wait a minute," Tommy says, "we want to see if this is for real."

"Jeffy, go tell José to read everybody a numbers book. I'll wait for the movie."

After Jeffery leaves, Molly seats herself on the edge of the sandbox. She stares at Tommy and Matt, who have already begun to survey the main school yard for roaming adults. After a few minutes they begin to fidget considerably.

"We gotta get going," Tommy says, looking over his shoulder. "The kid's probably hiding out in the bathrooms or somethin'."

"Look!" Matt says, staring in the direction of the office.

Grinning from ear to ear, Craig enters the kindergarten's interior gate waving over his head what is obviously a movie.

"Next time," Molly, says standing up. "Craig's maybe gonna take a note on you guys."

Tommy and Matt step away from the fence as Molly holds the red notebook in front of her to punctuate her threat. The two boys offer Molly their friendliest smiles, then wave to Craig, before running off to their classrooms.

It is uncertain exactly how many of the school's classrooms have teachers the following spring. There have been mixed reports from the school's office. Officially Mr. Reynolds, the school's principal, refuses to comment, while his secretary has unofficially stated that the school seems to be running better than ever. In town, there is a rumor that not a single teacher returned after winter break.

On the Friday before spring break, there is a fight between a few of the older children. This scuffle breaks out between the swings and the kindergarten playground. It is only after several noses are bloodied that Mr. Reynolds arrives to escort the injured to the nurse's office. After the crowd breaks up, Tommy tells some of the kindergartners in the small sandbox that the children taken to the nurse's office were fighting over the now controversial subject of Miss Conejo. It is almost certain that Mr. Reynolds is going to investigate.

Tommy barely finishes this warning when Mr. Reynolds appears at the interior kindergarten gate. Most of the small children hide in the playhouse while a few merely cover their eyes in terror.

Without taking notice of the half-hidden children, Mr. Reynolds walks directly into the classroom. A few moments later he reappears with the red notebook tucked under his arm and heads back to his office. Just inside of the interior gate he stops for a moment and then turns around smiling.

"Children, your attention please," he announces loudly. "The school year's nearly over. You've all been very good, and so I hope you all enjoy a well-deserved spring vacation."

Understanding this to be a dismissal for the day, the children cheer wildly as they rush about collecting their belongings before going home.

Standing beside the classroom door, Molly cries quietly.

Doug
Lawson

The Particular Lechery of Jacob

FOR A PERIOD OF TIME, a tall, blue-eyed man we called Jacob lodged in a small house near our shore. It was hot on the Island that year—a heat we no longer see. The sea winds held away and the Island, becalmed, sat off the coast of what we thought for months might be Venezuela. The trading boats could not sail; we could neither confirm nor deny our reckoning. The palm trees all along what was then the southern shore bent wearily under the weight of their own fruit, and our two white tigers swam in the lagoon during the hottest part of the day, paddling sloppily in opposing circles and growling.

At night, there were no comets, no insects. The children's school closed.

He was not our first stranger.

I am not sure, Jacob wrote, in a letter never mailed, *if wind or rains will ever come. These people are untrustworthy, ugly, and exceedingly odiferous, and I fear proper business between us is beyond the scope of possibility. They put the juice of the roots of trees into their hair. They go about unclothed and even the children speak of relations not suitable for the unwed. I hold to my memory of you, my beloved, of your long and golden tresses. You are my salvation here.*

On the only day he came into our market, he wore somber clothes, no hat, and an old condom adhered to his brown, dusty shoe, unnoticed by him. But we children laughed, pointed. He scowled. He wiped his forehead with a kerchief. He bought nothing, not even my mother's limes.

Afterwards, he did not emerge during the daylight hours for quite some time.

But we would not leave him be, despite his strangeness. It was not our way, then. Above his porch, on the roof, three older women made love every morning from nine until eleven, moaning like dogs and laughing, imagining him listening below up through the thatch. On the path, an old, beardless man—my father—rode a three-wheeled bicycle to his door, offered him scissors, a vegetable corer, long, thin knives with hardly any rust on them. Between the two back wheels was a large wire basket kept covered with empty sacks.

I like to think Jacob imagined that sack moved—perhaps it did. My father is a man filled with mischief even now, dead of shipwreck. He shakes the roof of our house in storms. He leaves toads in the water barrel to frighten the children. I can imagine some large, burlapped creature swaying between moving wheels, between my father's pumping legs growing in Jacob's mind beyond a simple chicken, or a brown, spotted dog. The rains, he might have thought, would bring the juices of women down on his hatless head like a curse. The wind will unsack what should be kept covered, and the creature will come through his open window, smelling of dirt and my father's toothless mouth. The wind will unhome him. He will have to leave his charts, and the strange alchemy of figures, behind. He would have been right.

I, a child then and free of husband or lover, knew things others did not. I would wait for him in the bushes. I stalked him silently, like the tigers could. He dined with The Doctor, a woman who had arrived seven months before to study our dining habits. He cooked voluptuous meals. He would speak of his numbers, first, for hours, and only later discuss her work, the observations she had made of us and her conclusions, with one of his hands up her dress. *Knife and fork*, he would say, teasing, *in the left hand or right?* He would move his hidden arm back and forth. *The arrangement of food on the plate—is the filet on the right or the left, the brown grains above, rising clockwise, the vegetable—seaweed, perhaps? Or okra? On the right, perhaps? falling toward the half-hour? Yes? I want to appear cultured.*

Jacob, she said, quietly, naming him in return. *From the Hebrew. One who takes by the heel. Supplanter.* Sometimes she succumbed and took him into her mouth. She spit stray numbers and scraps of paper, pieces of old maps and charcoal into a pile beside his pale, parsimonious thighs.

I know also they met in her narrow office, a room once a closet with a window and a tiny fan she brought with her, to remove the smell of her thin, dark cigarettes. Beneath her gray blouse, her skin was dry and cracked, crusted and white like her critical texts. How much better a young woman might be for him was a thought I could not resist then; my young mind, filled with these visions, with the night sounds of parents and neighbors, of the tales of my brothers, spun scenes. We would meet in the street by chance, sit next to each other at a communal meal, eyes not meeting, thighs touching, the sound of the drums our heartbeats. We would judge each other's mood by the angles of slotted serving spoons, by the rising and falling of rhyming syllables thrown randomly into the air over our heads by the crowd, spinning there like the hands of an invisible clock. . . .

I ate coconuts and caramballos, and threw milk and seeds backwards between my legs. I avoided a boy who had offered me a green fern-bough three times in three nights. I stole the feathers of a tall white parrot and left them, crossed, outside of his door.

On the deck of a boat floating in the eastern shallows, I thought, I would be taken like a yellow-haired woman, pressed up against the wooden rail. The sun and shadows roped and rigged my skin, binding me to him.

There would be the sounds of pelicans, the smell of the white blossoms of lime and valerian.

There would be salt water in my mouth.

We do not know what became of Jacob. A storm came, as if all the winds had gathered all in one place to talk and had forgotten the time. The men hung sheets in the trees, dragged logs in the water to steer us and great waves sent us north and east. Later, I saw snow for the first time.

When my father once again passed by his hut, Jacob was gone. He'd left his books and letters, most indecipherable to us. His calculating machine ran for some time, aimlessly chattering, in a corner. His charts curled in the cold air and faded. His gray suits paced, restless and resolute, for seventeen days.

Some said he had been blown away, bodily; had drowned or grown wings. Some said he would soon be returning. My mother, a strong if not intuitive woman, thought that perhaps Jacob was onboard a secret ship he'd kept hidden, and had cut himself loose of us in the Sargasso. With his skill of numbers, she said, a pattern of sails would be simple magic to him, a heading just another minor computation for a mind like his.

My father and I knew better than to argue.

But I am a mother myself, now. I have watched as his notes were passed, as we clothed our children in material from his suits, how the men and women I had known since birth squinted at and studied the cribbed and folded handwriting of his judging letters to that yellow-haired woman, that woman who he did not name.

I have seen a strange and particular lechery, that unearthly lust of *otherness*, spread among us. The men build more and more ships, now. The women weave baskets and our once-wonderful hats in quantity. My own mother's fingers fly over the once tight weaving and the hats will no longer hold water properly, cannot be used over a flame. Physical relations take place behind closed doors, and the young people leave in search of something they cannot voice, now. Few return.

Supplanter, I think. He is among us still. I imagine he watches us like the tigers do, from the high, thick limbs of trees.

I teach at the children's school now. I have lunch sometimes with the woman who once studied food. She is also one of us now. We have children of our own and we share secrets.

This is one: Unlike any other children on this Island, when our firstborn sons emerged from inside us their brown eyes were blue for weeks.

| Rochelle Natt | *Elements* |

Water

UNTIL I CROSS THE BOARDWALK, Mom won't let me take off my shoes. "Splinters can go straight to your brain, making you crazy," she explains. Mom once got one in so deep it never came out.

She drives the stake of her umbrella into the sand. From under its circle of shadow, she watches me, her youngest, crawl into the foamy part, keeping my head above water. "That's not safe," she calls. "Wait! I'll teach you to swim."

"No," I say, but here she comes, her hair stuffed so tightly into a bathing cap it makes her eyes slant. She takes my hand and leads me farther than I ever want to go. Her outstretched arms become my raft. With that white cap on, her head against the sky looks like a lost moon. I shut my eyes. She yanks her arms away and lets me sink. I jump high as I can, water jetting from my nose, my mouth. "Help! Help!" I thrash my arms and legs. The Lady in the Moon shouts, "Hurray! She can do the Mad Dog Paddle."

Air

In the hallway, Mom pushes two chairs together, fits them out with pillows laid like a mattress. She covers me, kisses my forehead and leaves me on the see-sawing chairs. I hear my cousin snoring from *my* bedroom. I hold myself stiffly. When I close my eyes, I feel myself rise. Maybe Mom is carrying me to my own bed. No, in the darkness, a Lady Magician is passing me through a hoop. "See, no strings," she says. "Hurray," the audience shouts, "the kid can stay up all by herself!"

Fire

From the porch I smell scorching. Inside there's thick smoke. A pot hisses on the stove. Eggs burst their burnt shells, shoot to the ceiling. In the living room, Mom's parakeet screeches. I rush in. On the sofa, Mom, wearing a white slip, sits, frozen and smoky as dry ice, staring at a soap opera, her eyes streaming. Over her head, Lovey flaps, circling and squawking.

"Mom! Ma!"

"Fire!" she screams.

"I already put it out," I say.

She springs up, flinging open windows and doors. The bird takes off. Leaning out the window, Mom cries, "Lovey, come back!"

Earth

In a bucket, Mom mixes distilled water with dirt. Standing naked in the tub, her hair wrapped in dry cleaner's plastic, she slaps the goop all over herself while singing, "Nothing like mud to keep you young." She lies back, wet lettuce covering her eyes. On the sink, the oven timer ticks. The mud gets lighter, cracks into lines. It's as if I'm watching her get old. Unable to wait until the timer dings, I shake her shoulder. Cakes of earth fall away.

"Wake up, Ma!"

Slowly, she blinks the lettuce off her eyes. Lips barely moving, she whispers, "Honey, it hurts to smile."

Leslie
Stahlhut | *The Black Sun Rises*

STEPHEN WAS RIGHT. It is not so bad once the engines pass; still, the noise of the train coming through disturbs my thoughts. But then, everything disturbs me these days.

He wanted to marry me—either that or he wanted to get married or he wanted me. It wasn't clear.

I roll over and try to sleep, but a train is going past. I get up, walk across the floor, slide open the back door, and look out over the thirty feet to where the tracks run.

There are so many cars, I can't begin to count them. From a distance of a hundred yards or so, time is suspended as the train approaches, as the sound waves compress. The pitch of the horn rises.

It reminds me of my grandmother's house, it reminds me of my cousins, it reminds me that I am standing still, going nowhere, while the trains continue to pass, at all times of the day, at all times of the night.

Along the back edge of my grandmother's property, out past the apricot trees and an abandoned hen house, ran the railroad tracks.

Standing at the window of the room I came to think of as mine, I watched the trains and counted the cars as they went by. At first, I counted them indiscriminately; one was not different from another.

As I got older, I differentiated between the engines, the cars, and the caboose. Later, I kept track of how many were Southern Pacific or Santa Fe. A Burlington Northern was a special find. The cars were valuable because they were too many or too few to count. Others got lost in the middle.

The summer I turned seven, one of my cousins persuaded me to go out past the edge of the lawn across the freshly plowed field to where my grandmother's property abutted the tracks. Our feet moved slowly in the newly turned earth; sand collected in our shoes.

She showed me a hole next to the track and told me to put my foot there. I did, and as I stood with the side of my foot pressed up against the hot steel of the track, hot from the heat of the relentless summer sun, she held my ankle in place and told me about a boy who had gotten his foot stuck—in this very spot, she said. A train came but didn't see him. He was killed. In an instant, she said. She admitted that he might have been afraid at first, as he saw the engine coming closer and closer, but once it hit, once the impact of the locomotive moving forward collided with the boy going nowhere, he didn't have a chance to think, no chance for his body to send the message to his brain that he was hurt, that he was dead.

She was eleven and I did not want to run and let her know how afraid I was; how much I believed her lie. I stood there until she helped me get my foot free. The whole time she swore her story was true and that I should stay away.

Now I live thirty feet from the railroad tracks, edging closer and closer.

Stephen has his work, so he did not bother with me. But it wasn't always that way. When we first met, he painted me with sunlight directly on my skin. Every pore, every mole, every scar—each imperfection was magnified and took on a greater significance. Later he experimented with shadows that obscured some part of me, a breast, a foot, my head, until I was completely submerged in the absence of light. Hour after hour, I sat, I stood, I lay on my side, trying various postures and gestures, my muscles cramped at the artificial attitudes.

He got to know me so well he could paint me from memory, the lines blurring and contorting and bending so, so that I was barely recognizable, but still, there was something he captured. There in his paintings was something I could never get back.

After he painted me in every pose he could think of, and my body had begun to disappear in the shadows, he painted the trains as they rolled by. The back door was always open so he could get a good look as the light of the engine approached, the horn blasting, then the colors and the lines of the cars, fusing as the train passed. He captured the motion and held it in place for a moment.

Jose is back. He came to live with us accidentally. It started with visits after school. He'd sweep the floor, an endless job with the wind that always blows, the dust, the endless dust, and the film from the train that can't be scrubbed from the walls and the floors.

If it weren't for his mother, he would be my son. Sometimes, I can see myself in him. Our eyes are the same. Not the shape or the color, and I must admit that his are set farther apart than mine, but we would see the world in the same way. Every now and then he holds his head just so, and I can see that the two of us are not so different. Without biology to join us, the similarities are even more striking.

His mother didn't believe him at first, that we were living in the warehouse, but he brought her by one day to see. After that Jose began eating dinner with us, staying later and later. One night, it was past his bedtime, our truck wasn't running, and I had no way of getting him home. I called his mother to ask if it was all right for him to sleep over.

Soon, I was fixing him breakfast and trying to make him presentable for school, insisting that he wash up at the sink, stripped down to his underwear. I scrubbed his skin until the layers of dirt and dead cells were gone and there was a rosy sheen.

I washed his socks and underpants in the sink every night, an extra shirt, another pair of jeans. There was no excess. He moved in just as I had, little by little, day by day.

Stephen swore the carpet was magic. It was uglier than most cheap Oriental rugs, and not just because it was dirty and ill-trimmed. It looked as if something bled to death at some point on what was the southeast corner of the carpet. I made him move it. There was no way, I said to him with certainty, absolutely no way, I will sleep where something obviously has died. He didn't argue with me about this—he never argued with me—he just turned the carpet around so that the bloodstain was in the northwest corner by the closet.

Really, he continued, it's a magic carpet. When it's time for me to go, I'll just pack everything up, kick-start the damn thing, and go. Now—now I almost believe that the carpet is magic. Not because I believe in such things, but because I want to believe that it is that easy to go. That all it takes are a few magic words and a dirty old carpet, and I could be off to a new life.

Jose is not doing well in school and I feel that if I care for him enough, bathe him, scrub his clothes, check over his math problems and listen patiently as he reads, that he will somehow recover a portion of his former self, that he will once again be a little boy, if not for an entire day, then for one, irretrievable moment. This does not work.

Since he saw his sister's baby explode in her arms, he has not been the same. He cries in his sleep and sleeps during the day and he cannot shake the sense that nothing is as it should be.

And what can I say? That babies' heads occasionally explode for reasons we don't yet understand? He would know it is not the truth. How can I explain love that is violent and cruel? What he needs, I cannot give.

Stephen had the maps out again. He was trying to decide where to go next. The western half of the United States and parts of Canada were spread out on the floor. He thought of going to Nevada (he has friends there), he considered returning to Montana (unlikely, two women wanted to marry him), he ended up driving straight north on the interstate to meet some friends and go camping in Canada, bypassing Montana altogether.

I tried to talk him into going to Mexico, but he would have no part of it. Winter was coming and I might follow him if he went where the weather was warm. His feet had been badly frostbitten once and he had lost almost all sensation in them. The cold hardly bothered him at all.

He went out once when the wind was gusting up to one hundred and ten miles an hour. To get the mail, he told me. He said he hiked over four miles to see if his coupons had come. Coupons for what, I wanted to know.

For the grocery store, he said.

Why, I was always asking why.

He shrugged his shoulders and said why not. Might be a good sale.

I didn't believe it. Not the part about the coupons, anyway, but I tried to imagine what drove him out of his house to go to the mailbox. Why he had to fabricate a destination.

I thought he would never get the maps up, that they would always be spread out on the floor. That he would spend forever deciding where to go.

When he was five he was bitten by a bat. The house was filled with them. The bat that bit him lived on the utility porch and bit him without any provocation. They couldn't find the exact bat, so he had to get rabies shots. He was proud of this. He said that he was the first person in this country to undergo the treatment for rabies and that he started the treatment several times, because his mom would forget to take him after awhile.

I forgot to ask how many shots he had to have, how long the needle was, and where they gave him the shots, but the part of the story he liked to tell best, is how cool he thought bats were after that. How he would sit and draw them for hours.

One night at dinner he suddenly pointed to the east with his chopstick. The black sun rises there, he said with a mouthful of lettuce, just like the regular sun.

I didn't know whether or not to believe him. Not about the black sun rising in the east, but the whole thing about the black sun and the white sun, constantly battling to determine who would control the world. What about the moon? I asked. That's the silver sun, he told me, taking another bite of salad. It just watches.

One day he decided that February should have thirty-one days, so I worked on a new calendar. I based it on the introduction of the Corvette. For my purposes, B.C. meant "Before Corvette," and A.D. meant "After Demolition."

Something, he told me, has to be done about Christmas. Not that Christmas is a favorite of mine, but he was adamant that the entire holiday had to be done away with and quickly as the days were growing shorter and the holiday was nearly here. Too commercial, he said. Christmas, he said, is proof that the black sun is winning. I couldn't argue, so I made something up.

When I showed him the new calendar, he was impressed, but not satisfied. January first was leap day, so the new year came only once every four years. He liked that. What about August, he asked. I told him my plans to make the entire month a holiday, and he said he'd have to think that over.

The maps were still on the floor, but in addition to the western United States and parts of Canada, he had the Iberian Peninsula and North Africa strewn across the studio. I wished he would pick up these maps—at least put them on the wall—but it was not something we discussed. I did not want to hasten the end, although I knew it was coming, just as I knew a train would pass by as I was falling asleep.

Let's go to Morocco, Stephen said one morning at breakfast. Jose had just gotten out of bed and was eating a bowl of cornflakes. His hair was disheveled and some milk had spilled onto his pajama top. There was a jackhammer chipping away at the street that runs parallel to the tracks.

I have never been to North Africa. I have not even seen the movie *Casablanca*, but I suddenly had an invitation to travel halfway around the world, when he wouldn't consider letting me drive north with him. I sliced a banana and listened to the workmen's shouts over the noise of their machinery as they broke the street up into smaller and smaller pieces.

"Why," I asked, not expecting an answer.

"Can I come?" Jose wanted to know.

"I bet I could get a thousand camels for you," Stephen said. And then I saw that I was no longer a woman he was afraid of creating obligations and debts to; I was a marketable commodity.

"Let me see your teeth," he said.

I smiled at him, not really a smile, but not quite a grimace.

"Can I come?" Jose was insistent. He did not want to be left behind.

"Your teeth look good," Stephen told me.

My teeth are clean and white and well-polished. My mother has seen to this. Nothing, nothing is too good for her daughter. Stephen appreciated my mother's efforts.

"Do they really have camels there? I want to ride a camel."

Jose was awake for the first time in months. The thought of Africa, with all of its possibilities, had brought him to life.

Stephen believed that I could make him a comfortable living. Who knows? He was sure he could get a thousand camels and a house in Marrakech.

The day was growing warmer, and the sound of the jackhammer on the street was drowned out by the drivers honking the horns of their cars as they drove past. Jose had given up on his breakfast. The cereal grew limp and soggy. He only wanted to know more about Morocco and whether the camels had one hump or two. He left for school late, his shirt tucked in halfway, and his hair still not combed.

I rinsed the breakfast dishes in the sink and thought about what Stephen had said. I was fairly certain I didn't want to go. I was tempted, though. Tempted to drive through France, and tour through Spain, then ditch Stephen somewhere near Seville. I knew this wouldn't happen.

As I stood at the sink, my hands submerged in tepid water, Stephen grabbed my hair into a ponytail so he could see my face better. It occurred to me that he knew my face backwards and forwards, that he was searching for something new or overlooked.

He didn't find whatever it was he was looking for, and he let go of my hair and kissed me absently.

Stephen took the maps up off the floor, one by one, until only a detail of Alaska and the Yukon Territory remained. He swore that he didn't know when or if he would go.

Until the truck was packed and he was gone, he thought that he hadn't made a decision, that there was still something left for him to do here.

When Jose's mother comes over she speaks to him in Spanish. She doesn't know that I understand every word, every nuance. Every pause, every extra breath tells me more than I want to know. She wants to believe that she is a better mother than I; that this is her child and I am only an uninvited interloper. But I know the truth. He belongs to both of us and neither of us. He is our child, nobody's child.

Jose is asleep in the chair and there is nothing I can do to rouse him. Not even the promise of going out for ice cream will wake him from this sleep. But as soon as I put him to bed, pull the covers up to his chin, and turn the radio down, just after I have wrung out his clothes to dry and have called his mother to tell her that he is safely asleep, he will waken; not fully, but fitful tossings that go on through the night.

The train moves forward only at the expense of the tracks that are bound to one another by large, steel spikes. Year after year the tracks never move, the trains never stop moving.

Since Stephen left, the black sun rises and sets earlier each day. If we lived above the seventieth parallel in the middle of the vast white plains of Greenland, or at the very tip of Siberia, the white sun would set at almost the same moment it rose. It is hard for me to imagine this, an entire day given over to the inky blackness of night; to go out at noon and see the stars. I want to know if Eskimos sleep all day. And during the summer, how is it when there is not a night?

Jordan Randall
Jones & Forsyth

Waltz: The Secret Diary of an Underling at the Department of Water and Power

I am a slow waltz
Itching in my ears.

— Murillo Mendes

June 1

THE CHOICES THE DIRECTOR gave me are not choices at all. The street is damp and lions have invaded all the houses. How can I possibly accept the door or the proverbial nervous-breakdown vacation? I walk my lunch breaks away, dreaming enough fire through downtown to quench the Director's daily water quota of 20,000 acre feet.

Too many questions circle the globe. Like why have the lions arrived, what left the streets damp in this dry heat, will the fires save us? Hours fight and die, come and go, while I look for immortality in all I do. My wife is a cipher.

The Department of Water and Power channels my life through its ducts and pipes, wires and more wires, circling me through this small community infinitely without a stop. Most people would find my job intolerable as a day-to-day situation, but it doesn't bother me. Either I have resigned myself to this corrupting safety, or I have learned the simple art of denying that this community lives on the edge.

June 4

Luckily, the neither-beasts arrive. Being the size of our houses, they take us into their mouths. Their gentle gnawing reminds me of the whirring of the wheels in the factory where I was born: it lulls me to sleep and I dream of the watery womb, then of my father in his p.j.'s at the tap, holding a toothbrush, and of fire kissing wood.

Among the cherry trees that encircle the Central Divisional Office of the Department of Water and Power is a poplar. It has gotten there, it has stayed there, by assuming the voice, the table manners, the sense of humor, of a cherry tree. Also, it steals cherries from its neighbors—who scarcely seem to mind—and street people nail them to its branches. Cherry trees do not have wives.

What we do and where we go is determined by who we are or pretend to be. In this manner, Napoleon can become Wellington, or Bismarck Napoleon, and the Director of the Department of Water and Power can become that wanna-be cherry tree. Go on.

June 6

The Director snakes me wire to wire, speeds me through pipes around and blindly under the fires I set to blooming. The choices once hidden are ever and always really choices. There are no questions, only flies circling my head.

At the Department of Water and Power, plans are made for the duration and quality of my life. I know this and, finally, I have done something about it. I have broken out of those pipes and wires, those conduits I travel for the Director's joy. I choose to live free of his damp traps, in the fire-warmth the neither-beasts keep muttering about.

"Choices are choices," said Chaucer, and promptly fell dead, unwillingly. Small questions hit a man hard.

June 8

In the night, the fires seem like conspirators, like revellers. The circle I have set around our community is like the ring on a dead bridegroom's finger, and may follow us to the grave. The Department of Water and Power, along with the City Government and all its Fire/Police/Ambulance functionaries, wait on full alert, knowing that the beasts of the fire, the fire of the beasts, threaten them even in the night, even in their peaceful solitary slumbers.

What do they threaten us with? Mainly the cutting off of our water and power. What we have, they want. And so on . . . equals *Das Kapital* if you let it.

Which is my point, damn it!

June 19

When my name comes up in idle conversation at the Department of Water and Power, the Director grins snidely, like a lion or my wife. But who's he fooling? Everyone knows he's a wanna-be cherry tree. Still, being the Director, he gets away with mimicking me and then suddenly demanding my head on a St. John the Baptist platter. This is known as "Calling out the National Guard," or "Volunteering for the flesh patrol." What we choose, we choose. What we do not choose may choose us: conscription, scoliosis, the Presidency. Ring-around-the-rosie.

ANYONE IS POSSIBLE

June 22

Wake, and you are woken. Don't speak until you're spoken to. The hidden choices have been revealed. They possess no questions, but all of their statements end perplexingly and are written on the pages with question marks by the scribes. Among the choices revealed is that one may become a cherry tree by first being or pretending to be that wanna-be cherry tree in front of the Central Divisional Office of the Department of Water and Power.

The waiting list was full up on *that* choice when it was revealed. The Director and I head the list. That's why he hates me.

Lions do not climb cherry trees, nor do tigers, but birds arrive and eat the delicate fruit and even the Director dreams about the sexuality of *that*.

Yes, it's a strange and subterranean existence we lead. The Director tells me no one will acknowledge it if not me, so I do. We eat beasts, we are eaten by beasts; we abortively dream of Chaucer and cherry trees, of hummingbirds at the blossoms, of pilgrimages to Canterbury and the *Wife of Bath's Tale*.

All my dreams are bawdy, and fall to combustion. All my dreams simmer solipsistically hot and conundrumatic. . . . I could go on like this forever, but would he *let* me? I hear his henchmen running up the stairs.

June 29

False alarm.

What people find intolerable leads them into fear of more intolerable things, until, paralyzed by paranoia, they are eaten by the lions and tigers, befriended as *disjecta membra* by the neither-beasts, and stuck through with wires and plumbed through with pipes by the Department of Water and Power.

There are flies circling my head, no questions inside it. The fires burn summer down the street.

June 30

I wake and my lawn is all pipes. I turn to my wife. She has become a lion in the night. The phone is a web of hot wires. I cannot read or write these words; I am dead of the fire: A cherry tree, smoke drifting from me in the lack of a breeze, in my former living room.

Outside, yellow fire engine lights bounce up, refracted by hydrant water, from the asphalt. The street is damp yet aflame.

42

Kika
Bomer

Sing a Song o' Sixpence

Sing a song o' sixpence, a handful of rye,
Four-and-twenty blackbirds baked in a pie;
When the pie was opened the birds began to sing,
Wasn't that a dainty dish to set before the King?

THE PIE WAS a large expanse of the South, his piece of the black earth where the black people used to work. His father, also a war veteran, owned it and soon it would be his. He pushed the nighttime sky from slippery steps leading into the dark canal where he moved with his officer's uniform and stared at the full moon rowing into laces of water, loosening and easing free in the ripple of waves. This was a kind of ritual, pulling the warrior soldier out of the delicate light and making the war cry sing, reminding himself that a war was just another piece of pie for the country and now he had this land, and it would be owned by him. What could have happened without the Gulf War and Vietnam? The whole country could be communist now, full of watchtowers and signs in the anonymous black and white of the state. We have to take the past and see that the risk of history reveals the value of the future. Politics are a gamble and so is life.

Water. Walking into the water where the shadow of his body covers it. Water of the defrocked priest's baptism, water of the eagle eye, water of Bonaparte's winter in Russia melting, water as if. . . . The doctor explained it to him, something about wounds going septic after he himself had stitched them up, something about getting help before you're breathing under it. Water. He's under it and he has gills and he's in a room where there are men in cages against the wall like a dog pound and he's watching TV. There are black men and dark Arabs, all so tall, and he is looking up at them and they are singing. Then a bomb hits. Then the static and it's only static.

He's eating the past, it's incorporating into him and eating him, plunging through the thin uniform. A ritual like a stained glass window. Outside, the water. And the cry of the seagull smashes the glass.

The next day, the sun rises and everything seems smaller. His lover lies beside him, warm like the smooth skin of a seal sunning on rocks, the waves licking the beach. A dog barks somewhere. He rises to the morning and lets her sleep, proud that he has learned to cook. He will bake a cake for his father. He rolls out the dough from yesterday and pours the blackberries in the shell. The oven opens its mouth and its orange teeth are lined in perfect straight wires. Setting the pie into the oven, his hands shake and he returns to bed. The twenty-four blackbirds sing the morning song for the twenty-four-hour day. Everything seems to be in order.

| Kika Bomer | *Humpty Dumpty* |

Humpty Dumpty sat on a wall,
Humpty Dumpty had a great fall.
All the King's horses
And all the King's men
Cannot put Humpty together again.

IN THE DREAM, there was an egg but it was alive and had no shell, just a thin gauze of translucent membrane covering its tiny body. It was in a terrarium and eating leaves off a plant and I picked it up and thought how my hands were dirty, I shouldn't touch it; it slipped and fell in the dirt and I thought it was dead.

We shouldn't be any worse for our loss, he said. First you buy the wool and then you let the snow fall. Right. This is said by the one who humped me and dumped me years ago. Two abortions and I feel like he still kicks his heels and gambols about like a goat who has found his cliff. Every life has its walls, its cliffs. He seems particularly good about dealing with them. I see a courtyard and a garden full of poppies on one side and on the other, factories and the military and work, and it seems we build a house on the wall, that somehow whatever we create together has to lie right between the drug of our love-making and the world with all its incessant demands.

My body like a croissant. This body has been baked in butter. This body has no nutritional value for me. I peel myself off in layers to try to rid myself of the desire that has no life inside of it, nowhere that the arrow can aim. Like laughter, irrational grunts, the growl of a bitch while a man drowns the puppies in the river. The water looks flat. My mother ironed it. I take a fat piece of my leg and step in, watching it cut through like a spoon dunking in thick lamb soup. I wonder at the slaughter of it. The sun keeps rising, an egg with no shell, no white, only the yolk and I press my lips to see it hard-boiled. I'm afraid it's going to run. I'm afraid of things being what they aren't. I feel my body crack through the air. I'm walking through glass. I can see the other side too clearly. Who said there was a wall between us and the world? It's transparent. A glass wall. I suppose to let the sunshine in for our little jungle, a blueprint of conventions so we can see through this mess. What if I told you it was this simple, that I laughed at him, the other man, the one who told me he had "found" himself? It is that kind of thing that ruins relationships. It's that perfect plan behind them. It's laughing at the plan, cracking it.

Smooth, white, round. Curve of my thigh. The inside is too soft. We have to burn all the poppies to cook it. And then when the drug is gone? But the drug makes you see it run, so it's a Catch-22 either way. You can say you own it, you can build the barracks but the sun will always set and the whole cycle just repeats itself. The month ends, a new box of white puffy tampons to drink it up, if it doesn't happen, you make sure of it. You make sure no weed comes between. You represent and don't reproduce. You number the map. But it's a joke and the laughter attests to that. It's like creating design out of debris or really believing you can stand in the middle of two sexes without the tug or the war.

I took four showers today and I still feel dirty. Now I'm going to do the laundry and iron. Then I'll go to work and put my life together again. For a moment, for eight hours of my day.

Lance Olsen | *Cybermorphic Beat-Up Get-Down Subterranean Homesick Reality-Sandwich Blues*

I'M A, LIKE, POET. Mona. Mona Sausalito. I write lyrics for my boyfriend's band, Plato's Deathmetal Tumors. Plato's Deathmetal Tumors kicks butt. It's one of the best Neogoth bands in Seattle. My boyfriend's name is Mosh. Mosh shaved his head and tattooed it with rad circuitry patterns. He plays wicked cool lead and sings like Steve Tyler on amphetamines. Only that's not his real name. His real name is Marvin Goldstein. But so. Like I say, I'm a poet. I write about human sacrifices, cannibalism, vampires, and stuff. Mosh loves my work. He says we're all going to be famous some day. Only right now we're not, which bites, 'cuz I've been writing for like almost ten months. These things take time, I guess. Except we need some, like, cash to get by from week to week? Which is why Mosh one day says take the job at Escort à la Mode. Why not? I say. Which I guess kind of brings me to my story.

See, I'm cruising Capitol Hill in one of the company's black BMWs when my car-phone rings. Escort à la Mode's a real high-class operation. Escortette's services go for $750 an hour. We usually work with foreign business types. Japs and ragheads mostly. Politicians, too. With twenty-four hours' notice, we can also supply bogus daughters, brothers, and sons. You name it. Except there's absolutely nothing kinky here. We don't even kiss the clients. No way. Handshakes max. Take them out, show them the town, eat at a nice restaurant, listen to them yak, take them to a club, watch them try to dance, take them home. Period. We're tour guides, like. Our goal is to make people feel interesting. Therma Payne—she's my boss—Therma says our job is to "give good consort." Therma's a scream.

But so. Like I say, my car-phone rings. I answer. Dispatcher gives me an address, real chi-chi bookstore called Hard Covers down by the fish market. My client's supposed to be this big-deal writer guy who's reading there. Poet. Allen something. Supposed to've been famous back in the like Pleistocene Error or something. Worth bazillions. So important I never even heard of him. But, hey. It's work.

Now I'm not being like unmodest or anything, okay? But I happen to be fricking gorgeous. No shit. My skin's real white. I dye my hair, which is short and spiked, shoe-polish black, then streak it with these little wisps of pink. Which picks up my Lancôme Corvette-red lipstick and long Estée Lauder Too-Good-To-Be-Natural black lashes. When I talk with a client, I'll keep my eyes open real wide so I always look Winona-Ryder-surprised by what he's saying. I'm 5'2", and when I wear my Number Four black-knit body-dress and glossy black Mouche army boots I become every middle-aged man's bad-little-girl wetdream. So I don't just *walk* in to Hard Covers, okay? I kind, what, *sashay*. Yeah. That's it. *Sashay*. I've never been there before, and I'm frankly pretty fucking impressed. Place is just *humongous*. More a warehouse than a bookstore. Except that it's all mahogany and bronze and dense carpeting. Health-food bar. Espresso counter. Dweeb with bat-wing ears playing muzak at the baby grand. Area off on the side with a podium and loads of chairs for the reading. Which is already filling. Standing room only. People are real excited. And books. God. Books. Enough books to make you instantly anxious you'll never read them all, no way, no matter how hard you try, so you might as well not.

I'm right on time. So I ask the guy at the register for the famous rich poet. He points to the storeroom. Warming up, he says. So I go on back and knock, only no one answers. I knock again. Nada. My meter's running, and I figure I might as well earn my paycheck, so I try the knob. Door's unlocked. I open it, stick my head in, say hi. It's pretty dark, all shadows and book cartons, and the room stretches on forever, and I'm already getting bored, so I enter and close the door behind me. When my eyes adjust a little, I make out a dim light way off in a distant corner. I start weaving toward it through the rows and rows of cartons. As I get closer, I can hear these voices. They sound kind of funny. Worried, like. Real fast and low. And then I see them. I see the whole thing.

Maybe five or six guys in gray business suits and ties, real like FBI or something, are huddling over this jumble on the floor. At first I don't understand what I'm looking at. Then I make out the portable gurney. And this torso on it, just this torso, naked and fleshy pink in a Barbie-doll sort of way, rib cage big as a cow's, biggest fucking belly you ever saw. Out of it are sticking these skinny white flabby legs, between them this amazingly small little purple dick and two hairy marbles. Only, thing is, the chest isn't a real chest. There's a panel in it. And the panel's open. And one of the guys is tinkering with some wiring in there. And another is rummaging through a wooden crate, coming up with an arm, plugging it into the torso, while a third guy, who's been balancing a second arm over his shoulder like a rifle or something, swings it down and locks it into place.

I may be a poet, okay, but I'm not a fucking liar or anything. I'm just telling you what I saw. Believe it or not. Go ahead. Frankly, I don't give a shit. But I'm telling you, I'm standing there, hypnotized like, not sure whether to run or wet myself, when this fourth guy reaches into the crate and comes up with, I kid you not, the *head*. I swear. I fucking swear. A *head*. The thing is so gross. Pudgy. Bushy. Gray-haired. And with these eyes. With these sort of glazed *eyes* that're looking up into the darkness where the ceiling should've been. I could spew rice just thinking about it.

Anyway, after a pretty long time fidgeting with the stuff in the chest, they prop the torso into a sitting position and start attaching the head. It's not an easy job. They fiddle and curse, and once one of them slips with a screwdriver and punctures the thing's left cheek. Only they take some flesh-toned silicon putty junk and fill up the hole, which works just fine. And the third guy reaches into his breast pocket and produces these wire-rimmed glasses, which he slips into place on the thing's face, and then they stand back, arms folded, admiring their work and all, and then the first guy reaches behind the thing's neck and pushes what must've been the ON/OFF button.

Those eyes roll down and snap into focus. Head swivels side to side. Mouth opens and closes its fatty lips, testing. And then, shit, it begins *talking*. It begins fucking *talking. I'm with you in Rockland. I'm wuh-wuh-wuh-with you . . . But my agent. What sort of agent is that? What could she have been thinking? Have you seen those sales figures? A stone should have better figures than that! I'm wuh-with you in the nightmare of trade paperbacks, sudden flash of bad PR, suffering the outrageousness of weak blurbs and failing shares. Where is the breakthrough book? Where the advance? Share with me the vanity of the unsolicited manuscript! Show me the madman bum of a publicist! Movie rights! Warranties! Indemnities! I am the twelve-percent royalty! I am the first five-thousand copies! I am the retail and the wholesale, the overhead and the option clause! Give me the bottom line! Give me the tax break! Give me a reason to collect my rough drafts in the antennae crown of commerce! Oh, mental, mental, mental hardcover! Oh, incomplete clause! Oh, hopeless abandon of the unfulfilled contract! I am wuh-wuh-wuh-with you . . . I am wuh-wuh-wuh-with you in Rockland . . . I am . . .*

"Oh, shit," says the first guy.

"Balls," says the second.

The body is a prosthesis for the mind! the famous rich poet says.

"We should've let him go," says the third guy.

"When his ticker stopped," says the first.

"When his liver quit," says the second.

"One thing," says the fourth. "Nanotech sure ain't what it's cracked up to be."

"You got that right," says the third.

Thirty thousand books in 1998 alone, the famous rich poet says, *but they couldn't afford it. Tangier, Venice, Amsterdam. What were they thinking? Wall Street is holy! The New York Stock Exchange is holy! The cosmic clause is holy! I'm wuh-wuh-wuh . . . I'm wuh-wuh-wuh . . . wuh-wuh-wuh . . .*

"Turn him off," says the fifth one.

Pale greenish foam begins forming on the famous rich poet's lips, dribbling down his chin, spattering his hairless chest.

"Yeah, well," says the second.

"Guess we got some tightening to do," says the third, reaching behind the thing's neck.

But just as he pressed that button, just for a fraction of an instant, the stare of the famous rich poet fell on me as I tried scrunching out of sight behind a wall of boxes. Our eyes met. His looked like those of a wrongly convicted murderer maybe like one second before the executioner throws the switch that'll send a quadrillion volts or something zizzing through his system. In them was this mixture of disillusionment, dismay, fear, and uninterrupted sorrow. I froze. He stretched his foam-filled mouth as wide as it would go, ready to bellow, ready to howl. Except the juice failed. His mouth slowly closed again. His eyes rolled back up inside his head.

And me? I said fuck this. Fuck the books, fuck the suits, fuck Escort à la Mode, fuck the withered old pathetic shit. This whole thing's *way* too fricking rich for *my* blood.

And so I turned and walked.

| Joe | *Now, Now* |
| Malone | |

THE TOURIST-LULLING OPULENCE of the Rose Garden behind them, Larry and his father entered the wide greensward of the Cherry Esplanade. They sauntered over the early summer grass toward where Daffodil Hill seemed to swell in haze beyond the hot breezeless trees. The father walked with his pudgy hands clasped behind his back, now and then dropping his head toward his chest, perhaps for respite from the humid sheen of the sun refracting in his rimless glasses. In submission to the pressing heat he had removed his tie, but still wore his watch-chained vest.

Larry felt in vague oppression the massive loom of the Brooklyn Museum, to the west outside the grounds of the Botanical Gardens where they now walked. Nor could he draw any comfort from the knowledge of Ebbets Field just to the south, that colossal cathedral of baseball and truth from summers past. And he sensed in low-key panic the caliper squeeze of Washington and Flatbush Avenues at the ultimate end of the flowered fields of their walk.

"Dad . . ."

"Mm?"

"Nothing."

They crossed the pathway at the edge of the Esplanade, and onto the lawn on the far side. The brook from the lake in the Japanese Garden trickled on beside them, ducks now and then paddling to little islands in the middle of the stream. Lucky ducks, Larry thought. More than lucky. Blessed.

"Dad . . . Were the saints always happy?"

The father walked on for a moment in silence.

"Well, Larry, that depends on what you mean. The saints sometimes felt troubled, even very troubled. But profoundly, in an essential way, I'd say, yes. Perhaps they were indeed always happy."

It was Larry's turn for a moment of silence.

"Yeah, okay. But I mean . . . Well, did they always know what to do? Were they sure what they should do?"

"God gave them guidance, Larry. God is always ready to give guidance."

Guidance. Larry saw himself wandering through the empty night-time streets, fearing to do any more than glance at the beckoning windows of strangers.

"Sometimes . . . sometimes I think I can't be good. It's . . . it's like my head, or my soul is being pushed from the outside. Y'know? And, well, and like a thin fence. . . . Remember that time in the wind storm when the backyard fence came down? It's like that."

They were climbing Daffodil Hill now, the father beginning to pant and perspire in the diffuse humid sun.

"Let's sit down a while, Larry."

They settled on a bench beneath a crabapple tree, its sour fruit strewn at their feet.

"God will always shore up fences, Larry."

Larry remembered coming down in the morning to find the fence caved in onto the yard, opening up the alleys behind the tenements on Eighth Street. The murderous Eighth Street alleys.

"Sometimes I almost kinda think that God is, well, too hard on us. . . ."

The father stopped in the motion of patting his damp forehead, clutching the handkerchief tightly. He looked at Larry as if hurt.

"Now, now, Larry. God is never *too* hard on *anyone*."

From the south across the moist air came a dull roar, as of surf breaking on a stony beach. Was there a game at Ebbets Field today, the crowd jubilant for their blessed Dodgers? His own blessed Dodgers, just last summer. Blessed.

"Like in Mass, when the priest has to say the words about changing the bread into Christ's body. Why does he have to pronounce them *perfectly*!"

"Because they describe perfection."

"But . . . but . . . It's so *hard* to say anything perfectly."

"Ah, yes. But hard is not impossible."

Hard. Hard. Impossible. Larry thought of himself at his tiny desk faced away from the window four flights above the backyard on the highest slope in Brooklyn. The window which only the grim Eighth Street tenements cut off from the dazzling expanse of the Upper Bay, from the sun setting flamboyant behind the jagged woods atop Staten Island.

"What if someone sat at their desk and . . . and wrote *vows*. Vows to God. And then couldn't keep them."

The father looked at his son with quick tenseness, but then seemed to soften.

"Did *you* do that, Larry?"

Larry didn't answer.

"Vows must never be made lightly. . . ."

"It's *not* light, it's *not* light!"

" . . . *or*, Larry, without consultation. You must seek the advice of your confessor first."

"Yeah okay, but what if . . . if somebody *didn't*!"

Another diffuse roar spread across the hot sky from Ebbets Field. The father stood up, patting down the front of his trousers.

They emerged from the Botanical Gardens at the Palm House onto Washington Avenue, walking southward in the afternoon shadows of the lush grounds they had just left. Toward the intersection with Empire Boulevard, the subway trench of the gloomy Franklin Avenue line cut them off from the Gardens receding to the west—from the spot called the Children's Garden. Beyond the burgeoning hedges across the trench might have been sweet young girls kneeling in the loam, their grammar school skirts fluttering down around their cookie-warm legs, planting flowers. Girls not much younger than Larry himself. Might have been . . . But his vows said: *no*. Counterpoint, the Franklin Avenue line. With its dull rails lying too low for the sun. A barren stretch of open track between two dead tunnels lost in the earth. And when a train clattered by, the smell of ozone came creeping up from the dead green cars.

From across Empire Boulevard, Larry dared to gaze down Washington Avenue. At the end, he knew, there was a wedge where the roadway joined Flatbush Avenue. A wedge of sterile concrete under a gas station. And a tinny red and white sign proclaiming TEXACO. That sign, he knew, was there now in the wet opalescent sun. And that sign had been there under the sodium-lit cold of last winter's night. Last winter's night when he stood at that sign, numb. Stood and gazed down the rectilinear desolation of Washington Avenue toward the unseen winter sleep of the blessed Gardens they had just now left.

When he was little, Larry had a jack-in-the-box that could talk. Tinny talk, as when last winter's night he struck the tinny Texaco sign with his fist. And it clanged cold and alone under blinkingless sodium light. Tinny talk:

Back up. Back up to the bus stop at the corner of Beekman Place. There. Now. That bus. Will take you past the other side of the Botanical Gardens. Along Prospect Park, to Grand Army Plaza. It will circle the Plaza under the Library. And cross over four streets. Eastern Parkway. St. John's Place. Butler Place. Vanderbilt Avenue. Stop in front of number 20 Plaza East. And you will get off and walk into the courtyard. Up to the doorway to your right. You are in the apartment on the second floor. Overlooking the courtyard. Standing at the window with your nonpudgy hands clasped behind your back. You see a woman in a light tan trenchcoat get off the bus. And walk slowly into the courtyard. It is SheSheShe. SheSheShe disappears from sight, unseen but certain into the doorway to

HerHerHer right and your left. You tense in the mahogany twilight of the room, its stately glassed-in bookshelves sparse with antique tomes. To your left, the corridor to the front door. Which you hear open. And close. A light step along the long corridor. Now. SheSheShe is standing in the room, not five feet to your left. Now. SheSheShe is smiling. And slowly unbuckling HerHerHer trenchcoat. The trenchcoat slides down around HerHerHer body to the floor. And SheSheShe is standing in a slip. Now. Now not three feet to your left. Now not two. Smiling. The straps of HerHerHer slip slide down. Now not one. HerHerHer breasts rise like cakes hot from the oven. Cakes topped with swollen syrupy cherries.

There had been a night, last summer, when he sat around the fin-de-siecle dining room with his mother and father eating metropolitans, moist and lovely with coconut, pinnacled in glazed cherries bursting. Bursting in the coming summer night's heat. It would come in waves, down from the oven of the sky. "Larry," his mother had said, "run down to Ebbingers and get some metropolitans for dessert tonight." They seemed to eat in unison, to the ticking of the grandfather clock. "According to the forecast in the *Journal American*," his father said, "there will be a storm tonight." His mother flicked her tongue. "Mm," she said. But hadn't that summer then passed in sweetness, good and open-eyed and smiling? Blessed sweetness. With the long warm weeks beaded between the blessed returns of Mass on Sunday mornings. Perfection. And safety. Mass, and the communion of safe, safe saints.

There had been other gardens, other parks. Sometimes during his father's brief vacations, the three of them up by train to Springfield, Massachusetts, Dad and he would leave the summer morning fragrance of Grandma O's kitchen right after breakfast with the promise to bring back berries for pie. They would bus out to Forest Park, rent a boat and row to all the woodsy nooks and dells along the lake, to return late in the afternoon with buckets of twinkling raspberries and shining blackberries and glowing blueberries. And sure enough, for evenings thereafter, instead of the four of them strolling up to Friendly's on State Street for ice cream on the hoof, Larry and Dad would lug back ice-misty quart packages from Mr. Jonstone's drugstore on Maple Street, and pie would be high piled with mounds of mellow vanilla, tutti frutti, peach, and, of course, butter pecan (HerHerHer favorite). Pie a la mode and the life of evening summer porch behind the leafy trellis, after the flowers went to sleep. From rainbow through verdant to black. Black for the night. Silhouettes. And silence.

How did he know that SheSheShe wore black and white striped elastic panties? The impression was buxom. As if he were watching a scene through the polished glass of a revolving door, and the door started to revolve. And unscrew. And levitate wobbling up into the canyons of steel (because he and Dad, little and harmless, had earlier been traipsing around Sunday Manhattan after seeing the Lionel and American Flyer train exhibits off Madison Square, and then up to Central Park South and the other Grand Army Plaza where he became glass-withheld voyeur of Gotham's elite, Protestant and Jewish professional names black lacquered on gold plates, all that unfathomed and forever unreachable world so distant and un-Catholic and enviable. . . .) —rise wobbling and ocular warbling up up toward Paradise it seemed, but the scene he had been stolidly viewing now swirled into incomprehensibility, like the rings of Saturn, the slow dervish of clouds of Uranus, blue and white and distant distant gray.

Walking just a week earlier through a defile in Prospect Park, his head full of the song "Blue Velvet," and all feeling so right with the world. But, from the sky between the far treetops in front of him growing closer, the hammer came. It flew straight at him, blacker and bigger with every dust mote of the seconds it took. To CRASH.

Where Empire Boulevard crossed Flatbush Avenue, they stood and wavered in the damp sun. Across Flatbush, in the dolmen portical entrance to Prospect Park, they saw a snack cart, and beneath its mosaic umbrella an alembic fountain of orange drink, bubbling up, cascading down through its fretwork of cool glass tubes. Without a word, they crossed over and partook. Then, refreshed if only in body, they moved along northward in the shadow of the park, the western flank of the Gardens they had left shimmering behind their picket fence in the lowering sun.

"Dad . . ." Larry was about to say when he noticed his father's face. At first he thought it was sweat, and it may have been in part, discreetly patted away with the father's wide white handkerchief. "Dad . . . ?!" but all sound stayed in Larry's head. His father was crying.

Larry looked to the roadway, to the passing cars. Some northward, others southward, they passed on soft humming tires, the sun of this day momentarily blazing crescents of glass, jigsaws of chrome. This moment I will remember, said Larry soundlessly. This moment's cars, and this moment's life-propping people inside those cars, I will remember. This moment, come what may, I will never forget.

They entered the park at the zoo, passing in silence among the cages and pens of fragrant non-understanding creatures. On the slope upward toward Monument Hill, dark with pines, the father broke the silence.

"Larry. I am not homosexual."

Mute, Larry felt himself flush violently. He began to tremble.

"Do you remember, last week, when your mother . . ."

Before his father could finish, Larry knew and remembered. After supper, when his father came back late from work, HerHerHer stomping around the kitchen table with balled fists and eyes yellow with fury. "Oooo *John*, sometimes I think you're *queer*. A *queer*! A *queer*!" His father had lurched back against the doorway, as if blown there by a hurricane. "*Queer*! *Queer*! *Queer*!" It had become a shrill singsong, and SheSheShe now hurled pieces of dirty laundry onto the floor from the sideboard where SheSheShe'd been feeding them into the Maytag. "*Queer*! *Queer*! *Queer*!" and SheSheShe jumped up and down on the shirts and towels and handkerchiefs like a jill-in-the-box shocked into life. . . .

At the top of the ridge, nearly panting, the father dropped onto a bench along a gravel path between the slope they had just climbed and the crest of Monument Hill. Larry sat down too, the pair of them gazing sightlessly down into the obscure pines of that slope with the shadow of the silhouetted monument dropping over their shoulders. The father's breathing slowed, his perspiration cooling in this brief haven from the falling sun.

"Larry, St. Thomas Aquinas spoke eloquently and truly of the debased nature of homosexuality."

Larry didn't know what to answer.

"Larry . . . your mother said that some people were worried that *you* might be homosexual."

Larry felt as if he'd been kicked in the stomach. In a flash, the electric presence of a young girl appeared before him and overwhelmed him. The coarse green cloth of a girl scout uniform lay rumpled and hot on her tanning body, as if beneath it she wore nothing else at all. She seemed to hover closer in the air in front of them, but when Larry blurted out in confusion "*NO*!" she receded in an instant down into the needle-tangled trees of the slope, and disappeared.

"'No', Larry? Thank God! For there are few sins graver than violation of God's natural law."

The girls in uniform milling around the large ground floor room which in Larry's house would be the dining room. Margie, the lone campfire girl, petite and poutish in her white blouse under the blue jumper, the wedge of an overseas cap tilted on her full curly hair. And the girl scouts: Samantha, big and summer dark and already breasted, smiling in her eyes, peering around, warily. And Colleen. Colleen with all her freckles, over the bridge of her pug nose and down her neckline where secretly across the soon-swelling mounds of her beginning breasts and . . . As in a twinkling jerk of the hand the slats of a venetian blind may change day to night, Larry is suddenly aloft on the third floor, in a bedroom with Colleen. She says, "Wanna see me bare, Larry?" And she drops her clothes to the floor her body so freckled as almost to be red and her new breasts mound in swelling nipples themselves like big berry-tart freckles, her hips are lilting back and forth, if he could see the nest between her legs it is the same color as her freckles but rolling rolling out like rolled up turf unrolling across Ebbets Field. "Wanna kiss me, Larry? Come on-n-n-n. . . ." Behind her in the frame of the bathroom door there is a clothes hamper, made of wattled straw, or shingled wickerwork, with a band of berry-colored knitting around the circumference of its lid, its lid which lies crooked, not covering the entire mouth of the hamper, its lid tilted subtly toward the floor. "C'mon-n-n-n . . . Chicken? Scaredy cat? C'mon, Larry, kiss me nice. . . ." He's backing toward the door to the hallway, backing, backing. "All right, you little fag! You don't like girls, huh? Don't like girls! You're a *queer*! *Queer*! *Queer*! *Queer*!"

Larry and his father ascended to the pinnacle of Monument Hill. For a moment they stood there, squinting against the liquid diffuse prism of the sun down in the west over the green grass sea of Second Field. Then they descended toward the place they were forced by God and Holy Mother The Church to call home.

Mark
Blickley | *Dear Miss*

THE CAPTAIN'S DEAD but hard to forget. He has to be dead. Nobody's liver could survive all those years of poisoning.

That's the word he used. Poison. Never drinking or booze or alcoholism. It was poison that ruined his life.

The Captain was a romantic. So was I.

Years ago I tended bar in a flea-bag dump called The Second Hand Rose. I wanted to experience life and write about it so I dropped out of Rutgers for three semesters and poured the vinegar that my boss called wine into small cups for customers like the Captain and his mates. Mates. That's the word he used for the sour smelling people he drank with.

The Captain was different though. He had enough pride not to make excuses unless he thought they'd be believed. When the Captain spoke he nearly always made sense.

Last week I found a sealed letter the Captain gave me. I was supposed to deliver it to a woman customer who came into the Rose every Tuesday night. She always stayed for about an hour and sat at a table by herself, never saying a word. She told me she liked Scotch and that was the only time I ever heard her speak. But we communicated. She sipped Scotch until her glass was empty and then she'd nod in my direction and I'd bring her another one.

I never knew her name. But then I didn't know the Captain's name either, until I opened his letter.

One day she just stopped showing up so I wasn't able to give it to her. I tucked it in a vest pocket where it lay crumpled for years. How many years? I'm not sure. There's no date on it.

DEAR MISS:

I give this note to Big Bob to give to you cause I know Big Bob's gonna be tending bar Tuesday nights. You aint been here in weeks. For a year now you been real important to me and now you aint here no more. Please come back. I'm ready for you Miss. To meet you I mean.

ANYONE IS POSSIBLE

The Second Hand Rose aint the same place anymore. Your perfumes gone and now piss and farts is all you smell on Tuesday nights. Even Big Bob said so. I miss you very much.

Hello Miss. My name's Eddie but friends call me the Captain. I aint a real Captain or nothing. I mean I'm sorta a Captain. I'm the floor man on the Scrambler at Coney Island. I mean I use to be. I'm the guy at the bar with the sailor hat on. To be honest with you Miss I wear the hat all the time cause of my bald spot. It aint that big you know.

You look real pretty Miss. I mean there aint been no lady in Rose's looking like you in years. Not by herself anyway. Not alone. I hope you aint sad or nothing. I aint sad. Being a little scared don't count right Miss?

You like music? I'm musician. Play harmonica. Grandfather taught me when I was a kid. I'm what they call a street musician. Mostly old Italian songs. I play across the street from S.P.Q.R. in Little Italy. Ever been there? The Arabs in the kitchen treat me real good. On Saturday nights when its warm there's a lot of bucks to be had.

You gotta come back to Rose's Miss. I blown too many chances. You can't take my Tuesday nights away like that. You can't Miss. Your making me scared.

I know you don't like talkin to people Miss. You don't like being bothered. Me too. Big Bob'll give you this. Its sorta like a letter of introduction right Miss? You gotta show Miss. Please. I'm the Captain the guy in the sailor hat at the bar. Or you can call me Eddie.

I wanna see you smile Miss. You don't drink that much. I mean your never blitzed after your hour on Tuesday night. I respect that in a woman. You got all your teeth so I know you aint a tramp or nothing. Your a lady Miss. A real lady. And you aint fat at all.

Forgive me Miss but your real important to me. You make me feel like a man again know what I mean? Last year before you started showing up Tuesday nights I sorta let myself go. You know relaxed myself.

I dream about you Miss. I aint dreamed about a woman in three years since that Puerto Rican jerked me off behind the control booth at Coney. She didn't like me or nothing just wanted a free re-ride.

Dear Miss

I gotta be honest with you Miss. I aint much. I'll tell you a story that might help you figure out who I am. Its something my brother told me. He once said I was the type a guy that sits in his room masturbating and thinks its an explosion. I aint exactly sure what he means but it sounds truthful.

I don't know if you noticed Miss but I been cleaning myself up a bit each Tuesday night. I seen you looking over at me but I don't think you seen me. You gotta come back to Rose's Miss. I'm starting not to like myself again.

You make me feel like a man Miss. No disrespect Miss but my prick feels alive. I mean it kinda sings to me now. I forgot about that. You know after a while it just pissed all that stinkin juice I drink.

I dream about you Miss. I dream I see you with nothing on. Your beautiful woman Miss. You gotta return to your table at Rose's. You gotta. I aint dreamed about you in two weeks. I need that dream Miss. I need to dream about me rubbing my nose against your belly and you laughing and smiling. I never seen you smile Miss.

Listen Miss. I don't want this note to make you nervous or something. You don't got to see me if you dont want. Not right away anyway. Things take time sometimes. But give me back my Tuesday nights ok Miss? Sit down at your table and have some drinks. I'll spring for some. I won't spin around and stare at you. I like watchin you in the mirror over the bar. Lots a times I got to tell Big Bob to move the hell outta way cause he blocks my view.

Miss please please come back. Tuesday night I left Rose's with pee stains on my pants. That don't happen when your here. I'm real careful Miss.

Thank you for reading this note. I miss you Miss. Thats sorta funny aint it Miss? Missing you Miss. I wanna make you laugh.

BEST WISHES
The Captain (Eddie)

Kate
Gale
| *Steve as Altar Boy*

1
Hotdogs

SOMETIMES MOMMY takes me to the hotdog stand at the beach where the girls wear white and yellow. The girls do not notice me much; they notice my brother. He is older than me and seems more exciting to girls who have long legs. My brother leans on the hotdog stands and smiles. His long hair floats behind him in a ponytail, and the girl's long hair floats behind her in a ponytail, and they look like a couple of ponies, there by the hotdog stand by the water.

Above the stand is a huge hotdog in a bun, and I love that hotdog, also called a wiener, my sister says. A wiener, I say this over to myself because I like the sound of that word.

I also have a wiener, my own wiener, I know this because my sister told me in the bathtub when I ducked my dinosaur toy underwater and made him swim straight up to my parts. Touch my parts, I told him.

Your wiener, my sister said, that's what it is.

It's not a hotdog.

It's a wiener, that's what that thing boys have is called.

Do you want one to play with?

They're yucky.

She says that because she wants one. I know it. So she could stand up like me to go potty, and not have to sit down. In the woods, when we go camping, she has to squat down, but I can stand up. With my wiener in my hand, my hotdog.

2
Superman

I have a stack of superhero books, *Spider Man, Batman, Ninja Turtles*, all of them, but I like *Superman* best. Because he can fly, because he can do anything he wants to. He can fly and rescue people, like girls from under buildings. Girls notice Superman. I worry about Superman though. What if he gets bored, then what would he do? He has to have jobs to do, if he doesn't he might get into trouble. He needs people to save, things to do, I think of things I could do to help keep Superman busy. If I did something, could he undo it? He can make things happen too, he can make the world spindle backward.

3
Spindle

It's not spindle backward, my sister tells me, it's spin. But I like spindle, like my mother's old spindle that she hangs her underwear on to dry. Like the spindle in *Sleeping Beauty*. She touched that spindle, and something happened, she went to sleep, and when she woke up, things were different, things were changed, things were better.

4
My Dad

My Dad never noticed me at first. He noticed my sister. She has long blond hair, silky, down her back, she can read already, and she does her homework, also she never runs away. I am practicing to be Superman, is what my Daddy doesn't understand, I am practicing making things happen. That's why I like elevators, I like to go up and down. I think about flying.

My Daddy wanted another girl like my sister, then I was born. At first, I lay around like babies do, I'm pretty sure of this because Mommy told me. I ate a lot. I played with my wiener, I got big, not big enough to be noticed, but big enough to be me. My Dad likes me sometimes now. Especially since he doesn't live with Mommy. When she was around, he never noticed me at all.

I think the reason he started to notice me now is because I got so big. I am almost big enough to have a girlfriend. My Daddy can't carry me anymore. Sometime, I will do something big, and my Daddy will notice me, and he will see my flying.

5
Mommy's Magazines

My mom gets these magazines in the mail, and I say, Mommy, can I look at these magazines, and she says sure, and keeps chopping onions and garlic. I like the smell of her cooking, and she drinks red stuff, wine she calls it, while she cooks, and she laughs. But I don't like to eat the food. I like plain pasta, macaroni and cheese, pop tarts.

I like my mom's magazines too. There are pictures of ladies like my mom wearing small clothes that are green and orange or with flowers. The girls look like they could nurse a baby, like my babysitter does with her baby. My babysitter nurses her baby all the time, and I watch. She lets me sit beside her, and I watch the baby drinking. In the magazines, the girls look ready to nurse a baby. I would like to see these girls. They have long legs, I like the legs, I wonder if those girls would notice me. I bet they would if I was Superman.

6
Bathing

Spindle me this, spindle me that, I say to my sister in the bathtub, and she passes over the dinosaurs and letters that we play with in the tub. We'd stay in the bath for the whole afternoon, if they'd let us, but they make us get out, and they make us wash our hair, which we don't like.

My sister does not have anything to nurse babies with, but Mommy does, and sometimes I get to take baths with her, and I watch her in the bathtub, and when she looks at me, I say, I'm not looking at your *pechos*, and she smiles, like she knows everything.

I wonder how much she knows, my Mom, whether she is like Superman, only a woman, but it doesn't seem possible. Super people are always men. Like me and Daddy.

My mommy lights candles when we are in the bathtub, when we are eating, when she is writing, thinking or reading. I like these candles. Long ones, blue ones, white ones. I want to have a long candle in my room to watch while I go to sleep at night, but she says no, they're too dangerous.

Daddy puts his finger through the flame of the candle. He does this too many times. Puts the candle flame out. Then finds he has no more matches. Looks through the cupboard for matches. Finds a pile of bullets instead.

What will you do with bullets? we ask him, but he doesn't answer. I think he misses my Mommy or maybe he hates my Mommy, I don't know.

7
God

My Daddy wants me to be an altar boy, and I like the idea. It's something I can do that Daddy notices. I get to wear special sheets, and I lay out food and wine with the other boys. The wine doesn't taste nearly as good as Mommy's wine, and once I spilled some on my white sheets, but I never told that it was because I was drinking it so fast. The other boys are older than me. They say words that I would like to say, but my Daddy would spank me. They say, goddamn, and fucking shit. My Daddy says these words sometimes especially when he is talking about Mommy, but he says if I say them, I will be spanked hard.

I hear about God while I am at church. He is Superman in the sky, and he wears white and rides a white horse, and he can send people to hell. He sends people to hell all the time which is a bad place full of fire. I think God is not as good as Superman. I would like to put God in a fire and see how he likes it. Maybe Superman would rescue him, maybe not, I think so, I think Superman would come down on one of his boring days, and rescue God. Or maybe God could rescue himself like Gulliver.

8
Gulliver's Travels

Gulliver went travelling among the little people, and when there was a big fire, he put it out with his wiener. I like to think about this because maybe, if there was a fire, the hotdog of God would appear out of the sky and put it out.

9
Airplane

My Dad took me on an airplane flight for my birthday. From up there, we saw the church where I am an altar boy. It is a big church with a big thing spindling up to the sky. Daddy calls it a steeple.

In the plane, Daddy was my friend. He talked to me. He noticed me.

10

The Hotdog of God

I spent a weekend at my Daddy's house, but he was gone. He was at his work. He came home Saturday night and talked with my stepmommy, and he went to bed and they made noises. I sat on my bed and sucked my thumb like I am not supposed to do. I went into the room. He told me, Get out of here.

I leave the house quietly and go to the church next door. I walk down the aisle. I find my white sheet clothes and put them on. I light all the candles. I drink some wine, I eat some crackers. I hear noises. I want to see Superman. I call him, but he doesn't answer. Maybe he is sleeping like my Daddy, maybe he is bored to death, maybe he has nothing to do. Maybe God will rescue himself.

My Mommy says God is in everything. Even in chicken? I ask.

Everything, she says.

Even in this hotdog I'm eating right now?

Everything.

So, I know God is a hotdog.

Or at least he has a hotdog because he is a man.

I sit and watch the candles for a while. I think of some stuff to do, and I cry since I am by myself and God and Superman won't see, and when I'm finished and I've played with the fire from the candles a bit, I go home and watch out the window hoping to see something.

Marlene	*The Story of the Fish*
Joyce	*and the Man who Took Her*
Pearson	*from the Sea*

IN ONE LIFE I was a fish—a blue, flared-finned fish, and I lived in the sea, at least until this hand waved cracker crumbs over my water. The man caught me at a ravenous moment, and I almost bit off his fingers sucking in such salty, white crumbs. He smiled and told me the crackers were leftovers from church. It was Sunday, and he was God or something like that. He had been preaching on the cross. After I removed the splinter festering in his wrist by waving my fin across his arm, we became good friends. He said to call him Charles, that I had a nice mouth, and then proposed.

He took me home to meet his mother, Edna. She wiped her hands on her apron when he explained we were to be married. She had never heard of such a thing. But she calmed down when he promised to keep me in a small glass bowl in the bedroom.

In the bedroom he mostly kept the door closed when company—especially Edna's friends—came over. And the other thing was—he had to promise to change my water a lot, so I wouldn't smell. She hated the smell of animals, and even though Charles tried to explain that I was not an animal—just a little fish, she put cotton balls inside her ears, rubbed cold cream on her face and sat down to watch Johnny Carson.

The man was not a bad son. The woman wasn't a bad mother either, really, but I could see that I had better learn to breathe and paddle out of there like a legged animal, a dog or something, soon because fish gills did not rate much in that house. So I practiced holding my breath for long periods of time. When I came up for air, I blew piles of bubbles in the corner of my bowl. Edna began to like me, she squinched up her eyes and wrinkled her nose, like a puffer fish. She began to believe in me. I think she saw me as a relative. She began talking baby talk into my bowl. That's when Charles said, She's never done that for me.

2

Charles had been one of those genius child-prodigies, a prophet type, his mother called him. He had even gone to Aimee Semple McPherson's funeral when he was three and clapped his hands to the songs. Mrs. McKinzie was sitting next to Edna and said, Praise the Lord! That child is sure to be a somethingorother! Edna did not hear due to the high-pitched, loud notes she was trying to reach with her own voice.

On that day, he told me that no one brought up the gossip about Aimee, who it seems had a lover, and her story had filled the papers for months, how they flew further than the world together, one reporter exaggerated. Although Charles said that what he had seen happen with his own eyes was quite spectacular. He told me how gossip hung light as air on the wings of mosquitoes right there in the church during the funeral. Then toads jumped up, licked the gossip right off the mosquito's wings, onto their tongues, and kissed all the young girls sitting very still, with their legs crossed, next to their fathers and mothers. When each little girl was kissed by a frog, she had an orgasm which shot her straight up to the roof. Little girls bounced up beyond the double balconies and hit their tiny, bobbed curls on the dome ceiling of Angeles Temple. One bumped into the painted John the Baptist right there in the imitation fresco of Jesus with the apostles and saints gathered at a table. It was supposed to represent the last supper. For these little girls, it was a big burp and then, of course, each one died.

After three days, the whole neighborhood got together for a barbeque and a massive funeral for all the little girls of the four-square church who had passed away at Aimee Semple McPherson's funeral and all the families came. But it seemed that the little brothers missed their little sisters tremendously already, more than seemed appropriate for siblings, because who else could they get to retrieve their baseballs that had accidentally flown over the fence and landed on Mrs. McKinzie's parrot's cage? And what if they fell off their scooters? Someone had to run inside and get mom and the Band-Aids. It had always been the sweet sisters. So the brothers' cried the most while they swallowed hot dogs with extra mustard. And that was the beginning of emotion in boys—or so Charles, brilliant man that he is, tells me.

3

Somehow I have wandered from my story, and I want to tell you about my life as a fish, and the man I knew named Charles. He was always cleaning the side of my glass bowl with his shirt sleeve so I could see better. He was remarkable. But he felt so sorry for me, locked away in that tiny bowl in the bedroom that the hair on his arms stood up red when he tried, but could not tell his mother how he wanted to move me into the living room, into a larger aquarium, large enough for him to swim in too once in a while. When he tried to utter the words to Edna, she stood stiff as a broom and his mouth clamped shut like lock-jaw. She slapped a hand in the air, said, Shhh! and swiveled her chair around to watch the rest of *Jeopardy* and talk to Mrs. McKinzie on the telephone.

Charles wanted to cry, really cry—the way he had done with the neighborhood boys when he was little, but all that emotion had stopped suddenly one day, and he couldn't remember much about that, not when, not why. He only remembered the hot spot on his cheek where his mother slapped him for crying. She told him boys don't do that.

Since that day, Charles didn't think he had ever gotten angry. He'd done a few things, slammed his fist through the bedroom wall once, when his door was shut and Edna was in the living room sitting in her velour swivel chair laughing at TV, but now crickets occupied the hole in Charles's wall, and his mother never noticed a thing. She thinks that because he is this genius and so religious to boot! that the hole must represent some God thing or maybe he was practicing a sermon and this is the miracle God sent to show them that there really are demons and a dark scary place. Charles just grew quiet, and then one day my dear husband saw no alternative other than to close his bedroom door, sit down and slit his eyes open with thorns he'd grabbed off Edna's rose bushes. He even tried poking his arms, trying to slice through the veins he said, get back to the fish he claimed to have been in a previous life. Imagine it! I thought he'd certainly lost his mind. But Edna said, Be quiet son, practice your preaching in whispers, *Wheel of Fortune* is on, and she took the cotton balls from her ears when Vanna White popped on the screen. Charles planned to cry for the rest of his life. I watched it all from my little glass bowl, until blood splashed onto the side of the glass.

4

I gave him time, then I blew bubbles to get Charles's attention—a huge spire of bubbles, and out of the top of the spire like sending organ music, you know, something he'd understand, I tried to remind him that it was Sunday and he would be expected to minister to his congregation. How would it look if he didn't show up? Or killed himself yet? Why, didn't he remember suicide was a sin? And wouldn't he be damned in some fiery lake? I wonder if fish swim in that lake? Can I go there too? Are fish allowed in hell? Probably like an aquarium with the heater turned on high. Maybe he'd just end up in that black hole in his wall with the crickets preaching sermons to dust balls. Oh, I never believed a word of the fiery place, but the bubbles and organ music worked. Charles wiped away the blood, took a deep breath and pulled himself up from where he had collapsed to the floor.

It took a few minutes, but finally he was dressed—a long-sleeved shirt and grey suit. Nothing special, but the long sleeves hid the thorn cuts, and I convinced him to wear dark glasses though he complained he'd look like one of the Blues Brothers; well, what's so bad about that? I told him. Why don't you take a saxophone to church and play "When The Saints Come Marching In?" People love that stuff. Anyway, finally Charles was ready and, just my luck, this Sunday Charles took me along in my glass bowl, after he cleaned it off. He said he didn't want to be alone at the pulpit, so he put me beneath the podium on one of the shelves where preachers keep a glass of water, or sometimes they put a white hankie there so if they sweat during the sermon, they grab the linen thing and dab their foreheads; it looks serious. Charles placed my bowl next to the hankie and the glass of holy water he used to pray for people who wanted extra attention, they called it healing.

When he finished the sermon—which was short, I suppose, because he was still recuperating from his suicide earlier that afternoon—he asked people to come to the altar. Anyone who wanted salvation or to be healed—that magic word. The first one to dash down the aisle was, of course, Edna. While the audience sang, Amazing grace, how sweet the sound . . . I saw her elbow past an old, crippled man who slouched and tripped backwards, luckily, landing in a wooden seat. She said her eyes hurt and she wanted Charles to anoint and pray for her. Of course, he did. As he prayed she whispered, Louder, son, louder, and opened her eyes a bit to make sure that Mrs. McKinzie saw.

When I heard her whisper, I tried to keep quiet. But I couldn't, I bubbled out to Charles, Tell her the truth—to turn off her damn TV and talk to you once in a while. He said, No, no, I can't, and pushed my bowl into the back corner. When my bubbles spilled over the top and dribbled down the wooden shelf onto his black shoes, he covered me with the Sunday church bulletin.

But no sooner was she home than she turned on the damn TV again, sat two feet in front and watched a re-run of *Truth or Consequences* and then two segments of *I Love Lucy*. Edna sang all the commercials and did not budge until the late news was over and the test signal glared from the glass screen.

5

Back in the bedroom, Charles stroked my little glass bowl and apologized, but he begged me to understand his mother. He just could not contradict that woman, not since he had been four years old. That was when he tried to join the neighborhood boys playing football, but they kept nudging him out of their circle of muscles and balls. So he offered the boys lemons from his mother's tree. After all, Edna had said she grew the biggest lemons on the block. All the boys scuffled up the tree and threw lemons, the size of basketballs, at each other. They played dodge ball with one until the lemon squashed on the asphalt driveway. Then the biggest boy told Charles the way to their clubhouse.

Charles remembered feeling good inside until his mother came to the screen door. The screen was dark with rust and dust, so the boys could not see her through the steel webbing. She took one look and dashed at the knob. It was a double lock, but took only an instant to scoot the metal chain off and flick the other lock open. All the boys heard her screeching like a crow, and they beat it out the gate.

Edna hollered at Charles, slapped her hands on her apron, stomped one foot into the asphalt. Get over here and sit down! You stay right here! It sounded like she ordered him to move the way you'd tell a dog, he said. She went back inside and came out with a large knife. His eyes grew large like the lemons. She cut all the sour fruit in half, piled them one on the other beside the boy, pointed her finger from the lemons to his mouth.

He heard a loud noise, he said. It must have been her words. But he was not sure because of the ringing in his head which grew louder than her voice. He picked up a lemon and started to eat. He saw her go back inside the house and slam the door shut. The screeching door sounded like the sour taste he tried to swallow without crying because, of course, boys were not supposed to cry. He heard the locks turn and slide, and he knew she would never let him back inside until he had sucked, chewed and swallowed all the lemons.

She hollered out the window, loud so Mrs. McKenzie would hear, And if your stomach aches, don't tell me about it, Charles, this is for your own good! I swear you won't come in until the test patterns are on TV!

So he sucked and sucked and puckered and swallowed all the lemons right down to the skins. And his stomach ached. It ached until he heaved with cramps, but he did not tell his mother. He only crawled inside late that night when she unlatched the locks, and he sank into bed, deep into the covers where he dreamed of living inside a giant lemon; of the neighborhood boys kicking the lemon all the way to the boulevard and he could roll down the gutter to the bad side of town—which he dreamed must be lovely, peaceful—red lights, women standing beneath doorways. He heard his mother laughing with them, cackling, he called it. And when he woke up, a worm crawled out of his ear, changed into a butterfly and told him to pray.

So he did. Charles called the wormy thing the Holy Spirit and said it was wonderful to tell God all about his mother. Or was it Jesus? I guess they think those two are the same one. What is it? Some god with two heads? He asked, No, three heads. So I tried to imagine it—a god with three heads, six arms and six legs. Sounded to me like an insect.

6

It has been a long time, something like a year, my husband said, since he first sprinkled the crumbs over my water. Charles told me they were leftovers from communion. Well, now I know what communion is. It's a game where people close their eyes and the preacher is dressed in black and he drops crackers, like rolling dice, into their mouths, and the people pretend they are eating the body and blood of one of their gods. I remember big fish in the sea doing the same thing—they would swallow—whole—a small fish like me.

Charles's mother grew older, weaker and smaller, but continually watched TV, unless it was Sunday, then she ran to the podium. He's my son, she stammered like she was speaking in tongues, running past everyone, and she'd beg him to pray for her first. She loved that. One day she died and Charles had her cremated and her ashes thrown over the ocean. I hope she didn't gag any fish!

Charles just kept putting on his black suit and preaching. He seemed to forget his plans for us—moving me into the living room, our swimming together. But I guess his routine was good for him. As for me, I never returned to the sea in that life, and Charles was pretty good to me.

He put me in a bowl that was a bit larger, square instead of round, one with a pump and filter and a nice little heater. He even put a castle with a hole big enough for me to swim in and out of at the bottom of some sand. But to tell you the truth, I would like to have moved out of his bedroom like Charles wanted a long time ago, into the living room and into a larger aquarium. But he did move me near the window, so I spent the remainder of my days watching the sun rise through my glass and watching Mrs. McKinzie's parrot sitting in its cage eating crackers.

Cameron
Fase

Some Kind Of Smorgasbord

I OPEN MY EYES to darkness. I feel a milky cool substance caressing my body, and my eyeballs seem to swim in the substance apart from my skull. I feel cramped and try to stretch, but I can't seem to escape the fetal position I am bound to. I am swimming in pudding but can't do the backstroke. Frantically I wiggle around, but my actions are in slow motion due to the resistance of the substance. I am like Houdini chained and locked in a trunk in the bottom of the ocean. From outside observation I seem to be in a comfortable stasis. The truth is panic. I ain't no escape artist.

I see a crack of light swim through the different textures of substance; jumping, bending and shooting in all directions. The substance begins to drain through the crack of light, and as the crack widens, I wiggle frantically until I find my naked body in a pool of iridescent ooze, with sharp pieces of eggshell all about me. My pupils shrink as they are flooded with a fluorescent green light.

As I wake, my eyelids slide away from my corneas, revealing myself buried nipple deep in cool dawn sand. My bald scalp is covered in snails. Where they came from I do not know. The sun peaks over the dunes with a violet existence that silhouettes my alligator skinned luggage, which lies out of reach.

I wiggle my body in a patient attempt to free myself of this granular prison in the desert. My attempt seems worthless, but I do free myself before the sun turns red. With no energy left I rest naked, noticing that the snails have journeyed elsewhere leaving a glittering trail toward the horizon.

I take my red polka dotted clown suit and big red wig out of my suitcase and get dressed. I unzip the small pocket on the front of the suitcase to get out my make up case, and precede to paint my face white with blue triangles pointing north and south around my eyes and great big red dots on my cheeks. I shape and twist a balloon into a pink elephant and leave it near the hole in the sand where I slept.

I begin to walk across the desert, my big red Ronald Mac Donald shoes filling up with hot sand. I walk for about half an hour before reaching what looked like the ruins of an old highway. The black asphalt has turned white almost dissolving into the ocean of sand that surrounds it, and the dotted spine of the highway has turned from yellow to a faded mustard color. The skeletal remains of the highway have been taken advantage of and thrown away, probably never to be used again.

With a sweaty face hiding behind the caked layers of white foundation, I decide to take my chances and wait for a passing car to rescue me. With an alligator skinned pillow and a fat thumb hanging in the middle of the highway, I fall asleep.

I open my eyes to the sight of beings with oversized craniums, large obsidian eyes and tiny slit mouths that drooled as they gathered around my body. "Am I some kind of smorgasbord?"

I clutch my suitcase and wake up to see my reflection in the mirrored glasses of a highway patrolman. It is quite startling to see the reflection of a smiling clown in your face, when you know you're not smiling. It's quite ironic that a clown can't frown because the painted smile forbids it. My eyes wander down his face past a drop of jelly and some powdered sugar in his beard (I didn't have the heart to tell him). My eyes continue down the bulbous trunk of his body, down past those ugly tan pants that flare out at the thighs and stop right below the knee caps where the tall boots began. I see his motorcycle and think how fun it would be to kick this guy's fat ass and drive off like a rebel fugitive into the horizon. But I am too tired to be thinking crazy shit like that.

"Can I help you son?" chunks of apple fritter flying off his hairy face.

"Ain't ya got no respect fer yerself, wit' all that shit flyin', off yer face n' shit. And why ya callin' me son I ain't yer son. I probably even am older than yer sorry butt."

Well, he starts whimpering about something and gets on his motorcycle and leaves. "Now there's a real cop!" I say to myself. "Why you're so stupid that was probably your only way out of here, and where is here? What am I doing? How did I get here? Oh well." You know I really don't care. I sort of have my health and I am alive so what should I care?

I notice a blue four-by-four coming toward me from the horizon. As it comes closer, it looks like a big Tonka truck with flood lights on the roll bars and all that tricked out off-roading stuff. As it gets closer, I begin to jump up and down waving my hands to get them to stop. It is full of a bunch of yuppie college students, and I hate that kind of kid. They think they're so much smarter than you as they drive around in their daddy-bought toys. Anyway they stop, so I have to swallow my opinion, as I run to get in the truck, and when I am about five feet away from the yuppie toy truck, they do a brody and take off laughing. I give then a big one finger salute and call them as many curse words as I can think of.

I turn around and see a beat up old pickup colored in various shades of primer pull up and stop. The two men in it ask, "So where you goin' Bozo"

"I don't know . . . where am I?"

"Well, you's about twenty minutes out a Vegas, hop in we'll take ya?"

I throw my bag in the back of the truck and sit up in the cab, squished next to a scruffy older man who has whiskey on his breath and probably hasn't showered yet this month. However, I must smell rather good to him too.

"Hiya I'm Bud and this is my older brother Tom. He don't talk much," the driver says. "We's saw them punks showering' ya wit' dirt. We hate them college brats thinkin' they's better n' stuff 'cause they got edacation. Ya know they ain't so bright. Once me n' Tom here saw one uv 'em on the side of the highway with a flat, har har *HA!*" Bud has an interesting laugh, it starts in a soft har and stopped short with a strong *HA*, that lasts no longer than a second. "Any ways we stopped to sees what the matter was. He said he had a flat and couldn't change the tire, har har *HA!* Well we's said neither did we and we left his dumb self sittin', there crying in the dirt. Hey, ya see that burlap bag in the back. Me n' Tom here just knocked off a liquor store, and plannin' ta make it rich in Vegas." For some reason I don't care about driving down the highway with a couple of felons, if they didn't care about driving with a big goofy looking clown.

Bud is a talkative guy and talks the whole twenty minutes to Vegas. I don't even get to say a word the whole way there, but that is good, because I am too tired to speak anyway. He talks so much I don't really remember most of the drive except when I see the Tonka truck pull over on the side of the road, and everybody getting frisked by that fat cop I scared off earlier. I make all sorts of faces at them; it feels so good.

I see the bright lights of sin city. It reminds me of a carnival and I know I am going to like it here. I feel that a great life change, is about to happen. My body fills with such an energy I am no longer hungry or tired. Bud and Tom stop just before entering Vegas to get a bite to eat at some five-dollar steak dinner joint. As soon as the car stops I run out of the truck toward the great towering, dancing lights. I am skipping and jumping around like a kid and must look like some joker on PCP. I am so wrapped up in the excitement I don't notice the squad cars that surround the pickup, and arrest Bud and Tom. I fling my arms up to the lights and scream, "I'm home!"

I run down the neon lighted streets of Vegas hugging and kissing everyone I see. Yeah, I get punched a couple of times by some homophobic white trash, city cowboys, but I don't care. I love seeing the blurred lights and faces of the thousands of people as I run down the street. I run into a casino, rummaging through my pockets for a quarter as I dance around the money hungry gamblers. You know it's really funny to watch people gamble. They spend fifty dollars, and when they win a buck they get so happy, as if they won a dollar instead of loosing forty-nine. I find a quarter, drop it into a slot machine, not really expecting anything, just playing for the fun of it. Then lights and sirens go off as I win a million bucks or something. I fall flat on my face and pass out.

I wake. There are guys in tuxes with platters full of stacked bills overlooking me. "Sir, here are your winnings." I just stand up, drool in amazement. Cameras are going off everywhere, reporters are coming out the walls asking all kinds of stupid questions like, "How do you feel, about winning a million dollars?" or "Why are you wearing a clown suit?"

I get a room at a hotel. I order everything on the room service menu. I eat until I pass out watching nudy shows on pay-per-view. The next day I meet a showgirl and get married in a drive through chapel by an Elvis impersonating priest named Father Priestley. I live happily ever after.

Travis Hodgkins	*75 MPH*

"DO YOU REALIZE YOU'RE AN ACCOMPLICE?"

I guess I could keep iffing all night and I'd still be here answering what I can and making up what I can't. I don't know what he thought or was trying to think. All I know is that if we had changed cars in New Mexico, like I had wanted to, they would have never traced the car back to L.A. and they would have never matched it up to the murder.

We must have been six states away before she called the cops; her conscience must have gotten to her. Even though she swore she hated Paul's guts, and mine even more, I knew it would be awhile before she picked up the phone. But he was still all go, go, go! He only puked once, but it was in his eyes, the scene played over and over.

"The Bitch and the Bastard" must have been how he saw it. He saw everything like that. Big, white, block letters laid up flat against that black background "The Bitch and The Bastard." He was always quoting films. It was all just shit as far as I'm concerned, the only thing I liked about him was that he knew you had to live life before you could tell people about it.

I think that's why he picked me. It's not like he picked me like I was the forsaken one or there were a lot of people for him to choose from, but Mommy and Daddy had plenty of cash to send him out to C-A. He didn't need me, they could have flown him right into C-A, but that's not living—that's not good material. The best thing that could happen on a plane is a hijacking or crashing in the Rockies during a horrible snowstorm and end up eating the other passengers. No, he knew the best way, my way.

He got in my car talking.

First thing he did was ask a stupid question and he asked this same question every time I got a new car, "Is this stolen?" Don't ask me stupid questions. I've never wanted anything more than to meet the person who started that fucking saying. Just let him ask me a stupid question, and after I told him what an anal crock of shit his stupid question was he'd probably turn around and tell me "sticks and stones." There are two kinds of people, the ones who ask stupid questions and the ones who answer them. Then there's me. I've got your fucking answer, but if you don't know it you can shove it and keep stumbling through life half-witted.

What did he expect me to tell him? No? He'd picked me for two reasons. I always had transportation and I knew the roads. I stole my first car when I was a fish. I couldn't even drive yet, but here I was in the seat, flooring Michael McCall's new, blue Mustang through red lights and all, eating up corners and snaking through traffic on the belts.

Paul couldn't believe it. That Christmas break I stole a Chevy Nova and drove to New Orleans for my first time. The piece of shit didn't even make it through Alabama and I had to steal another car, a Honda Prelude, just to make it the rest of the way. Then I was nailed on my way back through Alabama, but I was pretty much slapped on the wrist and sent home. You learn real fast, change your cars a lot and you won't get caught and you won't have to make your dad mad and get belted.

Paul and I are true of any two junior high pals. Once you reach high school, you break away and start finding your own kind of people. While I was sitting in PE learning how to steal cars, he had his nose plugged in some book or was auditioning for a play. While I was at a show getting stoned and moshing, he was at prom getting stoned and dancing slow with some prissy cheerleader who probably gabbled his ear off all night with stupid questions.

And even though we lived in two separate worlds, by the time he needed to go to C-A, we still nodded to each other in the halls and said hello and actually talked when we ran into each other outside school. He'd ask me where I'd been lately, then he'd tell me about some flick he'd seen that supposedly was filmed there, but was probably mostly shot on some set somewhere. We had that kind of friendship where you can always seem to trust that other person and depend on them. Paul said it was because "we're keen on each other's instincts." I don't know about that, but I do know that where I had gaps he filled in and the reverse.

He surprised me when he asked if I would take him to C-A. I mean, the guy had a life to live. College, maybe a future, but he knew it and so did I. He could spend his time in college, in the dorms, living with a bunch of preppies who go home during the holidays and talk about how much they miss Mommy and Daddy and little Toto because they've never been any further from home than their family summers on the Virgin Islands. No, he needed out, not to mention he didn't want to make comedies.

I considered not taking him, and if I hadn't, they wouldn't still be picking pieces of him out of the Toyota Corolla I smashed into the side of a hill. Anyway, he was set on going and this was probably his only chance to go in style like this. He'd had some girl in high school he'd supposedly fallen in love with who had moved to C-A just after graduation. She was starting right away in summer session at some school in the L.A. area. He had to see her, and why not have some fun on the way.

He should have listened to Peckinpah, the only one of those Hollywood assholes Paul liked and I could stomach.

She was some girl in drama he'd met, worked with, and then worked. The only damn thing I ever liked about her was her hair. It reminded me of wheat fields in the Midwest. I imagined her hair smelled like it too with the windows rolled down on an early summer morning. Its thick odor pushing on your face at eighty replacing the stale stench that settles in a car after driving across the states all night.

There was one thing that I'd agreed with Peckinpah first off, there are two kinds of women. He said, "There are women and then there's pussy." Callie was pussy, and rank pussy at that. He said that a woman will take a man three times further than he could normally go and pussy was immature and, in my opinion, most importantly, naive in the ways of life.

While she was stroking Paul with one hand, she was stroking two others. While she was lying in bed with Paul filling his ear with stories about marriage and love, she was telling everyone else that he was a bastard. He may be a stupid bastard, but not a bastard like she was making him out to be. He didn't want to hear about it, and when he did listen, all he'd say was, "Well, at least the sex is good."

I still don't know if not telling her we were coming was the best thing that ever happened to me or not. All I know is that I don't have any place left to go. The air smells different, a way I've never smelt it before and the colors all seem more like how they should look.

All he could talk about was going west. New Orleans was too far south for him. But the fact remained, I steal the cars, I pick the routes. But there was one thing he wasn't going to do and that was sleep on the ground. His parents gave him some plastic and he was determined that we were going to stay in a hotel everywhere we went. I don't know why they didn't just buy him a car, and save me the labor and Paul some neck pain from always looking over his shoulder.

"This is real Morrison style."

Paul had this serious problem—he was hypnotized by the legends and myths that had been spawned by literature and Hollywood. Anything we did had something to do with someone. When he got in my car, he had a bag full of books all about being on the road. As soon as we got on the beltway, I threw them out the window. He heed and hawed about it, about that they were classics, and these people knew how to ride.

"Then, they might have. Now, these roads are mine." It didn't really matter, he'd read them already.

He felt that driving across the country—especially West—in a stolen car was just how Morrison would have done it. That is, if Morrison had actually had the nerve to steal a car. I was willing to teach Paul, but he preferred to wait in the room and believe me, sleeping in hotels made life easier when it came to stealing. I'd go into the parking garage and have my choice of automobiles and because I'd driven in with a stolen car I'd have a parking ticket so I could get back out of the garage. Not to mention who knows how long it would be before the owners would go back to the garage to get their car.

"Fingernails" is what I call it. There isn't another feeling like it. You don't feel it until you step out of your room with the intention to steal. It's real light at first like someone is tickling me, but with each footstep, the closer I get, the harder the nails scrape across my skin. And when I've slipped that jimmy down into the car door it feels like some mad lover is scraping their fingers through my hair, over my scalp, and all I want to do is roll my eyes back and just fall into this feeling. But once that monster under the hood coughs and then leaps up it all goes away and all that's left is a light sting that would come from a red welted scratch.

Morrison didn't have the nerve to face life, he'd probably stand in the hotel lobby, if he got that close.

There are certain rules to the road that if you follow you won't have any problems. I broke one of these, and not a little one. I fell asleep at the wheel. We'd gotten to the L.A. area early in the morning, about five, after driving for almost fourteen hours straight from El Paso. Then hell erupted in our faces and we skipped out of town headed back to N-Y I started popping No-Doz to stay awake, another rule broken. When I came down I came down hard. I woke up in a hospital bed with an escort to County, where they told me that my friend who I'd smashed up in the car had his prints all over a gun that had filled some schmuck's face full of holes back in L.A. Then they started asking me stupid questions.

I knew better. I'm not even sure if that shit keeps you awake. The only thing you notice is that your whole body starts shaking all over. I've decided that's probably what keeps you awake. Then, when you're coming down, you don't think you're coming down, you start telling yourself things like, "I'll hear the reflectors when the car goes over them and I'll wake up," or, "I'll feel the car jerk when it hits the shoulder." All I had to do was wake Paul, but he hadn't slept since we'd left C-A, and he'd taken some cough syrup to make himself drowsy when I took No-Doz.

The crazy things you think when you're running trying to find a safe place. Callie surely had told them where we live, but in our panic we ran for home when we should have been going to Mexico or Canada. We needed familiar people. If there is one thing I know, it's that no matter where you go, the cities are all pretty much the same. The further west you go the newer things are, but they're still the same. It's the people that change. We wanted far away from California, from Los Angeles.

We were on the road in Texas flying down the 10, probably one of the longest stretches of pavement in the world. The fucker just keeps going and going. All there is to do is listen to the radio and talk. Paul talked about making our trip into a movie someday. He'd call it "Seventy-five miles per hour."

"I'd open it with this keen guy I met at that diner in New Orleans. I was talking to this guy, well, actually, he sort of started talking to me, and he asked me where we're headed and I told him L.A. He got real interested and told me he'd been all through L.A. and San Diego and Santa Barbara, and all up and down the West Coast. I asked him if he'd been to New York and he said yeah. Come to find out he drove trucks and now he lives behind the diner and comes in there every morning to eat breakfast."

"So, picture this. It opens on one of the main characters, the one playing me, maybe Val Kilmer because not only is he a good actor but he has blond hair too. So here's Val and this old guy just sitting at this counter eating breakfast when the old guy starts talking to him and they have this conversation. And then Val, who's me, asks, 'What's it like in L.A.?' And the old guy responds with—and he really said this—'They're crazy.'"

I had to laugh. They couldn't be any nuttier than the ones in N-Y I didn't talk to the old man and Paul didn't bother to ask him what he thought was so crazy. But I can guess now.

I always got a kick out of going to the South. It's like one constant freak show. I mean in N-Y, you can spot normal-looking people, beautiful people, and the freaks. You know where they are and which you are. In the South, I don't think they know and that's part of the problem. Whereas other places try and hide them, the South puts them on display.

Paul's first real run-in with the South was a few hours into Virginia at a gas station. He came back from the bathroom and got in the car and looked at me and said, "It's like we're in a David Lynch film." I guess the bathroom was in the back of the quickie down this long hallway that had half the lights out and some guy was sitting on the floor with his baseball hat just touching his greasy brown hair, one of those "bad eighties hair cuts," with the back long and the top short. His legs were stretched out on the tile floor and between them was a styrofoam cup. Supposedly it looked like he was trying to bend at the middle of his body to try and get a drink while his eyes followed Paul all the way to the bathroom, then back out as if he'd never stopped looking at the door.

On his way out, some skinny, but real tall guy walked by Paul with his shoulders swishing from side to side, but it wasn't the funny way the guy walked, or maybe it was the combination, it was the T-shirt he had on that announced that, "The South will rise again."

If you ever want to know what a place is like go to the bathroom at a gas station and read the walls. In most places like N-Y or L.A. the most interesting things you'll read are blowjob offers. I was in Arcata once in a Chevron bathroom and on the wall was a poem about a guy who lined two hundred girls up and fucked each and every one and by the time he finished his balls were blue. The most impressive part was that it all rhymed. I mean, the guy didn't miss a beat. Whether or not he got it out of a book, it didn't matter because he had taken the time to write something on the wall that not only made me laugh, but had some quality to it as opposed to, "I'll bet you a hundred dollars that when you're reading this you're touching your dick."

In a Chevron in Baton Rouge, I actually spent twenty minutes reading everything on the walls.

There wasn't an empty spot for you to put your initials on that wall without writing on something somebody else had written. Out of everything that was in there, only one was a blowjob offer and above that it said "Fuck you AIDS fucker." Above that, it said something like "Only niggers are queers," but "nigger" was crossed out and replaced with "honkey." From that branched every homophobic remark I've ever read and more.

The wall next to that was like a bulletin board for the KKK. I'm surprised there weren't meeting announcements and sign-up sheets. There were quotes from Hitler and people I'd never heard of. They weren't penny quotes, either. They were like passages from books. The wall next to that was the same as its neighbor except it was passages from Malcolm X and Martin Luther King Jr. and more people I'd never heard of. Both walls had passages from the Bible, and all three walls just kind of bled onto the wall with the door.

That wasn't the only one. I saw others just like it in Florida, Alabama, and Georgia. If I ever get a camera, I swear I'm going to take pictures of these walls and show them to any and everyone. I told Paul he had to put them in his movie. They're like shrines of hate hidden in little no-name towns.

Our conversation drifted every so often back to girls. I don't think either of us has ever been with a woman. As someone who is in love does, all he could talk about was Callie. I never really knew anything about her. The most I knew was that she was originally from C-A and moved East her sophomore year. As to things like statistics and such, I was in the dark. All I knew was the fat, and that's more often than not more important than anything else.

I'd heard her name in my ring of friends before she actually hooked up with Paul. So it was no surprise when he told me he didn't start experimenting with drugs until he met her. What surprised me was that he said she didn't start experimenting until then either. They didn't get together until the end of our senior year, and I'd heard stories about her long before then.

We'd go on for hours talking about girls while the car pounded down the road. He'd tell me something and then I'd tell him about some broad I was banging and then he'd ask me some stupid questions, and would end up talking about Callie again. And then he asked me:

"Women are scary, aren't they?"

This got me. It wasn't a stupid question, but there was still something very obvious about it. Like if I said "yes," I'd be joining some kind of secret society and if I said "no," I'd be cast out and never offered this opportunity again.

"I don't know. I like to think they're a lot like us." It was a denial, but not exactly.

"No, I don't think so."

"Why not?"

"They're just not."

"Well, that doesn't make any sense."

"It's not supposed to. It's just the way it is."

"They're human beings. What can make them so much more different?"

"They're raised different."

"So."

"They think different."

"We all think different."

"No. Not like them."

"What are you talkin' about? Next thing I know you'll be telling me that women are this strange alien race sent to Earth to rid it of human beings. Come on."

"That sounds pretty keen to me."

"If Callie's that bad then why are we going to C-A? Just—"

"It's not."

I looked at him. "Surprise me."

"Have you ever thought about how women are always put second to men?"

"What?"

"I mean think about it. Really. Even in the Bible, Eve gets her life from a man. They're raised with some kind of sense of being submissive. I mean it's even more than that. Their bodies are made submissive to the man's."

"So."

"Wait. Wait. It works both ways though. Men are raised with this sick idea of superiority. They base their entire lives on their dick size and the need to maintain their high-maintenance arrogance."

"You're all fucked up in the head."

"No. No. I'm not."

"Then what the hell are you talking about?"

"I'm talking about how we've been raised differently. How men have been raised to under estimate women and how women have been raised to count on that. They depend on our reactions. I mean if you think about it women have been responsible for every war and means of destruction men have created."

"You can't possibly think that's true."

"I'm serious."

"How can you—"

"Think about it. What is any animal's main purpose for being alive?"

"I don't know. Reproduction."

"Exactly, and who gets to reproduce?"

"The strongest animal in the herd, right?"

"Right."

"But man has something over animals. We can reason."

"Yes, yes, we can, but that's exactly why man has suppressed his natural urge to procreate. It's our arrogance that we think we're no better than any other animal, and that's why we've pushed back our natural urges. That's why our society looks at it as something dirty and obscene. We're no different than a pack of wolves or lions. Instead of fangs or claws we have advanced minds that can reason, but that doesn't mean we aren't animals."

"So, anyway."

"Anyway, anyway, what the hell was I talking about?"

"Uh—women are the cause of war and . . ."

"Right, right. So, realizing that we're animals and we have this constant need to reproduce, and we have this idea that we're dominate over women which makes us arrogant to begin with, and realizing that women realize this we can understand that women will use this to make us kill each other off."

"What? Why? Without man they couldn't reproduce either."

"True. I don't know. Maybe women are just naturally evil. They could be the devil that we so often refer to. It was Eve who plucked the apple from the tree, and it was a man who wrote the Bible."

"So what you're getting at is that the man who wrote the Bible was trying to protect us from women."

"Yep."

"You're full of shit."

"Then why is our God and our savior a man? Think about—no, I'll tell you, Jesus was a virgin, and a woman was his last temptation so are they ours. It's like in *Grimm's Fairy Tales* when the princess keeps making these demands of her suitor before she'll agree to marry him. You see men will do anything in order to be the strongest in the herd."

"What? I can't believe that women are alive only to be our temptresses, and that they'll force men to kill each other before they'll submit. Look, you want to know what it is? You're in a fucked up relationship and so you think all women are fucked up."

"What are sperm banks I ask you?"

"Now you're just getting ridiculous. What about your mother? Huh?"

"Perfect. Women hold the motherly role and can ensure that we are raised with the ideas of the male and female roles."

"When did you start thinking this?"

"I don't know. It's just been coming to me since we've been on the road. You know, I've been reading this interview with Sam and it just kind of makes sense."

"Jesus."

"What?"

"No."

"No what?"

"No, I don't think women are scary."

There must be some kind of bug people plant in the brains of others that just makes them oblivious to the obvious. That sets them on some kind of self-destruct mode, and no matter what anybody says to them they just don't get it. You just want to shake them, and scream, but you don't. I don't. I let him walk his path.

When we got to L.A. we asked for directions to the school. She lived in an apartment off-campus within walking distance of the school, so we found it pretty quickly. The sun was just cracking in the horizon, and I wanted to get some breakfast before we went to see her. The longer I waited before I had to see her the better, but Paul wouldn't hear of it.

We knocked on her door, then knocked some more. Finally a muffled, "Who is it?" cuing Paul and this great smile on his face, "It's me." The door cracked, "Wait just a sec." The door closed again and the chain latch slid back. Then there she was.

Wrapped up in a blue bathrobe and her hair all slept-in. If there is one thing I believe; it is that all women are the most beautiful when they first wake up.

"Paul?"

"Hi."

"What are you doing here?"

"We drove three thousand miles and all you can think to say is 'What are you doing here?'"

"I'm sorry."

I guess I must have been standing too far off to the side for her to see because as she took a step to give Paul what looked like a hug, she stopped.

"What are you doing here?"

"He's my driving partner."

She repeated the question, ignoring Paul.

"I'm fine. How are you?" I smirked and walked on in.

She hugged Paul and then led him in. I didn't wait for an invitation, I figured it wasn't going to come, and I took a seat on the couch while Paul sat in a chair next to the dining table with Callie in his lap. We spent the next hour like that. Me on the couch and those two arm-in-arm, and all I could think about was my stomach. Paul talked about our drive out and about his movie idea. She was stuck on the Mississippi.

"I've always wanted to go to New Orleans. I mean where else in the world does a river like the Mississippi run into the sea?"

I didn't want to ruin their moment by telling her that the Nile River does the same damn thing. I just wanted to go get something to eat, but it bothered me.

"How is it you're going to school on a scholarship and you keep asking stupid questions like that?"

"Who're you to correct anyone?"

"That's another stupid question."

"You aren't even going to college. You're some thug who barely graduated. I bet you can't even read."

"I can."

"Do you? Have you ever read any Shakespeare or Tennessee Williams?"

"Why? I'm not an actor."

"How about novels? Have you ever read any of Anais Nin or Margaret Mitchell?"

"Nope."

"What have you read?"

"Not much of anything."

Then the doorbell rang, calling her away from the fight. When she walked back in with a dozen roses I'm not sure who was more shocked, me or Paul. Either way it, was Paul who got up and walked over to her.

"What's this?"

"I don't know."

She picked up the little green envelope stuck in the arrangement on a plastic pitchfork and opened it.

"Well, what does it say?"

"Nothin'."

I laughed. Paul ripped it out of her hands and read it.

"Who is he?"

"No one."

There was something new in his eyes. I wondered if my eyes looked like that when I was stealing a car.

He let out that big booming stage voice of his and asked again, "Who is he?"

"No one."

"No one doesn't apologize, then say 'love'. Do they?"

"Look, it's none of your business."

"Are you fucking him?"

She let out her own stage voice. Fucking actors. "It's none of your business."

"What's he apologizing for? Huh? What?"

She ran into the bedroom and slammed the door. He opened it and then slammed it again. I shrugged, figuring this meant we'd be leaving sooner. I laid down on the couch and was about to fall asleep listening to their muffled yelling, when everything went silent. My eyes popped open and they walked out of the bedroom, Callie tucked under his arm, her body shivering with hysterics, and every vein in Paul's pale face was popping out.

"Get dressed Callie."

"Why? Paul, why?"

"Just do it."

She disappeared again in the bedroom and Paul sat down next to me.

"Well?"

"I guess she's been dating this Jim guy without my knowing about it, but she hasn't slept with him."

"So we can go get something to eat then?" I won't ever be sure if that was a stupid question or not.

"He sent her those flowers to try and make up for raping her."

I almost asked another stupid question, but he looked at me and pulled a handgun out of his coat pocket and gave it to me.

"Do you know how to use that?"

"Do you?"

"Yeah."

"Paul, what—"

"It's a twenty-five auto. It's not as small as a twenty-two, but it's not as big as a thirty-two."

"I know what it is, Paul. Why am I holding it?"

"We're going to beat the shit out of our keen friend Jim. You'll keep this handy in case he has any friends with him."

"Who cares—"

I heard Callie's door and shoved the gun into my pocket. I don't know what he had said to Callie in that room, but when he told her that we wanted to meet her friend Jim, she hesitated for only a moment before leading us to some apartments on the other side of campus. She told us the room number and Paul told her to stay in the car.

We walked up those stairs and all I could hear was our rubber soles on the cement and all I could feel was the weight of that gun in my pocket. When we got to the room, Paul asked me to do the talking. I started to feel the "fingernails" in my hair and something new. I began to itch all over.

I'd been in fights before, but this was different. Going into someone's apartment not knowing who's behind that door or who's with them. I took the gun out of my pocket and knocked on the door.

"Who is it?"

I didn't know what to say. I just stood there, and God I wish he would have never opened that door to look and see. When he did, Paul kicked the door so hard it flew back and hit Jim in the face. He was stumbling around on his knees when we walked in, one hand on his face, the other groping the floor, trying to balance himself.

As Paul smashed this guy in the face all I could think was the guy was still in his boxers. Light blue cotton boxers. Paul turned around and told me to shut the door. I did.

He kept punching him and kicking him for what seemed like forever. I was lost in the feeling of the "fingernails" in my hair and on my body. Then Paul took the gun from my hand and said something about me being a stupid idiot for almost dropping it on the ground where this guy could get it.

For the first time I got a good look at him. His nose and lips were mashed into one big bloody hole in his face. One of his eyes were swollen shut. I was surprised he was still conscious. A spurt of blood suddenly gushed from his cheek arcing in the air like water from a drinking fountain. His body instinctively curled into the fetal position and then popped back to its original position.

I heard the second and the third shot, and suddenly the "fingernails" were gone and all that was left were their scratches. I grabbed Paul and threw him against the wall, and I started screaming something that I don't remember. The sick smell of sulfur and the salty smell of blood clotted the air. I told him to drop the gun, I remember that, and we left.

When we got back to the car Callie started screaming and crying and beating on Paul's chest, face, and finally the arms he put up in self-defense. He tried to hold her and comfort her, saying things like, "I did it for you," and, "He deserved it." I just drove. Nowhere in particular. I just drove.

When we got to wherever, I pulled over and turned off the car.

"Get her out of the car Paul. I can't listen to her cry anymore."

She had pulled her knees into her chest and just sat in the seat and cried.

"I want to talk to Damien alone, Paul. Please."

"No. If you got something to say to me, you can say it in front of both of us."

"No."

"Say it, or don't. It doesn't much matter to me, Callie."

She paused, and hardly moving her lips, said, "He didn't rape me."

Paul opened the door and threw her out of the car. Right over himself, like she was a little ball, he tossed her on the sidewalk.

"Go," he said.

I watched Callie in my mirrors until I turned at the end of the street. She never even got up.

"Girls are scary aren't they?" I didn't even bother to look at him.

If our conversation wasn't about girls it was about movies. And, man, did he ever talk about movies and actors and directors. Supposedly, his favorite director was Sam Peckinpah. I guess he was the king of violent films before any of the schmoes of today, but Paul thought there was more to his films. To prove it, he'd point out quotes from this interview he had in this magazine he kept with him.

"Peckinpah was keen on the ideals of the person who would not compromise. He likes the loners, the person who will say, 'fuck off.' And it's amazing, he said, at how many people there are who don't say that. He said that we have to stand up sometime in our life for what we believe is the right thing to do, and not sway from it. Whether it be right or wrong."

And he would go on like that with me not really caring one way or another. I guess everyone's got their thing they feel they need to do or say, and then there are those of us that are just there for the ride.

Thaddeus

THE SUN IS WARM on the back of my neck. Taylor sits, without moving, on the porch. He's been sitting there since this morning, and now the afternoon sun soaks into his black hat. He doesn't notice that the shade left that side of the house two hours ago. The only sign his body gives of the heat is the wet fringe of hair where the hat band ends. From inside the house, I hear Zelma moaning. They're digging the grave in the front yard behind me.

I wonder what people will think a hundred years from now when they pass this yard and see that grave. Foster says some day we'll be able to come and go as we want. The border guards won't be here anymore to kill us and Kansas City, Kansas will just be another part of a much bigger place, the way it used to be. When I go with him up Wyandotte Street to get the granite for the grave markers, he tells me about how they lived in the old days. Foster's hair is white and his face is the color of the granite that he chips to make the grave markers. He runs his fingers through his wiry hair as we stand inside the barn that used to be a warehouse. The sun, seeping through a crack next to the one boarded up window, marks the air and the floor. Dust floats lazily in the ray of light, making the illusion of peaceful life and movement. A chicken cackles, and the pig, just now noticing us, squeals and comes loping from behind a stack of hay bales.

"The people used to work in the factories over in Lenexa," he says. "They'd go there days and work as assemblers. We even used to have some tool and die makers over there. We had old cars and some of the skilled workers even had new trucks. Back then, the people went over into Missouri and the other counties in Kansas to work. The trouble started in Kansas. Those were the wealthiest Howlies. First, they made sure we left their towns as soon as the factories closed. Then, we began to get on their nerves just passing through. The town fathers said it didn't look good for visitors to see our old cars junking up the freeways; and sometimes when one would break down, a policeman would see it before we could get our friend and his car off the freeway. Our friend would be arrested, his old car impounded and turned to junk to pay for their trouble. In the jail, the police always beat the people and sometimes killed us." He studies the pieces of granite, looking for one that he can turn into a grave marker. "You can imagine how the people felt about that; and the Howlies began to talk about how we didn't appreciate the work they provided for us. Said we were not only bad workers, but had become a threat. They closed the factories and moved them other places. Like now, everything started coming into their airports by plane; and if we were caught in their towns things became even worse for us." Foster picks a piece of granite and rubs the shiny side. It's been honed and polished some time in the distant past. The name *Lillian Washington 1995-* is carved on it with the date of her death left off. Washington is Foster's name. I can see his eyes fill up and he wipes them with the rag. "She disappeared during the time that the Howlies were still coming into Kansas City. They would come down here in the daytime at first, to get things that they couldn't have in their towns. Then they started kidnapping little girls between the ages of eleven and fifteen. Someone came and took pictures of them on their way home from school, and later, thugs would come and kidnap them. The people began to kill any Howlies that crossed into our section of town. Life was over then. That was when the helicopters started flying over and soldiers strafed the streets." He picks up the two hundred pound block of granite, his arms bulging, and rests it on his shoulder. "Check the door, Henry," he says. I push back the bolts on the warehouse door and look up and down the street to make sure nobody sees us, and will know that we have stuff in here.

It's almost dark now and Taylor hasn't moved. I can see two coal oil lamps lit at each end of the coolin' board, inside the house. Thaddeus is wrapped in a winding cloth. I can see the imprints of the parts of his body, and I see his face looming into view as if yesterday was now.

Thaddeus is tall and blond. Zelma found him seven years before I was born. She said he was four years old, walking down 52nd Street as if he was on a mission. He walked past her; and, instinctively, she realized that he was alone and had been for some time. His curly blond hair was dirty and he was barefoot in October. "Thaddeus," she said, naming him the most obscure of the twelve disciples.

Thaddeus is dressed in the border guard uniform that Taylor brought home late one night. It fits him; and Thaddeus is the only one of us that can pass for a border guard. He's over six feet tall with blonde hair and blue eyes; and, unlike the rest of us, he's not missing any parts, like fingers, teeth, or an arm, that would identify him as one of the people. Zelma took good care of him when he was a kid and he's quick. In a fight, he never gets hurt; and he's made more trips across the border than were ever made before he started.

"Henry," he says; and I put down my book. "Go get dressed. I need somebody with me this time." He smiles. Damn! He's been teaching me to fight with my hands and feet. I can even fight with a gun and a knife. Now I get to go over into Lenexa, maybe even Mission. There may be a library over there where I can get more books. I've read the last one he brought me five times already.

Thaddeus is going over the maps that Foster makes from memory and that Thaddeus updates when he returns from his trips across the border. Taylor hands

Thaddeus

Thaddeus the new border guard IDs that he makes up each trip. "Be careful," he says and grips Thaddeus' shoulder.

"How can we lose?" Thaddeus says; and he turns to me, smiling. I smile back, trying not to be too enthusiastic, imitating his smile. "What I miss, little brother will see."

I ride behind him on the Harley Davidson motorcycle that came with the border guard uniform, my hand just above the Smith and Wesson 38 on Thaddeus' hip. The further south we go, the more houses are still standing; but they're empty. I'm watching for other border guards and thinking of Thaddeus and myself as the police class, because that's important. Thaddeus says that people think about you exactly what you think about yourself. Our survival depends on our imagination and our ability to act. "Lie and believe your own lies," he says; and I can tell by the way Thaddeus straddles the Harley like the power between his legs is alive and invincible that he *is* a border guard. He doesn't even appear to be looking around. He better be one if anybody sees us.

I'm amazed at the difference as we enter Lenexa. There are crowds of people everywhere. The streets and the shop windows are alive and noisy. Electricity isn't historical here. I notice as we cross 95th Street on Kenwood Avenue that the lights have pictures on them, telling us when to wait and when to walk. Thaddeus tells me that the Howlies don't read like we do, that they've become so accustomed to pictures that their language is a kind of pictograph. He says they respond to the sights, smells, sounds, and tastes that they've been programmed with. "That's important to know," he says. We are standing in an electronics store, watching a movie on a giant screen. Gigantic blond border guards are subduing and killing a rabid crowd of the people. A particularly ugly and deformed leader of the people is trying to kidnap the wife of the captain of the guards; but the guards and the captain overcome the mob, first with laser guns and then hand to hand combat when the numbers are almost equal. Of course the snarling demon from hell fights dirty; and surprises everyone by snatching the eleven year old daughter of the captain. They cannot conceive of such evil. The daughter puts up a superhuman struggle, frees herself and the next thirty minutes is devoted to the bloody battle to rid the world of demons from hell.

From here we go to the library. Our last stop will be the gun shop. Thaddeus tells me that there used to be book stores, but no one reads anymore. The libraries are museums where a few aging media professors still go to read about propaganda, marketing and formula drama before laser disk.

The white haired ancient at the guard station recognizes his superior in uniform and salutes without requesting identification. Thaddeus casually returns the salute; and we enter the STACKS. That's where the books are shelved. Thaddeus goes immediately to fiction. I pick out McNickle who writes about the people in the early days. Thaddeus uses his I.D. to check out the book, casually mentioning to the flirting young Howlie behind the desk that the book is for the guard researcher, and telling her that it's about ancient warfare. She smiles warmly and says, "I didn't think someone as handsome as you would be reading." They both laugh at the idea. She punches the picture of a book on her computer key; then she scans the bar code on the spine of the book; and we're on our way to the gun shop.

I'm a bit worried about being both related to him and carrying a book. He just laughs, saying they've probably never even seen one. Then it happens. We've both relaxed into the situation. He's a handsome guard and I'm his nephew. What could be simpler? We aren't even to the gun shop when a Howlie pulls up beside us, riding in a limousine, and asks Thaddeus to get in. Thaddeus explains that he's on duty; and when the Howlie shouts, "Do you know who you're talking to?" Thaddeus turns to me and says, "Take the Harley and go home." I do.

That was the last time I saw Thaddeus alive. Taylor heard the car in the night; and looked out in time to see the limousine driver dump Thaddeus' body onto the front lawn. He won't tell me how they killed him.

Taylor is kneeling by the body. Zelma kneels at the feet, and Foster kneels by the other side. I stand at the head of the coolin' board, telling Thaddeus goodby. I keep thinking he might have gotten away if it hadn't been for me; and Taylor reminds me that I have the talent to take his place. One of us must live.

We pick up the body on the board, carry it into the front yard and lower it into the grave with ropes. Foster puts a tin box at his feet. I put his journal in the box, his obituary and some life history that I have written. Zelma puts in the few pieces of jewelry, his watch, a toy train and the picture of his first girlfriend, who is now buried somewhere else. We promise that someone will come back and get him one day. Taylor lays his own black hat on top of Thaddeus; and we shovel in the dirt.

Early Sunday morning, we catch the south bound train at Union Station. I change my name to Thaddeus and carry in my mind all our conversations and our stories.

Fernand Roqueplan | *The Monarch of Hatred*

1

WHAT ON EARTH is all this fuss, and why? Nathan Allen Waterson. Twenty-seven years four months eight days a citizen of America, in the state of Georgia, township Half Moon. He darkened column after column of boxes on an endless sheet of questions so he could eat. "No test no BLT," the overseers warned Waterson after he had torn up the third "Minnesota" or MMPI, a test designed to isolate disturbed areas of consciousness termed "splinter psyches." There were splinters lodged in Waterson's body as well as his mind—shards of bone and copper jacketing. His wounds healed slowly, severed facial nerves caused his left eye to twitch. Nathan smudged his chin and forehead as he worked, littering the table with soot and broken stubs; one box of the friable charcoal sticks and counting. The overseers didn't mind the mess. No one wanted to facilitate matters by giving Nathan a long, hard, sharp No. 2 pencil.

The police psychologist studied Waterson. Revolted and fascinated, his gaze unwavering, he watched—jotting notes from time to time, inhaling small fragrant cigars. At 2:45, the police psychologist asked softly, "What are you thinking?" Nathan replied just as softly "Nuh nigger," because he was still reluctant to play their game and describe his dream.

"Nothing at all?"

"Nuh."

"Can you express anything, put it into words?"

Nathan thought about it. Could they read his mind? Was the police psychologist a devil? Why were the freedom words—secrets with which he could purchase food and solitude—so infuriatingly obscure? He struggled to think clearly then it came to him in a blinding flash that smote his vision with a thousand silver stars and yellow tracers: God's work was never done! Nathan spat on the floor. "Nuh."

"No what?"

"Nuh, nigger!"

"Why *nigger* again?" The police psychologist was not a physically imposing man but his voice was bitter. He leaned forward. "Well?"

"Wuh?"

"You keep calling me *nigger*."

91

"Yuh." Nathan, concerned they might refuse him food, stalled. "Daddy . . ."

"Yes? What about your father?"

Nathan scowled. "Nuh."

The police psychologist leaned back. "Do you hate black people?"

"Nuh."

"Do you hate women?"

"Nuh hate."

The police psychologist nodded, scribbled a note. "Are you thinking anything else?"

"Yuh—hungry."

The police psychologist sounded disappointed. "Nothing else? Aren't you at all concerned about your fate, about what's going to happen to you?"

"Nuh. Y'all do anyhow."

"What do you want us to do?"

"God's judge," said Nathan. He rubbed his nose. The nagging fairy tale paradoxes made his head ache—how could a boiled egg like Humpty Dumpty talk, when everyone knew that the mess inside an egg contained only the soggy outline of a mouth? Or a fox eat grapes when anyone with a lick of sense knew that foxes ate mice and chickens. And how could a witch with devil's ESP be duped by Hansel, a mere child? A bride of Satan unable to distinguish a chicken bone from a boy's finger! Nathan chewed his blackened thumbnail and pondered that *Once upon a time* the world was a black hole and the spirit of God the face of the deep. He dug his fingers into his skull until a memory of strawberry ice cream flooded his tongue. He sucked saliva, a noise like birds chirping burst from his throat.

The police psychologist leaned forward. "Nuh," said Nathan, sick of questions. *Once upon a time* he was free and he'd be free again to do his favorite things—gather pomegranates, masturbate in the gold-token booths at The Adult Pleasure Palace porno arcade with the cassette tape sex-grunts of whores taking it deep and the company of other men surrounding him. He'd clean a clogged carburetor jet with a toothbrush dipped in gasoline and inhale the fumes until he did not have to remain earthbound—he could fly. Nathan closed his eyes, smiled at images of old women pink nyloned with silver belled like bird-hungry cats dancing the Gasoline Cancer at midnight. Naked one-breasted women skipping through fields of okra. Mother.

What are you thinking?

He shook his head back and forth to spill it all out: death, offal, ice cream. He needed cigarettes and food but would get nothing, not one puff or bite to eat until he completed the MMPI. He peeled the flap of a dressing and scratched a scab. He ached deep inside where the high-velocity hollow points had broken his bones. So many unmarked boxes taunted him—what did darkening squares have to do with Percodan and Pall Malls, coffee (double cream and sugar) and bacon-lettuce-tomato sandwiches? Nathan savaged black into the endless hollows. "Uh!" he said, stabbing, stabbing *Do you see things others can't see?* "Nuh!" he cried, poking *Do you anger easily?* He would never finish, not now, not ever; each hour someone would enter with a fresh sheet of questions—interrogations worded, like a magician's knife, to lift his scalp and peer into his brain.

He was full of pain and the smell of bacon and coffee all around him was maddening. He answered "Yes" to *Have you ever wanted to be a florist?* because the dank, musty cubicle reminded him of roses—off-white Kennedy roses—and when the police psychologist took advantage of Nathan's agitation to repeat "Why did you rape the Hawthorne girl?" Nathan shook his head and kept on coloring.

2

For sixteen years, Dana Hawthorne shared the township of Half Moon with Nathan Allen Waterson. Dana's precocious world-view was based more on rigid self-adherence to homework and Scripture than any natural talent. "Who cares?" was often the stock response to her biblical ejaculations, and while the attention given her was often cruel, she retaliated with loving kindness. She was a cordial girl—eager, and not at all unbeautiful with her clear complexion, but not exactly beautiful with her gaunt face and crooked teeth. Dana knew Nathan only through gossip that called him queer, thieving, perverted, retarded. From her school bus window Dana would see him in the sun or rain or snow, dragging sacks of aluminum cans or beer bottles or an old car battery to sell at the Mavis Recycling Plant. She watched him dragging his scraps and she'd shiver: the world was a brutal place, after all, and it shamed her Christian conscience to admit that she really didn't want Nathan in it.

Dana's older siblings hadn't fared well. Troy pick-axed through the roof of a dentist's office and died inhaling nitrous oxide—the tube frozen to his lips, his lungs a graystone butterfly. Hirschel owed society forty more years at Huntsville where he wrote Dana now and then for cigarette money and to curse the parole board; he wouldn't get out until the next appearance of Halley's comet. Melinda, the first-born and a transient flutist, had disappeared following a bonfire on Alki Beach, Washington. The police speculated that Theodore Bundy had liked the way she played, her waist-length auburn ponytail pot-scented and breeze-tossed, and took her for a ride. The police speculated but couldn't say for sure the precise location of Melinda's grave (a twenty-mile forest between Snoqualmie Falls and Seattle) and Ted wouldn't tell, not even when he was sentenced to die or before he died or as he sat dying, rigid and strapped.

Denouement. A word Dana learned in school so pretty she wrote it in her bible.

Lust. "The Devil's magnet," her mama always said.

"The everything of nothing," Dean wrote on the cover of his diary.

"Sex," Hirschel once told Dana when he was drunk and she made his coffee those semi-happy times before he robbed Fort Worth Savings and Loan. "That's all the little bastards want from you. You stay away and get yourself in college, you hear? Forget about fucking." She'd nodded and cracked his eggs into sizzling oil. Sex, sex, sex. Floyd, the one boy who had tried to touch Dana's minuscule front while endeavoring to work the point of his tongue past her pursed lips (in the front seat of his '81 Camaro half an hour into *Die Hard*) had been sternly rebuffed and lectured to about the ephemerality of flesh. "Mankind," she'd told Floyd, "is utterly incapable of pure devotion." His erection had withered like lettuce at high noon.

But *Jesus* loved her, and you soon knew about it. You knew about it if you sat next to Dana on the bus as she brushed her straight ropes of uncut dark hair, the skin of her hands inflamed and split from multiple ablutions with lava soap and boar-bristle brushes. The redness in stark contrast to the paleness of her throat, when she tweaked the mole there, an almost constant nervous habit. Her pallor was striking—a white face framed by complete darkness within two close-set eyes the color of maple—the demeanor of one who had spent her short life suppressing carnal urgency. The face of a girl who had surrendered willingly only to the steadfast desire to evangelize. Who had, as Floyd told his locker room brigade to howls of agreement, *spread only the word*.

To anyone seated next to Dana, the day of her tragedy, what was notable? Flesh scented with Ponds and buried under a rough sweater that stank gently of bacon grease pancake, straw, and Bag-Balm. To anyone seated so close—staying and not moving away as children invariably did—she'd nod and exclaim, "Beautiful morning, isn't it—praise God!" then press upon him or her a tract with a bold rubric *Repent! Jesus is Coming* or *Pray For Middle East Apocalypse!*

Dana was the last-born—conceived by a father addled from alcohol and sunstroke and the mother pleasantly surprised, as she put it, "to be in the family way at my age." Doctor Warren didn't share her enthusiasm. "Thea, you can't take this chance. It could have Down's Syndrome or Spina Bifida or God knows what."

"God *does* know!" And Thea delivered without complication. The only incongruity or blemish Dana exhibited was the star-shaped purple birthmark crowning her skull—invisible after Dana grew hair. Scrawny and good-natured, self-righteous and friendly, a Bible expert full of that racist love which is the spiritual prerogative of all practicing and would-be missionaries, Dana considered herself happy.

3

The day of Nathan's crime, the last of the unpicked pomegranates had shrunken, resembling tiny skulls which, soaked by dog-rain, had sprouted caps of green mold. The semblance of the pomegranates to rain forest talismans—morose shrunken heads with stitched lips bobbing in the chill wind—exemplified Nathan's macabre imagination. He watched Lights Out Theatre and National Geographic on his Lloyd's black and white. He knew all about the jungle: cannibalism, nakedness, torture and head-shrinking. Nathan's obsession was decapitation. He drew pictures of the guillotine and the Grim Reaper; he nailed a velvet Jesus above his bed for protection, knowing all the while the leather collar of his coat that he'd fashioned from a harness strap wouldn't stop the blade when it swung from shadows. Nathan backed up Jesus with a mojo alligator tooth, a double-heads quarter which had cost five dollars from the Cree Trading Post, a string of purple and green Mardi Gras beads, and a rabbit's foot. In his nightmares, the scythe continued to hit and his blood gushed in smoking jets onto the frozen concrete while his severed head rolled, fire ants stinging the tongue.

Nathan drew Death as a wolf with rheumy eyes full of crusts, black snout dripping foam, nostrils snorting over the scent-trail of man: *Monarch of Hatred* crayoned under in red. Always sniffing, always a leap and a bound away. . . . But pomegranates earned Nathan fifty cents a pound and picking fruit for the witch-widow forced him into the open where devils could zero in, voices babbling endlessly at his ears. At such times Nathan looped FM antenna wire around his waist, a ten-foot tail dragging behind him—he knew that the fillings in his teeth could magnify minute sounds. He'd stuff his sacks with fruit until his early-warning wire screeched, then he ran until he was tired. He'd stop to eat a pomegranate, his thumbnail splitting leathery skin to reveal glistening rows of wet garnets, the pungent aroma of the juice filling his nostrils, the bitter tang of inner pith on his tongue as he ate. And always one eye out for the wolf, the Monarch.

That day, as he feasted on pomegranate, Mrs. Troy stamped across the porch of her battleship-gray home to scream at him. The Troy lawn was littered with rusted tricycles, big piles of dog shit, beer bottles and cans. Dry-rotted shutter slats poked from the walls like punji sticks, tattered awnings flapped from rusted bolts. The screen door—aviation silver and blue-glass topped, was the only newness. The slavering, crazed face of the Troy's Doberman pushed the bottom screen into a hellish death-mask. It wanted to break through, it had broken through before, but now it mashed its face into triple-strength nylon mesh—OWOWOWO roaring from the giant speaker. Mrs. Troy's mouth opened, round and hungry like the sex-book girls under Nathan's bed: "*Get* yer *ass* off my *yard!*" Nathan's response was to smile for he loved the heavy-breasted fat ones with short oily hair. Then he'd cupped his crotch to demonstrate his love for Mrs. Troy and the woman, cursing and falling down in her excitement to free the dog, had torn the latch from the aluminum door, locking herself out.

Denouement. Whatever would kill him, Nathan drew: things on the ground, under the water, but especially the beasts in the air. It's a universal psychosis: Dean suffered from it (brain sarcoma) and Dana knew it as sin and the police psychologist wrote a beautiful paper about murderous rage and necromancy, explaining how the sky actually was falling—the collapsing ozone layer exacerbating societal suffocation—the instinctive paranoia, agoraphobia, claustrophobia the doctor termed "collective dread." No journal would touch the essay, even his alumni magazine called it "aberrant." But the police psychologist was definitely on to something: that December afternoon Nathan borrowed a cigarette, he forgot from whom. But the cigarette-giver would remember and correctly identify Waterson from a lineup: where he was (9th and Jefferson, exiting the Flying W Cafe), what he was doing ("wandering aimlessly like a damn fool in the rain, kicking through puddles of water and mud like a kid") what he was wearing (Red Wing boots, blue overalls, Coors t-shirt underneath, knee-length plaid jacket with the collar pulled up to his ears and his greasy hair spilling over his shoulders) what he said: "*Watch the air mister, it's killer air.*"

The justice system of Half Moon would have Nathan cold, a process which mystified him. Much later in court he would glare at witnesses not with hate but envy: how on earth did they do it? Their heads were huge Mason jars capable of storing the vegetables, jams and sauces of human detail indefinitely. When the judge asked Nathan if he remembered anything he shook his head, "nuh!" But he did, yes he did: *Breathing in is impossible. Breathing out adds to the death.* The soot from Half Moon's coal-fired powerplant filled Nathan's lungs, compounding the damage from the Pall Malls he chain-smoked (three packs every day and whatever he could borrow or shoplift). And then he tried to confess: "It was the witch-widow," but no one heard him, otherwise they pretended not to hear him. That December day Nathan spent the last of his mushroom money. The wild mycelium pockets he scavenged until the weather turned cold were depleted, the remaining woodears and bonebuttons and morels had decayed into a tarry mess topped by toadstools and Fly Agaric—the *amanita* or Death Angels. Nathan stamped through the toadstools, preparing his poison-boots for the witch-widow. He was thrilled by the power of his poison-boots. He made a mushroom burger for the Troy hound but his Siamese ate the meat, it was over so quickly there was nothing he could do but hold the body and cry, but at least he knew it worked, that his Vibram soles toadstool-toxic could kill! Just up and kick a man in the face and that man would die as quickly as if pierced by Amazon arrows. Nathan thought of all the faces he would kick after he finished off the witch-widow: the sheriff, Mrs. Troy, the Presidents of the world. To travel, to afford to accomplish good deeds, Nathan needed money; all he had left were persimmons—spicy orbs the flavor and texture of cinnamon wax.

Enemies. Darkness-bound days which kept time in a barrel—a barrel Nathan dreamed of kicking open with his poison-boots, then he'd be free—the millions of words descending from outer space to clap his ears would stop. Like a prophet, he'd turn over everyone's whitestone, see the names underneath and thus control them, as the Bible ordered. Nathan Allen Waterson would know the right ordering of names; he would have knowledge of all good and evil. But for now he'd have to stomp and stomp the mushroom patch, prepare like David for Goliath.

On the rich side of town, at exactly the same time that Nathan Allen Waterson cashed his final widow's check, Dean walked out of Jacksonville Memorial Hospital and vomited into the shriveled four o'clocks. Someone stopped to help him up. He was, after all, the prosecutor; a very nice guy and generous loser at five card draw. Dean wiped his mouth on the sleeve of his Banana Republic sportscoat. *Air. The air is making me sick.*

4

The Waterson case was Dean Evan's first participation in democracy, justice, and due process the *way*, his brother Roy insisted, Andrew Jackson *intended* democracy to be practiced: hard and fast and damn the liberals. Roy had wrecked his Hawk 650, staining Half Moon speedway with strips of metal and flame, "looking," he said appreciatively at the videotape played to him in the hospital, "as if the devil wiped his ass on the blacktop." Dean saw less a daredevil than a torn fat man spread-eagled over a hay bale and spare tire barricade, miraculously alive. Roy recuperated three weeks at Honeygrove Memorial, complained about the food and cable television, offended the nursing staff at every opportunity. Example: "What's your social, sir?" "Surcingle?" (with a wink to Dean) "Hon, I musta left that under my codpiece." Roy wasn't as funny as he thought himself, and from the evidence gathered it appears Dean hated being his brother's keeper. Page thirty-four of Dean's diary ($5.95 from Walmart, vinyl with a plate-brass lock):

> Shiny chrome bars like meat spits pierce my brother's leg from ankle to thigh. Wounds—tiny anuses (anusi?) pucker pink donuts where the chrome bars enter and exit his flesh. Nurses (nursi) swab the leg with iodine, looks like Roy's being barbecued—disgusting but I continue to visit, soonhe'll have the bones plated, pinned & screwed with titanium.I do his job, he's proud of me. Blood & continuity. ThoughI rebel against populist spoils systems (& doing so is open-season on all I Love) I must, humdrum child of the ethical nineties, continue on, Bad Brother. Daily our bourgeois *noblesse oblige* between god & clod, Moneyed Christian Soldier & white, black, brown, yellow; slips. DENOUEMENT, the poor girl scrawled in her bible. She had no idea. Roy's South will rise again, when it does I hope to be comfortably settled on the West Coast . . .

Dean called Judge Wilbur "a man subdued by custom doing wrongly the right thing." The reason for Dean's statement, and the brain fever brought on, as he told Roy, by "half-truths and perverted allegory" is best answered in his own words—the essay found in his briefcase—*The Suicide of Jeffrey Scottsdale Wilbur*, subtitled *The Socriatic Anomic Immolation of Alexander the Freud*:

> The Hon. Wilbur devoured his favorite dinner of chicken, marshmallow-baked yams, fried okra, peach cobbler and four pralines. He unwrapped and lit a King Edward, aimed peanuts at the heads of grandchildren Paul and Melody as they fought for the paper cigar-ring. He swallowed three table-spoons of Pepto-Bismol, fouled the parlor with flatulence, then retired to his study. Judge Wilbur inserted the letter (drafted in his copious Ciceronian script) between the marble board and preface of an autographed *Billy Sunday, the Man and his Message*, removed his tortoiseshell reading glasses and placed

them atop the book. He loosened his silk ascot but left it noosed around his fleshy neck.

He drank Old Overholt, finished one bottle, then sometime close to midnight broke the tax seal on a fresh bottle but didn't drink any but instead grasped a Model 1911 Colt, pulled and released the slide, chambering one round. He removed his dentures, pressed the barrel into his upper palate and triggered one .45 hardball round at 1,025 feet per second through the center of his bald dome, directly underneath the autographed photo of Lyndon Baines Johnson. The report would have reverberated thunder in that quiet room, but no one heard. The household continued to sleep around Judge Wilbur, the roar and stench of powder contained within oak-paneled walls. When asked if it was her custom not to check on the Judge before herself retiring, Mrs. Scottsdale-Wilbur replied that she never did. She thought he was reading Duns Scotus, or reviewing a case, or drinking himself to sleep upright in the chair as he often did. She preferred not to disturb the old man as she had preferred a thousand times the final decade of their marriage to *leave him be.*

The .45 ACP is a massive cartridge, composed of a 230 grain lead bullet enclosed in copper jacketing, a load designed by the military to kill Krauts, Hippies, Fascists, Japs, Tax-evaders, Moonshiners, Drug-dealers, and whoever else the agents of democracy blast it into. The .45 hollow point implodes soft matter, creating a cratered exit-wound. Former president Johnson received a string of tissue across his upper lip and in the subdued light of the study it looked like a moustache. Johnson looked like Hitler. We thought, until inspection proved otherwise, that Judge Wilbur had killed himself under a picture of Adolf Hitler.

Dean, driving in the dark from his office, spotted a possum trotting along the soft shoulder and swerved over it with his Ford. "Bonzai!" he screamed. Persimmons hung from denuded limbs—glistening balls of scarlet-splotched orange twisting in the wind. Possums were everywhere, squalling over windfalls in the persimmon groves and stagnant ponds west of Old Military Road. Their shrieks and cries of hunger could drive anyone crazy.

5

December fifteen a mist thick with ice pellets struck Nathan's face as he worked. Dana was on foot, having missed the bus. She missed the bus every Thursday to preside over the school's four member Youth For Christ. Nathan gathered persimmons, his hands tarred with orange pulp. He sold the fruit in five-gallon buckets to the witch-widow. Mimi Ezell Parson (Parson's widow, Half Moon called her) boiled the raw persimmons into jam distributed by TRENDSTAR, an Atlanta-based health food chain. Four dollars for a jar of *Grandma's Organic Aprisimmon Preserves* and new orders outpaced stock. The widow sold six other flavors of jelly, and loaves of pumpkin, squaw, and anadama breads. Mondays she drove to the Amtrak office in her Buick to ship goods and talk profits with Travis over sour cups of station coffee: a dollar every jam, forty-cents each loaf. The widow considered herself a shrewd businesswoman, and she was.

Nathan despised her because she cheated him and never offered him anything to eat. He'd stand at the doorway of her immaculate kitchen-workshop, sniffing, his body sour with hunger and drunkenness. He stared at the bins of buckwheat graham, rye, corn, and oat flours; canisters of brown, turbinado, powdered, rock candy, and red-beet sugars; glass chimneys of vanilla bean, cinnamon stick, allspice, anise, granola, and citron; the squat tubs of candy sprinkles, M&Ms, and jelly beans. Then Parson's widow brought his check, her cunning eyes scanning the floor for signs of his filth. "Nuh!" Nathan would say, slapping the check (short as always) into his coat pocket. The widow always dismissed him with "Shoo," her neck, jutting from the humpback like a twisted branch, the meat-curtains of her throat tied with a string of pearls. Nathan tried to make sense of it: the Bible said kill witches but he was afraid of her eyes. Hansel and Gretel killed a witch and everyone told the story to children as a parable of valor, courage, and redemption.

December fifteen Nathan delivered four gallon-buckets of persimmons, received a short check, uttered "Nuh!" to the hag's spiel about supply and demand. He clenched his fists. He wondered how loud she'd scream, how long she would take to die after he poison booted her clean floor and kicked her into one of the back rooms. The widow slammed the door in Nathan's face. He peered through the pane. She stood over the sink, washing his persimmons. Nathan rapped the foggy glass and she yelled "Shoo! I'm expecting company and I don't want you around!"

He cashed his check at the Flying W and bought hamburger, a carton of Pall Malls, Puss 'n Boots for his cats, oil for his pickup, a liter bottle of Popov vodka that tasted like disinfectant. His money gone, the day still early, Nathan returned to the persimmon grove. His eyes itched, his fingers burned, his tongue was swollen. He drove slowly, filling his mouth with vodka. The pickup rattled and back-fired. The sky was ugly, mirror-gray, but Nathan noted with satisfaction that his Mackinaw was the same brown of the leaves and rotten fruit underfoot.

Dana Hawthorne enjoyed the walk home. She discerned in every rock, puddle, twig, scrap of paper and broken beer bottle God's glory. She chewed a strip of licorice, mentally catalogued the dozen chores left to perform before dark. She finished the candy. The drizzle slackened and with a crack of thunder the clouds parted, revealing a crescent moon. Dana stopped and stared. It was a sign—*all is well*. She splashed on, her stockings plastered with muddy leaves. She scraped at the mess, circled the cemetery behind Half Moon Soldier's Home, cut across the road and into the persimmon grove. The old Smith place had burned in 1987, a foundation of blackened concrete remained. An owl huddled in a hackberry tree; mistletoe had killed the hackberry, its shaggy branches drooped, kudzu clutched the trunk. Dana hurried on, her sudden unease crowded out with psalms and algorithms. She only stopped to talk to a good-for-nothing like Nathan Allen Waterson because he was killing a possum. The possum had filled its pouchy jaws with persimmons, and was reaching from its limb for more, when Nathan lunged and struck it with a rake. The possum barked, caught itself with its tail, swung in a dazed arc, a thin string of blood slipping down from its mouth.

"Stop!" Dana raced through the spongy grass and vetch of the grove-bottom. "Leave it alone!" She twisted the rake from Nathan's hands.

The possum, coughing with fear, stared stupidly at them, its slack lips revealing bloodstained teeth. Its urine dribbled, spattering the leaves below. The piss sounded louder than the rain. Nathan lit a cigarette. Rain dotted the white cylinder, hissed into the ash. His fingers trembled as he drew. "Nuh—you queer, girl? Queer on possums?"

Dana stared into the black sodden pupils of his bloodshot eyes. She read danger and glanced back up at the safety of the road. "I feel sorry for the poor things, is all. Everyone kills them for no good reason." She hung her head. In his presence, mercy sickened her, goodness was inconsequential, caring diabolical. Her wet hair shielded her face like a veil.

Nathan pushed the hair from Dana's face. She recoiled from his touch with a cry of disgust, stepped back and he followed, surprise in his eyes hardening to hate. "Queer," he said. "Understand? The problem, this whole goddamn world's queer." He thrust his hand again into her hair, crimped his fingers around the base of her neck. He looked at Dana's birthmark—purple through the part in her hair—his eyes widened. "Nuh!"

"Stop it!" she screamed. "Don't touch me!"

"Gotta witch-mark, girl! What witch ever felt sorry?"

"Stop it!"

Nathan struck her, pulled her back, struck her again, wrapping her hair in his hand like a windlass until the nape of her neck was under his nose. His stormy, triumphant eyes bored into the birthmark, he touched it with his tongue, his breath stank smoke, alcohol, chili. Orange strings of persimmon pulp clung to his thick, drooping mustache. "Bible dropt in the dirt. Bad luck, girl, dropt God's Word." He twisted her head savagely until her eyes focused on the leather-bound King James, a gift from Reverend Fray. "Blazfemur! Jezbel!" He squeezed until bones in her neck popped.

"Don't touch me you ugly bastard!"

Nathan kicked his poison-boots behind Dana's legs, sweeping her off-balance, then crashed down on her with his knees. He unzipped the Mackinaw, steam wisped from the chest of his sweaty Coors t-shirt before the equilibrium of nature balanced his heat with its cold and he quit steaming. Nathan patted his pockets for the knife. He sighed, remembering he'd left it on the tailgate. He'd just have to make do with his hands. "Wuh got to say now?"

Dana clawed at Nathan's face, he beat her down. "God, don't let him kill me!"

He tore her dress down the middle, peeled each half across her ribs—tucking and rolling the flap of material into a ball—the squirrel skinning method one of his daddies had taught him years before. Nathan didn't kill her and when it was over—when he cried out and sprawled over Dana with his face in the leaves and his mouth gasping like a fish's—she crawled from under him, dazed with shock and pain, certain he would pounce again with his hurting hands and club her senseless like the possum. Nathan watched Dana crawl. He yawned. She fell into the ditch and struggled up. He zipped his trousers and bit into a persimmon. Dana made it to the road and began to stumble home, crying "help!" and shielding her nakedness with scraps of torn gingham.

6

The law came looking for Nathan at the Flying W. Sammy fed them chili con carne, then Sheriff Owens and his deputies searched the trailer at 473 Meadow Park. "Kick it in," said the Sheriff, standing back to let his boys do their work. It took some doing. The three pounded, kicked, and rammed the door with a fence post, pried out the siding with a crowbar. They smashed the small glass portal, buckled the aluminum frame, rocked the trailer, but still the lock held. "Stand back!" Owens blasted buckshot into the lock, forced the door and charged in, getting the drop on five frantic cats. The officers smoked, ground butts onto greasy linoleum. Then Son-of-Owens drawled, "I seen Nathan at Casey's. Seems he's always there when I drop in. Sits in the comer. Don't play pool. Don't talk. Just sits there drinking."

Away they roared—Owens and Son in a '93 Crown Victoria, the other two deputies making do with an '89 Thunderbird—lights flashing and sirens wailing. They skidded into the gravel lot of Casey's as if making a play for home, burst into the tavern with guns drawn. Casey thrust his arms into the air. "Don't shoot! You boys need a beer just say so!" Everyone had a good laugh, settled onto stools with bottles of Miller and Pabst, and the investigation proceeded. "Waterson, huh? Hawthorne girl? Sumbitch. How's her folks taking it? Hell, I know where he lives—Meadow Park—he ain't there? Well, he ain't been here." They talked about the Hawthorne girl, how strange she was. They talked about Nathan, how crazy he was. They talked about Dean, how crazy he was getting. They talked about taking time off to shoot deer. They talked about Judge Wilbur's arraignment for racketeering and extortion. Imagine—the Judge a crook! They drank another round then lapsed into silence. Casey wiped his mouth. "Say, where exactly did *it* happen?"

The law arrived at the grove with sirens screaming, lights circling, as darkness fell. Nathan had loaded the last pail of persimmons into his pickup. His back was to the officers, his hands moved over something on the tailgate. The cops sprinted across the grove at Waterson, their matching black sharkskin Acme boots slinging ropes of mud. They yelled "Stop! Freeze! Turn around!" until Nathan turned, a bloody knife in his hands. Four revolvers intersticed dusk with flame and the stench of chemical burning; bullets tore high into the air. Nathan spun face-down into the buckets of fruit—it was the heavy, quilted lining of the Mackinaw, a gift from Half Moon Salvation Army, that slowed the .357 magnum slugs and saved his life.

The story was a national sensation: *Drunk Sheriff Guns Down Mentally Retarded Boy!* (this headline glued to page one hundred-five of Dean's diary, first sentence of text written as a caption under a photograph of Sheriff Owens, a line drawn from "Now" to his mouth):

"Now how in HELL were we to know he was skinning a god-damn possum?"

Owens was BLASTED by Mayor Cole who in turn had been ripped and torn by Governor Colfax who had the day before been drawn and quartered by "that bitch" (Senator Susan Ryan, PDAA author)—the Protection of Disadvantaged Americans Amendment—the allegations of Hate Crime have everyone pointing the finger at someone else: Half Moon has, according to PDAA, only one victim: Nathan Allen Waterson, luckless since birth when he became a ward of the State after his mother died in alcoholic coma. It's terrible what he did to Dana Hawthorne but I disagree with Roy (better, though his leg's wasted away to a bluish-white, pale stick, pitted and staphscarred like a wino's). Roy says I'm "Xanthic," then he laughs. He says the problem with the whole damn world is "Xanthism." I took Art 101, so I understand the insult, his imagined cleverness. Roy says "we'll make laws, genetic test all babies so that the Nathan Allen Watersons can be isolated and drowned in gunnysacks like unwanted cats. Better yet, we'll kill 'em in-utero."

7

"What are you thinking?" the police psychologist asked.

"Dreamt." Nathan had finished the MMPI and sat drumming his fingers, anticipating the bacon-lettuce-tomato sandwich, coffee, and Percodan.

"Describe them."

"Nuh, nig . . ." He stopped, grinned slyly, then replied, in a voice mimicking Robin Leach, his favorite television personality, "Florence—Florence Nightingale."

The police psychologist did not smile at this absurdity, he considered it a breakthrough. "Why Florence Nightingale?"

Nathan placed the crown he'd woven from dirty bandages atop his head. "Because I am the Monarch of Hatred."

"Why did you rape the Hawthorne girl?"

The Monarch waggled his finger at the police psychologist *no-no*. The Robin Leach voice continued, scoured with Delta twang: "I guess recurring dreams are most significant, ain't they? I dreamt Florence Nightingale every night this week. You ever read her book, *Cassandra* I bet you ain't. One of my mothers kept it on her shelf. I read everything on that shelf. She called me an Idiot Savage 'cause I interpret God's Message in everything I hear or read. In the dream I'm a British major in the

Crimean. That was 1853 to '56, you don't know. Florence was assigned to my post. Wouldn't let men touch her, no sir, had to keep that babymaker pure. We drink brandy in my tent. She's on my cot, starch-white cotton uniform blood-spattered her eyes bright with excitement; I can tell she gets off on fightin' and killin'; bloodlust. Maybe she's lesbo or a girl who goes both ways. She's let her hair down, she smells of sweat and soap and guts and perfume and iodine. I hike up her dress and peel down her panties. That girl make a noise, that girl moans . . ."

The police psychologist puffed the rapidly dwindling stub of his cigar and pretended, as he had pretended countless times as Nathan's diagnostician, to be unfazed by this outburst. He pushed aside his tape recorder and notepad, slipped his gold Cross pen into the pocket of his Arrow broadcloth shirt, opened the box of Swisher Sweets and lit a fresh cigar. Time to prove his diagnosis. "That's enough for today, Monarch."

"You don't want the rest?"

"No. What's the point? You're mentally capable of standing trial. You raped Dana Hawthome because you hate—it's as simple as that—you hate everything."

The Monarch sagged, tore the bandage-crown from his head. "Nuh!" Nathan dug his little finger deep into his ear, tasted the wax. He kicked over his chair and limped to the window. A flag of gauze fluttered from his wrist.

The police psychologist stared at the gauze. The gauze made him sick. The gauze made him remember the razor-sharp elephant grass, the festering wounds of those green blades and the maddening swarms of flies attracted by the pus, the sweat, the decaying feet. The gauze made him remember the zip-zap thud of 7.62 rounds punching holes through his flak jacket, driving powdered glass, lead and copper deep into his flesh. Medically retiring him at the insulting rank of First Lieutenant from the only job he really ever loved. It hurt even to remember. "Nathan! What are you thinking? Why did you rape Dana?" He could barely voice the words around the boulder of rage lodged in his throat. His fingers itched to hurt the boy, hurt him deeper than bullets in places that could not be healed or bandaged, places that would leach out all the cases never understood, all the help not given. All the miserable condemned *faces*.

"Nuh!"

"Don't you want help?"

"Nuh, nigger."

"Then it's over. You'll stand trial."

Nathan shrugged. The police psychologist signaled for the tray of food to be brought in. There was no BLT, only a brown patty of textured vegetable protein called "salisbury steak" by the corporate cafeteria serving the jail. The police psychologist extracted a Swisher Sweet from the box, his fingers trembling, placed fire at the end of the cigar, and handed the cheroot to the boy. Nathan nodded and puffed. The police psychologist waited until Nathan smoked it down before handing the guard several dollars. "Buy him a pack of Pall Malls. That's what he likes. So long, Nathan."

"Mister!"

The police psychologist waited.

"Up there (Nathan pointed to the ceiling) you boys and girls is on your own; the first last and the last first" He limped back to the window and stood chewing the cigar butt, grinning.

"Matthew 19:30."

"Wrong," said Nathan, triumphantly. "The *other* one. Mark 10:31."

Outside, Sheriff Owens picked at the brim of his hat. Son-Of-Owens picked a pimple on his biceps, his uniform sleeve rolled to the armpit. "Well? You wire him to some machine or something? I'd love to watch you give him a good electro-shocking. Is he really crazy or what?"

"That's confidential, sheriff."

"Bah!" Owens mashed the brown Stetson onto his head. "Mum-jumbo! I should've reloaded and made sure Nathan Allen Waterson was dead. Shit." He stomped to his car, punching at his son to follow.

Dean's diary, Pages one hundred-thirteen through sixteen:

"So what are we dealing with?" Magistrate Brady inquired of Dr. Alan Crowley. I snorted into my snifter of VSOP in spite of the gravity of our situation. I wondered if Crowley knew that Brady was a former Grand Wizard; I thought Crowley couldn't possibly know or he'd give some sign just how difficult he was making it for our Aryan Christian Soldier to rule solely on the diagnosis of a Black Shaman—sent by "that bitch" Senator Ryan. I thought for sure I'd bite my glass in two! Did Crowley have any idea how tough it was for the Magistrate to extend goodwill to a representative of the enemy plethora? To drink HIS cognac (good Caucasian liquor) from HIS snifter, in HIS chambers? The doctor sprawled fully relaxed in a leather chair, gulped his brandy. He slurped three glasses as quickly as beer, declined Brady's Cubans to smoke those horrid Swisher Sweets. God, I loved him! God! Magistrate Brady had discovered that Dr. Crowley was a Medal of Honor recipient. The good doctor didn't know the Aryan knew. I snorted and chomped down on my cigar: HYSTERIA! I would have made it if they hadn't continued on so, if they had given up and parted company. I bit the snifter, inhaled Louis fumes, choked down screams of laughter. "SCHIZOPHRENIFORM. Affect-laden Paraphrenia," Dr. Crowley said. Magistrate Brady nodded gravely that he understood perfectly. "He meets all criteria for acute severe bipolar multipersonality disorder. I've recommended immediate neuroleptic therapy, contingent of course, upon your releasing him to the care of Dr. Osborne at Jacksonville State Hospital." "So that's it?" Brady sighed. "We can't try this animal? Positive?" "Yes. Believe me, Nathan's a very sick boy. Dr. Osborne will confirm the biochemical basis of my diagnosis. Nathan's so far gone that as of this morning he has become non-communicative. The term is retrograde aphasia; I'm afraid that my prognosis at this time is contrary to any hope of remission." Brady kept nodding. "And Senator Ryan's Protection of Disadvantaged Americans?" "They'll drop the lawsuit." Crowley smiled. "So will the ACLU." I let them have it then. I tipped cognac over my shirt and trousers, the shocked expressions on their faces made it worse. I soaked myself with booze. "Stop!" they say I howled. "You're killing me!"

Greg
Boyd

The Further Adventures of Tom, Huck and Jim

1
The Usual Shit—Drought—Riches to Rags

IT HAD BEEN THE KIND OF DAY that made his neck chaff—in spite of the slipped collar button and the loose tie—and he was heading home through rush hour traffic with a headache and an attitude. After crisscrossing the city chasing minor accounts all morning, getting stung for lunch by some publicity peon from W. F. Scott, and then jerked around for hours in the afternoon only to be curtly informed that there was no final decision yet on the new campaign his guys had worked up for one of The Big Three—in short, the usual shit—Tom was in no mood to wait for oncoming cars or anything else. His last cigarette was burning itself out in the ashtray. He needed a new pack and he needed it now. Gunning the engine of his luxury sports sedan, he slipped the transmission into gear and whipped across two lanes of traffic. Tires spinning, radio pumped up and blasting, he pulled into the over-crowded parking lot of a convenience store and double parked behind a battered white Impala.

As he exited the car and moved toward the store's entrance, Tom flipped his shades up, clicked the remote door lock, and patted his wallet through his hip pocket. Though a mid-winter evening, the air was warm and dry. A stiff Santa Anna breeze blew dust and candy wrappers across the pavement. In the distance, the mountains loomed brown and massive, their tops chopped abruptly by the dirty twilight haze.

There had hardly been a rainy day since he'd moved from Missouri six years earlier. Half that time he'd lived with water rationing regulations so strict he wasn't allowed to use the expensive automatic sprinkler system he'd installed on the new lawn at the house he and Becky bought out in the Valley. A crew of Mexicans had done the job in one day, arriving at first light with a rototiller and a truck full of rolled sod and white PVC pipe. Now the grass—Kentucky Blue—was long dead and the desert seemed to be bent on reclaiming the city. The newspapers kept calling it the worst drought of the century. Scientists predicted that if they didn't get some snow pack in the Sierras this year the reservoirs would dry up completely in the coming months. In the past they'd diverted one big river and now there was even talk of building a pipeline from Canada. Hell, maybe they could re-route the damned Mississippi while they were at it.

Somehow things had been drying up all over. When he'd first brought Becky to California not long after they were married, Los Angeles was still booming. Real estate prices had soared to unbelievable highs, defense contractors were building enough fighter-bombers and missiles to police a dozen planets, and people on the inside track were still optimistically babbling about expanding Pacific Rim trade and investment opportunities. It didn't take a genius to figure out that there was money to be made if you weren't shy about it.

Back then Tom had plunged right into real estate, signing on as an agent and taking courses for a broker's license at night while he hustled other people's listings during the day. Within a month everybody in the office was talking about how good he was. Clients trusted him, especially people with money. He made them laugh, told them stories about his childhood, complimented the wives on their looks. They liked the way he talked, his boyish enthusiasm, his home-spun humor. For him, selling big property was as simple as selling a dream. And no doubt about it, he had the gift.

Within six months he'd earned over a hundred thousand dollars in commissions and started his own office. Then he really racked it up and cashed it in, stuffing his pockets, rolling in dough, laughing all the way to the bank. Weekends when he wasn't closing yet another deal, he took Becky on all-day shopping sprees to Rodeo Drive and dressed her up like a model. When he had the chance, he picked up the house in one of the best hill sections of the valley. To celebrate, on the same day he closed escrow he bought himself a new car and one for Becky, too, insisting on ordering for her a customized license plate that read, MY BABE. Of course there were other women, too. Lots of them. Women pretty enough to star in their own television shows. He met them everywhere he went. They liked the way he talked. They liked his car, his style. It was all too easy.

But it didn't last. One of his biggest clients, a high-rolling, big-time former network television executive named Pinkston, had warned him it would eventually dry up. "Get out while you're ahead," he'd advised. He even invited Tom to come on board as a partner in a new advertising venture he was putting together. "You're good, kid. Good enough to get in on some of the action out there, to turn a real profit." But Tom, pumped up by his own success and put off by Pinkston's blustering, had just laughed him off. No doubt he'd been a fool not to jump at the opportunity. And sure enough, when the bottom dropped out of real estate six months later, Tom was stuck with huge debts and a failing business. Somehow he'd managed to save the house. But his marriage was beyond salvaging, for Becky had already left him and gone back to Missouri.

After he'd straightened out the mess—laid off his agents, secretary and receptionist, closed down the office, got the creditors off his back—he looked up Pinkston, whose agency was located in a downtown high-rise with impressive views on clear days. Since the whole business depended on creating images, the executive suites of

M.T. Media were designed to impress visitors. Pinkston's own office was situated in a prime corner of the building, giving him a panoramic view of the city below. The desk and chair sat on a platform elevated a foot above the floor. "Sorry to hear about your tough luck, kid," Pinkston told him, as they shook hands. They talked idly for a few minutes before Pinkston checked his watch and made excuses about a meeting. Just as Tom was standing to go, Pinkston said, "Look, buddy, I think I might be able use somebody like you in the field. Give me a call me next week."

So Tom had signed on as an account representative. That was two years ago. Since then he'd been hustling media advertising, selling concepts. It was a living.

2
The Shit gets Thicker—Robbers and Cops—An Old Friend

When Tom stepped into the store, the first thing he saw was the barrel of a shotgun. A giant of a man with long black hair, wearing a sleeveless, embroidered jeans jacket, sunglasses and a black felt hat with a feather in the headband, held the gun inches from Tom's face. Another smaller man with a short-cropped red beard stood behind the counter aiming a pistol at the head of the store clerk, who was filling a paper bag with cash from the register. Several customers lay spread-eagle behind the magazine rack, their faces pressed against the floor. "Get down on the fucking floor with the rest and close your eyes," the one with the shotgun yelled at him. As Tom eased himself carefully onto his hands and knees, he felt the cold metal of the gun barrel kiss his temple. "Hurry up, motherfucker!"

When the register was empty, the man with the pistol filled the rest of the bag with cigarettes, snack cakes, and donuts from a rack adjacent to the counter while his partner collected the wallets and purses of the customers. They also took Tom's keys. "Shouldn't park behind another car," shotgun told him, laughing. "You never know when people might be in a hurry." Then they instructed everyone to remain on the floor for ten minutes. Behind him Tom heard a woman whimpering. When he was sure the men had had enough time to start the engine, he rolled over and watched through the glass as they pulled his car out of the parking lot and turned right into traffic. The blinker was flashing and they didn't seem to be in any hurry. "Shit," he said.

Tom spent most of the evening at the police station, where a detective asked him to describe as accurately and completely as he could, exactly what had transpired during the robbery. As he talked, another officer transcribed his statement in short-hand. Next he looked through a dozen thick binders of photographs of possible suspects, none of whose faces matched those of the robbers. Based on the descriptions he, the clerk and the other victims had provided, a police artist produced accurate composite drawings of the two men. Finally, a detective who seemed to be in charge of the investigation or perhaps the whole section, asked what seemed like dozens of irrelevant questions. "Do you think I'll get my car back?" Tom said, finally.

"No telling," said the detective.

When he finally got home that night, Tom tried to call one of his tennis buddies to talk about the ordeal. No one answered. Then he tried two different women he'd been seeing, but neither was home. He even tried Becky in Missouri, but hung up without speaking when her father picked up the phone, for he was in no mood to deal with the Judge. Finally, he poured himself a whisky and sat down in front of the television. Halfway through the movie he was watching, a commercial for pantyhose aired. The camera panned across a dozen pairs of chorus-line legs kicking out at the screen, settling finally on one sheathed in hideously run nylons. "Guess who isn't wearing Hotlegs?" the voice-over asked. Then the legs resumed their dance to the tune of an insulting jingle. It was an old spot, one of the first big deals Tom had cut by himself. He'd since lost the account. In this business everything happened quickly and there was no such thing as loyalty. Tom got up and poured himself another drink. When, hours later, half-drunk and numb from the day's events, he finally went to bed, the jingle was still playing in his head.

Tom called in sick to work the next day. He spent the morning replacing his lost keys, cancelling his credit cards and arranging a car rental. He took a taxi to the rental agency, then drove to a hardware store and bought new locks for the house. The following day the police called, interrupting an important concept presentation his team had arranged to show a new client. The detective he'd spoken to before at the station told him they'd arrested someone who fit the description he'd given them and wanted him to come down to try to pick the suspect out of a lineup. "We need positive identification to hold him. It will just take a minute," the detective said. And no, he added, the car had not, as yet, been recovered.

Inside the station yet another detective escorted Tom to a screening area where, safe from view behind a two-way mirror, he could view the men in the line-up. "If you're so sure you got the right guy, then who are these other people?" Tom asked when six men entered the room in front of him.

"Just some creeps we picked up for questioning in conjunction with this and other cases. Now, take a good look and tell me. Is our guy out there?" Tom looked carefully at the six men, pausing to study each one in turn. None seemed to match the appearance of either of the two gunmen. He shook his head.

"Sorry to disappoint you, lieutenant, but I'm positive it's none of these men." Still, something bothered him about the man on the far left, a thin, worn-looking fellow about his own age. Though he was sure he wasn't one of the gunmen, Tom nonetheless felt a strong sense of recognition. "Who's the guy on the left? I'd swear I know that face."

The lieutenant shuffled the papers in his folder. "Let's see," he said, frowning. "Small-time hustler by the name of Sawyer. Huck Sawyer. Lists his occupation as an actor. Currently unemployed." The cop snorted. "No address. Brought in on a drunk and disorderly. Probably a street person." He paused and took a sip of coffee. "Why, you know this bum?"

3
Bailed Out—Huck's Tale—The Cost of Housing

On his way back from the bank, Tom wondered if he wasn't making a terrible mistake. He knew that in all likelihood he and his childhood friend had drifted so far apart that they would probably have little in common except for their past, and thus little to say to each other. Still, his conscience told him that to turn his back on someone who'd once been like a brother to him would be an unpardonable sin.

Huck looked dazed as they led him out from the holding cell. When the police pointed to who had made his bail, he stared from across the room with eyes half closed into narrow slits of suspicion. When he'd collected his billfold and pocket knife and was free to go, Huck shuffled slowly toward Tom, his head down. "Mister," he said, "I don't know you from Adam, but I'm much obliged."

Tom offered him his hand. "Tom's the name," he said. "We're a long way from St. Petersburg, Huck, but it's good to see you again."

Suddenly Huck looked up and a smile cracked across his face. "Well I'll be goddamned," he said, shaking his head in disbelief and taking Tom's hand in his own. "Say, Tom, you wouldn't have a cigarette, would you?"

Of course there was lots of catching up to do with so many years gone by, and as they got into the car and headed out of the underground parking structure, Huck soon enough persuaded Tom that the best way to go about it was with a bottle of bourbon. "This here's a fine car you got, Tom. You musta got lucky. Though you always was one for books and such. What are ya now, a lawyer?"

"Nope, just a salesman," said Tom.

"Well, I reckon everybody's got something to sell. Me, I done sold everything I own at one time or another." Tom thought better of asking him to elaborate. Instead, he told Huck about how he'd been robbed, his car stolen. "I maybe seen those fellers you're talkin' about," said Huck. "Just give me a couple of days and I'll foller 'em next time I see 'em. Then me and Jim'll get your car back for you."

"Jim?"

"Yeah, sure. You remember ol' Jim, don't ya? Me and him been on the road together pretty steady near to twenty years now. Ever since he come back from the war. Messed him up somethin' awful, that did. We seen a lot, him and me. Traveled all over. Worked in construction—shovel work mostly—back when things was easier. Then Jim gets this brainstorm and says we ought to come to Hollywood an' get us some into the movies, maybe westerns or something. Play little parts like the guys who get shot or beat up. So we did her. Me and him both started waitin' 'round the studio gates, talkin' to the guards and shakin' hands with everyone who went in and out. Finally they run us off, but not before this one guy told us how to go about it proper. That is to read up on all the casting calls and such and to stay informed about which picture needs what kind of extras and all. And sure enough we started gettin' on. Me in a couple of commercials and Jim as an extra on all kinds of movies where they want black folks in the background. Things was surely lookin' up for us. We had us a car and a hotel room and everything we needed. They feed you meals, too, just for being there. Big spreads of stuff piled on long tables, with paper plates and plastic forks. Then one day we both got fixed as extras on the same movie. Of course there's lots of waitin' around on these sets, so Jim, he figures why not him and me slide off somewhere to blow some weed. Next thing we know they're running us off the studio and telling us never to set foot there again. But we settled in here, nonetheless. Gonna stay, too, on account of the weather."

Tom nodded his head and pulled into the parking lot of a liquor store. He set his cigarettes on the dashboard. "I'll get us some refreshments and be right back," he told Huck. "Help yourself to a smoke if you like." When he came back to the car, carrying a bag with a half gallon of Jack Daniels, some snack food and a carton of cigarettes, Tom found Huck going through the contents of the glove box. The pack of cigarettes had vanished from the dash.

Tom had no more set the bag down between them on the seat of the rented Cadillac and was fastening his shoulder belt when Huck cracked the seal on the bottle and took a long pull. He wiped his mouth on the dirty sleeve of his work shirt and held the bottle out before him. "That does a man a world of good," he said.

Tom frowned. "There's a law against open containers in cars, you know."

"Yeah, I know. Me and Jim done time in Mississippi once on account of that one." He took another pull and screwed the cap back on. Then he opened the carton of cigarettes and flipped a new pack onto the dashboard. "I'll just set her back in the bag and rest that down by my feet till we get where we're goin'," Huck said. "Say, we ought to go check up on Jim. I bet he could do with a snort of this here Daniels. And that way you can see our place, too. We been buildin' it ourselves. It's a ways from here, though. Out near to Burbank in the San Fernando Valley."

"You live in Burbank?"

"Well, not exactly. But nearabouts."

"I'm in Encino."

"Well that makes us just about neighbors, then," said Huck. He reached again for the bag, then thought better and pulled back, sighed, and instead grabbed the cigarettes off the dash. Huck and Tom smoked until they got on the freeway. Then Huck pressed himself against the door and closed his eyes. He snored as Tom drove.

When they descended into the valley Tom exited the freeway and reached over to gently shake his companion. Huck woke with a start, blinking his eyes and turning his head in both directions.

"Where we at?" he asked.

"Burbank," Tom answered. "How do we get to your place from here?"

"Just keep headin' straight till you get to the light yonder, then turn left and go a piece more. When you get to the river make another left and keep drivin' till I tell you to stop."

"The River?"

"Yeah. The L.A. River."

Tom nodded and turned left. "You mean that storm drain?" Tom asked, pointing to a fenced-off concrete channel. Years ago every former stream in Los Angeles had been systematically transformed into a network of wide, deep ditches collectively called the Los Angeles River. Dry most of the year, during the rainy season, these concrete channels turned into raging torrents that carried the runoff from the surrounding hills and mountains quickly to the sea.

"That's it," said Huck.

Tom made another turn and headed into a warehouse district that ran parallel to the flood control channel. "Hey, wait a minute," said Huck. "Stop the car and back up. You see that?" He pointed over his shoulder with his thumb. "There's a full sheet of half-inch plywood lying out by the curb like they was fixin' to throw it away. We can surely use a board like that. You give me a hand with it now and me and Jim won't have to fetch her all the way back on foot."

Tom turned the car around and pulled up by the curb. He left the engine running while Huck got out to inspect the wood. "Nice and straight and dry besides," said Huck, lifting it so that it set on its edge. "Now why don't you turn the car back around and we'll set her on the hood. It's only another quarter mile or so, and if you drive real slow it won't go noplace."

Halfway down the street the board slid off the front of the car, caught an edge on the pavement and ripped the driver's side mirror off the Cadillac. "Damn sorry about that, Tom," Huck said, standing in the street with the broken mirror in his hand. "But I know we can fix her up again no trouble. Jim'll know where to get another one."

4

The Great Graffiti War—In Country—Huck's Confession

"That you, Hucky?" a voice called out when they got close to the shack beneath the bridge. They'd pushed the plywood over the chain-link fence and were carrying it down the sloping concrete wall, Huck clutching the bag with the whiskey close to his chest with one hand. The board wobbled considerably and Tom had just collected a handful of splinters trying to keep it from falling. When he turned around he was staring at a man with a blanket over his head. The man pointed a revolver at Tom's head.

"Whoa, Jim, put that thing away," said Huck. "This here is ol' Tom Finn from St. Petersburg."

"No shit?"

"Straight up, man," said Tom.

"And we brought us a bottle of Jack Daniels and a nice piece of plyboard might serve as a new roof," said Huck.

Jim grinned in the moonlight, then waved the revolver in the air. "Got to be careful," he said to Tom, tucking the gun into the pocket of his fatigue jacket and extending his hand. Tom set his end of the board down and they shook hands.

"Good to see you again, man," Tom said.

"Yeah. Lotta water under the bridge," Jim laughed, pointing with his chin toward the dry channel bottom. "Anyway, like I was sayin', you never know who might come poking around here. It's a dangerous neighborhood for sure 'cause we right in the middle of a fucking gang war. Seems about every night some of them kids in big pants come down here marking their territory like wil' animals with spray paint cans." He pointed toward the graffiti on the walls of the channel. "'Bout a week back, two sets of them sprayers showed up on the same night, one either side of the bridge and us stuck here between. Pretty soon they was taking pot shots at each other to the point where we all had to clear out 'fore the police come. I thought for sure they were gonna root us out after that, but all them cops did is park their cars on the street and wait for their chopper to come shine some big-ass lights down here. Can't see nothing much 'at's under the bridge that way. We watched 'em from the sewer mouth yonder. Safest place to be, much as I hate crawling into tunnels. Reminds me of them fucking death holes in the Nam."

"I told Tom you was in the war," said Huck. He took the bottle out of the sack, uncapped it and took a pull. Then he handed it to Jim. "Jim's a hero. Got hisself a Purple Heart and every other kind of shit, too."

"Now don't get yourself started up on that again, Huck. Ain't nobody wants to hear about them troubled times. Least of all a visitor. Ain't that right, Tom?" Jim said, handing him the bottle.

The whisky burned down Tom's throat as he drank. "I don't know," he said, "might be something to hear."

"Oh, yessir, it's somethin' all right. Somethin' I'd as soon forget about altogether only I could. But you wanna hear it, I'm one for the telling." Jim paused to strike a match and Tom saw how his hand shook as he tried to touch the flame to his cigarette. "You see, two or three times a week I wake up in a big sweat, screaming my damn head off—ask Huck—the sound of AKs going off all around me. Other times I get these dreams where I'm ordered down a motherfucking tunnel at's booby-trapped. Man, I seen enough guys buy it in Nam to keep me in nightmares the rest of my life. One buddy of mine lost his legs to an anti-fucking-personel mine with me walking not fifty feet from him. Blood soaking into the muddy grass all around him and the bunch of us standing around quiet as church not knowing what the hell we could do about it. Looked like a piece of meat chopped up on the sideboard. Dead in nothing flat. Another time I got tagged for a search and destroy and saw a head blown clear off a pair of shoulders. Christ hisself only knows all the death I seen."

Jim looked hard at Tom as he took another long pull on the bottle. "But I'll tell you somethin', Mr. College. All that ain't shit compared to what we done to them. No fucking shit. You understand what I'm sayin'? We butchered those motherfuckers. If a ville looked hostile we pulled first and asked questions later. You ever seen what a napalm strike can do to a bunch of them houses of sticks and grass? Jesus H.

Christ, man. I seen kids and little babies looked like burnt toast after we went through some of them places. And that ain't all. The worst part is living with what I done myself, Lord forgive me. You see, I'm a killer, Tom, sure as our Father sits in Heaven. I shot men—maybe girls, too, for all I know—took 'em down like I was huntin' for rabbits. And let me tell you this. I'm sorry as hell for my part in it. So damned sorry that now I figure I got it comin', those bad dreams and all. Livin' like a damn rat under this here bridge is all a murderer like me is fit for."

"Aw, come on, Jim. You ain't no murderer. You was only doin' what they told you to," said Huck. "I done just as bad or worse."

"Maybe that's why the good Lord threw us into the stew together, Huck. You ever think of that?"

"Can't say as I ever did," Huck said. "But if you'd quit huggin' that bottle like it was a new borned baby and pass it over this way, a man might have the chance to slack his thirst some." Jim handed him the whisky and Huck drank. "Now Tom, I'm gonna tell you somethin' I ain't never told nobody before 'cept for Jim, here, on account of him thinkin' he's the only blasted sinner on the face of this earth. You remember when I first lit out, don't you? I was no more than a child. I just up and disappeared one day and I ain't never been back. You wanna know why? It's 'cause I killed my own father, Tom. I killed that son-of-a-bitch, Pap."

"*You* killed Pap?"

"That's right. I know they figured it was one of them biker outfits that did him in, 'cause he had it comin' for cheatin' one of them outta his Hog in a card game. But it was me that done it. He was drinkin' every night and whippin' my ass to beat the band and I just got tired of it. So one night I laid for him and when he come in to whip me I fixed him good and that was that. I ain't never been sorry about it neither."

"He was one mean bastard, your daddy," Jim said, shaking his head. "There was plenty folks around glad enough to see him laid out."

"Well I reckon I fixed it for 'em," said Huck. "I stopped Pap for good and forever." Huck spit over his shoulder. "You think we could have some of them Vienna sausages, now, Tom? Maybe open that bag of chips and bean dip too? All this jawin' done given me an appetite."

5

An Ominous Suspicion—The Wonderful Meal—The Cave —Bad News

After Huck had passed out from drink that night, Jim told Tom a bit of disturbing news. "I didn't want to say nothin' in front of him, Tom, but Huck's not been feelin' too good of late. Been losing so much weight there ain't much left to him but skin and bone. That much you can see yourself. Most days he just want to lay around and not do much of nothin' no more. I suspicion something bad, Tom, real bad. I don't reckon he'd of told you nothing about exactly how we been gettin' on all these years, but there been more than a few times we gone hungry and cold for days on end. That much you gotta understand. I mean such as what can drive a man to go so low he ain't even a man no more." Jim sighed deeply and fell silent, as if saying another word would cost him his last chance at salvation.

"What are you saying, Jim?" Tom asked. "This may be important."

"What I'm sayin' is that Huck done things."

"What kind of things?"

"Things for money. Things I hate to say aloud or even think about. Things no boy or man should never have to do just so we could have us somethin' to eat and a place to lie down in for a night or two. And now I'm afraid the Lord is fixing to punish him some more for it, as if the doin' weren't a bad enough whipping at the time."

Before Tom left that night, he took Jim with him in the car and drove to an automated teller machine in front of a bank, where he withdrew two hundred dollars. When he dropped Jim back at the river, he gave him the money and one of his business cards. "Look, Jim, take Huck to see a doctor. Try make sure he gets plenty to eat and, if possible, keep him away from the booze. I'll come back here to check on you in a couple of days. We can all go to a restaurant and have a good meal together. And if there's anything you need before then, call me at this number."

After Jim had promised he'd get Huck to a doctor and thanked Tom, they shook hands. Then Jim slipped through the hole in the chain link fence and vanished into the darkness.

At work the next day Tom was tired and hungover. He pushed papers around his desk, made a few phone calls, drank coffee. Every time his phone rang, he jumped. That afternoon he called on clients. After work he played tennis and tried not to think about Huck and Jim living under the bridge. He felt bad, but here was nothing more he could do for them.

Two days passed and he still hadn't heard any more from the police about his car. He called his insurance company and began making plans to lease a new Lexus. He'd almost completely forgotten about Huck and Jim when the phone rang.

"Say, Tom. We done found those robbers of yours."

"Good, Huck. That's wonderful. But I'm tied up right now. You can tell me about it later," he said.

It took several minutes to get the information across, but Tom finally arranged to drive down to the storm drain after work and pick them up. He'd promised to take them to a restaurant and now he realized, with dismay, that he'd have to. Luckily, Huck suggested they go to a coffee shop close by, where they all ordered hamburgers and coffee. Jim, winking at Tom, insisted Huck drink a glass of milk besides.

"Say, this is wonderful, eating together here like this," Huck said.

Everybody agreed. Then Jim told Tom, "We got some good news and some not so good news. First off, I seen that guy in the feathered hat you was talkin' about not a mile from our place, walkin' along the river bed. He and his buddy was each carrying something, though I couldn't tell what, on account of I was on the street above. I watched 'em crawl into one of them sewer holes. When they come out again a few minutes later, I waited for 'em to get clear of the channel, then I went and fetched back Huck. He went into that ol' sewer while I kept a look out from up above. Well, Huck, he wandered around in there a little ways, 'til he come to a kind of room down there with a ladder going up to a manhole that was padlocked shut. And sure enough, they been putting all kinds of stuff in the room for safe keeping. You tell him, Huck."

"Yes sir, Tom, there was jewelry and guns and lots of silver pots and such they'd stole from who-knows-where. They was hidin' it all away down there. I even found this." Huck pulled a billfold from his coat pocket and handed it to Tom.

"My wallet," Tom said, opening it. The cash and credit cards were missing, but everything else was intact.

"Yeah, I figure they's probably plannin' to hit up at your place one of these days, since they got aholt your address off the drivers license."

"Well, they ain't got it no more, thanks to Jim," said Huck, laughing.

Tom said that he'd call the police and that they'd probably want to stake out the area to catch the robbers.

For a while after, no one said much. They were all waiting for the bad news to be sprung. Finally, Huck cleared his throat. "I been to see that doctor, Tom." He looked down at his plate, picked up his fork and poked at a french fry. "Well, I guess it ain't gonna go so good for me. You see, they run some kinda tests on my blood and when I called for the news yesterday the doctor told me I better get over there and talk about it. Me and Jim rode in a taxi to the clinic where this one feller tells me I got it bad. Said I'm already real sick and only gonna get worse. Said I been infected with some AIDS virus. Said I oughtta go down to County Hospital, but I told him I'd just as soon take my chances where I'm at."

6

The Bust—Law and Order—Huck and Jim on Television

The next day, acting on the information Huck and Jim had provided through Tom, the police staked out the sewer and caught the robbers red-handed as they brought in an armload each of stolen merchandise. Huck and Jim watched from behind the chain-link fence on the street above as a dozen policemen wearing bullet-proof vests and blue baseball caps dragged the two criminals, handcuffed, out of the tunnel. "Sure glad they ain't here for us," said Huck, as they watched the police shove the smaller of the two into the back seat of a squad car.

As they were poking at the bigger man, herding him into yet another car, he suddenly turned on the officers and began kicking his legs wildly, in spite of all the drawn guns. "Jesus H. Christ," said Jim, "That one's a wild feller." They watched as half a dozen police officers began beating the giant with their nightsticks. One of them ran toward him with a strange-looking device, an electric shock-gun, which knocked him to his knees. Then another officer cracked him hard across the back with his billy club and the big man fell face forward onto the street. The police continued kicking him in the ribs. Finally, they dragged him roughly up under the arms and threw him into the car.

Just then a white mini-van with a big number eight painted onto a three-dimensional billiard ball on the door pulled up beside Huck and Jim. "We just got an inside tip from a detective that two homeless men had a hand in breaking up a theft ring," a woman said, unrolling the passenger side window. "You boys the heroes who reported those guys to the police?"

"I reckon," said Huck, shrugging his shoulders.

"How about giving us an interview?" she asked, getting out of the van.

Jim scowled. "I don't see much use of us gettin' mixed up in all that," he said. "Less 'o course you offerin' to pay."

The woman tossed her hair, insulted at the mere suggestion. She was, after all, a journalist.

"I didn't figure." Jim spat on the sidewalk.

"Aw, come on, Jim," said Huck. "What's it gonna hurt?" By now the cameraman was setting up his equipment. He handed a microphone to the woman and shouldered the video unit.

"I'm Amy Lawrence, KSXY News," the woman said. "If it's okay, let's start out by me asking your names. Then I'll introduce you on camera and ask a few questions about how you helped the police apprehend the suspects. Try to forget about the camera and just act natural."

"Oh, don't worry none, Miss, acting natural comes easy to us. We both been on television and even in the pictures lots of times. We used to do extra acting all the time for the studios," said Huck. "I do believe I even got a knack for it."

That night, relaxing at home after work with a whiskey sour in hand, Tom switched on the local evening news to find news reporter Amy Lawrence interviewing two homeless men who had helped solve a rash of burglaries, robberies, and thefts. "'Tweren't nothing," Huck said, grinning into the camera. "Jim, here, done all the work. All I done is crawl into the sewer yonder and check for where they was stashing the loot. And it was our friend Tom what called the police." (Watching Huck on camera, Tom cringed. He hoped that Huck wouldn't pronounce his last name, for in spite of himself, he couldn't help from thinking he'd never seen a more pathetic and ridiculous human being.) "And then when all them police started beatin' on that big feller, I thought they was gonna kill him they was hittin' him so hard and then kickin' him all over whiles he was on the ground. I been beat a few times by the police myself, but I swear I never seen such a whippin' as they gave that poor son-of-a-bitch. Guess that'll learn him not to steal televisions and such that ain't his."

7

Mud—The River—Tom's Car—Lights Out

The rains came while Tom was on a week-long sales stint in the Big Apple. While he hustled new accounts, staged presentations, and did breakfast, lunch, and dinner with one client or potential client after another, a huge low pressure front slowly moved in from the Pacific Ocean and blanketed the entire west coast. Tom wasn't even aware of the storm until he picked up a copy of the *Los Angeles Times* on the flight back and saw the lead story concerning the record rainfall. After two straight days of torrential downpour, the hills were saturated and the runoff had turned many low lying areas into lakes. Severe mud slides now threatened several exclusive canyon housing developments and had shut down the coast highway near Malibu. From Tom's window seat, visibility was zero until the airliner broke the cloud barrier and Tom could finally see the wet and blurry lights of the city, closing rapidly below.

As he drove his newly-leased car from the airport, water rushed down the streets, pushing over the curbs and spreading like shallow rivers. Movement on the freeway slowed to a walking pace as accidents—cars that had slid out of control as they tried to change lanes, trucks that had jackknifed into the center divider or else overturned along the flooded shoulder—closed lanes of traffic. As he drove, Tom listened to reports on the radio of people in the valley who had become stranded while trying to drive their cars through an intersection in the flood control basin that normally passed for an expansive park and traffic network. Some had to be rescued in inflatable rafts as they clung to the rooftops of their stalled vehicles, water rushing dangerously around them.

As he moved his foot back to the brake pedal, he switched on his defroster. The car ahead of him crawled forward again. He lit another cigarette, and listened to the quick, rhythmic ticking of the windshield wipers. While the car was nearly new, the rubber on the wipers had been corrupted from sunlight, heat, smog and disuse, and they left wide streaks across the glass. "Bloody fucking hell," he said out loud. Nearly two hours later he had finally made it the thirty-five or so miles from the airport through the canyon and into the valley.

When he got home he knew something was wrong immediately. Cardiff Lane was all but completely blocked by cars, fire trucks, and city vehicles. Crews in yellow rain slickers and hats were on his neighbor's front lawn, shoveling a huge pile of sand into canvas sacks, while others carried them into the darkness beyond. A torrent of muddy water cascaded down the street.

"What's going on here?" he asked a fireman.

"You live here?"

Tom nodded, pointing to his house.

"Part of the hill behind collapsed and came down. We got a lot of damage already and I don't know if any of these houses will survive the night unless the rain lets up."

Inside, Tom could hardly believe what he saw. The mud had come down so suddenly, and with such force, that it had completely overwhelmed his entire back yard, filling in his pool. It had broken the sliding glass doors and covered his living room, kitchen and master bedroom with six inches of wet clay. "Jesus Christ," Tom muttered. Suddenly he thought of the river, the shack beneath the bridge. "Jesus H. Christ."

By the time he got to Burbank, it was nearly midnight. The rain was falling, if anything, even harder than before. Tom parked his car on the street above the river, pulled his jacket over his head and ran to the chain link fence. Beneath the street lights, the white water roared through the channel. Under the bridge there was nothing but water, swirling and raging.

Tom ran up and down the street calling out Huck and Jim's names, but got no answer. The rain water soaked his clothes and dripped down his face. He ran until he was out of breath, then leaned, gasping, against the fence.

Then he saw it bobbing crazily down the river channel. It approached with amazing velocity, carried weightlessly along. Yet he'd sat in it, secure in its heaviness, aware of its solid construction. Four doors, leather interior, a thousand-dollar stereo system, a goddamned burglar alarm. Loaded with all the options. His stolen car. He watched it pass by and charge beneath the bridge, disappearing on the other side. One last wild ride to the sea.

A lot of water under the bridge, Jim had said. A lot of water under the bridge.

Richard
Grayson

Moon Over Moldova

IT IS A LANDLOCKED AREA bounded by Ukraine on the east and, to the west, Romania. Because of its close ties to Romania, culture and language reflect the make-up of its population: Romanian and Russian are spoken, as well as Ukrainian, Bulgarian, and Turkish (Gagauz).

When postage stamp prices were raised to twenty-nine cents for the first ounce and twenty-three cents for additional ounces, the stamp machines in post office lobbies would spit out one or two one-cent stamps along with the stamp that the customers really wanted. It always amazed me how many people left those one-cent stamps sticking out of their slot at those vending machines. I felt no embarrassment at tearing off the coil of penny stamps, sometimes in front of the very people who had disdained them. But then I'm the kind of person—like my father—who picks up pennies in the street. When I see school kids spurn pennies that have dropped out of their pockets as they board buses, I shake my head, bend down, and retrieve the coin. Once, after I picked up a penny outside a bagel restaurant on Waverly Place in the Village, a drug dealer or wino standing nearby called out sardonically, "Hey, buddy, I hear somebody dropped a dime up on Fourteenth Street!"

With an area of only 34,000 square kilometers (13,000 sq. mi.), it is the second smallest of the former Soviet republics and the most densely populated.

What I miss most about not living in a large metropolitan area isn't the fact that without cable TV, I can only get one of the old three major alphabet networks. No, that's a plus. When someone knocks at my door at dinner time and I hear that it's the town's only cable TV provider, I shout out without opening the door, "Sorry, I use your competitor!" and they just laugh or get confused.

A hilly plain, it occupies most of what has been known as Bessarabia. About two-thirds of the republic's 4.4 million people are Moldovans with Ukrainian (14%), Russian (13%), Bulgarian, and Jewish minorities.

No, what I miss most is the sound of airplanes. I miss seeing them in the sky. The neighborhood where I grew up was far enough from a major airport so I wasn't bothered by the sound of planes landing and taking off, but close enough so I grew comfortable with the sight and sound of jets overhead. Even when the Concorde started its daily flights to and from Europe and the noise level was at its highest, I was always delighted to hear that sleek silver roar. I've seen the Concorde take off and land in New York, Washington and Miami.

The weird thing is, there are few things that make me more uncomfortable than being on an airplane. Especially on a slow non-Concorde transatlantic trip whose final destination is a country I don't know, a country nobody knows.

Its location has made it a historic passageway between Asia and Southern Europe, as well as the victim of frequent warfare. Greeks, Romans, Huns, and Bulgars invaded the area, which in the 13th century became part of the Mongol empire. An independent state emerged briefly in the 14th century but fell under Ottoman Turkish rule in the 16th century.

It's like being in a strange country when you find yourself attracted to the lover of the person you keep fantasizing about. On the Sunday before the anti-gay referendum, at a meeting at which there weren't enough seats, I was on a dumpy couch next to a middle-aged lesbian when Bryan asked if he could sit there too. Sure, we said, and he squeezed in between us; it was only about as uncomfortable as you might be on a subway ride during rush hour. Daylight Savings Time had ended the night before and it was already dark; I'd noticed the full moon already out when I drove to the meeting. But it was still warm, and Bryan and I were both wearing shorts. His right leg couldn't help brushing up against my left leg. Bryan had nice legs; his blue jeanish shorts were longer than mine but rolled up once with that perfect crease that I could never get. His legs were paler than mine because I'd put on self-tanning cream that morning. His legs weren't really hairy, but a little hairier than mine, and suddenly my mind wandered from the pep-talky meeting to Bryan's body and his face. And then I looked across the room to the back of the guy who had introduced Bryan as his partner back at the start of the campaign, the guy I thought I'd been in love with for over a year, Javier.

After the Russo-Turkish War of 1806-12, its eastern half between the Prut and the Dniester Rivers was ceded to Russia, while Romanian Moldova (west of the Prut) remained with the Turks. Romania, which gained independence in 1878, took control of the Russian half in 1918. The Soviet Union never recognized the seizure, creating an autonomous republic on the east side of the Dniester River in 1924.

When I was in high school and not sure if I loved the first guy I was sleeping with and he admitted he wasn't sure if he loved me, we decided that if you think you love someone, then you love them. That had always been good enough for me. But although I thought I was in love with Javier, I knew it would be ridiculous to say I was in love with him. Instead, I told myself I had a huge crush on Javier.

Does it matter what you call things? I heard Bryan use the term boyfriend to describe Javier even though Javier referred to Bryan as his partner.

In 1940, Romania was forced to cede its eastern half to the U.S.S.R., which established a Soviet Socialist Republic. Romania sought to regain it by joining with Germany in the 1941 attack on the U.S.S.R. It was ceded back to Moscow when hostilities between the U.S.S.R. and Romania ceased at the end of World War II. The present boundary between it and Romania was established in 1947. It declared independence on August 27, 1991.

For a couple of years I hadn't given Javier a thought and a half all the times I saw him around town. We used to nod to one another sometimes and sometimes not; it was no big deal. Then, at the rally, just before the city council passed the anti-discrimination ordinance, a lesbian activist introduced Javier and said, as a flip afterthought, "And he's cute, too." I sat somewhere on the grass of the downtown plaza and thought, She's right. He *is* cute. Why hadn't I noticed that before? And as he spoke about gay rights and Nazi Germany and Castro's Cuba in an unpolished yet sincere manner, he got cuter and cuter and cuter. Within a few weeks I was sure I was in love with him.

The United States recognized its independence on December 25, 1991, and opened an embassy in the capital of Chisinau in March 1992.

But I left town for a while, and when I got back and saw Javier again, I made a perfect fool of myself trying to make small talk whenever I ran across him. So I tried to forget about my crush. But I joined the Vote Against Bigotry campaign only half because I believed it was important. I always figured we'd lose, and I didn't like trying to convince local yokels whom I felt superior to that I didn't deserve to be discriminated against. I joined the campaign half because I knew it would give me a chance to see Javier.

At the first meeting I attended I had a feeling that the great-looking guy who sat next to him was more than just his friend. Then came the "partner" introduction to this visiting bigwig from a national gay rights organization while we were sitting at a table, stamping envelopes for a mass mailing appealing for contributions.

Training and technical assistance programs have been provided in law school curriculum reform, rule of law, law enforcement, assessment of the draft constitution, political parties and elections, independent media, pluralism, protection of minority rights, and diplomacy and foreign policy.

I've always liked having these wonderful hopeless crushes on people. In college there was this girl with no waist and luscious shiny straight black hair down to where her waist would be, a friend of my ex-boyfriend and maybe more than that, whom I deluded myself into thinking I loved hopelessly. Years later, she told me it wouldn't have been hopeless at all but it meant we could be friends in a way we couldn't otherwise.

One night when her parents were out of town, we were smoking grass and lying on the living room floor with some Indian sitar music coming from the stereo and the TV on with no sound—which was weird, since it was playing the opera *Nixon in China*. Now I wonder if the love I felt for her on that stoned, full-moon night wasn't as real as anything.

A trade agreement providing reciprocal most-favored-nation tariff treatment became effective on July 2, 1992. A bilateral investment treaty was signed in April 1993. The Export-Import Bank has not begun operations there.

When I e-mailed a friend in Scotland and mentioned my crush on Javier and said something like, "And the funny thing is, if I didn't know him, I wouldn't look twice at him," my friend e-mailed back, "Then it *must* be love." But why? When my bare leg brushed against Bryan's, for a second our eyes met, I felt a little something, I'd use the word "frisson" if I didn't want to be accused of pretentiousness.

I never felt that when I talked to Javier. I could have been a ninety-year-old man or a twelve-year-old girl for the way Javier looked at me. That night I realized, maybe not for the first time, that Bryan was very attractive, much more attractive, in fact, than Javier.

It has accepted all relevant arms control obligations of the former Soviet Union. It has not acceded to the provisions of the nuclear Non-Proliferation Treaty but has expressed its intention to do so. It does not have nuclear, biological, or chemical weapons. It joined the North Atlantic Treaty Organization's Partnership for Peace on March 16, 1994.

I knew there was nothing to it on Bryan's part, and I hoped so, because in order to maintain my hopeless love for Javier I had to keep this image of his and Bryan's relationship as a perfect one, trusting and passionate and platonic (in the old sense, not in the nonsexual sense) and beautiful. Also, loving Javier as I did—albeit secretly—how could I even think of flirting with his partner? Imagining that Bryan loved Javier as I did, how could Bryan even think of flirting with me?

It declared its independence from the former Soviet Union on August 27, 1991. Parliament elected Mircea Snegur to be president in October 1990. A former Communist Party official, he endorsed independence and actively sought Western recognition.

But if Bryan had flirted with me, I would have been tempted. Bryan was very sweet in addition to being good-looking. He didn't have Javier's sharp intelligence. (There's nothing sexier to me than a high I.Q.) But even when Bryan admitted that he was so depressed on election night in '92 because Bush lost that he cried, as idiotic as it sounded, I thought there was something cute about that. Bryan hadn't come out before he met Javier and he'd been raised by fundamentalist Republicans as a good Southern Baptist. I think Bryan knew that even though I made fun of him, I liked him. One evening, when we were folding letters from Coretta Scott King to send to black voters, this lipstick lesbian at our table kept ribbing him about being "Mrs. Javier." He tried to ignore her but was embarrassed, and I suddenly felt very protective of Bryan. "Oh, leave him alone," I said gently enough so that I knew she'd stop.

Its transition to democracy has been impeded by an ineffective parliament, the lack of a new constitution, and continued unrest in the Trans-Dniester region where a separatist movement has declared a "Dniester republic" which has attempted to meet the Russian minority's demands by offering the region limited cultural and political autonomy. On July 21, 1992, the government negotiated a cease-fire arrangement with Russian and Trans-Dniestrian officials.

"Bryan is our knight in shining armor," I e-mailed my friend in Scotland. He was the Vote Against Bigotry's official spokesperson, and as such he was the one debating the right-wing nuts on local talk radio, commenting on the campaign on our one TV station, and being quoted in the newspaper. We wanted one message, and that was easier if one person spoke for the group.

I loved to listen to him. Only if I concentrated could I hear the slight accent that appeared when he too carefully pronounced some English sounds. Mostly he was getting more polished and more eloquent. At our campaign work sessions I often made sure I didn't sit with him, and sometimes he and Bryan didn't sit at the same table, either. Sometimes I did sit near Javier, though, and on those occasions I would do everything in my power to say something that would make him smile. He didn't smile that often, but when he did, I felt it was some incredible gift.

The ineffective parliament elected in 1990 to a five-year term was replaced after new elections were held on February 27, 1994. The election for the new parliament was conducted peacefully and received good ratings from international observers for its fairness. Authorities in the Trans-Dniester region, however, refused to allow balloting there and tried to discourage inhabitants from participating.

I liked to watch Javier and Bryan interact. Something about them when they kidded each other made me feel really nice, like when Javier told me, with Bryan sitting next to him, how they'd often go to the lake but Bryan would not go in because he was afraid to swim. Obviously that was something they joked about when they were alone. After Javier spoke to a sympathetic women's group for ten minutes one night, I overheard Bryan tell him: "That was pretty good, 'cause I only looked at my watch twice." Javier cocked his eyebrow and nodded once, a gesture I took to mean a dozen things. I began to revel in their relationship.

Moon Over Moldova

The largest political group in parliament is the Agrarian Party, which holds a 56-seat plurality. The Socialist Bloc holds 28 seats, while the pro-Romanian unification parties—the Peasants and Intellectuals Bloc and the Popular Front—hold less than a dozen seats each. Other parties did not receive a sufficient percentage of the popular vote to be represented.

At the meeting where Bryan and I were sitting on the couch, the people in charge of the campaign and the out-of-town activists from Washington were telling everyone how great we had been in the campaign, but that everything really gets done just before the election because people really haven't gotten focused on voting yet. Right, I thought, like with all these lies these creeps are spreading about child molesting and special rights and having sex with animals and dead people. I knew the people in charge of the campaign had to say this to make sure everyone worked hard.

But I didn't raise my hand to do what they wanted everyone to do: stand on a corner where there's heavy traffic on Election Day and carry a Vote Against Bigotry sign. I'm less closeted than the majority of the gay and lesbian people in town, but I'm not going to stand at an intersection with a sign. Whenever I saw candidates for city council or the school board standing at an intersection holding a sign and waving, they always looked like idiots. Anyway, I volunteered to set up the victory party at a hall they'd rented. That meant I had to get there before just about everyone else.

Freedom of speech, press, assembly, and religion are widely respected. Political parties and other groups publish newspapers which often criticize government policies. An independent news service, Basa Press, was established in November 1992. However, dependence on government subsidies inhibits complete objectivity by the press.

That morning at 8:00 a.m. I saw Bryan and Javier standing on the big intersection I have to pass to get to my first class. At least they weren't waving. There were a couple of lesbians with them, and on the opposite corner were the religious right guys with their Save Our City/Vote Yes signs.

I voted in the afternoon in the United Church of Christ, which is a pretty gay-friendly church in a neighborhood with a lot of students and liberal yuppies, and then I called the guy handling the catering to ask him what time I should come. He wanted me there right away to help with the food, but once he saw how I laid baby carrots and broccoli and cauliflower and celery on a dish—"Not like that, you've got to make it *pretty*"—he decided I was a loutish jock and told me I should just use my muscles to carry stuff the two blocks down to the victory party. I would have said something, but it isn't often that people think I'm dumb, and as I lugged the soda and beer and wine and food over, I thought how easy it would be if I really were dumb.

I did like being the first person at the hall, even if the catering guy didn't allow me to do very much in terms of setting up. But I got to see people as they came in.

125

We'd all worked pretty hard getting out enormous mailings and making those em-barrassing phone calls to voters (Democratic women were our targets, then Demo-cratic men) and hadn't had much reward except for some camaraderie and pizza.

Bryan came in with a couple of friends. He dressed well, unlike Javier, who looked like he had no taste in clothes. (I noticed he had only one belt, a Pierre Cardin belt, so I figured maybe his family didn't have much money.) I wandered over to where Bryan was talking to some people and heard him say Javier had a terrible headache, probably because of the tension, and was over at city hall with the rest of the cam-paign leaders to watch the votes come in.

"I have a terrible stomachache myself," Bryan said. I wanted to put my hand on his shoulder, so I walked away and said hi to this lesbian couple I'd done telephoning with.

There are no independent broadcast media. Peaceful assembly generally is allowed. Per-mits for demonstrations must be obtained, and private organizations, including political parties, are required to register with the government. Legislation passed in 1992 codified religious freedom but required that religious groups be recognized by the government.

Javier and the rest of the Vote Against Bigotry bigwigs walked in around half past eight. They'd obviously decided among themselves to put on neutral expressions and not answer the questions that people peppered them with. Javier looked terrible. Coincidentally I was standing by Bryan at the time and I whispered to Bryan, "Go fix his collar before he goes on TV." Bryan went over to him and smoothed down the collar, tucking it in. He said something to Javier, who nodded, and then the woman who was officially managing the campaign gave the first results.

They were actually better than I'd expected: 54% yes, 46% no. I had told myself that we'd be lucky to break 40% in this town, where most people are idiots. One of the times I'd made Javier smile during the campaign work was one night when, talking about our town, I paraphrased a Morrissey lyric and said I was just passing through here on my way to someplace civilized.

It surprised me how stunned everyone seemed to be. The real young people espe-cially looked as if they were going to cry. I went around trying to be philosophical and telling people we did better than I expected, that these anti-gay referendums nearly always go through, but I don't think that really helped. One guy, our speakers' bureau coordinator, seemed so bummed out, I didn't even know what to say to him.

By and large, I think, the women took it better than the men, but maybe that's just my irrational belief that lesbians are more sensible than most people.

I didn't talk to Bryan or Javier that night. Javier gave a nice little talk for the 11:00 p.m. newscast and left with Bryan before I'd finished cleaning up.

A 1991 parliamentary decision provides for independent trade unions. However, the Federation of Independent Trade Unions, successor to the former Soviet labor organiza-tions, is the sole structure. It has attempted to influence government policy in labor issues and has been critical of many economic policies.

I didn't see them for a while, didn't see much of anyone. I did a lot of work and went out of town to see my sister and a Green Day concert, and I read Yeats and rented videos and tried to teach myself to bake bread. That was when I decided to apply for the Moldovan fellowship. I saw the announcement posted one morning, and by that night I'd finished what was a very complicated application form.

I knew Javier's schedule and sometimes I'd plant myself where he'd be, coming out of class, but I didn't see him for months. Finally one time I caught him and surprisingly, he talked to me for a long time. He and our campaign manager had just come back from D.C., where they attended a weekend training session for gay activists and he said, "Now I understand why we lost." He explained to me what they'd explained to him about organization and starting early and identifying your voters and all that stuff and his face lit up with excitement when he talked about it. I loved standing there listening to him discuss political strategy. Mostly I just nodded, said "Uh-huh," and nodded some more.

It wasn't me. If it had been anyone he'd known even slightly, at that moment he would have gone on like that because he was filled with passionate intensity.

There have been increased tensions among the ethnic minorities of the region due to civil unrest, but no serious violations of human rights have been reported. Language policy is an increasing source of friction. In August 1989, the Supreme Soviet adopted Romanian as the official language and replaced the Cyrillic alphabet with the Latin. Although the law protects the use of Russian and other languages, it has raised much skepticism, especially among Russian speakers. A new constitution that will provide a legal framework to protect minority rights is not yet in place.

Months passed.

The day after I got the thick envelope from the Soros Foundation, I was in the post office after hours to get a change of address card in the lobby (I was going to have my mail sent to my sister's while I was gone), I saw Javier and Bryan standing by the stamp machines.

They seemed really surprised to see me. Bryan didn't even say anything, except maybe hello. I talked first, telling them about the fellowship and then of course explaining about Moldova. "I hear you guys are leaving town, too," I said. I'd heard it from a reliable lesbian.

Javier said yeah, he was moving to Miami, where his parents lived. "You know us Hispanics," he said, "We like to be with our family." I knew Javier's parents worshipped their only son; they missed maybe one beat when he first came out, but he was the sun and the moon to them.

"Well, we should get together before we both leave town," I said. "I'll give you a call."

I was oblivious to how Bryan was reacting. I'd heard Bryan was moving with him, but Javier didn't say anything about Bryan and Bryan didn't say anything. He was at the stamp machine, collecting the stray one-cent stamps Javier had left there.

Parliament approved its membership in the Commonwealth of Independent States on April 8, 1994. It is a member of the United Nations, the CSCE, and the North Atlantic Cooperation Council. It has worked with its neighbors, Romania, Ukraine, and Russia, to seek a peaceful resolution to the conflict in the Trans-Dniester region. It has cooperated with CSCE and UN fact-finding and observer missions and called for international mediation.

That afternoon I took a deep breath, practiced, and dialed Javier's number. I left a message asking if we could have lunch because I had some business (yep, I actually said "some business") I wanted to talk to him about.

The next day I constantly monitored my phone, and when it rang at 6:00 p.m. and was Javier, I was delighted. He'd actually called me back.

I ran on about a mile a minute and he said that we might as well have lunch sooner than later because he was going to get busy, so we made a date for the next day. I couldn't believe he didn't know the very popular restaurant I'd already picked out before we even talked, but I realized that Javier lived in a world where things like restaurant locations weren't that important.

The hour we spent at the restaurant was incredible. After I'd got through my ridiculous pretense about asking if he knew anything about the gay community in eastern Europe, I got to find out stuff about him I'd always wanted to know. When his family left Cuba. The different places he'd lived. That he'd majored in comp lit as an undergrad and wanted to be a philosophy professor "but my parents didn't think that was too practical" so he went to law school. He had no idea what kind of law he planned to practice, and when I brought up movement stuff, he told me that they have way too many people all wanting to work for Lambda Legal Defense or other gay rights organizations.

It was raining when we left the restaurant, and only I had an umbrella, so I walked him to his car and we talked more. I told him I thought he'd be a great candidate and asked him if he'd ever thought of running for office and he said maybe someday and I said we should keep in touch so I could send him a campaign contribution. Then, as I was about to walk away, I told him to say hello to Bryan for me. All along that had been the last thing I'd planned to say.

Like many other former Soviet republics, it has experienced economic difficulties. Since its economy is highly dependent on the rest of the former Soviet Union for energy and raw materials, the breakdown in trade has had a serious effect, which was exacerbated by drought and civil conflict. Despite its difficult economic situation, it has made substantial progress in economic reform.

A few months later someone called me about helping out with a mailing the follow-ing night. I arrived a little late and couldn't get to sit at the same table as Javier so I folded the cover letter and second sheet at another table and passed them over to the guy next to me, who added a contribution slip and a little return envelope, and the old lady with us put them in a regular envelope for mailing. We'd done this so many times during the campaign, it went pretty fast.

Bryan came in later, and before the evening ended I was placing pressure-sensi-tive address labels on the envelopes with him and Javier.

"So," I said to Bryan, trying to sound hearty, "are you going to like living in Miami?"

"I'm fixing to find out," Bryan said with a smile. Javier smiled too.

"You'll both do fine," I said, and then I just listened, mostly, letting them talk. Bryan told me how he made sure Javier studied like crazy after the election was over so he wouldn't screw up his grades because of being so busy as our campaign spokes-person. Javier said he'd done better than he ever did before, despite doing much less schoolwork than usual.

"That's always the way it is," I said.

The government has liberalized most prices and is phasing out subsidies on basic con-sumer goods. It has International Monetary Fund standby and systemic transformation programs in effect. Its economy resembles those of the Central Asian republics more than those of the other states on the western edge of the former Soviet Union. Industry ac-counts for only 20% of its labor force, and agriculture's share is more than one-third.

We had a bunch of meetings trying to re-energize the community after the referen-dum defeat. Several people—not just Bryan, Javier and I—were moving out of town. A lesbian couple had left already, for San Francisco. We tried to find new people who weren't so burned out for the steering committee. And we planned all the activities for Pride Week. The guy who had been so bummed out on election night was coor-dinating everything.

I usually don't like marching, but I figured it would be interesting this year. Also I was leaving in a couple of weeks and figured it would give me one more chance to see people I wouldn't see otherwise. I made sure I wasn't too obvious about marching next to Javier and Bryan and so I ended up starting the march with this older couple. There were some "straight but not narrow" college students right in back of me and their dog kept straining at her leash and bothering me, so I picked up my pace until I was walking on Bryan's left.

He was holding Javier's hand.

"In two days I'll be thirty years old," he said to me. "I'm so depressed."

"Oh, Bryan," I said. It was probably the first time I'd ever called him by his name. I don't think I'd ever heard him call me by mine. "You look like you're twenty-three, you're great-looking, you're smart, you're a good guy . . ." I took a breath.

". . . Plus you've got what's-his-name here, the guy who everybody worships the ground he walks on."

It didn't come out right.

Javier laughed. He looked at me. Bryan looked at me. They both were smiling. It was obvious they had no idea how I really felt. I didn't care, or else I was glad.

Later that day I got to hug both of them, but I also hugged a lot of other people.

Its proximity to the Black Sea gives it a mild and sunny climate, making the area ideal for agriculture. Its fertile soil supports wheat, corn, barley, tobacco, sugar beets, and soybeans. Beef and dairy cattle are raised, and beekeeping and silkworm breeding are widespread. Its best-known product comes from its extensive and well-developed vineyards, which are concentrated in the central and southern regions. In addition to world-class wine, it produces liquors and champagne and is known for its sunflower seeds, prunes, and other fruits.

Somewhere over the ocean, on my way to someplace semi-civilized, I thought about the guys in town I'd been involved with.

There was the tall black guy with perfect SAT scores and washboard abs whose effeminacy I found charming. Every time I went out to eat with him, I heard someone referring to us as "faggots," something that never happened to me otherwise. He thought I was really sloppy and I tried not to act uncool when he showed me a photo of himself in drag. But he was obviously still in love with his horrible promiscuous ex who had punched him in the eye the last time they'd been together, and when I ran into him at the health food store one day we realized that we had nothing to say to each other, nothing in common except that we'd been born in the same hospital, or maybe on the same planet.

There was that short Pakistani computer engineering guy whose roommates didn't know he was gay. He had impossibly long eyelashes and despite some acne was spectacularly handsome, but it didn't take long to figure out that he was going to marry a nice Muslim girl and spend the rest of his life lying to her the way he did when he told his roommates I was working with him to invent a new kind of CD-ROM drive or something.

Then there was this Chinese exchange student who seemed grateful that I could pronounce his name correctly. He had great calves and was older than I was, although he looked about twelve. Back in Shanghai he'd been a chef, and he once fixed me drunken chicken, a dish I'd never heard of before. But his accent was so thick I couldn't understand half the things he said in English and I was embarrassed to tell him, so I stopped calling.

Mostly, if only in my brain, there was Javier. And Bryan, of course.

The moon that can be seen from Moldova rotates on its axis every 27.3 days, the length of time it requires to revolve once around the earth. It has a diameter of 2,160 miles. Contrary to popular belief, the moon does have a diffuse atmosphere whose dominant gas is thought to be oxygen, although it has yet to be detected. All volcanic activity on the moon ceased nearly a billion years ago. Like other heavenly bodies, the moon wobbles, and because of this, 41 percent of the moon is always turned toward the earth, 41 percent is always invisible, and 18 percent is occasionally visible. Details of the lunar surface are best observed near the terminator, the line dividing the light and dark portions of the moon, where shadows help highlight the topography. The large dark blotches on the moon's surface, designated as "maria," the Latin word for seas, are occasionally discernible from Moldova.

Leonard Gray | *It's for You*

THE PHONE RANG at 10:45 as he was in bed next to his wife, and he looked up from his reading, slightly annoyed. His wife picked up the phone from her low bookcase. She answered, paused, and said "Yes," in a flat voice. After a few seconds of listening, she said nothing—just handed him the phone. She left her light on and picked up a magazine.

"Hel-*lo*." The voice was soft, husky, phony-seductive, with the second syllable emphasized. It might have been his sister, pulling his leg, but he always knew her voice. He hoped this was a wrong number, instead of a nut. "I decided to call you early, before—"

"Just a minute. Who were you trying to call?"

"Oh, have I dialed the wrong number? I'm *so* sorry. I was calling Edwin Jarvis. Please forgive me."

"Who is this? How did you get my name?"

"If this is inconvenient, I'll call you back later . . . or would you prefer to take care of our business now?"

"Do you know this is a federal offense, annoying people by telephone?"

"It's up to you." She paused for a few seconds, and he didn't reply. (What did she expect him to say?) "Okay—talk to you later." Click.

"Well, that's a new one." He handed his wife the receiver, and she stretched to put it back.

"Who was it?" she asked.

"Nobody I know."

She turned to look at him. "But she knew your name. It wasn't a wrong number."

"Got it from the phone book, I guess."

"You mean picked it at random?"

"I'm going to call the phone company."

"Don't be ridiculous," she said. "They're closed."

"Not *now*—tomorrow."

"And tell them what? That a woman you don't know called you, and you don't know why, or from where? Or *do* you know?"

132

"Don't be absurd."

"*Is* it a federal offense?"

He put his magazine on the table and turned out his light. "I have no idea," he said. She thumped around, shaking the bed before she settled, to show her annoyance—instead of talking about it, so they could dispose of the matter. She knew he didn't have a mistress, and she'd never had a reason to doubt his fidelity. Why couldn't she have sympathized—helped him deal with the problem?

He slipped out of bed and went to the bathroom—not the big one connected to their bedroom, but the one down the hall. He needed to pass some wind. He blew his nose on a Kleenex, flushed it down the toilet, and came back to bed.

It would be ridiculous to lose sleep over that woman's malicious joke—whoever she was. His wife was lying there silent and brooding, and he got in quietly and stayed on his own side. The night was ruined—for no reason. It took him an hour to get to sleep.

When the phone rang, he woke up with that out-of-whack, stripped-gear feeling in his heartbeat that he got sometimes when he was jolted out of a deep sleep. "Jesus Christ—not again!"

She turned on her light, picked up the receiver without a word, and handed it to him.

"Jarvy?" No one ever called him that.

"Who the hell *is* this?"

"Our business—remember? You wanted to wait."

"I'm going to unplug this phone, and report you in the morning to the telephone company."

"You haven't paid me for the last five times. I'll have to turn you over to a collection agency if I don't get your check by Wednesday."

He didn't answer.

"Oh, well, make it Thursday."

"You're in trouble if—"

"I won't keep you—"

"Wait a minute. Do you have the wrong Edwin Jarvis?"

"Edwin D. Jarvis, thirty-nine Berkeley Way?" Silence. "Well, have a nice day. Bye bye."

His wife was lying rigid, staring straight ahead, and he got up and walked around the bed to hang up the phone.

"Well—you'd better tell me about it."

"Is that how much you trust me, after thirty years of marriage?"

"Who was it?"

"How in hell do *I* know who it was?"

"Who might it have been?"

"You know as much about it as I do. Why are you treating me like a perpetrator?" This was straining sanity, normality. He felt on the verge of uncontrolled nervous laughter, and had to turn away for a few seconds to compose himself. They were deep into a bad situation, all over nothing.

"Well . . . what did she *say*?"

As soon as he'd told her, he realized his mistake. The caller must have guessed he'd repeat her outlandish story, without thinking, and make his wife even more suspicious. What a dirty, rotten, fiendish trick!

He snapped off the light, rolled over with his back to her, and tried to think who could possibly do such a thing. She apparently knew him, or knew of him. It could hardly be a former business associate. None of them were crazy, or even borderline. He had left his job two years ago, and was working full time managing his investments and serving on boards of directors. Could he have unknowingly harmed someone in a financial deal? Possible, but not likely. He might never have the answer. He dozed, then jolted himself awake, all snarled up in a bad dream.

The next morning, he dressed and shaved, brought in the paper, and poured a cup of coffee. His wife gave him the financial section and started on the front page as he put bread in the toaster. They commented on the news and weather and their plans for the day. He hadn't told her the unbalanced woman might call again on Thursday. Before then, he'd figure out how to deal with her.

Two days later, they went to a restaurant with friends. As they sipped their drinks, waiting for their order, his wife told the other two couples about the bizarre calls, and joked about being furious with him—in effect (by treating it lightly), repenting her initial lack of understanding. The others laughed. Thank God things were back to normal!

The subject changed, and a woman at the table asked where he'd been traveling to, lately. Los Angeles, he said.

A young woman had sat next to him on that flight. Her name began with an "S"—one of those distortions of an ordinary name to make it fancier. He tuned out his friends' table conversation and thought about her. Even before take-off, she had leaned across the empty seat and started talking, like someone from a small town. She told him she wanted to work in a bank—not as a teller, but in management. She had a certificate from a two-year college, with a lot of work in computers, and had completed an assignment for a bank-modernization plan. On and on she went.

He put away his magazine and took a good look at her. "You ought to be on the stage."

"Everyone says that. They're joking—and so are you. Only a fool would try for an acting career." They both smiled. "Don't you think I should be a banker?"

"No reason why you shouldn't." Maybe she *could* do it. She was certainly assertive enough.

"I've got an interview in Los Angeles . . . entry-level job. I'll be nervous, but I expect to get hired."

"Maybe I could help."

"Oh—are you with a bank?"

The attendants came around then with their cart, and he bought her a glass of champagne. He had one, too.

"I've got some stock in an L.A. bank, and I know the director. Nice guy. He wants to modernize. You might be just the person he's looking for."

"Oh, neat. Could you give me his name?" She took a pen from her purse, looked for paper, then tore a page from the airlines magazine in the seat pouch.

"I'll do better than that. I'll introduce you to him."

"Could you, really?" She shifted in her seat to face him. She was bright-eyed and enthusiastic, with a hint of shrewdness—like some successful business women he knew.

"Sure."

"You're serious about this? I've got a time problem, and I can't change my flight back."

"He owes me a favor. Could I see your résumé?" She took a copy from her purse and watched him skim over it. "Hmmmm. Not bad . . . not bad. My friend will probably offer you a job. He's desperate for good people. I don't know what he'd pay, of course."

"Are my credentials that good?"

"No, but your personality is."

She didn't seem to mind that he was looking at her intently—her face and her body and her legs, nicely revealed in one of those new short dresses that reminded him of the miniskirts of the sixties. She had a lovely smile and a nice, assured manner. She must be older than she looked. She didn't talk like a teen-ager, and wasn't dressed like one. He turned back to the first page of her résumé. She was twenty-three. He bought more champagne when the attendants came back.

"Where are you staying in L.A.?"

"With friends—not in a hotel."

When a flight attendant popped the top on a soft-drink can next to her, the drink frothed out, and Sherri (*that* was her name—Sherri) squirmed out of the seat, with a lovely wiggle of her bottom. He grabbed her hand when she thrust it out to steady herself. They were going through a patch of rough air, and he held her hand as the plane dipped again. She said "Oooh," and lowered herself to the seat next to him, as if she were enjoying this.

"I don't even know your name. I'm Edwin Jarvis."

"Sherilee Bedford."

"Shirley?"

"*Sherilee.*"

She gave his hand a little squeeze for emphasis as she spelled her name. Holding her hand for those few moments shot a jolt through him like falling in love. He knew it wasn't real, of course, but his body stirred to that brief touch and to the intent way she looked at him.

Was there any harm in that? he'd thought at the time. His wife loved casual flirtations—with the young lawyer at a party who got her off in a corner and talked and talked, the small-business CEO she charmed at dinner. He let her enjoy it, knowing there was nothing to it—and how was this different? No complications, no damage to anyone.

Before their plane landed, he arranged to pick up Sherri at her friends' house, off Western Avenue, at three the next day. He'd introduce her to the banker, he said. After her interview, the two of them could have dinner and maybe do something else. He gave her his business card.

"How nice of you," she said, "doing this for me. You know what? I'm going to cancel my other interview—otherwise, I could miss my flight back. Your idea sounds much better. You're serious. . . . Are you?"

"Of course I'm serious." He suppressed an urge to foolishly grab her hand again, when she looked at him that way.

He barely had time to check into his hotel, then get to his first meeting, so they started saying good bye at the luggage carousel. She took both his hands, looked up at him, and said, "I appreciate what you're doing for me. You won't forget, will you?" He smiled. "Get busy with your work and forget all about me?" She gave him the phone number where she'd be. "If I'm out, leave a message. I'm counting on you."

They walked to the exit with their carry-ons. She casually hugged him—with one arm, because of the bags—and they said good bye. She had a nice walk that understated her sexiness. She didn't turn and wave.

After the meeting, he took off his clothes and flopped on the bed in his hotel room. In the dream that came to him, he was having a sexual romp in El Dorado Park with Sherri. He woke up, with the room getting dark, lay there a few minutes returning to reality, and went to the bathroom to rinse his face.

Standing on the bathmat, looking in the mirror as he combed his hair, he thought of hazards lurking behind the smiles of innocent-looking women. But he wasn't going to bed with Sherri—that wasn't the kind of thing he did. Even if he was tempted, he certainly wouldn't jeopardize his marriage. But maybe he should buy a pack of condoms, anyway. What if she made it hard to resist? It was exciting to think about it, even though it would never happen. He felt good about having a pleasant, attractive young friend like Sherri, and to be doing something for her.

That night, a frantic phone call from an associate summoned him home to Connecticut. He'd have to drop everything in L.A. and rush back to help bail out an ailing company he had invested in heavily.

As he ate in the smaller of the hotel's dining rooms, alone at a table for two, he worked out what he was going to do when he got there, and made some notes on a pad. No—that plan wouldn't work. This would take a lot of finesse. He'd have to— the waiter cleared his throat. He hadn't realized the man was standing there. One reason for his business success was his ability to concentrate.

He went to bed with the problem still churning in his mind, not at all sure he could save the company. In the morning, he checked out of his hotel, grabbed a quick breakfast, and took the first flight home. There was nothing available but first class, which he often took anyway. With his first sip of champagne, he thought, Oh, hell—I didn't call Sherri.

All that was several days before the night of the two phone calls. He'd thought Sherri was genuine—she hadn't seemed vicious or psychopathic—but how can you tell in a few hours? He felt a small stab of guilt. Why hadn't he at least called her when he got home? He ought to look up her number and call her now and apologize. He'd explain why he'd been so distracted that he'd left her in L.A. without a word, and would promise to arrange an interview for her. But if it *was* she who called him that night—if she was that vindictive, that weird . . .

She (Sherrilee or whoever it was) had threatened to call back on Thursday. That evening, he and his wife had supper as usual. While she was clearing the table, he went to the bedroom and unplugged the phone.

As they were going to bed, at eleven-fifteen, she asked him, "Why was the phone unhooked?"

"Cleaning woman, I guess."

"No matter. I plugged it back in." She opened her closet and took off her blouse and skirt, half hidden by the closet door.

After he had his pajamas on, and had been to the bathroom, he went downstairs and quietly opened the liquor cabinet. He drank from the brandy bottle, screwed the cap on, then unscrewed it and took another slug. He picked up the latest copy of *Time* from the coffee table and went up to bed. His wife was reading a book.

When the phone rang, at eleven-thirty, he went on reading. His wife lowered her book and stared straight ahead. As the phone rang and rang and rang, he got up and unplugged it.

He took off his pajamas and let them fall to the floor, turned out the light, and got in bed. His wife startled him by pulling the sheet down to uncover them both in the dim light, to display her body to him. Her wet lips touched his neck as her hair fell across him, and her hand went to his belly. Her cool naked legs were against his, and her breasts were against his back as she curled herself around him. How strange that she was sexually excited tonight, in spite of the phone business. No—it was because of the masterful way he'd disposed of the problem. He chuckled silently at the thought.

It was then that they heard the downstairs phone ring, and keep ringing.

Nancy Krusoe | *Hens, Cows, Canoes*

Romeo said about his name:
"Had I it written, I would
tear the word."

1

FOR LUNCH COLD HOT HEN is offered to all the men who wait to be fed at a table in town. Already they are toweled, knifed, and forked. All at once they want it now. Who cares if it's hot or cold!

Steadily a red-hot dish is brought to the table. It is Hen who serves the men. Think of this as a phase of a country hen.

"I am giving you my most red one," she says to the men.

"First time?" one asks.

Already read-red and on the wing: "Not the first," she says.

2

What country are we in? Hen is not totally new at this; nothing is the first time. In town a hen is always red.

3

Hen says, "In the country I am in love with a blues singer; my singer's words come out of my mind-mouth. He licks like my mother. The first time I heard his mouth working like my mind, I thought *between* is a place that is not caught as it is."

At the table the men are laughing now. Hen has made them happy.

"What's in the future?" they ask.

Hen says, "If I fall into the lake, you will have cold wet hen."

4

Then she jumps into the lake which is blue to a bird and is wet until the eating act is over.

5

After work Hen goes home where she and her mother are alone with cows that long like cows sometimes do when they are in love. It's madness—Hen is sleepy thick with licorice, but they wake her in the night in her dreaming time and time again leaning into her, melting large AM-OOU-ISSES on her very red mouth.

Alone with cows you can say anything. Swear to a cow and she laps you with her long fibered tongue. Pour hot flames into a cow and quicker than you think she licks in Hen, taking her easily swinging into the night mountains—who cares about that?

6

In town, the men at Hen's table peck at their food. They are lonely and they are sad; they say they are tired of waiting and eating and working. Hen has been to a fortuneteller, and there is fortune in the air where they sit—not theirs but hers.

"What is it?" they want to know.

She says, "When I was young, my fortune was my name—my father's name. Then he died and the name he had given to me and my mother made no difference. We could have been anyone—no telling who we were."

7

Sometimes Hen wants to see the word *hen* in her brain.

Thanks to her father, Hen had a name—Hen House.

Thanks to the mother, too, who stretched thick red sentences, embedded with secrets. All those gagging words cannot be forgotten; strung together they mean home, place, calling us there, making us names—hens, cows.

8

Hen says, "Even then already I knew what I wanted to become was a singer." "Maybe your name will sing you to fame," my mother said.

"Or a man will sing it for you," a man all hands on the table says. Then they all begin to sing for Hen in unison, "When Johnny Comes Marching Home."

9

Lunch is between: wet/grow, better/red, beyond town/what country are we in?

10

Hen says, "In the country I am in love with a blues singer. He mouths my mind."

Then she takes off her clothes, waves goodbye, and jumps into the lake, the warmth of her skin soothing water. "You're My Little Buttercup," the men sing to her from the edge of the tips of their shoes at the lake.

Underwater Hen is not silent, she is not a quiet good girl; inside the lake she shrieks and bellows, building her body to a flame.

11

What is your fortune, Hen?

12

Lower your voice, city boys will say to her. Mouthing her mind out her mouth she'll try it lower she'll sing: My mouth will wolf you down. Laughing they'll love to eat up her song.

13

Don't sing, says her mother. Don't try to sing. Don't ever sing. There's no pleasure in it, it's no good your singing, none whatsoever. Your father is dead, his name is dead, now be quiet and be good and believe in your future.

But what does a country mother know about mooing lakes or cows that canoe? What does she know?

With cows you can sing anytime.

With cows it's la-la-la all day and night; they stare and watch you as if they are trying to figure out something and then they begin to harmonize: "If ever I would leave you." It is very pretty cowsong. But they get tired—cows, too, must sleep—so Hen is alone far away with her dreams of lakes and fires.

14

This is not a lonely place in the country. This is the mountain alive at night. Here Hen talks to the places where her mother's warnings lie between mind and mouth and mountain—turning into poultry.

15

Don't wait, her mother says. One day it will be too late.

16

At home Hen writes, "In the country I am in love with a blues singer; his words come out of my mind-mouth. Every time he touches me he's in me. He says to me 'you are cold' and I shiver, inviting him in. He pulls me away with him and comes inside me. One moment it's him, then it's me. Can he be hen? Can he become inside me me?"

It's tempting to say so. It's tempting to pretend, for Hen to spread her legs and never look up, to fill in—to put a whole there, right there where his hand is—to have a hole that isn't filled and let it be filled—a hole you cannot see but seeing isn't everything. To feel and touch it. Seeing isn't everything, but the hole is everywhere; there are many and it's tempting to fill them all but he can't be everywhere at once—she is a walking giant hole.

In this place now he's inside Hen. It's time for her to decide—it's time to come—it's time to be now. Hen's mind is racing with hard hot words. "Can I be inside you?" she asks him, her lover whose words are the same in her mouth—does he mind? "Can you let me be inside you you? Is one whole enough? I am making the whole of you and I am what is made inside out. Can you hold me there like this oozing, losing my mind in you?"

Hen's lover pulls away. "Remember how it was?" he says. "Remember how we said we were? You wanted how I wanted you."

Now he lets go, he undoes love, he remembers what came before what they are doing now, and he forgets the place they are in this moment they have led up to, this mixed up place. Can we see the country we are in?

17

Hen moves to the city where she sings for her fans, but in the city there are bodies everywhere wanting to be someone—you or him or her. But how do you get to be

one of each of everything without being once someone yourself?
   Can this hole be filled?

18

Moved by your grieving, he marries you, they say.
   When you are in pain, he intoxicates you.

19

Back in town for a day in the middle of things, all the men at the table wait for Hen.
It's a reunion. Napkins, forks, sharp knifes—everything is ready for that very special
number, that make-my-dreams-come-true meal-of-your-life for Hen and the men
who eat.
   "You!" they say. "It's you we are waiting for."
   One man, fanning a fire with his knife, pushes her face toward the flame—it is a
telling of fortunes for Hen.
   "You are back at last," they say.
   For a moment Hen thinks she might tell them that once she caressed cows, that
they are better than anything else, oh better, better, much better!
   All those people who know her in the city do mouth her songs, putting hen into
their eating act.
   There are messages in her songs: what has to die will over and over on the surface
of poultry sounds, separate from the rest, and don't turn to the fire in a lake, don't go
underwater in turn, you know already what sounds to make, you know how to kill,
under fire connect this part to that side by side and burn in slow motion concentrated.

20

Chicken parts—hands down—hen/sine/die/sin/ge/Hen/her

21

What's wrong is it's inside, its insides, its poultry parts. To be chicken penned—the
girl caged written into a state of fire.

Half out of the country now.
   Lying in wait.

Hens, Cows, Canoes

22

Lunch is between: wet/grow, better/red, red/red, beyond/town.

Before going to the city, Hen was the girl part of herself awaiting the fortune around her, flying out and back, scratching and pecking a commotion of sounds in her head, the way cows sing and canoe in the mountains at night—turning monsters into mouths for mountains.

23

Back in the country where the cows come in, first you hear their voices, they are hot and steamy, they heave and snort. They swing their heads, and in every swing is a moment of hurrying pleasure in deeply muddied air. Marching through the mud, they've been singing "Where the girls are," singing all the words in the woods, riding a canoe they sing and bellow. They break the silence at the foot of the mountain at night on fire in the country where hens are from. In Hen's house the air is foggy and wet with their breathing. That's how she knows they've come in swishing fuzzy daylight.

Gary D. Wilson | *Promises to Keep*

EIGHT-THIRTY SHARP the phone rang. He knew it was eight-thirty without looking at his watch or a clock because he always had his second cup of coffee Saturdays
at eight-thirty as he sat in his easy chair and planned his day—like trying to decide
when to take the car in for an oil change so he'd be sure not to miss the opening
kickoff of the Notre Dame football game—and he said what now and pushed himself back up.

It was the kind of thing Marge would have told him he should be thankful for
instead of complaining about. Something different. Something to break the routine.
And he was thinking, as if she were right there beside him and not gone six months
now, out the door clean as a whistle because she said she couldn't stand it anymore.
He was thinking if she's so hot on different maybe she should be the one talking,
only she wasn't the one the guy asked for. He said Ray Stevens with a big question
mark at the end, like somebody calling about insurance or a fantastic new long distance service or one of those I'll-only-take-five-minutes-of-your-time telephone con-
sumer preference surveys.

"Yeah, this is Ray Stevens."

"Ah. Well," as if the caller couldn't decide what to think of someone who would
admit to being the person he was looking for. "My name is Morrissey, Mr. Stevens,
Dr. Berwyn Morrissey. I'm with the Medical Examiner's Office and there's something I need to talk to you about, if you have a moment."

"*Doctor*, you say?"

"Yes."

"A *medical* doctor?"

"Yes."

"Something wrong? Somebody—?"

"No, no, Mr. Stevens. Don't misunderstand. No one's sick, or anything like that.
In fact, we don't even deal with sick people in the normal sense of the word. You see,
I'm a pathologist, Mr. Stevens. My primary interest is in what kills people rather
than what makes them sick."

"Oh my god!"

"I'm afraid I'm not making myself very clear. Let me explain: about six o'clock this morning we got a call from a rooming house in Fells Point saying they had a dead body on the premises, could we come and take a look? Of course we said we would, since that's part of our job, and one of our people went down to investigate and didn't find anything out of the ordinary. An apparent heart attack, he thought, although you can't be absolutely certain in a case like that without an autopsy. But nothing from a visual examination that would indicate an unnatural as opposed to a natural death. Murder or the like."

"Okay, but what does all this—?"

"I'm coming to that. The man in question here left a note, it seems. Pinned to his shirt."

"Yeah?"

"It instructed the person who found it to call you."

"Me?"

"It said—here, let me read it to you—and I quote: 'Call Ray Stevens. He'll know the decent thing to do.' Unquote."

"This a joke, right? Something one of my weird friends put you up to?"

"I'm afraid not, Mr. Stevens."

"What then? What's the idea?"

"We were hoping you could maybe help us out. You know, come down and have a look at the man?"

"Why?"

"To see if you might have known him."

"Get outta here!"

"I realize how hard this must be to—"

"I mean, you haven't even told me his name, for chrissake."

"Joe."

"Joe what?"

"Just Joe. Unfortunately that's all we could come up with. He had no ID on him and nobody had ever heard him called anything else—or at least wouldn't admit to it if they had."

"You know what I should do? I should hang up. Put the phone down and go drink my coffee and forget this ever happened."

"I understand. If I were you—"

"You're not, though."

"Let me assure you, Mr. Stevens, that this whole matter is nearly as awkward for us as it is for you. We would vastly prefer that we had another open and shut case on our hands, another unidentified body. But we don't. And when something like this comes up, we're obligated to follow though with it. We need your help, Mr. Stevens. I can't make it any clearer than that."

Ray glanced down the hall at the empty living room, then the other way at the tangle of sheets on the floor beside the bed and wished he had someone to talk to.

Marge: You could've told him no.

Ray: What the . . .

Marge: Watch out, you're gonna have a wreck!

Ray: You shouldn't sneak up on people like that.

Marge: If I'm a sneak, you've made me that way.

Ray: Right.

Marge: Well it's not my idea to be here.

Ray: Go away then.

Marge: I can't, and you know it.

Ray: You mean out of mind, out of sight?

Marge: Exactly. You don't want me around, send me away.

Ray: Yeah, I wish it was that easy.

Marge: Don't let that guy cut you off!

Ray: You wanna drive?

Marge: Real funny, Ray.

Ray: You used to laugh at my jokes.

Marge: I was a captive audience.

Ray: Hmm. So what did you mean I could've told him no?

Marge: Just that. You never had any trouble telling me no.

Ray: But that was different.

Marge: How so?

Ray: Because you're my wife.

Marge: Was.

Ray: Are.

Marge: Not.

Ray: Are, too.

Marge: No.

STOP IT!

Marge: Who said that?

Ray: What?

Marge: Stop it.

Ray: The guy in that car over there. He was yelling at his kids.

Marge: Oh. You still haven't told me why you didn't.

Ray: Didn't what?

Marge: Say no.

Ray: Because I wanted to be sure.

Marge: About?

Ray: Him. Whether I knew him.

Marge: But he was a bum.

Ray: How can you be so sure?

Marge: Who else lives in a rooming house in Fell's Point?

Ray: Maybe he was rich, but didn't like being alone all the time.

Marge: Then why didn't he pay somebody to stay with him?

Ray: Why all the questions? It's so out of character for you. Normally you'd be the first one in line to have a look.

Marge: You don't like the way I am, change me.

Ray: I wish you hadn't left.

Marge: I was waiting for you to say something like that the morning I did. Something like no, please don't go, but you just stood there at the door with your hands in your pockets and your shoulders shrugged, saying but. But-but. Sounded like a lawnmower that wouldn't start.

Ray: We were so good together.

Marge: That's what you remember maybe.

Ray: But I miss—

Marge: I know what you miss. Here's your turn. He's waiting.

Dr. Morrissey met him at the door. Pumped his hand, thanked him again for coming. He just didn't realize what a help he was being. "Not everybody would agree to do a thing like this, Mr. Stevens."

"Ray."

"What?"

"Just call me Ray."

"All right, Ray," he smiled, peering out of the tops of his eye sockets the way people do who wear half-glasses, a tall thin man with a halo of faded red hair and pale, freckled skin. "Shall we?" guiding him with a hand to his back down a dimly lit corridor, exposed brickwork on one side, unpainted wallboard on the other, toward a red-lettered sign on a door at the end: "AUTHORIZED PERSONNEL ONLY."

"Oh, yes, one final thing," he said, stopping before they entered. "In the event that you do find out he was someone familiar to you—and that's not totally out of the question; it happens far more often than you might think—I want you to remember that you have no obligation to us other than identifying him. That's it. That's all we care about. As far as we're concerned, this is purely an administrative matter. All right?" The smile, the stare. Ray Stevens nodded.

The room was just like in the movies, bright white and shiny, antiseptic-looking. A wall full of what appeared to be oversized file cabinet drawers. Dr. Morrissey crossed to them, read the labels with his finger until he came to the one he was looking for and pulled the drawer open.

Ray Stevens could clearly see the outline of a body under the sheet. Head, chest, a white valley between parted legs.

"Are you all right?" Dr. Morrissey asked.

"Yeah, I just—"

"It helps sometimes, if you're not used to this sort of thing, and I doubt you are, to take a couple of deep breaths."

He did, trying not to shudder, telling himself how this couldn't be much worse than seeing a body at a funeral—and he'd had to do that far more often than he liked to think about—only there they'd already been fixed up, dressed up, made to look as good as they could dead.

"Ready?" Dr. Morrissey asked.

He nodded, looked away, even though he told himself not to. Swallowed. Took another deep breath. Looked back.

Grey. Like he'd been washed with mud. But not quite, because it was under the skin, not on it. Scrawny, scruffy grey, with no teeth and a mangled left hand, pinky finger missing entirely, the next two cut off on a perfect diagonal up from it. But an old wound. All of them were, whitish nicks on the face, the arms, a longer "smile" under his left ribcage, sworls of shiny flesh paralleling the right shin bone. And god knew the last time he'd shaved, had a haircut, bathed, knees and elbows covered with dark patches of skin.

"Well?" Dr. Morrissey said.

Ray Stevens glanced up.

"You recognize him?"

"No."

"Positive?"

"Yes."

"All right." Dr. Morrissey lowered the sheet, straightened it, himself, fished around in the pocket of his white coat. "Ah, there it is. The note. I thought you might want to see it." Reaching across the body to hand Ray Stevens a single piece of paper the color of a yellow legal pad, only smaller, three-by-five maybe, torn clean at the top and folded lengthwise down the middle, pinholes near the upper two corners, but otherwise not a wrinkle in it, black ballpoint handwriting inside in round, even letters, saying exactly what Morrissey had told him. But he read it again anyway, and again, to be sure he wasn't missing anything.

"Something wrong?" Dr. Morrissey said. "You seem—"

"I don't know, I. . . ."

"If you're wondering how he got your name—"

"No, it's not that—anybody can open a phone book—and it probably doesn't amount to a hill of beans really, but, well . . . it's this, I guess." Showing the note. "This *decent thing to do*."

"Oh. I see. Well, I wouldn't worry about that, if I were you. Sometimes these old guys have a pretty bizarre sense of humor."

Ray Stevens looked down at the body, Joe, imagining him imagining him standing there now, what he was thinking as he pinned the note to his shirt, grinned a toothless grin and started to laugh, but coughed instead, something catching in his throat as he lay back just right, wiggled in for comfort and died.

"So it probably was a joke after all."

"In a manner of speaking, I suppose. From his viewpoint at least."

"Huh." Felt himself shrug.

Dr. Morrissey nodded in agreement that there wasn't much else to discuss. "I'm ready if you are."

"Yeah, I guess I am. Except for one thing."

"What-might-that-be?" drawn out in a cautionary way.

"I know this is going to sound odd. Weird. But I can't get it out of my mind. Doesn't it seem strange to you, even a little bit, that at exactly that moment he opened the phone book to exactly that page and found *me*? Out of all the others? Out of any other possibility?"

The doctor cleared his throat, glanced toward the door. "We don't get into that sort of . . . *speculation*. Not that it's uninteresting, mind you, but in this business it would be neverending and. . . . Well, quite frankly this isn't the only case we have."

"I'm sure you're busy."

"That doesn't mean this case is any less important than the others, however, or that what you've done is any less appreciated. As I told you on the phone, it's simply a matter of—"

"Yeah, I know. So what now?"

"I'm sorry?"

"What happens now? With him," a nod toward the body.

"Standard procedure. We'll try missing persons, check his fingerprints, that sort of thing; and if we don't get any leads, which I doubt we will, we'll contact one of the medical schools to see if they need a cadaver. They take pretty good care of them— treat them with respect and all. After they're finished, they'll have a nice service, talk about his contribution to mankind, and bury him. If they don't want him, we'll turn him over to a funeral home and—"

"And?"

"Well, it's pretty bare bones," the half-glasses smile again, only less patient, more patronizing, his hand raising to Ray Stevens's back, urging him toward the door. "Now I promised you this wouldn't take a lot of your time, and I want to be good to my word, so if there are no further questions—"

There'd been an accident near the Washington Monument and he was stuck mid-block in traffic, the air thick with the smell of hot asphalt and antifreeze. He rolled up the window and turned on the airconditioner. Thought how chilly the morgue had been, how good the sun had felt when he stepped outside. Watched now as a young Asian woman—Chinese, he guessed, probably a Peabody student—strolled up the sidewalk beside him, her hips swaying beneath a long t-shirt, straight black hair hanging half way down her back.

Marge: Nice, huh?

Ray: She's all right.

Marge: Young.

Ray: Yeah.

Marge: Pretty.

Ray: Yeah.

Marge: Full of energy. Enthusiasm. Lots of deeply felt urges. You wish you were with her, don't you?

Ray: Maybe.

Marge: And instead of looking at a dead body you're holding onto a live one. One that you woke up next to and watched sleep a while and then touched—on the neck probably or the lips—because you couldn't help yourself and you made love and went back to sleep. Got up finally and decided to go out for a late breakfast somewhere.

Ray: Nice story.

Marge: What's stopping you?

Ray: I still—

Marge: Ha! Tell me, how long were we married?

Ray: I don't know—eleven, twelve years?

Marge: Exactly to the day thirteen and a half.

Ray: What's the point?

Marge: Did you love me?

Ray: Do.

Marge: *Hate* me?

Ray: Come on.

Marge: They are one in the same, you know. They each take oomph, commitment. Did you?

Ray: You shouldn't have to ask.

Marge: Exactly. But I do because I don't know. Didn't. May never. Although I did see a spark back there. With him. Joe. Something beginning to click. I mean, I was impressed that you went through with it. I wanted to gag.

Ray: It wasn't easy.

Marge: But the point is you did it. Actually stood there and looked at him. In detail. Head to toe, so to speak. I couldn't believe it.

Ray: Thanks.

Marge: Well think about it. Mr. No. Mr. won't take any chances. Mr. never won or lost a thing in his life.

Ray: Until you.

Marge: That's what you say, but I don't believe it for a minute. I think you *think* you miss me, but what you mean is that you miss having somebody else in the house and an occasional partner in bed. Isn't that right? And isn't that the way it was with everything? Look at your job. How long have you been there? Twenty years or something like that and you haven't missed a day, yet you always said you could walk away from it in a minute. And remember that vacation in 1978? The one to the Eastern Shore where you were bored out of your mind. Or at least that's what you told me. And you must have been serious since you never took another one. You'd rather work, you said, or stay home. So you can say whatever you like—She's turning. You see her?

Ray: Yes.

Marge: Better hurry then. You don't want to miss your chance. There aren't that many in life. Go on, get out. There's a parking place right over there. Go catch up with her. Take her hand in yours. Tell her you just want to be her friend. That you're tired of being lonely, getting older, with no end in sight. Or the end you see not being the one you want. Not yet anyway. Not like him. Joe.

The traffic jam broke and he headed to nearest liquor store to buy a bottle of whisky. Picked one off the shelf without even looking at the label. Drove the rest of the way home in silence, parked in front of the house, but didn't get out right away, staring instead at the oil marks on the street.

Ray: Wanna come in for a while?

Marge: I don't think that would be such a good idea.

Ray: Suit yourself.

He locked the car, unlocked the front door, went from room to room turning on lights. The place even smelled empty.

Damn her.

It was too early to start drinking, but he did anyway. Took a glass and the bottle to his chair, flipped through the TV channels until he found a golf match. Filled the glass. Drank. Tried to hate her. Couldn't, except for a few seconds at a time, since whenever he'd reach a peak of loathing, she would fuse in his mind with the Asian woman on the street and he would end up, hand over his tingling crotch, thinking of Just Joe, cold, dead, feeling nothing.

By evening he didn't care what was on the screen, since he could no longer focus on it. But something was. Some noise. Some company.

That night Just Joe emerged naked as a baby one piece at a time from a dark corner of the room—head, shoulders, arms, torso, legs—lay a moment on the floor as if collecting his thoughts, then stood, brushed himself off and came and sat on the edge of Ray Stevens's bed, elbow on one thigh, mangled hand on the other as he leaned forward, lips puckered, left eye squinted shut. "First off, let's get the name straight. It's Joe, all right, but it ain't *Just* Joe. It's Joseph Michael Robertson McGrew. My mamma was Mary Robertson and my daddy was Michael McGrew. His daddy was Joseph. His daddy before that, I don't know, except he came on the boat from Ireland hungry as hell and ready to do anything to stay alive. So there you got it all. I never married, never had no kids that I know of, and out of the five of us in my family, even though I was the oldest, I was the last to go. My first brother drowned, the next was trampled by horses. Had one sister die of childbed fever and another go to the nuns before the polio took her. There was a couple of cousins here and there, but none of 'em close. Aunts and Uncles, too, only they're all gone now of course. And that's it, and I wanted somebody to know. Also that I ain't no bum, no matter what she says. I ain't tryin' to get nothin' for nothin' outta nobody. I worked my whole life, just like my daddy and his daddy. Damn hard, too. For the B. & O. Made a livin', but that was about it. Put a little aside, not a lot. At least I did later in life. With that and my retirement I got along all right. Until Bushnell anyway. He was the husband of the sister of mine that died having his baby. He died, too, though, the baby. So Bushnell was there with nothin', like all the rest of us. Only a little more so. Pretty sad case, or that was the way he liked to play it up, folks told me. They all said he was a fake, a no good who was just out to take anybody for anything he could get. I don't know, I can't judge a man like that when all he's doin' is askin' a favor. He wanted money, of course, and I give it to him. A lot of money—for me, anyway— and I never seen hide nor hair of him after that. Now you wouldn't be alone if you called me a fool, and maybe I was. It sure as hell cleaned me out. It wasn't long after that I got sick and ended up havin' to sell my place and move into a hotel to begin with, then to the rooming house where they found me. But I still never regretted it. It's like givin' a real bum a dollar, or five, or even ten like I done once. You just can't go around worryin' then what he does with it. Probably gonna buy a bottle, but that's his business. Just like it was Bushnell's business. I done it and that was it. I never looked back. Never thought I was a fool. 'Cause I got this idea you just never know how somebody's gonna pay you back—by kickin' you in the teeth or returnin' the favor, passin' it on to somebody else, your little kindness. And if you don't do it, who's gonna? Somebody's got to. Otherwise—well, you can just about imagine how bad things would get if nobody ever did nothin' for nobody. Think about that. But— and this is the damn truth, too bad about it—most people *don't* do nothin' but set on their butts most of the time. You know it, I know it. And that means, of course, that it's up to the ones that's left to do even more. To take up the slack, so to speak, so the whole damn thing don't just fall apart in a heap." At which point he stood, walked backward to where he had lain earlier, got down on the floor, and once situated, was reabsorbed piecemeal into the dark corner, legs, torso, arms, shoulders, head, paus- ing long enough for one last piercing gaze at Ray Stevens, huddled against the head- board of his bed, sheet wadded in his fists beneath his chin.

He called the Medical Examiner's Office as early the next morning as he thought civil. The woman who answered said Dr. Morrissey wasn't in, it was Sunday, after all, and they shouldn't be expected to work seven days a week, could she take a message? He asked if there was some way he could get in touch with the doctor and she said no but maybe she could help him, and he told her he doubted it, unless she knew what, if anything, had been done with the bodies that were there yesterday. She said it depended on who he was inquiring about, and he said he wasn't sure, except that his name was Joe. He'd been in to identify him and couldn't. Not then anyway. But now— She said she'd have to check the records, did he remember the identification number of the body in question? No, he couldn't say, didn't remember ever seeing one, and she told him in that case it made her task doubly difficult, if not impos- sible, since she didn't have a lot of free time on her hands just now to go look. It hadn't been what she would call a slow night. He told her she could say that again, but she said nothing and he asked once more about Dr. Morrissey's number. It *was* urgent. Even an emergency, if that made it any easier for her.

"Dr. Morrissey?"

"Ye-es."

"Ray Stevens here," imagining him peering over the tops of his bifocals while he tried to put his name with his face. "You remember yesterday when I—?"

"How did you happen to come by my number, Mr. Stevens?"

"Woman at your office."

"I thought as much. That would be Lattimer. I'll have to speak to her about this."

"It's not her fault. I told her it was an emergency. It's about Joe."

"Oh?"

"I think I know him after all. And I, um, I wanted to see if it was too late for me to—"

"Take possession?"

"If that's what you call it. I just want to do right by him."

"Well, there isn't anything . . . at least not on the surface to stand in the way of. . . . But this is a bit of a surprise, you understand. I do hope I made it clear to you yesterday that you are under no obligation whatsoever. Even if overnight you've started feeling sad or guilty about what might become of him, you still—"

"I know that."

"I see. It won't be cheap, you understand."

"I'll take care of it."

"And the time involved—"

"I said I'll take care of it."

"All right then. If that's what you want, come to my office tomorrow to sign the release forms, and we'll go from there."

"Eight o'clock?"

"Make it eight-thirty."

"See you then."

"First, before you go, if you wouldn't mind, Mr. Stevens, would you be so kind as to do me the favor of explaining something? A small personal matter: why the hell didn't you tell me this yesterday?"

"I didn't know it then."

"But surely—"

"It came to me in the middle of last night. I realize that sounds corny, but it's the truth."

"You had a revelation of some kind, or what?"

"No, it was more like a *visi*tation."

"I see. . . . Tomorrow then."

Marge: He thinks you're nuts.

Ray: So?

Marge: *I* think you're nuts.

Ray: Sorry you feel that way.

Marge: Wouldn't you, for god's sake? I mean, do you *really* think he was there? This Joe?

Ray: I don't know. He seemed real enough at the time. But that's not the point anymore. What's done is done. I can't back out now. Not again. Couldn't even if I wanted to, because the one thing that is clear is that if I don't go through with this, nothing will ever seem right again. Will ever *be* right. Does that make sense?
Marge: No.
Ray: I'm sorry, but it's the best I can do.
Marge: That's too bad.
Ray: Oh?
Marge: I was hoping for something a little more—
Ray: What?
Marge: I guess I'm not sure.
Ray: If I didn't know you better, I'd say you sounded worried.
Marge: Would that be so bad?
Ray: Are you?
Marge: Answer me!
Ray: I can't.
Marge: Won't.
Ray: Either way.

He had driven about as far out Belair Road as he'd ever been—or had ever wanted to be—and he was trying to be patient, reminding himself that you always think it takes longer than it really does to get to someplace for the first time, as he passed through a seemingly endless commercial strip of bars and doughnut shops, fast food restaurants and run-down malls, car dealerships, grocery and liquor stores, an occasional bowling alley or movie theater, all with flags, mostly American, large and small, a few lines of pennants and silver and gold tinsel intended to divert attention from the otherwise seedy sameness of the area.

At the top of a rise, he could see in the distance a large sign in the middle of a line of large signs bunched together like commuters waiting for a bus: "PRESTON & SON FUNERAL HOME, Serving the Public since 1925, Phone: 932-7600." In fact, the sign seemed larger than necessary, larger than what it announced, an unpretentious brick and frame building set back off the road that could just as easily have been the office of a small construction company or, judging from the array of vehicles to either side of the door, a used car dealership. He hadn't expected anyone else to be there and idled a moment at the entrance to the lot, wondering where he should park—next to the cars, or a few spaces away. Smiled at his old indecisiveness, pulled up directly in front of the door and was met immediately by a woman shaking her head and saying, "No, no," as she waved him back, like someone directing an airplane. "No parking."

She waited as he pulled into a space nearer the street.

"Sorry, but we have a funeral in progress and need to keep that space clear for the hearse."

"No problem."

"Are you here for—?"

"I'm supposed to meet with Mr. Preston."

"And you're—?"

"Ray Stevens. I called him earlier."

"Oh. Yes. He did mention—"

What? he wondered. That it takes all kinds? That you thought you'd seen it all and then—?

"This way, please."

Nice legs, hips, hair. But you're not supposed to think of things like that at times like these. He could at least ask her her name.

Down a short hall past a room with a casket, people sitting in rows in front of it, a preacher reading from the Bible. Another room, someone arranging flowers around an empty space. Something else he'd forgotten about, of course. Flowers. What kind would Joe like? Anything but mums. He hated mums. Or at least Ray Stevens was going to imagine he did. Another room with closed doors.

She stopped in front of what looked like an office on the left, turned, held her arm out— "Please be seated. Mr. Preston will be with you shortly."—and was gone before he even noticed the color of her eyes.

It was a small room. Papers on the desk. Books and diplomas on the walls. Mortuary Science. The chair wasn't nearly as comfortable as he'd expected.

"Mr. Stevens?"

He stood.

"Philip Preston," hand extended in greeting.

He wondered whether at mortuary school they taught people to look pasty, or whether being around the dead so much eventually sapped the life out of you. The voice, too, the whole manner. Soft, smooth, like hand cream.

"So sorry about your loss," Philip Preston said, indicating that he could sit again.

"Loss?"

"Yes, your . . . *friend*, wasn't it?"

"Oh. Yeah. Thanks."

A tick of a smile that involved nothing more than his mouth. Maybe he knew Morrissey. Maybe they'd worked together sometime, rubbed off on each other.

"But I wouldn't call it a loss, I don't think. Not as such. It's actually more of a gain on my part. You see, he—"

A raised brow, a look in the eye that said no matter how much he tried to explain himself he would never be able to. He glanced down. Philip Preston continued.

"Now we have several packages for you to consider." And he went through them, all more or less elaborate and expensive, depending on style and composition of casket, flowers, type of service, music or not, preacher or not and who, number of limousines, location of cemetery, pall bearers hired or volunteer or none, and so on, not to mention clothes, which Ray Stevens hadn't even considered.

"What do people usually do about that?" he asked.

"Bring something from the deceased's wardrobe. Something nice. A favorite suit, shirt, tie. Did he wear glasses?"

"Not that I know of."

"Jewelry?"

"I don't think so."

"Not even a watch, a wedding band?"

"He was single. That's what he told me anyway."

"How about shoes?" Philip Preston asked.

"Shoes?"

"Some people insist on them, others don't. The feet are covered, of course."

"It's up to you," Ray Stevens said.

"I beg your pardon."

"I mean, what do you think?"

"I would, I believe. It makes for a more complete costume."

"Shoes it'll be then."

A yellow pencil as his guide, Philip Preston read down a list on a sheet of paper in front of him. "Hair style—anything special there?"

"A part's all. Left side, if I remember. But it's hard to with things like that."

"Of course. Don't worry a minute more about it. You can usually tell right away by looking. We'll take care of it."

"He will get a bath, won't he? A shave and maybe a trim to spruce him up?"

"Oh, yes. Absolutely. We do a nice job, Mr. Stevens. I'm sure you'll be satisfied."

"Because I want the best for him. You know, sort of a going away present."

"I understand," Philip Preston said, making a note of something, straightening a stack of papers to his right, looking up again finally. "Any other questions?" as though he hadn't been the one asking them.

"Not that I can think of."

"If you're ready then, perhaps we should—"

Ray Stevens nodded and was escorted through another door at the end of the hall into a room filled with caskets, lids open to display their plush interiors, set out at different heights and angles, soft lighting behind them. But no music, and there should have been, he was thinking, because otherwise all you could hear was your own breathing, which seemed somehow out of place.

He chose a grey metallic box with wood trim, brass hardware and a white satin interior, but no vault, no clock, no five-year guaranteed surroundsound stereo, solar power panel discretely located above ground near the grave marker.

Back in Philip Preston's office, they decided on flowers, no mums, music, a priest, if possible from St. Peter the Apostle Church, burial in the churchyard beside Joe's family—which Ray Stevens had already arranged for—order and time of service, newspaper notices, obituary— "You know, highlights of his life, that sort of thing." —and other details to be taken care of by Philip Preston and Son, except for method of payment, which of course only Ray Stevens could provide.

They both stood then, shook hands and said they would be in touch.

At the first mall he saw on his way home, he stopped in to buy a suit—a brown pinstripe, size 38 or 40, he guessed—medium shirt, brown tie, brown shoes, nine and a half C.

"You'll be taking this with you?" the clerk asked.

He said no, deliver it to Philip Preston and Son. You know, the funeral home? The clerk stared at him, as if waiting for him to break out laughing at his own joke, then looked away, not knowing what to say.

The morning of the funeral he woke early, showered, shaved and dressed. The weather was fine, the headlines in the newspaper harmless. Even the traffic in front of his house seemed more orderly than usual. He ate, washed up his dishes, turned to the obituary page to help pass the time. "Joseph Michael Robertson McGrew, native Baltimorean and devoted Orioles fan, died July 12, 1991, after a long illness at his Fell's Point home. He was 78 . . ." A whole life in two or three paragraphs. A bunch of words—his at that—telling about somebody who may never have been more than a bad dream. But there it was. There *he* was. Right there in black and white. A man had lived now and died and was soon to be buried, all because of him. It made him dizzy to think about it. He closed his eyes, held his hands to his head until the feeling went away, got up and left for the funeral home, even though it wasn't time yet. Just to see him. To be sure.

The woman who had shooed him away, and whose name he now learned was Betty, escorted him to a room nicely arranged in the way things like that are. But it was too sweet-smelling, too obviously bright. Joe as well, his face a cosmetic caricature of itself. But he had to admit the suit was nice, the shirt, the tie, and he nearly thought how good he looked before remembering how he'd always hated it when he'd heard people say that at funerals. How stupid and insensitive it had seemed. He wondered if the shoes had fit as well. Tried to lean in over the rim of the casket to see down to the foot of it. But the view was blocked by a satin border across Joe's midsection. Why? he wondered. Why was only the upper half of his body exposed? It might not even be him in there. It might be a statue instead. A wax dummy with no shoes on at all because someone had kept them, thinking they'd be damned if they'd see brand new shoes get buried. And the suit pants too. Maybe the same person had taken the pants home to a closet filled with black, brown, grey, blue, green, god knows what color pants from corpses nobody had ever asked about; and if it was really was him in there, he was bare-assed, or bare but for the shoes, which the person maybe didn't like after all. He couldn't stand to think about that and motioned for Betty to join him.

"Is something wrong?" she asked.

"No. I mean I don't know. I mean maybe. I need to see all of him."

"I beg your pardon?"

"All of him. Head to foot."

She frowned, cocked her head. "We don't usually—"

"I don't care about usually. I want to see him! And if you can't manage it or okay it, get Preston in here."

She studied him a moment, raised her brow, smiled a nervous smile and hurried from the room as quickly as he imagined she was allowed to.

"It's all right," he said. To himself. To Joe. Reached out without thinking and patted him on the hand. It was skin. No doubt about that. Or at least what used to be skin when it was alive. "It's gonna be okay."

"Now what seems to be the problem, Mr. Stevens?" Philip Preston asked as he swept into the room.

"Like I told her, I want to see him. *All* of him."

"You seem agitated," he said. "Here, why don't we sit down and relax."

"There's nothing wrong with me. You have something to hide, or what?"

"Of course not. It's just that a request like yours is usually an indication of stress, and we like to keep everyone as calm as possible."

"By refusing what they want?"

"You have no idea, Mr. Stevens, of the effect of exposing people to a full-body view. It's quite amazing. They're much more comfortable with what we have now."

"But we're not talking about a whole bunch of people here, are we? There's just me and you and her, and I'm guessing you've already seen him."

"That is a point, of course," glancing at his watch. "Ten till ten. I can give you five minutes at most."

"Fine. Great."

"Betty, please ask Charles to come over from Parlor C."

He had no idea what he was looking for or why, except the shoes, and there they were, bright, shiny and somehow propped toe-up. The pants, too, creased and dressed off to the proper length. So what else? What was missing that he hadn't thought of? Mourners maybe? The room did seem awfully empty. Why hadn't he told Dr. Morrissey—or even Marge? They probably would have come. Rolling their eyes for sure, but they would have been there, filling a seat. Wouldn't they? Or would he have had to hire somebody like they do other places? He'd read about it once in the paper, where they get old women in black scarves and dresses to come in and weep and wail to show the right amount of grief. But that didn't sound right either and someone behind him was clearing his throat—Preston probably—turning it into a cough to disguise the signal that his time was up. He stepped back and watched Charles close the bottom lid again, asked him to seal the top, too, a sinking sensation settling in his gut that made him feel about half sick, and he sat down and closed his eyes and tried not to think. Watched and listened instead from his seat in the middle of the front row to the organ music, the priest reading scripture, praying, reading more scripture, the vocal solo, the homily on the selfless, righteous life of Joseph Michael Robertson McGrew, the final prayer asking God's blessing on all lives past, present and still to come, amen, and hoped with every ounce of strength he could muster that what he'd done, what he was doing, was good, was right, was even, for god's sake, *decent*, and would probably even have shed a tear for all concerned if Betty hadn't suddenly and quietly appeared to stand with him while the casket was lifted onto a dolly and wheeled out.

Once enough time had passed for them to have loaded it into the hearse, Betty ushered him to a limousine where she sat in front with the driver and he in the back with the priest, but at an angle that gave him a clear view of the curve of her ear and her pulse beating in her neck.

Marge: You're hopeless.

Ray: No, hope*ful*.

Marge: Sure, and I'm—

Ray: More than I have been in a long time.

Marge: All because of a pretty neck?

Ray: Other things too.

Marge: For instance?

Ray: This stuff with Joe. I've done the right thing. I know that now.

Marge: So?

Ray: So it carries over. It makes me wonder—*hope*—that maybe you and I—or just you—

Marge: We've been through that already.

Ray: And god help us if we repeat ourselves, right?

Marge: Make the same mistakes again.

Ray: Hurt the same people.

Marge: Nothing ever changing.

Ray: I need you, Marge.

At the cemetery they unloaded the casket, wheeled it to the gravesite. Ray Stevens stood by himself opposite the priest who pronounced ashes to ashes, dust to dust, made the sign of the cross and prayed again.

And it was over. And they lowered the casket into the grave. He picked up a clod of dirt and dropped it in, heard it thunk like a rap on a door.

"Who is it?"

<table>
<tr><td>Gary
John
Percesepe</td><td>*Chase*</td></tr>
</table>

HUMPHREY WANTS MORE from me, would like to be the brother I never had, but we both sense that we can't top our first conversation. I wandered into town, lost, looking for someone to talk to about my wife, who was hunched over a corner table in Humphrey's bar talking to his wife, Jan, whom she'd just met. We closed the place down and spent the night with them, and the next day Anne drove back to L.A. and I started teaching at my new job. Now, six months later, when Humphrey and I talk, it always comes down to women, but the story about Anne isn't as edgy as it was. It sounds boring to me, and worse, predictable, something you'd want a friend to censor, out of mercy. And now there's Chase.

At the mall I'm thinking about Chase, who spoke in class today for the first time, when I see a retail art director with big hair undressing a mannequin in the window of Victoria's Secret. The guy has his hands on her breasts, which are razor-sharp, fitting a purple wired bra over her simulated nipples, and there's a crowd of kids booing. He dips her, lays her out flat, and when he kisses her there's an enormous clap of laughter.

I search the mall until I find a hair place, and ask for a shampoo. A woman with a name tag that says "Charbe" leads me to a back room and motions me to a chair. When she puts her hands to my hair I shudder, startling her. Charbe asks if the water is too hot. I shake my head, embarrassed, and tell her I've been cold for three months. She smiles and tilts my head back further, so that the warm water pours over me, then trickles lazily into the sink. I cross my arms around myself in a hug, trying to get warm, and smile back at Charbe. I want to tell her about Chase, but when I start up she puts a pretty finger to my lips and says, "Sorry, I don't do girl advice anymore." She bats her eyes a few times, then says, "Oops. I'm not reading from the script, am I?" I tell her it's okay, I'll figure it out, and she says, "Sure you will." Then she lifts my damp hair off the back of my neck and starts to blow it, waving the drier back and forth like a wand so that the warm air hits my neck, shoulders, and ears as well as my hair. As I turn to leave she gives me a top to bottom look, hands me her card and says, "For later. When you need this mess cut."

Later, I sit in bed and re-play the day's events. Before today, Chase hadn't said a word for seven weeks. There had been plenty of looks, and once, walking around the classroom as I lectured, I had glanced down and seen my full name in her notebook, with two dozen question marks arranged neatly around it in a square: North, east, south, west. Then today, she hands in her mid-term and says, "So. You got your coat and hat at Nick's, right? I shop there all the time. Nick's a friend." Her voice is whiskey and soda, sexy. I turn towards her but she's already gone. It's confusing, I remember, with students swarming all around the desk trying to hand in exams, and I have difficulty recalling more about this non-conversation. There's the voice, sure.

I live alone. "Freelancing," Humphrey calls it. When it's not crowded in the bar Humphrey sometimes pulls the Springsteen tape from its place next to the Frito stand, picks up his four month old kid, turns him upside down like a guitar and plays him while The Boss does "Born to Run." The kid wails but what's he going to do? About then Jan will come up and give Humphrey one in the gut, tell him to put the kid down. Which he does. She kicked him out once, and he spent a week camped out on some land his father owned. When I came in the next day he told me that Jan was busting his balls again. "She's pissed because we didn't do mega-thousands on the Violent Femme promotion, so now I'm freelancing."

It's an eight-block walk from my apartment to the Humanities building, but the blast of cold that blows off the lake adjoining campus is pitiless. On the way is Humphrey's bar. Mid-mornings, I stop there to get warm. I help him set up, he gives me a shot of Bushmills. We talk. To be fair, he does most of the talking. Anne calls the bar a lot, usually late, and if I'm not there she'll talk to Jan or Humphrey, then call the apartment. The next day the three of us hash out what it all means. Two of us have positions.

Humphrey thinks I need to go back out there, claim what's mine. "Show up during one of her rehearsals, rock her socks," he says. Jan's skeptical about this. "What's the hurry?" she says. "You do that, she'll know you're desperate. Anne's cruising, she's trying out her new girl stuff. This guy Dominic's necessary to her now, he's Transition Man. Let 'em dance the dance, it'll make a man out of you. Besides, what can you do?" Dominic is Anne's producer, a guy with a gold Mercedes and big teeth. Anne says he's been hanging around rehearsals, looking hungry, but that she can handle him. "You want my advice?" Jan says. "Get a divorce, then give her a call. Marriage is a beast, it's ruined otherwise normal people. It's totally overrated, everyone knows that. See if she wants to date. After you get a job out there, of course."

All of this tends to depress me, so then I walk to campus. Jesuits dart in and out of offices in darkened hallways. They look at me like maybe they should know me. Sometimes they ask if they can help, thinking I'm somebody's student. It's a huge department, and this is my first job. I was lucky to get it. Tenure seems, at the moment, unthinkable.

Anne didn't want to leave L.A. We argued about it some, said things we'd come to regret, and finally I just left. We didn't talk for a month, and I made no travel plans. Not even for the holidays.

I'm from California, and this is my first winter in the Midwest. On Christmas Eve I bought myself a black coat at a thrift shop, along with a gray scarf and a gray Greek fisherman's cap. That night Anne called. Scattered on the bed were letters from the big journals, with much white space, telling me that the projects I was working on weren't what was wanted. I had them arranged, these letters, according to style, from mildly interested to vaguely hostile. When Anne called I was getting set to burn them. I had a Windex bottle in my hand, filled with water, in case things got out of hand. It was midnight in L.A. and she was calling from a pay phone at the theatre where one of her plays was being mounted. The play was called "All Those Crazy Sweaters," and had Evel Knievel's son in the lead role, with sisters fighting over him and swapping clothes a lot. I asked what she was wearing, and she said, "You mean right now? Mmmmm. Panties, white. Black bike pants over a black lace leotard. There's a skirt with that, maybe eight inches worth of skirt. Silver on the wrists. My orphan boots, you remember, the Oliver Twist ones? A black Doors T-shirt I made with gold glitter letters over Elmer's glue."

"What's it say, this T-shirt."

"Fuck Oliver Stone," she said.

"Cute. So, how's Dominic," I asked.

"He's still got the teeth, if that's what you mean. He's being separated from his money. Theatre-wise, of course."

"Of course," I said.

I lit up one of the letters. It broke up into a bunch of fiery pieces, moving upward in a dozen directions. I blasted them with the Windex bottle and in the process dropped the phone.

"Tom? What was that."

"It's okay, I'm back. Small fire crisis here, some flames, possibly some burn damage, nothing serious."

"He likes it. The theatre, I mean. He's in real estate full time, so this is a new venture, here, for him. The arts thing, he calls it. He tells me he's starting to feel a little human."

"Great. I mean, considering the alternatives."

"He reads all my shirts. He can read."

"Maybe I'll send him a card," I said.

I don't hear from Chase Whitney again until two weeks later when I find a note in my campus mailbox:

> *Professor Cioffi:*
> *Can we talk? Today? Especially today. 6 PM. Your office.*

It's signed simply Chase, but it needn't have been. I know it's from her. I'm expecting it. I say that because at the end of that mid-term, two weeks earlier, after answering the essays on skepticism and the mind-body problem, she had written on the last page, in tiny handwriting,

You who never arrived
in my arms, Beloved, who were lost
from the start,
I don't even know what songs
would please you. I have given up trying
to recognize you in the surging wave of the next
moment. All the immense
images in me—the far-off, deeply-felt landscape,
cities, towers, and bridges, and un-
suspected turns in the path,
and those powerful lands that were once
pulsing with the life of the gods—
all rise within me to mean
you, who forever elude me.

I remember thinking at the time: This is a bit much, no? The professorial moment. Then: O God! O shit! O shit! This was pretty much the sum of my thinking at the time, as I recall. Luckily, I had assigned a grade to her essays before I found Rilke's poem written in that cramped, childish hand. I closed the booklet and placed it with the other W's. Strict alphabetical order.

At five minutes after six, Chase knocks lightly on the door of my office. She's wearing a ripped up pair of Guess jeans and a heather ski sweater that brings out her eyes. She's blonde and deadly.

"Look," she starts out, "I don't know why I'm here, exactly. Shit, that's not true. Shit. This isn't going to work. Did you read the poem?"

I check it out with the part of me that approves, then silently I rehearse Rilke's poem, looking past Chase to a point over her left shoulder, to a spot I imagine myself sucked into, without remainder. Then I give her the second stanza, in a voice that sounds as though it's coming from the other side of the room.

"You, Beloved, who are all
the gardens I have ever gazed at,
longing. An open window
in a country house—, and you almost
stepped out, pensive, to meet me. Streets that I chanced upon,—
you had just walked down them and vanished.
And sometimes, in a shop, the mirrors
were still dizzy with your presence and, startled, gave back
my too-sudden image. Who knows? perhaps the same
bird echoed through both of us
yesterday, separate, in the evening . . ."

163

What happens next is what I'm still thinking about, what makes me think. It's like a test. I wait to see how she'll do. If she speaks too quickly. If she makes a sound. If she talks about how she really likes Rilke, how she can't get enough, how he speaks to her directly, how he *is* poetry, or anything like that, I'll be embarrassed for her, for us, I'll lose interest, there won't be room to audition even one more word.

What happens is she reaches across my desk and grabs my keys. Then she stands and takes my coat off the peg, grabs my hat and scarf, turns off the light.

Most of my life I've spent waiting. Not waiting for something, a taxi, or the waiter to come to your table—no, just waiting, like whatever the wait was for would soon be announced. Was coming soon. Before long. A vocation of waiting, then. This is what I'm thinking as we walk out on the frozen lake, trying to keep our footing on the sleek black surface. The northerly wind at our backs blows us faster and faster. We're holding on to each other in a half-run when my feet go out from under me. I know right away that Chase is going with me, we're falling, falling, and there's this exquisite moment when we're both suspended over the surface of the lake, in movie time. I think we're never going to hit, we're going to stay up here for as long as we want, for as long as it takes. But of course we don't. We land heavily, and the unyielding ice feels malevolent and sinister as I turn my head to look, seeing it really for the first time, this element of life gone cold, undrinkable, suddenly strange. The ice is scarred from the blades of skaters. I place an ungloved finger in the wounded, glassy surface and feel a chill pass all the way through me. Just then Chase laughs. I turn in the direction of that laughter and see her small white teeth fully exposed, the pink gums gleaming, the tip of her tongue tilted upward against the roof of her mouth. I imagine her mouth pressed against my ear, firing hot moist pockets of air into the cold, warming me, those teeth closing on the skin of my neck, spitting out gray and black thread till they find human flesh. It is snowing. In the silvery winter air we sit there on the ice, mute and expectant. We haven't said a word since the office.

"Is there a word for this?" I finally say.

"Selection," she says. "I've selected you. It's really out of your hands." She studies my face, sees how I'm taking this, then says, "Hey, you're a lucky guy."

Humphrey's Amstel neon gives a softness to the street below that I hadn't noticed before as we climb the three steps to the bar, stomping our feet clumsily as we enter. Chase's green mittens are clumped with snow from when she made a snowball and hurled it at a stop sign, hitting it from twenty feet between the S and T. She doesn't throw like a girl, the result, she tells me, of playing shortstop in the Whitney infield with her father and two older brothers. This would be Nantucket. It's a close family. She's Dad's girl.

Too late I try to steer her to the left, into the restaurant part, but Humphrey's quick, in a Ralph Cramden way, and he's on us before we can sit down. He peppers me with questions about the Bulls-Lakers game and makes furtive glances at Chase. Finally he pulls himself into his full butler pose and goes, "Ahem."

"Oh, uh, Humph, this is Chase. Chase, this is Humphrey. He owns this dump."

"With the claw," Humphrey says. "Over there."

"With Jan, he means." I give Humphrey a look, but it must have been too professorily correct because I can see him tugging on his ear diamond, which is our code language for "Listen to this shit." Humphrey wears a large red button on his XXL rugby shirt that says, "Sounds Like Bullshit To Me." I try not to think what Humphrey would think about my Rilke quoting earlier. Not pretty.

"I've been in here once before," Chase says, smiling. "For the turtle soup. Can we get some? With some brandy, maybe?"

"My mother's recipe, three generations. She cooks it herself in the back room," Humphrey says. He looks pleased. "Mom!" Humphrey bellows, "get your elderly ass in gear, these people want the soup!" and waddles off. As he turns the corner I catch Jan with hands on hips, making this impossible-to-imitate face at Humphrey. She's radiant. The bar is humming. People are in their whimsical blizzard mood. It reminds me of a scene from Little House. I expect Pa to come in next, maybe with Victor French, singing Old Man Tucker.

Jan delivers our order herself, waving off the waitress. She looks at me, maybe a little too tenderly, then puts the food down. We drink a pitcher of beer with the meal, follow that with Irish coffees, then shots of Frangelica with hazelnut Hagaan Daaz. It's snowing fiercely when we leave. We fall into the street, laughing like children, and walk a block to Chase's BMW. It won't start. We blow back into the bar. Humphrey is only too willing to help. He grabs his parka and steers us back out into the storm. Parked outside is his car, a hearse with a Ghostbusters insignia on the rear window, and an orange sticker on the side that says "Vacancy." I look at Humphrey, then at Chase. She says to Humphrey, "I'm going with him. To his place."

The hearse is roomy and dark inside, with the faint smell of honeysuckle. It is unbelievably cold. The three of us huddle together like soggy Scouts in the front seat while Humphrey fumbles for the ignition. Snowflakes melt on Chase's lashes, and her snow-whitened hair falls on her shoulders in disarray. Humphrey drives slowly through the narrow, darkened streets, aiming the hearse through deep troughs of snow on the straightaways like a slalom skier, then crossing through the wake on the corner turns.

"What are you thinking?" Chase says.

What am I thinking? I'm thinking of Rilke. How he loved Clara, his artist wife, and Rodin, his mentor. How he slipped the knot of his marriage within a year, unable to work. And the letters they exchanged, letters about solitude and art and news about little Ruthie, whom they had abandoned to the care of grandparents. I'm thinking how dumb that was, how little of anything seems to connect to me. I'm thinking how maybe I'm wrong, about this, about everything. I'm thinking of an alternate Ulysses, one loosened from the mast to chase the sirens, to chase the voices of a thousand distant fires.

"Do you know Rilke's definition of love?" I finally say, leaning into her so Humphrey won't hear.

"I know about Anne," she says. "Jan told me, when you were in the bathroom."

"I wasn't in the bathroom," I say. "I was on the phone to L.A., to Anne. And I'm the one that asked Jan to tell you."

Humphrey is strangely silent. He stares straight ahead, trying to pick out my apartment in the swirling snow. Buildings that shelter strangers rise suddenly from the whitened sidewalks, which are empty of people. An abandoned car sits with its rear end jacked up, its grillwork grinning.

Humphrey steers the hearse to the curb. We get out. Wordless, we watch the hearse's taillights glow fainter, then disappear. The traffic light on the corner flashes yellow in what seems a miraculous way. Snow fills the mock Bernini fountain in the courtyard, giving it a false, fugitive beauty. Everything shines with a queer, antique light.

We climb the stairs to the apartment and shake ourselves off at the top of the landing. I find Chase a clean towel and an old flannel shirt and direct her to the bathroom. I hear her in there, showering. I turn on Letterman. He's got some woman on the phone, live, in her office. He asks about her boyfriend, wondering how serious they are. Is there a chance, does she think, for him, for Dave? She laughs, plays with her hair, tells him she can't believe he's calling her. He says, "Look outside your window." She does. He's got a high school marching band in the street playing Happy Birthday. "How did you know!" she squeals.

Chase comes out of the shower. The tails of my shirt hit her mid-thigh. Her smooth brown calves are beaded with water. She sits beside me on the couch, curling her long legs beneath her. I nuke Letterman.

"Rilke's definition of love is neighboring solitudes that border, protect, and greet one another," she says.

"You're young. You're supposed to say dumb, wrong stuff."

"Is that what you want me to do? And you're young, too."

"What I want you to do doesn't matter. What I want you to do is sleep in my bed tonight," I say. "I'll sleep out here."

"What'll happen to you and Anne, do you think? I mean, what's the plan here? Jan says you guys have a complicated history."

"Jan only met Anne once, the day before I moved into this place. We stayed with them one night. It's amazing the business women can transact in one night."

"Will you guys get a divorce?"

She asks this with a perfectly even tone, mild inflection at the end. I choose to hear it as a child's question.

"My parents almost got a divorce, I think. Last year," she says.

"When in America."

"How did you meet Anne? I want to know."

"Anne was a theater major at UCLA. I went to see a play on campus one night. Anne played Cher in Nicaragua. I went backstage looking for Cher and found this woman in a Belinda Carlisle T-shirt and black jeans with a buzz hair cut sitting splay-legged against the wall, lots of cheekbone. I was dressed in black. She asked me who I was. I told her. She told me she used to like philosophy but that now she thought of it as 'Socrates, Inc.' I told her I thought pretty much the same thing. Then I said I know a place where they play the Go Go's all night, not a contra in sight. She did this squinty thing with her eyes and hands, like she was sighting me along the barrel of some dangerous but still secret military weapon, then said 'Sure.' We spent the night in my car out in the desert, listening to tapes."

I stop there. I don't know how to continue, or if I should. It feels like I've been talking for a long time. I hadn't expected to tell this story again. The family voice in my throat sounds strange. My words seem suspended in the air between us, as frozen as the fountain outside. Beneath them, the space of memory.

I look over at Chase. Her eyes are clear, her gaze steady. She listens like this is the most natural story in the world, like if there's more and I want to tell, then she's the one to hear. Everything passes softly through us.

"What do I call you? I mean, it's awkward, isn't it. Can I call you by your first name?" Chase says.

"Look, Chase, I'm sleepy. What time do you want me to get you up in the morning?"

"It doesn't matter, silly. It's Saturday."

"Right."

I get up and walk into the kitchen. I run water from the tap, then try to find a glass, searching all the cabinets until I find a blue one that I like. I put the glass under the stream and try to understand why I feel so lost, why I have trouble locating the simplest things. Listening to the water run, overflowing the glass and spilling out over my hand, I think about the playful way Charbe had tousled my hair after telling me she didn't do girl advice any more. Her girlish giggle after she said that, and her smoky, bubblegum smell, but mostly her touch. Two weeks ago. I start to think about Anne, try to imagine what she's doing or what she's wearing, but decide to kill that thought before it gets going. I turn the water off, draw the edge of the curtain aside and try to look outside. The window has frosted, and I have to scratch a spot clear with my fingernails to see the snow, still faintly falling. Covering everything, what wants covering and what doesn't. I let the curtain fall back and feel the draft circle my wrist. Shivering, I go back into the living room with my water. Chase hasn't moved.

"Tom?"

"Yes?"

"Anne? She loves you, you know. I promise."

I put the glass of water down. I lift her, sliding my hands under her back. Her legs stick out over my outstretched arms. She laughs, and tucks her knees into my chest to keep from knocking pictures off the wall of the hallway as we head to the bedroom. I smell my scent on my shirt, on her. I lay her down on the bed, pull the covers up to her neck, fan her long hair out over the pillow. She sighs contentedly, smiling up at me. I turn off the light.

In the night, what will happen is this: She will get up to use the bathroom and get disoriented in the strange space. She will grope for the hall light. I will look at her, startled, the harsh white light framing her shadow on the wall. I will get up and go to her, watch as she sits to pee, then guide her solemnly back to bed. Neither of us will say anything. Minutes later I will return to the bed, stand over her, and study the line of her legs beneath the thin cotton sheet. I will crawl into bed beside her, noiselessly. Breathless, I'll put my hands to her hair, raise it to my face, feel it tickling my skin. The perfect ends I'll put in my mouth. I'll curl up alongside her till we're shaped like spoons in the chilled night air, my stunned fingers resting in the small of her back.

Charles | *Flood Show*
Baxter

IN LATE MARCH, at its low flood stage, the Chaska River rises up to the benches and the picnic areas in the Eurekaville city park. No one pays much attention to it anymore. Three years ago, Conor and Janet organized a flood lunch for themselves and their three kids. They started their meal perched crosslegged on an oilcloth they had draped over the picnic table. The two adults sat at the ends, and the kids sat in the middle, crowding the food. They had to walk through water to get there. The water was flowing across the grass directly under the table, past the charcoal grilles and the bandstand. It had soaked the swing-seats. It had reached the second rung of the ladder on the slide.

After a few minutes, they all took off their shoes, which were wet anyway, and they sat down on the benches. The waters slurred over their feet, while the deviled eggs and mustard-ham sandwiches stayed safe in their waxed paper and Tupperware. It was a sunny day, and the flood had a peaceable aspect. The twins yelled and threw some of their food into the water and smiled when it floated off downriver. The picnic tables, bolted into cement, served as anchors and observation platforms. Jeremy, who was thirteen that spring, drew a picture, a pencil sketch, the water suggested by curlicues and subtle smearings of spit.

Every three years or so, Eurekaville gets floods like this. They spill over the top banks, submerge the baseball diamond and the soccer field, soak a basement or two along Island Drive, and then recede. Usually the waters pass by lethargically. On the weekends, people wade out into it and play flood-volleyball and flood-softball, but, as Jeremy says, you have to be half-assed or stoned to enjoy it.

It's the sort of town where floods are welcome. They provide interest and variety. This year the Eurekaville High School junior class has brought bleachers down from the gym and set them up on the paved driveway of the park's northwest slope, close to the river itself, where you can get a good view of the waterlogged trash floating by. Jeremy, who is Conor's son from his first marriage and who is now sixteen, has been selling popcorn and candy bars to the spectators who want to sit there and chat while they watch the flotsam. He's been joined in this effort by a couple of his classmates. All profits, he claims, will go into the fund for the fall class trip to Washington, DC.

By late Friday afternoon, with the sun not quite visible, thirty people had turned out to watch the flood—a social event, a way to end the day, a break from domestic chores, especially on a cloudy spring evening. One of Jeremy's friends had brought down a boom box and played Jesus Jones and Biohazard. There was dancing in the bleachers, slowish and tidal, against the music's frantic rhythms.

Conor's dreams these days have been invaded by water. He wakes on Saturday morning and makes quiet closed-door love to his wife. When he holds her, or when they kiss, and his eyes close, he thinks of the river. He thinks of the rivers inside both of them, rivers of blood and water. Lymphatic pools. All the fluids, the carriers of their desires. Odors of sweat, odors of salt. Touching Janet, he almost says *we're mostly water*. Of course everyone knows that, the body's content of liquid matter. But he can't help it: it's what he thinks.

After his bagel and orange juice, Conor leaves Janet upstairs with the twins, Annah and Joe, who conspire together to dress as slowly as they possibly can, and he bicycles down to the river to take a look. Conor is a large bearish man with thick brown hair covered by a beret that does not benefit his appearance. He knows the beret makes him a bit strange-looking, and this pleases him. Whenever he bikes anywhere there is something violent in his body-motions. Pedaling along, he looks like a trained circus bear. Despite his size, however, Conor is mild and kindhearted— the sort of man who believes that love and caresses are probably the answer for everything—but you wouldn't know that about him unless you saw his eyes, which are placidly sensual, curious—a photographer's eyes, just this side of sentimental, belonging to someone who quite possibly thinks too much about love for his own good.

The business district of Eurekaville has its habitual sleepy aura, its morning shroud of mist and fog. One still-burning streetlight has its orange pall of settled vaporish dampness around its glass globe. Conor is used to these morning effects; he likes them, in fact. In this town you get accustomed to the hazy glow around everything, and the sleepiness, or you leave.

He stops his bicycle to get a breath. He's in front of the hardware store, and he leans against a parking meter. Looking down a side street, he watches several workmen moving a huge wide-load steel platform truck under a house that has been loosened from its foundation and placed on bricks. Apparently they're going to truck the entire house off somewhere. The thought of moving a house on a truck impresses Conor, technology somehow outsmarting domesticity.

He sees a wren in an elm tree and a grosbeak fluttering overhead.

An hour later, after conversation and coffee in his favorite café, where the waitress tells him that she believes she's seen Merilyn, Conor's ex-wife, around town, and Conor has pretended indifference to this news, he takes up a position down at the park, close to the bleachers. He watches a rattan chair stuck inside some gnarly tree branches swirl slowly past, legs pointing up, followed by a brown broom, swirling, sweeping the water.

Flood Show

Because the Chaska River hasn't flooded badly—destructively—for years, Eurekaville has developed what Conor's son Jeremy describes as a goof attitude about rising waters. According to Jeremy's angle on it, this flooding used to be a disaster-thing. The townspeople sandbagged and worried themselves sick. Now it's a specta-tor-thing. The big difference, according to Jeremy, is sales. "It's . . . it's like, well, not a drowning occasion, you know? If it ever was. It's like one of those Prozac disasters, where nothing happens, except publicity? It's cool and stuff, so you can watch it. And eat popcorn? And then you sort of daydream. You're into the river, right? But not?"

As early as it is, Jeremy's already down here, watching the flood and selling pop-corn, which at this time of morning no one wants to buy. Actually, he is standing near a card table, flirting with a girl Conor doesn't quite recognize. She's very pretty. It's probably why he's really here. They're laughing. At this hour, not yet midmorning, the boom box on the table is playing old favorites by Led Zeppelin. The music, which once sounded sexy and feverish to Conor years ago, now sounds charming and quaint, like a football marching band. Jeremy keeps brushing the girl's arms, bumping against her, and then she bumps against Jeremy and stabilizes herself by reaching for his hip. A morning dance. Jeremy's on the basketball team, and some-thing about this girl makes Conor think of a cheerleader. Her smile goes beyond infectiousness into aggression.

Merilyn is nowhere in sight.

The flood has made everybody feel companionable. Conor waves to his son, who barely acknowledges him with a quick head-flick. Then Conor gets back on his bi-cycle and heads down to his photography studio, checking the sidewalks and the stores to see if he can spot Merilyn. It's been so long, he's not sure he'd recognize her.

Because it's Saturday, he doesn't have many appointments, just somebody's daughter, and an older couple, who have recently celebrated their fiftieth anniversary and who want a studio photo to commemorate it. The daughter will come first. She's sched-uled for 9:30.

When she and her mother arrive at the appointed time, Conor is wearing his battery operated lighted derby and has prepared the spring-loaded rabbit on the table behind the tripod. When the rabbit flips up, at the touch of a button, the kids smile, and Conor usually gets the shot.

The girl's mother, who says her name is Romola, has an errand to run. Can she leave her daughter here for ten minutes? She looks harried and beautiful and profes-sionally religious, somehow, with a pendant-cross, and Conor says sure.

Her daughter appears to be about ten years old. She has an odd, eerie resem-blance to Merilyn, who is of course lurking in town somewhere, hiding out. They both have a way of pinching their eyes halfway shut to convey distaste. Seated on a stool in front of the backdrop, the girl asks how long this'll take. Conor's adjusting the lights. He says, "Oh, fifteen minutes. The whole thing takes about fifteen min-utes. You could practice your smile for the picture."

She looks at him carefully. "I don't like you," she says triumphantly.

"You don't know me." Conor points out. He checks his camera's film, the f-stop, re-focuses, and says, "Seen the flood yet?"

"We're too busy. We go to church," the girl says. Her name is Sarah, he remembers. "It's a nothing flood anyway. In the old days the floods drowned sinners. You've got a beard. I don't like beards. Anyway, we go to church and I go to church school. I'm in fourth grade. The rest of the week is chores."

Conor turns on the little blinking lights in his derby hat, and the girl smiles. Conor tells her to look at the tin foil star on the wall, and he gets his first group of shots. "Good for you," Conor says. To make conversation, he says, "What do you learn there? At Bible School?"

"We learned that when he was up on the cross Jesus didn't pull at the nails. We learned that last week." She smiles. She doesn't seem accustomed to smiling. Conor gets five more good shots. "Do you think he pulled at the nails?"

"I don't know," Conor says. "I have no opinion." He's working to get the right expression the girl's face. She's wearing a green dress, the color of shelled peas, that won't photograph well.

"I think maybe he did. I think he pulled at the nails."

"How come?" Conor asks.

"I just do," the girl says. "And I think they came out, because he was God, but not in time." Conor touches the button, the rabbit pops up, and the girl laughs. In five minutes her mother returns, and the session ends; but Conor's mood has soured, and he wouldn't mind having a drink.

The next day, Sunday, Conor stands in the doorway of Jeremy's bedroom. Jeremy is dressing to see Merilyn. "Just keep it light with her," he says, as Jeremy struggles into a sweatshirt at least one size too large for him. "Nothing too serious." The boy's head, with its ponytail and earrings, pokes out into the air with a controlled thrashing motion. His big hands never do emerge fully from the sleeves. Only Jeremy's calloused fingertips are visible. They will come out fully when they are needed. Hands three-quarters hidden: youthful fashion-irony, Conor thinks.

After putting his glasses back on, Jeremy gives himself a quick appraisal in the mirror. Sweatshirt, exploding-purple bermuda shorts, sneakers, ponytail, earrings. Conor believes that his son looks weird and athletic, just the right sixteen-year-old pose: pleasantly scary; handsome; still under construction. As if to belie his appearance, Jeremy does a pivot and a lay-up near the doorframe. It's hard for him to pass through the doors in this house without jumping up and tapping the lintels, even in the living room, where he jumps and touches the nail hole—used for mistletoe in December—in the hallway.

Satisfied with himself, Jeremy nods, one of those private gestures of self-approval that Conor isn't suppose to notice, but does. "Nothing too earnest, okay?"

"Daad," Jeremy says, giving the word a sitcom delivery. Most of the time he treats his father as if he were a sitcom dad: good-natured, bumbling, basically a fool.

Jeremy's right eyebrow is pierced, but out of deference to the occasion he's left the ring out of it. He shakes his head as if he had a sudden neck pain. "Merilyn's just another mom. It's not a big puzzle or anything, being with her. You just take her places. You just talk to her. Remember?"

"Remember what?"

"Well, you were married to her, right? Once? You must've talked and taken her places. That's what you did. Except you guys were young. So that's what I'll do. I'm young. We'll just talk. Stuff will happen. It's cool."

"Right," Conor says. "So where will you take her?"

"I don't know. The flood, maybe. I bet she hasn't seen a flood. This guy I know, he said a cow floated down the river yesterday."

"A cow? In the river? Oh, Merilyn would like that, all right."

"She's my mom. Come on, Dad. Relax. Nothing to it."

Jeremy says he will drive down to the motel where Merilyn is staying. After that, they will do what they are going to do. At the back stairs, playing with the cat's dish with his foot, and biting his fingernail, Jeremy hesitates, smiles, and says, "Well, why don't you loosen up and wish me luck?" and Conor does.

Five days before Merilyn left, fourteen years ago, Conor found a grocery list in green ink under the phone in the kitchen. "Grapefruit, yogurt," the list began, then followed with, "cereal, diapers, baby wipes, wheat germ, sadness." And then, the next line: "Sadness, sadness, sadness."

In those days, Merilyn had a shocking physical beauty: startlingly blue eyes, and a sort of compact uneasy voluptuousness. She was fretful about her appearance, didn't like to be looked at—she had never liked being beautiful, didn't like the attention it got her—and wore drab scarves to cover herself.

For weeks she had been maintaining an unsuccessful and debilitating cheerfulness in front of Conor, a stagy display of frozen failed smiles, and most of what she said those last few evenings seemed memorized, as if she didn't trust herself to say anything spontaneously. She half-laughed, half-coughed after many of her sentences and often raised her fingers to her face and hair as if Conor were staring at them, which he was. He had never known why a beautiful woman had agreed to marry him in the first place. Now he knew he was losing her.

She worked as a nurse, and they had met when he'd gone up to her ward to visit a friend. The first time he ever talked to her, and then the first time they kissed—after a movie they both agreed they disliked—he thought she was the meaning of his life. He would love her, and that would be the point of his being alive. There didn't have to be any other point. When they made love, he had to keep himself from trembling.

Women like her, he thought, didn't usually allow themselves to be loved by a man like him. But there she was.

When, two and a half years later, she said that she was leaving him, and leaving Jeremy behind with him, and that was the only action she could think of taking that wouldn't destroy her life, because it wasn't his fault but she couldn't stand to be married to anybody, that she could not be a mother, that it wasn't personal, Conor had agreed to let her go and not to follow her. Her desperation impressed him, silenced him.

She had loaded up the Ford and a trailer with everything she wanted to go with her. The rain had turned to sleet, and by the time she had packed the books and the clothes, Merilyn had collected small flecks of ice on her blue scarf. She'd been so eager to go that she hadn't turned on the windshield wiper until she was halfway down the block. Conor had watched her from the front porch. From the side, her beautiful face—the meaning of his life—looked somehow both determined and blank. She turned the corner, the tires splashed slush, the front end dipped from the bad shocks, and she was gone.

He had a trunk in the attic filled with photographs he had taken of her. Some of the shots were studio portraits, while others were taken more quickly, outdoors. In them, she is sitting on stumps, leaning against trees, and so on. In the photographs she is trying to look spontaneous and friendly, but the photographs emphasize, through tricks of angle and lighting, her body and its voluptuousness. All of the shots have a painfully thick and willful artistry, as if she had been mortified, in her somewhat involuntary beauty, under a glaze.

She had asked him to destroy these photographs, but he never had.

Now, having seen Jeremy go off to find his mother somewhere in Eurekaville and maybe take her to the flood, Conor wanders into the living room. Janet's sprawled on the floor, reading the Sunday comics to Annah. Annah is picking her nose and laughing. Joe, over in the corner, is staging a war with his plastic mutant men. The forces of good muscle face down evil muscle. Conor sits on the floor next to his wife and daughter, and Annah rumbles herself backwards into Conor's lap.

"Jeremy's off?" Janet asks. "To find Merilyn?"

Conor nods. Half consciously, he's bouncing his daughter, who holds on to him by grasping his wrist.

Janet looks back at the paper. "They'll have a good time."

"What does that mean?"

She flicks her hair back. "'What does that mean?'" she repeats. "I'm not using code here. It means what it says. He'll show her around. He'll be the mayor of Eurekaville. At last he's got Merilyn on his turf. She'll be impressed."

"Nothing," Conor says, "ever impressed Merilyn, ever, in her life."

"Her life isn't over."

"No," Conor says, "it isn't. I mean, nothing has impressed her so far."

"How would you know? You didn't follow Merilyn down to Tulsa. There could be all sorts of things in Tulsa that impress Merilyn."

"All right," Conor says. "Maybe the oil wells. Maybe something. Maybe the dustbowl and the shopping malls. All I'm saying is that nothing impressed her here."

A little air-pocket of silence opens between them, then shuts again.

"Daddy," Annah says, "tip me."

Conor grasps her and tips her over, and Annah gives out a little pleased shriek. Then he rights her again.

"I wonder," Janet says, "if she isn't getting a little old for that."

"Are you getting too old for this, Annie?" Annah shakes her head. "She's only five." Conor tips her again. Annah shrieks again, and when she does, Janet drops the section of the newspaper that she's reading and lies backward on the floor, until her head is propped on her arm, and she can watch Conor.

"Mom!" Joe shouts from the corner. "The plutonium creatures are winning!"

"Fight back," Janet instructs. "Show 'em what you've got." She reaches out and touches Conor on the thigh. "Honey," she says, "you can't impress everybody. You impress me sometimes. You just didn't impress Merilyn. No one did. Marriage didn't. What's wrong with a beautiful woman wanting to live alone? It's her beauty. She can keep it to herself if she wants to."

Conor shrugs. He's not in the mood to argue about this. "It's funny to think of her in town, that's all."

"No, it's not. It's only funny," Janet says, "to think of her in town if you still love her, and I'd say that if you still love her, after fourteen years, then you're a damn fool, and I don't want to hear about it. It's Jeremy, not you, who could use some attention from Merilyn. It's his to get, being her son and all. She left him more than she left you. But I'll be damned if I'm going to go on with this conversation one further sentence more."

Both Annah and Joe have stopped their playing to listen. They are not watching their parents, but their heads are raised, like forest animals who can smell smoke nearby.

"All I ever wanted from her was a reason," Conor says. "I just got tired of all that enigmatic shit."

"Watch your diction," Janet says. "And I told you about that one further sentence." Annah gets out of her father's lap and snuggles next to Janet. "All right," Janet says. "Listen. Listen to this. Here's something I never told you. One night Merilyn and I were working the same station, we were both in pediatrics that night, third floor, it was a quiet night, not many sick kids that week. And, you know, we started talking. Nursing stuff, women stuff. And Merilyn sort of got going."

"About what?"

"About you, dummy, she got going about you. Herself and you. She said you two had gone bowling. You'd dressed in your rags and gone off to Colonial Lanes, the both of you, and you'd been bowling, and she'd thrown the ball down the lane and turned around and you were looking at her, appreciating her, and of course all the other men in the bowling alley were looking at her, too, and what was bothering her was that you were looking at her the way they did, sort of a leer, I guess, as if you didn't know her, as if you weren't married to her. Who could blame you? She looked like a cover girl or something. Perfect this, perfect that, she was perfect all over, it would make anybody sweat. So she said she had a sore thumb and wanted to go home. You were staring at your wife the way a man looks at a woman walking by in the street. Boy, how she hated that, that guy stuff. You went back home, it was cold, a cold blister night, she got you into bed, she made love to you, she threw herself into it, and then in the dark you were your usual gladsome self, and you know what you did?"

"No."

"You thanked her. You two made hot love and then you thanked her, and then in the dark you went on staring at her, you couldn't believe how lucky you were. There she was in your arms, the beauteous Merilyn. I bet it never occurred to you at the time that you aren't supposed to thank women after you make love to them and they make love to you, because you know what, sweetie? They're not doing you a favor. They're doing it because they want to. Usually. Anyway, that was the night she got pregnant with Jeremy and it was the same night she decided she would leave you, because you couldn't stop looking at her, and thanking her, and she hated that. For sure she hated it. She lives in Tulsa, that's how much."

Conor is watching Janet say this, focusing on her mouth, watching the lips move.

"Son-of-a-bitch," he says.

"So she told me this," Janet says, "one night, at our nursing station. And we laughed and sort of cried when we had coffee later, but you know what I was thinking?" She waits. "Do you? You don't, do you?"

"No."

"I was thinking," Janet says, "that I'm going to get my hands on this guy, I am going to get that man come hell or high water. I am going to get him and he is going to be mine. Mine forever. And do you know why?"

"Give me a clue."

"To hell with clues. I wanted a man who looked at me like that. I wanted a man who would work up a lather with me in bed and then thank me. No one had ever thanked me before, that was for goddamn certain sure. And you know what? That's what happened. You married another nurse. Me, this time. And it was me you looked at, me you thanked. Heaven in a bottle. Are you listening to me? Conor, pay attention. I'm about to do something."

Conor follows her gaze. A living room, newspaper on the floor, Sunday morning, the twins playing, a family, a house, a life, sunlight coming in through the window. Janet walks over to Conor, unties her bathrobe, pulls it open, drops it at his feet, lifts her arms up and pulls her nightgown over her head. In front of her children and her husband, she stands naked. She is beautiful, all right, but he is used to her.

"I'm different from Merilyn," she says. "You can look at me any time you want."

Now, on Sunday afternoon, Conor cleans out his pickup, throwing out the bank deposit slips. When he's finished, with his binoculars around his neck, and his telephoto lens attached to his camera, the 400 millimeter one that he uses for shots of birds beside him on the seat, he drives down to the river, hoping for a good view of an osprey, or maybe a teal.

He parks near a cottonwood. He is on the opposite side from the park. Above him are scattered the usual sparrows, the usual crows. He gets out his telephoto lens and frames an ugly field sparrow flittering and shivering in the flat light. A grackle, and then a pigeon, follow the sparrow into his viewfinder. It is a parade of the common, the colorless, the drear. The birds with color do not want to perch anywhere near the Chaska River, not even the swallows or swifts. He puts his camera back in his truck.

He's standing there, searching the sky and the opposite bank with his binoculars, looking for what he thought he saw here last week, a Wilson's Snipe, when he lowers the lenses and sees, at some distance, Jeremy and Merilyn. Merilyn is sitting on a bench, watching Jeremy, who has taken off his sweatshirt and his talking to his mother. Merilyn isn't especially pretty anymore. She's gained weight. Conor had heard from Jeremy that she'd gained weight but hadn't seen it for himself. Now, through the binoculars, Merilyn appears to be overweight and rather calm. She has that loaf-of-bread quality. There's a peaceful expression on her face. It's the happy contentment of someone who probably doesn't bother about very much anymore.

Jeremy stands up, throws his hands down on the ground and begins walking on his hands. He walks in a circle on his hands. He's very strong and can do this for a long time. It's one of his parlor tricks.

Conor moves his binoculars and sees that Jeremy has brought a girl along, the girl he saw yesterday at the flood show, the one who was dancing with him. Conor doesn't know this girl's name. She's standing behind the bench and smiling while Jeremy walks on his hands. It's that same aggressive smile.

Goddamn it, Conor thinks, *they're lovers, they've been sleeping together, and he didn't tell me.*

He moves the binoculars back to Merilyn. She's still watching Jeremy, but she seems only mildly interested in his display. She's not smiling. She's not pretending to be impressed. Apparently that's what she's turned into. That's what all these years have done to her. She doesn't have to look interested in anything if she doesn't want to.

To see better, Conor walks down past his truck to the bank. He lifts the binoculars to his eyes again, and when he gets the group in view, Merilyn turns her head to his side of the river. She sees Conor. Conor's large bear-like body is recognizable anywhere. And what she does is, she raises her hand and seems to wave.

From where he is standing, Conor thinks that Merilyn has invited him over to join their group. Through the binoculars a trace of a smile, Conor believes, has appeared on Merilyn's face. This smile is one that Conor recognizes. In the middle of her pudginess, this smile is the same one that he saw sixteen years ago. It's the smile he lost his heart to. A little crow's foot of delight in Conor's presence. A merriment.

And this is why Conor believes she is asking him to join them, right this minute, and to be his old self. And this is why he steps into the river, smiling that smile of his. It's not a wide river after all, no more than sixty or seventy feet across. Anyone could swim it. What are a few wet clothes? He will swim across the Chaska to Merilyn and Jeremy and Jeremy's girlfriend, and they will laugh, pleased with his impulsiveness and passion, and that will be that.

He is up to his thighs in water when the shocking coldness of the river registers on him. This is a river of recently melted snow. It isn't flowing past so much as biting him. It feels like cheerful party icepicks, like happy knives. Without meaning to, Conor gasps. But once you start something like this, you have to finish it. Conor wades deeper.

The sun has come out. He looks up. A long-billed marsh wren is in a tree above the bank. He cannot breathe, and he dives in.

Conor is a fair swimmer, but the water is putting his body into shock and he has to remember to move his arms. Having dived, he feels the current taking him downriver, at first slowly, and then with some urgency. He is hopeless with cold. Tiny bells, the size of gnats, ring on every inch of his skin. He thinks, *This is crazy.* He thinks, *It wasn't an invitation, that wave.* He thinks, *I will die.* The river's current, which is now the sleepy hand of his death waking up, reaches into his chest and feels his heart. Conor moves his arms back and forth but he can't see the bank now and doesn't know which way he's going. Of course by this time he's choking on water, and the bells on his skin are beginning to ring audibly. He is moving his arms more slowly. Flashcard random pictures pop up delightedly in his mind, and he sees the girl in his studio the day before, and she says, "I don't like you."

He doesn't want to die a comic death. It occurs to him that the binoculars are pulling him toward the river bottom, and he reaches for them and takes them off of his neck.

He swirls around like a broom.

He pulls his arms. It seems to him that he is not making any progress. It also seems to him that he cannot breathe at all. But he has always been a large easygoing man, incapable of panic, and he does not panic now. His sinking will take its time.

The touch of the shore is silt. The graspings of hands on his elbow are almost unfriendly, aggressive. Jeremy is there, pulling, and what Conor hears, when he starts to pay attention to sound, through his own coughing and spitting, is Jeremy's voice.

"Dad! What the fuck are you doing? What in the fucking . . . Daddy! Are you okay? Jesus. Are you . . . what the fuck is this? Shit! Jesus. Daddy!"

Conor looks at his son and says, "Watch your language."

"What? What! Get out of there." Conor is being pulled and pushed by his son. Pulled and pushed also, it seems, by his son's girlfriend. Perhaps she is simply trying to help. But the help she is giving him has been salted with violence.

"What do you think?" Conor asks, turning toward her. "Do you think he pulled at the nails?"

Conor's trousers are dripping water on the grass. Water pours out of his shirt. It drains off his hands. Now in the air his ears register their pain on him; his eardrums are in pain, a complex aching inside the ravine of his head. And Merilyn, the source, the beneficiary of his grand gesture, is simply saying, with her nurse's voice, "He's in shock. Get him into the car."

"Merilyn," he says. He can't see her. She's behind him.

"What?"

"I couldn't help it. I never got over it." He says it more loudly, because he can't see her. He might as well be talking to the air. "I never got over it! I never did."

"Daddy, stop it," Jeremy says. "For God's sake shut up. Please. Get in the car."

Jeremy opens the door of the old clunker Buick he bought on his sixteenth birthday for four hundred dollars, and Conor, without thinking, gets in. Before he is quite conscious of the sequence of one event after another, the car's engine has started, and the Buick moves slowly away—away from Merilyn: Conor remembers to look. She grows smaller with every foot of distance between them, and Conor, pleased with himself, pleased with his inscribed fate as the unhappy lover, tries to wipe his eyes with his wet shirt.

"I won't tell anybody about this if you don't," Jeremy says.

"Okay."

"I'll tell them you fell into the river. I'll say that you slipped on the mud."

"Thanks."

"That can happen. I mean really." Jeremy is enthusiastic now, creating a cover story for his father. "You were taking pictures and stuff, and you got too close to the river, and, you know, bang, you slipped, and like that. Just don't ever tell Mom, okay? We'll just . . . holy shit! What's that?"

The Buick has been climbing a hill, and near the top, where a slight curve to the right banks the road toward the passenger side, there comes into view an amazing sight that has cut Jeremy into silence: an old wooden two-story house on an enormous platform truck, squarely in the middle of the road, blocking them. The house on the truck is moving at five or ten miles an hour. Who knows what its speed is, this white clapboard monument, this parade, a smaller truck in front, and one in back, with flashing lights, and a WIDE LOAD sign? No one would think of measuring its speed. Conor looks up and sees what he knows is a bedroom window. He imagines himself in that bedroom. He is dripping water all over his son's car, and he is beginning now to shiver, as the truck, carrying the burden it was made to carry, struggles up the next hill.

| Nora Ruth Roberts | *Adagio in Black and White* |

WE SHOULD BE ON A DESERT ISLAND, just you and me. The only people. Bunch of coffee-colored curly hair babies running wild around the hut. They would be the new people. The only people we'd ever have to worry about what are they thinking.

Deep pile carpeting fuzzing up against my back. Why did I still have panties on? Well, he still had his shorts. Candlelight from little stubby wax things planted here and there oozing glow out into the sleek ebony of his arm moving down now, his hand making slow circles at my breast. With a querulous little boy look—was he doing this the right way? Sad pulse of clarinet beating jazz from a stereo lit upon his bookshelf in the dark like controls on a jet liner traveling through space.

We're here now, darlin', just you an' me. Are you worried about what folks out there be thinkin'?

No, not at all, not me. It was you I was thinking about, the way you look around out of the corner of your eye when you touch me. For me, I was bringing only little coffee-colored babies into the world.

Hey, baby, wait a minute, darlin'. That laugh so gentle like a small boy's when I licked the broad perfect sculpture of his chest, tasting sweet and sour and salty all at once, a hint of ointments and long luxurious showers.

Babies, he said, not so fast. I got to finish school. You said that yourself, Mrs. Teach.

Love talk, just love talk. I need a fantasy sometimes to get the juices flowing. Sometimes it helps to think of making babies.

The sad wail of trombone cascading out into the quiet suburban city night. Poster of a tribal girl in corn rollers a million seed-thing bangles watching in the pale glow of candlelight, glowering down like she belonged here, did I dare usurp her place?

It was my turn for the Fiat, Alex's for the kids.

Movin' across the room like he walk on sofboil eggs. Where you goin'?

Wait your smart-pretty self right there. Daddy Steven be right back.

From the kitchen, brighter cubicle than mine, a once-familiar scraping sound. Grandma used to do that with a sifter when she made apple butter.

What the hell you doin'? I said.

Mexican shit. Has very tiny seeds.

I don't do reefer. Mellow do-wah from the jazz.

What shit do you do?

Reminds me, I said. I rummaged in my leather bag in a heap of off-duty clothes. Do you have a glass of water? Bare boobs feeling tingly in the naked rush of light. Didn't realize how the hair curled so tight across his vast expanse of solid chest.

Your dope? You won't tell me?

New anti-depressant. Just came out.

How long you been takin' that shit? Neat heap of baby leaves and dust in a lip of square white paper. Seals it off and twists. More compact job than Alex ever managed.

Can't remember, I say, swallowing, if it started before the divorce or the divorce talk started first. Watched him suck in deep. Before this the shit I had in class made your hands shake—did you see me tuck them in my inner arm? That bunch, you know what they'd think.

Could think it still, baby. How do I know what you're on? Deep inhaling suck. And you?

Reefer's in my blood, you musta heard that. Short exhale. Must be Tijuana. The smoke is sort of blue.

I don't believe what I read in the Sunday funnies.

Okay. Letting the ash burn a bit. Swiveling on a stool. By now my nipples burn. Cool wafts from the window cracks billowing starched curtains, trimmed sort of like my mom's. See if you believe this one. I didn't even take the least little hit till Nam.

Nam. I stop a minute in my tracks. The word conjures newsreels still. That pix of napalmed babies in the arms of close-cropped GI's the age Abie soon would be. Demos down Fifth with strollers. Hash brownies in rap parties in the coop. He offers me a toke, still sucking in his hit.

I shake my head. The two dopes don't mix. I've had bad results. I pause, not knowing whether to press the point. Is it still sore? Never mentioned it in class, but neither did the white one. Were you in the front lines? I finally say. Mai Lai? Like that? Kevin told me he was.

That red-haired dude? What was wrong with him?

Couldn't straighten out his verbs.

If I be in the front lines, sweetheart, you see shit here more than reefer. Or don't see nothin' here at all.

I took another glass of water. Gleaming stainless steel. Carved wood totem on a shelf. Tits droop worse than mine. Bet you hid out the entire scene in a Mekong Delta cathouse.

He sort of laughed. Sweetest boyish smile even behind black bush of beard. That be the first place Charlie hit. Small thoughtful suck, pushed away my embrace. Don't want to talk about it. You know what your babies say. Who want yesterday's papers? Nobody in the worl'.

I decided not to press.

He went on unasked. Get it down by your house. Projects. Same place your chil'ren do.

This hit me for a minute. I wasn't ready to deny. Abie seemed, even more so than his father, so godawful straight. Vergie left me helpless, staying out late with buddies from that new private school on their own bench in Central Park. I wouldn't be surprised, I murmured, stroking across his back. The jazz was sort of getting to me. I sashayed around his front. Like to pack up everybody's stash from all the projects, send it in a Red Cross box to the Capital and the White House, C.O.D.

They already got theirs, baby. Kind of town D.C. be. Here, seem like you need a hit. Help you enjoy the soun'.

Just one toke, I said, sucking the stinging smoke deep in. Pray it don't mess up my head.

You do bad things to my body?

Only if you beg.

We did not do bad things in his bedroom. Line of Essence pinups sultry-eyeing down. Both stripped off remaining underthings. Been awhile since I saw that little end of flappy flesh, but no pink inner eye ever winked. In the middle of the night, me still working hard, he finally pushed me off. Reefer got ol' Steven daddy, sweetheart. I'm surprise. Only had three sticks.

That would surely do it to me, I said. Or worse. I lay back on my arms, listening to soft snortly urps whisper in the night. Anti-depressants were the wrong shit for this kind of scene. I wondered if the drug of choice was ludes. It didn't seem to be true what they say about black guys. But then I'd only sampled four. And there was a whole career ahead.

| Mary Hazzard | *Playing Dead* |

"SORRY." Karl Compton came to a halt as he rounded the tall stockade fence on the corner of Channing Street. It was a rainy day in December, and Karl, walking back to his rent-controlled attic from the news kiosk in Harvard Square, had nearly collided with Joanna Schliemann, who was weeping into the hatchback of a blue Toyota. "Sorry," he said, as if he had.

Karl didn't know Joanna, but he really did; everybody did. She was one of the topics at the Thursday Club, which met for dinner at the round table in the Casablanca Cafe. "Right," somebody would say when somebody else mentioned her, with her plastic scoop and ungainly blond dog. "Just like the movies."

Because Joanna Schliemann's ex-husband was a prize-winning Cambridge filmmaker whose recent work featured a woman and a dog. In his last four films, as Greg the movie buff pointed out, the same character had appeared, in different guises. Compact or long-legged, Titian-haired or dark, she always wore an oversized English raincoat and trailed a mournful dog over brick sidewalks. A husband had appeared in earlier films, but the last one ended with the woman and the dog alone, fading away down a path in Mount Auburn Cemetery. Oscar Schliemann had shed his actual wife at the same time.

A freelance technical writer and lapsed novelist, Karl made a daily point of leaving his Macintosh and walking either to the Square for the *New York Times* or to Star Market for day-old bread. He often saw Joanna walking her dog between Fresh Pond and Harvard Square, and he'd even heard her speak. "Heel, Clytemnestra," she might say, or "Come on. It can't be *that* interesting." He hadn't spoken to her, though, before the December afternoon when, gripping the *Times* under one arm, he turned the corner and stopped short. "Sorry."

Oscar Schliemann's former wife stood just a few feet away, sobbing into the gaping blue car. A sprig of holly was pinned rakishly to the lapel of her London Fog. He felt he knew her, from those movies. "Is something wrong?"

She looked up and managed half a smile. "I couldn't let them dump her on some trash heap, could I? I didn't know she was so heavy."

Karl peered into the car and saw a pile of tawny fur, like a wadded-up coat with legs. It was Clytemnestra, either dead or very sound asleep. "Oh," he said, stricken.

"I had her killed." Joanna's voice was matter-of-fact.

183

"*Why?*" he protested. How could she?

She groped for a tissue. "Kidney failure. She was fifteen years old."

"I see." Of course there would be a reason. In Schliemann's films the wife was too sensible, if anything.

"*Not* put to sleep," she said sternly.

"No." Did he look like somebody who used euphemisms? "What do you want to do with her?"

"Bury her next to the compost heap." Her voice broke. "But my roomers' cars are in the way."

It was true. The driveway was clogged with two Volvos and a rusted BMW. "Can I help?" he asked. Though the inert dog must weigh eighty pounds, and the ground was probably frozen.

She looked at him through lank, pale hair. "Why would you want to?"

Karl wasn't sure, but there was a sense of fatality, as if he were following a script. He could feel his heart beating. He put down his newspaper, and together he and Joanna succeeded in rolling the body onto a tarp and dragging it up the driveway almost in silence, while the rain still fell. It was like the penultimate scene in a movie, in black and white, without sound. Karl cleared his throat. "What can we dig with?"

She found a spade and, without consulting him, attacked the matted, mossy area next to her garage. "Such a fool," she said, striking blow after blow and scarcely making a dent. "I was such a fool." She seemed possessed.

"I'm sorry," he said. "I'm really sorry about your dog."

"Clytemnestra? Oh, I won't miss her that much."

"You won't?" It wouldn't be this way in the movie.

"Don't you know animals are foisted on people?" She straightened, grasping the handle of the spade with both hands, and blazed her eyes at him. "Everybody else goes off without a care in the world, and there you are with the damn dog."

All right, so Karl was sentimental. "I wanted a Cocker Spaniel," he said, "but my father was allergic."

"She was so *humble*," Joanna said with disdain. "She used to stand there licking my shoes, and . . ." She took a breath, swayed alarmingly, and dropped the spade.

Karl reached across the grave and caught her shoulders. "Careful." He felt her weight against his hands.

"It isn't the dog." Her eyes were squeezed shut, leaking tears.

"No."

"Sixteen years," she said. "Why do I have to choose the wrong people?"

"Most of us do." Karl saw the caption 'Crying for her Lost Love' printed above her face. He moved his hands cautiously away from her and picked up the spade.

There was a layer of gravel a few inches down, but Karl kept digging. When he looked up, breathing hard, Joanna was leaning against the garage watching him. "This is so nice of you." There were smudges around her eyes.

"Not at all." Karl Compton was forty-two years old and had lived with a copy editor named Roxy until last January, when for no reason she had thrown all his clothes down the stairs. (Well, not really for no reason, but by the time he saw she was serious, it was too late.) After that, he had organized his life: Up by eight; tea and microwaved oatmeal with Morning Pro Musica; work at the computer till a ten-thirty break for calisthenics and grapefruit juice; back to the computer till one; then his therapeutic walk to the kiosk or the market, followed by soup or a sandwich; work again till six, when (except on Thursday) he would watch the Newshour on WGBH during some kind of thawed dinner. Then he might go to a concert or play or movie, or read a book.

Karl did see friends, and on Thursdays there was the Casablanca. His telephone rang sometimes, if not as often as he would have liked. But that day, when he turned onto Channing Street and nearly bumped into the famous Joanna Schliemann, it was an event, better than a personal letter or a UPS package. For years he had envied Oscar Schliemann, who could make trouble and turn it into art. However, it wasn't Schliemann who was here now, helping Joanna to bury her dog. "The privilege is mine," Karl said as he yanked out roots. Every word either of them said reverberated, like dialogue.

"Those could be poison ivy," Joanna murmured, and he felt even more energized, at the risk he was taking. He plucked the holly from her coat and dropped it into the hole. "Requiescat in pace," he said, then knelt to scoop up a handful of dirt.

"Just a minute." Joanna stooped and patted the dog's exposed ear into a more dignified position. "There," she said.

When the two of them had heaped the grave with stones and rotted leaves, their hands were muddy, and Karl was sweating in spite of the chilly air. "No gravestone, I hope?" he asked, still crouching. Her face was just inches from his, her cheeks glowing.

"The kids can take care of that." She stood upright. "Do you want to come in and wash your hands?"

But this felt aesthetically wrong. "No, thanks." He got to his feet.

Before he could reconsider, she held out a grubby hand. "I'm Joanna Schliemann, by the way."

"Yes." He felt dizzy, maybe from rising too quickly.

"Oh," she said ruefully. "You knew."

"Karl Compton. Any time you need help. With anything."

Walking home over slippery uneven bricks, Karl continued the scene: He followed Joanna into the tall gray house and washed at an old-fashioned marble sink, while she measured tea leaves into a Haviland china pot and told him how besieged she had felt, living with Oscar and having her private self plundered for other people's entertainment. And yet, alone now, she scarcely knew how to be.

They even had a quarrel, of a sort. "Do you know you've picked up Claudia's way of talking?" Karl heard himself fatuously asking over the antique tea table. (Claudia was the woman in Schliemann's second and third pictures.)

"*Her* way?" Joanna's imaginary face flushed. "Don't you think Oscar might have picked up something from *me?*" But she accepted Karl's apology and led him into the hall, to the foot of tall stairs mounting past grand faded wallpaper. "Thank you so much," she said at the front door, with a look that was only a beginning.

There she was in the Nynex White Pages, he discovered at home, Schliemann J T. His forgotten newspaper would provide an excuse for calling, but he couldn't; he would feel like one of those opportunists who lurk on the edges of singles groups, assessing the latest crop of divorcees. For today, it was enough that he had helped to lift the dog out of her car and bury it. He had seen her cry. Oscar Schliemann's wife. It was extraordinary. He went to the video store for tapes of Schliemann's films and played them on his VCR, noting gestures and phrases.

Walking in Joanna's neighborhood in the days afterwards, Karl didn't see her. And then he realized: Without the dog, she had changed her routine. In February a company in Lexington hired him for an in-house job, and he stopped his own daily walks. Roxy, in their final argument, had accused him of cowardice: This was why he didn't get on with his novel, she had said; if he finished it, he would feel obligated to send it out, and the thought of another person's eyes actually looking at words he had written was too intimidating. But writing wasn't all he was ambivalent about; he wouldn't take a chance on anything. And then she had done that thing with his clothes.

Maybe it was cowardice, but Karl still hesitated to call Joanna. If she even remembered him, might it not be with the same scorn she had shown toward her slavish dog?

One Sunday in November Karl saw a full-page ad in the *Times*, for *Winter*, Oscar Schliemann's new film. There was the usual dejected woman in a raincoat—a trademark by now—played this time by a blonde. Schliemann was heading straight into self-parody.

On Thursday night at the Casablanca, though, Greg was already talking about *Winter*, which had opened at the Nickelodeon. It was more serious than the earlier films, he said.

"Come on," Karl protested. "Oscar Schliemann doesn't even pretend to be serious. His dialogue jumps from God to Saran Wrap in the same sentence." Watching those rented videotapes one after another, he had been disillusioned. "He doesn't take responsibility."

"Wait till you see it," Greg said. "There's one scene . . . But I won't spoil it for you."

The *Sunday Globe* had a review. *Winter* dealt with the same old marital tangles, Karl saw; the lines might be clever, but the characters would stammer too much and be too sensitively photographed. If he chose to see the movie at all, it would be at a second-run theater.

But the next paragraph mentioned "the touching, bittersweet scene in which the family dog is buried." Karl sat up straight in his chair.

So Joanna and Oscar were in touch. No doubt she had described the whole thing to him—Karl's difficulty in lifting the dog, his refusal to come into the house. He saw the two of them over the tea table, leaning toward each other and snickering. Oscar's burial scene would feature some clown stumbling over the shovel and probably getting poison ivy afterwards (though Karl himself hadn't).

He threw the newspaper down and took the T to the first matinee at the Nickelodeon. How could she do that, he was thinking all the way on the screeching train, the bitch, how could she? Not that he had any right to consider the incident a private event in his own life; even at the time, he had thought of it in cinematic terms. But that didn't mean Joanna was supposed to think of it that way. He felt utterly betrayed.

In spite of a line at the theater, he got in. The picture was in color, he noted at the opening shot of a woman leading a bleached-looking pink-nosed dog (called Cassandra) over brick sidewalks strewn with orange and yellow leaves. All wrong. True, Clytemnestra's coat had been yellow-gray and her nose the rubbery gray-pink of an eraser, but the color made the movie look cheap.

At first, Karl's fury kept him from following the story. There was a married couple and another woman—as usual in Oscar's plots—and the husband's forbearance with his wife's anger only exacerbated it. A good touch; in spite of himself, Karl was drawn in.

The picture moved to the Harvard observatory, where the protagonist worked as an astronomer. (There were symbolic star-gazing scenes.) The burial occurred after the man had moved to Provincetown with his new love. (A beach scene, with crashing blue waves.) The dog died; the distraught wife called; and the husband came roaring up Route 95 in his new Saab with the sun-roof.

No, Karl wanted to announce to the whole theater: It didn't happen that way. *I* was the one. *I* did it. And yet he was still held. When the husband stood on his former doorstep and groped absently for his key before pausing one beat, slapping his pocket, and ringing the doorbell, Karl, with the rest of the audience, thought the man shouldn't give up so easily; there was still hope.

Not really, though. That was clear as soon as the actor leaned on the shovel, gazing into the grave. "Why do I have to choose the wrong people?" the mournful blonde asked. There was a single streak of mud on her cheek, artistically placed.

The actor took a sprig of holly from his pocket and stooped to tuck it into dead Cassandra's collar. "Most of us do," he said as he lifted a shovelful of dirt, and Karl, even as he recognized his own words, felt the back of his throat tighten. The scene, as Greg would say, worked.

It still shouldn't have been in color, Karl thought in the crammed subway car as he clutched the back of a seat in which an Asian woman hunched over a paperback copy of *Cranford*. The sight of books on the T always cheered him, proving that literature was not quite dead.

He was cheered now for other reasons. The movie, which he had intended to hate, had exhilarated him. Not that Karl wholeheartedly admired *Winter;* no matter how well Oscar Schliemann understood his own weaknesses, his entire oeuvre was one long self-justification, and Joanna was well rid of him. What excited Karl was a feeling of participation; he might not yet have produced a whole book of his own, but now, without even trying, he had become part of somebody else's work.

But it was more than that. After the burial of Cassandra, the protagonist had guided his wife—gently, masterfully—into the house and up the stairs to a high, inviting bed with pineapple-carved posts. (For the last time ever, it was implied in the solemn disrobing that followed.) At that point something in Karl's chest had made a sudden swooning plunge that wasn't quite pain: What was happening on the screen was too close to what he had declined to imagine a year ago.

It hadn't really happened, though, he saw. The subway car squealed toward Kendall Square and flung its passengers from side to side, but Karl held fast. Of course it hadn't. That final foreseeable embrace wasn't taken from real life any more than the scene before it; Oscar the genius hadn't even bothered to bury his own real dog. Joanna had described the burial—maybe even the stranger who had helped her—and Oscar had simply appropriated the material for his own purposes; that was all. There were no rules about such things. Oscar Schliemann could do what he liked, and so could Karl Compton.

At the Harvard stop Karl jumped from the car and ran up the escalator, past the patient waiting passengers, as quickly as he could.

John
Domini

Minimum Bid

BY THE NIGHT of the art auction Kath had achieved the look she wanted, the wallop of a freethinking woman in her fifties. Endless sessions at the Fitness Center had honed her for the role (that, plus the calcium pills), a New Year's resolution made a fact by mid-autumn. For the auction she chose a black pantaloon one-piece, a romper with a tank top, showing off flat and burnished pectorals. Round her waist she knotted a thong strung with native medallions, gargoyle faces, and she pegged on witty earrings. She was Katherine Wick, divorced and remade. If people wanted to talk about her, if they wanted to whisper and glance sidelong—then she might as well be the talk of the night.

And Kath's biggest coup was to arrive at the event with one of the artists. She paid the ticket for a prodigy, a pretty girl young enough to be her daughter.

Kath introduced the girl, Dory, as "my date for the evening." When someone asked, she made it clear that Dory was a housemate. Might as well be the talk of the night.

Kath wouldn't cling to the youngster, either. In the three years since she'd at last gotten out of her marriage, she'd made a few runs at this crowd, the money crowd, and she'd learned who she could count on for the least hypocritical reception. She introduced the girl to a few of those—heteros, but not entirely tongue-tied in Kath's presence. Then, alone, Kath found a table beneath the auctioneer's podium. She set down her bidding paddle and made it over to the art work up for auction. Local stuff, varied in size and splash, it was strung like a Miracle Mile halfway round the function room. Only after she'd checked the first several pieces against the descriptions in her program did the woman allow herself a look back at Dory.

The girl was as much an eyecatcher as Kath. Dory's skirt was carhop-retro, a cherry electricity well above the knee. She'd topped that off with a rockabilly shirt, a spangled tornado across its back; plus, God knows why, she'd torn away the sleeves. Did she want to call attention to her skin? That indoor skin, white, chilly? Kath suffered the chill; she dropped her chin.

Oh, Kath. Oh, didn't she get off on teasing the heteros, throwing around a word like *housemate*. The fact was, she'd never touched the girl. Kath had never come closer than sitting in a heap outside the youngster's bedroom door, buzzing with insomnia.

By this time she'd even come up with tricks to help through the worst of the infatuation, the mania; an old woman has her tricks. Now, raising her eyes once more, she forced herself to picture how Dory would lose her looks. The girl had a millworker's thick trunk, and those upper arms were already as much pudge as muscle. Tonight's event generally brought out a more hammered shapeliness.

Tonight was a fundraiser, a benefit for a proposed performance center in downtown Corvallis. The small Oregon city had one sizable hotel, the hotel had donated its largest basement room, and the space looked nearly filled to capacity. Clusters of auction-goers sidled past each other, exchanging smiles over their shoulders, while champagne stewards in starched coats circled outward from the rollaway bar. Nonetheless there was almost no one with a beer belly, no one with saddlebags over the hips.

In the Willamette Valley, the money crowd stayed in shape. Kath had seen more than a few of these people at the Fitness Center. She'd seen them hesitate between the Nautilus machines, heaving, doubtful, and then press on, no match for the social pressure. What other means of proving they'd made it did these people have? In the Valley, what wasn't farmland was suburb, suburb without a city attached, without a place for the more oddball glitter. You wouldn't find a colored face at the auction (other than in Dory's piece, a portrait), none of the Asian or African or Middle Eastern influence that supposedly carried weight in the faster-moving markets. The Valley was high-tech pastoral. Dory's getup had the women fiddling with their shoulder pads. And if a man found himself near the girl, he preened, cocking a knuckle at one hip and showing off a belt line crunch-trim. For a moment the people around her were nothing but a bunch of performing dwarves.

Kath downed some champagne, hiding in the cup. She had to watch it on these mean thoughts.

She turned back to the display, while others fell in beside her. The work was hung salon-style, crowded between the hinges of the room's unfolded partition. Nonetheless whoever stood next to Kath would concentrate on their program, keeping their elbows to themselves. She would have thought it impossible to move around in a sardine-tin like this and not at least bump a few elbows. No wonder she had mean thoughts. Only once did someone say hello, one of her so-called friends from the Clinic, and the man immediately asked about her children.

He flexed his mouth, but you couldn't call that a smile. Kath lifted her chin, showing off her shoulders and pecs.

"Oh," she told him, "I keep the kids at Christmas-card distance." She was divorced and remade.

Then came Dory's piece, in the corner. Kath couldn't bid on it; the girl had made that a condition of coming. Dory had wound up sleeping with her subject, a married man, a father. God knows he must have seemed fascinating, a surgeon born in Morocco. Plus Dory had worked in pastels, which required repeated sittings, long hours together. Even tonight Kath had to admire the layered effect, like a winepress in which the grapes bulged yet froze, forever just at the point of bursting.

The back wall held more, making sixty items all together. Dory's piece however had left Kath distracted, frowning.

"Who does these *landscapes*, anyway?" This was a stage voice, practically in her ear. "Do they have cars?"

Kath turned, frowning. But this was Leo Farragut, one of her patients, one of the terminal cases. He sounded more rheumy since last time.

"I'm asking, Mizz Wick. Do they have cars?"

Her face relaxed. "I believe most of our artists can afford cars, Leo."

"Oh yeah? Real cars? *American* cars?"

She opened her stance, the gargoyles clinking at her waist. "You're saying you find our offerings a tad precious? A tad, oh—out of touch with the hurly-burly?"

"I hear the Japs now'll sell you a car like this one." Leo raised a discolored finger towards a lithograph, a beige heron taking off over swoozy reeds. Every curve in the picture was a Coca-Cola wave. "They got a car that just floats out there."

"Not really."

"I'm telling you. The thing's *made* for a painting like this, it never touches the ground at all."

"We live in an amazing country, Leo."

"Yeah," he said. "Japan."

She chuckled, her cup to her naked breastbone. Above the man's ears, his grinning, his shaved head wrinkled. Cases like Leo had come her way a few times before. While she filled out the prescription forms they would stand around hitching their belts, loudly up front about their dying. *Gal, let me tell you about bad. Gal, it's got me nailed to the wall.* This when Kath had to work in a cubbyhole—the Clinic didn't allow much room for a physician's assistant. Nonetheless whenever Leo or one of her other terminals went into their act, playing cowboy past the graveyard, Kath found herself cheering them along. She let them strut all over her cubbyhole. Now she made a fuss over the man's hat, a stiff and short-brimmed black fedora.

"It's a rapper's hat," he said. "All the little black kids wear 'em."

"Looks like Bo Diddley to me," she said. "Bad to the bone."

The couples within earshot smiled wanly, not quite risking eye contact.

"Bo . . . Diddley?" Leo asked. "Where'd someone like you ever hear about him?"

"You remember my friend." Kath kept her tone sprightly. "The singer."

Of course he remembered. Kath's story had all but made the headlines— *Mother Of Two Dating Feminist Folksinger.* Her husband had actually found someone to serve her with papers at one of the woman's concerts. Kath was using a little stage savvy of her own, here: *Leo, let me tell you about bad.* The old man, give him credit, said nothing stupid. His nod and his grin remained decent.

"Say, Leo," she said then, "have you got a table yet?"

The two of them had to circle the room to pick up his bidding paddle, and then they slowed down for hors d'oeuvres. But Kath didn't mind the additional averted faces and uptight elbows. She enjoyed—though all appropriately jaundiced about what she was doing here, her debutante's ball for one—a mounting excitement. Under the stage lights, the auctioneer appeared enlarged, a Rockwell centerpiece in bow tie and suspenders. Around him the volunteers running the show fretted over clipboards and wads of champagne scrip.

Once she and Leo were seated, he asked if she were alone. Kath turned, pointing. Against the bar, the dark service entrance, Dory's arms and legs appeared to glow.

Kath hid in her purse, the stink of rain on leather.

Wonder Woman, she recalled, used to change costumes simply by whirling in place. Too sudden for the naked eye. But Kath lacked the power, especially after fifteen or twenty minutes polishing a different act. Since her last look at Dory, she'd been working the crowd, conventioneering, and it took effort to switch to a more intimate brand of theater. Yes, these three months sharing the house had been continual theater, more smoke and blue lights than Kath would have thought she had in her. She'd even learned to poke fun at the girl's determination to get back to art school. What Dory was really studying to be, Kath would claim loudly, was a martyr. And yet how many nights had she ended up outside the girl's door, buzzing with insomnia? How many times had she replayed her fantasies, imaginings by now as brown and worked-over as her showy new pecs and abdominals?

Even here at the auction, Kath realized, she might have some seduction scheme going. Kath might have a back-of-the-mind notion that Leo here, old Heparin-dosed Leo, would somehow make her interesting. Oh, Kath. Please. These days Dory found no one in Corvallis interesting.

She'd begun writing to New York, to Dr. Ossaba, the surgeon in her pastel portrait. Dory would vanish upstairs as soon as she saw the man's postmark; Kath knew only that the last two letters had been finger-thick. What could they have to say to each other? No question, the girl had wanted the doctor's picture out of the house. Kath had needed every trick in the book just to get Dory to come watch the item get sold.

The gavel sounded, *rick-kity wick.*

Everyone else sat heads-up. Earrings appeared elongated, under slant working-woman haircuts, and the men ate carefully, using both hands. Then Dory hurried over, a head-clearing tang of soap and baby powder. At first she wouldn't sit.

"Hey there, gal," said Leo. "You look like you've seen a ghost."

"You won't believe who's here," Dory said.

At the time of his portrait, Ossaba had been the hottest new arrival at the Clinic. He'd come to town as a transfer from Harlem Hospital, with a smart mouthed two-year-old and a wife who taught a section of French at Oregon State. The one thing that none of the gossips seemed to know was just how he and Dory had met. Now the girl came to Kath and Leo with the news that the wife—the ex-wife—was at the auction.

"Mrs. Glynde," she kept saying. "Mrs. Glynde."

Did she feel safer, using the woman's new name? Kath looked in the direction of Dory's nod. The French instructor preferred what used to be called a Jean Seberg cut, the only woman here besides Kath with such short hair.

"I see," Kath said.

The ex-wife lifted her champagne, oblivious. But then why should anyone watch her? What sort of fuss was Kath supposed to make, with Leo at the table? The man had tipped back his bowler, and his look carried the obvious question. Who is this girl? Kath fumbled ahead with the introductions ("Number twenty-three in your program, folks"), meantime trying to catch Dory's eye. But the youngster only made a face: I do *not* want to be here. She chose the chair beside the old man, across from Kath.

"Dorr," Kath tried, "in this town, you were bound to run into her sooner or later."

The girl stared away, showing her spangled back. Around them the bidding began, the paddles going up. Kath thought of flamenco dancers raising fans, hiding their heat.

"So," Leo said, "you're one of the artists."

"Well, I was." Now all of a sudden, Dory was smiling. "The money ran out before I finished sophomore year."

"Then tell me something, gal. Do you own a car?"

The girl allowed herself maybe two seconds of looking confused. Then she snatched Leo's paddle from the table, she jabbed him in the chest. Typical: Dory had him sheepish, explaining himself, and when a boy came by with champagne, Leo said he'd buy her a second glass. Another minute and he and Dory were playing tug of war. They gripped opposite ends of the paddle's wooden spine, almost giggling, and Kath took more of the bulk-order champagne herself. She got a mouthful, an eyeball-tickling belt.

"What's the *big deal* about the doctor's wife?" she asked.

The girl broke off the game, blinking.

"Dorr, you were bound to run into her." Levelly Kath reminded her that the woman's new husband—"Mr. Glynde"—was a vice president at the university. "Look, that's why they have the fundraiser in November. Most of the OSU people haven't had a decent paycheck since June."

Dory's mouth had gone square.

"Listen," Kath went on, "I used to think my husband was sentimental about November. It was the only time he ever took me to a restaurant."

"Oh, Katherine," Dory said. "Common-sense Katherine."

Kath fought an impulse to lift her drink again. "Common-sense?" she managed. She pinched up one strap of her top and with the other hand gestured at herself.

The girl refused to smile, she turned toward the stage. That left Leo. Kath kept her hand at her top-strap, making a fist. Tell me, Leo—you've never met our Dory? You didn't know our Dory won an undergraduate award?

The man's face wrinkled in new places, twitching.

"You didn't see the notice in the paper? You've never *heard* of our Dory?"

Leo wiped his lips; he licked them again. Kath had another question but lost it somehow in the man's doddering gesture, his undone flesh. One of those moments when her Master's of Health flickered in her mind's eye. She let go of her top. Dory's look was no fun either: like the girl had just come out of her Friday-night shift at the Video Circle. Kath checked out the stage. A volunteer beside the podium held up a miniature, a square piece that fit in one hand.

In her program Kath had marked this item a Maybe. A doll-sized robe, vaguely Oriental, it had hems and borders the yellow of split wood. From her seat Kath could see the sequins glimmer. Leo went on twitching, redoing his lips, and with that in the corner of one eye Kath put in the first bid, the minimum asked in the program. Twenty dollars more and the thing was hers. By the time someone brought the receipt the old man's face had better color. His finger steady, he pointed out a woman at the next table.

"That gal made the thing," Leo said.

The artist looked to be about forty, with an enjoyable swank in her grin. Her husband was dressed out-of-season, a canary shirt. Hello, Kath grinned back. Welcome to the party—the Desperate Debutante's ball.

Then came the heron over the reeds, the swoozy beige floater. A couple of rich men started a bidding war. Five-dollar increases went back and forth between Mr. Glynde from the university and, let's see, who was Dory looking at this time . . . of course. Another administrator wanted the print for his office. One of the muckety-mucks at the Clinic, his bidding sloppy with alcohol. Kath bent over her miniature; a runner had brought it to the table. But the fluorescents above her were reflected in the tiny robe, painful in its Chinese glitter. Behind her, some flunky loudly egged both bidders on: "Great piece! *Terrific* piece!"

The auctioneer socked his gavel against the podium. Applause rippled briefly through the underground room.

Dory was leaning into Leo. "I don't even want to know who got that one."

Kath lifted her head. "Don't be mean," she said. "It's for a good cause."

The girl turned. Her eyes were two quick hazel tree-dwellers, stilled at a sound they didn't understand.

"Don't be *mean*," Kath said. "I've got to live with these people."

"With what people?"

Leo broke in, extending one thin arm. A stage whisper: "Not now, ladies. This one's the best thing here." And Dory played to him again, her face reanimated: "Oh yeah, oh really. Check out the scumbling."

What? Dory and Leo were talking about a wall-size oil, a stretch of Peoria Road in winter, roughed out in descending swaths. Rain, road, scrub. Midway up the closest foreground there jetted an orange flare, some New-Year's blossom, which made it look as if the murmurous view might split down the middle. Was that "scumbling"?

But the artist had set too high a minimum, six hundred dollars. Nobody lifted a paddle.

"This is humiliating," Dory said. "It's like a ritual slaughter."

"You know," Leo said, "you really should be more generous. You heard our Mizz Wick."

"What, about living with people?" Dory faced her; it felt like too soon after last time. "Kath, I don't get it. You're a grownup. You don't have to live with anybody."

"Well . . ."

"I mean, the only people you really *have* to live with—right?—are your lovers."

Unexpectedly Kath found herself laughing. Her chin dropped, her hand felt its way across her loosening mouth—and what, had she *forgotten* about laughing? About giving herself a *break*? The auction program on the table before her for once looked nothing like an actor's promptbook; its print had turned to feathers, to bugs.

"What's so funny?" Dory asked. "There's your lover, like whatever you have with him. And then there's everyone else."

Kath's diaphragm rippled, and along her waistline the gargoyles winked. Yes, laugh, Kath. Just laugh.

"Mizz Wick?" Leo asked.

"Hey, I mean it," Dory said. "There's your lover and then there's everyone else."

After all, Kath reminded herself, it wasn't going to get any easier tonight. The item after next was Dory's. And God knows Kath could make herself crazy with that face up beside the podium. That proud glare: *Hey, Wick—I had her and you didn't.*

"Come on, Kath," Dory said. "At least get it together while they sell off my piece."

Kath fought for a breath, she reached for the champagne. With that she noticed the faces nearby. The woman who'd made the miniature was watching again, with her Broadway grin. When Kath caught her eye the woman nodded, and meantime the artist's husband, eyebrows up and grinning himself, tapped a thumb against his canary'd chest. Well, well. The acoustics in the hotel basement had protected her. The wrangling with Dory had gone unheard; all that had come across was an interesting threesome having themselves a time. Kath checked left-right, she knew how laughter freshened her look, and she was met with honest eye contact. One or two of the men licked hors-d'oeuvrey fingers, but that was better than the rigged faces she was used to. Well. The only meanness she could find belonged to Dory's Moroccan doctor, up beside the podium.

No doubt as Dory had laid on the pastels, she'd fallen into a recapitulation of her father. The family lived in Unity, in the high desert country, and the hint of home gave her sheeny layers a baleful depth. Now bidding was brisk. No surprise to Kath, after the team spirit she'd read in these faces. The closing offer came from Mrs. Glynde.

"I . . . can't . . . *believe* it," Dory whispered.

When the girl had no expression—other than those puzzled eyes—you saw the baby fat in her cheeks. She leaned across the table, closer to Kath than she'd been all night. "I mean, what's going on?"

Didn't Dory notice these faces? Suddenly the girl was everyone's favorite. They tipped their heads, congratulations, attaway, and a man at the next table, a circuit-trainer Kath recognized from the Fitness Center, sent a runner their way with still more champagne. Kath kept her own look party-hearty.

"Well Dorr," she said, "the woman came out a winner. Nowadays she's got too much money to have hard feelings."

Behind the girl, across the room, the Jean Seberg cut bobbed beside the boy who'd brought the receipt.

"Oh, Kath." Dory's mouth had gone square again. "Would you for once stop thinking about money?"

"Hey," Leo put in. "What is it with this Glynde woman? What's going on?"

"Hush now," Kath said, "both of you. This next is mine."

Actually she'd marked this a "Maybe." She'd found it agreeably weird, a collage that combined shredded IBM discs with a straw doll dressed as the Flying Nun. But the design was like calendar blocks and it had a ponderous title: *The Woman's Point of View*. Plus anything by this artist would cost. She was well-connected, a Hewlett-Packard wife. The men at the collagist's table were the most in-shape at the auction, and they settled back as the bidding began, sharps at the ball game.

Kath worked her paddle hotly. The auctioneer lead the crowd, pitch and yaw. She wound up ninety dollars over the minimum, duking it out with one of the wives at the artist's table. When the thing was gaveled sold—"To the lady in black!"—the room burst into applause.

Dory kept her hands in her lap. She sat stiffly, and Kath could see every stud on her rodeo shirt.

"That's what all this is about," she said, "isn't it?"

The kid with the receipt stood at Kath's elbow, but Dory felt closer. "Hey, I mean," she went on, "let's give the little lady a big hand. That's the whole point, right?"

"That's enough, Dorr." Kath tried to make it like Mother Knows Best. "We all know you don't want to be here."

"Oh, excuse me. I have some emotions, excuse me."

Behind the girl, the miniaturist wore a dandy smirk, worth a wink in reply. Hi, again; hi. But then that woman and her husband once more faced the stage.

"I should have realized," Dory said, "we have to forget all about *my* emotions. This is the Wicked Wick Show."

At the edges of the girl's sleeves, the torn threads were blue thorns. Kath was struggling for a comeback when Leo hooked her housemate by the elbow. The wine had threaded his cheeks but his eyes were purposeful. Did Dory have any idea, Leo asked, what Kath had been through when her marriage broke up?

"It was like a cyclone hit," he said.

"Don't give me that," Dory said. "She had money. She had a place."

Kath had more or less forgotten the old man was at the table. But he was wearing the girl down already; her cowboy buttons disappeared beneath her crossed arms. "Oh Do-ro-thy," Leo chided, "oh now, I certainly don't feel used." Kath let him take over, reopening her checkbook. That Flying-Nun piece had busted her balance down so far that anything else would have to go on plastic. Meantime Leo's tone grew warmer, more among-pals, and Kath understood that Dory didn't want a scene either. The gray nap on these walls, this plastic-wood furniture—it must have reminded the girl of the whispering rooms at the clinic. Now Dory was the one with a hand at her mouth.

"Leo, you don't know the whole story either. You're part of her hocus pocus too."

"Oh, what's the harm done?" he asked. "Why shouldn't the old gal go home with a few new friends?"

Dory shrank between them, her chin doubling against her collar, her looks briefly spoiled. Around their table erupted new laughter, the crowd was sensing success, and Kath brought up her head, open-mouthed. Oh, see. Numbers meant mercy. Besides her own, more than fifteen thousand homes had been mortgaged here, between the river and I-5, and given those numbers she was bound to find a few at least with whom she might laugh. Leo kept his eyes on the girl, his jowls limp. Not until the hubbub died did he reach for his paddle.

His paddle; right. After all, he'd come here looking to buy. Kath was watching Leo bid, his withered fingers ropy on the handle, when Dory angled towards her again.

"You know," Dory said, "Ossaba can get me into art school in New York."

The girl cleared out the night's commotion. She was a portrait and the rest was wall.

"He'll co-sign the papers for financial aid," she said. "He's already put down a deposit on a dorm room."

"He *told* you this?" Kath asked.

"In his latest letter, he told me." Thorns at her shoulders, studs across her chest. "I can move in the first of the year."

"Well—well, Dory—he'd have all the money."

"I'd have my own room, Kath. My own room, my own door."

"But it would still be his turf. His world, Dory. And you didn't even want the man's picture around."

"Oh, the picture. I mean, totally amateur work."

Leo was motioning for his receipt. Somebody made a crack, *Why don't they just keep a runner at your table?* Kath's own two pink forms however seemed suddenly flimsy, way too few. "Dory," she asked, "don't you understand?" But she was head-down, talking to her receipts; in this noise she might as well have been speaking another language.

"The picture's a separate question," Dory said.

At the Clinic, Kath recalled, the girl's story wasn't so special. An affair during the first year of a residency was a natural hazard. Ossaba's real problem had been that he lacked the necessary powerful insider to quiet the gossip. The man was black and Muslim, after all. But other doctors had seduced the occasional co-ed. In most cases the marriage survived, the rupture bridged with jewelry and trips abroad. Most households had the strength for only so much dislocation. Kath herself, just tonight, had lost a good half the wallop she'd come in with. It cost her to avoid Dory's stare, she felt it in the neck, and she couldn't believe the effort it took to finger together her receipts and weight them in place with the miniature. On an evening like this—cold and late in the year—that doll's robe itself mocked her, more substantial than her whole rattling getup. At least the little gilded coverall didn't pretend to be anything other than a toy, an Emperor's new clothes.

"I can be out of here the first of the year," Dory said.

What was the next item? A work in bright fiber, a picket fence and a peacock beyond . . . but what difference did it make? She'd given nothing here more than a Maybe anyway. Kath slung her paddle up in front of her face.

Afterwards, Leo offered to drive Dory home. Just as well; Kath couldn't even see the girl. Once the last item was in the books (the only piece left not taken was the ominous view of Peoria Road), ten or a dozen in the audience closed around Kath, picking at their sweat-stuck clothes. The husband of the miniaturist settled behind her, his hands on her shoulders, his fingers greasy with chicken. Volunteers brought the credit-card machine to the table, and she punctuated her conversation with the clack of each imprint.

"What *happened*?" Kath asked, grinning. "At the bank they're going to think a bomb hit."

At last Leo eased through the knot around her chair, quieting the crowd. His smile had paled again.

"The gal would like to go," he said.

Kath couldn't see her. She tried to catch a glimpse through the pack of aging bodies, and found herself thinking: I had a family, I had a man who loved me—and now the girl wants to go? The girl too? Kath's contact lenses couldn't hold a focus. They needed a soak.

"These lenses," Kath said, "are going to get a soak."

And then, finding the old man's face: "My hero."

Her looks wouldn't hold up much longer either. Just getting the receipts in her purse left her blinking, and it felt like her mascara had loosened. Her long coat, whew.

Outside in the parking lot, the black and white leaden with rain, Kath almost walked right into the Glyndes.

Not that they noticed. In the farthest corner of the lot, half hidden behind a Volvo station wagon, the Glyndes were scuffling. Actually scuffling; Kath couldn't help but stare. The couple staggered back and forth in an impossible mutual grip, their arms locked upright above them. Somehow, together, they'd hefted overhead the portrait of Dory's surgeon. It was like a workout station at the Fitness Center, the extended straining arms, the ungainly square weight. Mrs. Glynde's open overcoat had been forced back under her armpits, revealing a Gothic label stitched in golden thread. Now a word that might have been *please* came through the drizzle, now a grunted obscenity. What was going on? Who was trying to hit who? Kath couldn't even see which of them had hold of the portrait. The art work jigged above the struggling husband and wife, neon exploding off its glass cover. And those colors sweeping that foreigner's face—could this be a trick of the glare?— For a moment those colors looked to Kath like Dory, Dory the way she'd been tonight. Kath saw Dory's glimmering tornado, her up-a-tree staring and electric ruby skirt; she saw Dory's bruised pearl, scrap blues, profound whites: the whole wizard's wardrobe of the disappearing girl.

In the end she moved on without interfering, without lifting a finger. She kept to the hotel, the shadow. There the lights off the youngster's painting couldn't reach her.

Brad	*Family Fishing*
Wethern	*— Fairhaven Style*

I ALWAYS LIKED TO FISH. Ever since whenever. We fished in a stream behind our house in Oregon. Family fished, don't you know. Picnic lunch. Mother. Father. Brother. Sister. Big can of worms. At the edge of the apple orchard, I had my favorite spot in the tall grass where I felt safe and secure.

We caught wriggly little fish that we would sometimes throw back because they were too small. It was a big decision for little people. Life and death. Food or freedom. How big is not small? Keep or give back? How could I make such a quick choice, when it was forever? Mom! Dad! They are clear downstream. By the time they come and say too small, you'll be dead. I don't know. Back you go. Hey, I think he turned and thanked me. I wonder if that's possible? Okay, everybody! Who took the worms? I want to catch a really, big one now. That's family fishing.

Later, when I was ten years old and we lived on Humboldt Bay, we fished from a large, L-shaped dock in Fairhaven where two commercial salmon boats were sometimes tied. I fished with older kids, just after low tide with big lines, big hooks and giant mudworms we dug at dawn from the kelp beds. We fished for movie money. We needed big poles with long handles and star drag reels, but most of all, we needed to be alert and well back on the dock, because with no railing, it was a fast twenty feet to the water at low tide—and the only things we were there to catch were stingrays and sharks.

Without actually seeing it, we usually knew what was on our line. If a shark hit, it would go in all directions and try to wrap the line around a piling. If a stingray hit, it would take off for the middle of the bay in a straight ahead power thrust and when it had all of the line, we had to make sure we were secure on the dock so we could begin the long process of give and take, which we optimistically referred to as "reeling it in."

The sharks and rays were too heavy to bring up twenty feet to where we stood so they had to be coaxed along the outside of the long dock to the shore in order to be landed. We always did the best we could to land each one, but it was tricky. The shark could usually find a way to bite the line, break the leader or circle a piling, making it necessary to cut the line, while he pulled loose and headed back out to sea.

And the stingrays, with their Olympic quality butterfly stroke, would often over-power our small arms and strain the line until suddenly we would feel nothing but the tide. Then it was time to take a deep breath, feel the wind, look at the water and the clouds, then add new line, leader, hook and very carefully reach into the coffee can to select another mudworm. In Fairhaven, even the worms were treacherous. They had black pinchers on the front. If they sunk into your finger with their noto-rious worm poison, the head would have to be cut off and the pinchers removed with pliers. Then your hand would have to be doused in alcohol, and you would have to start biting and sucking your own finger and spitting out the contaminated blood. And never drop one inside your overalls, even on a dare. I don't know if that was all true, because I never saw anyone get pinched. The natural tendency was to be wide-eyed and coordinated around mudworms.

I remember this one Saturday. We are there on the high dock. Several of us. More than usual. The boats are out for the day. We have the dock to ourselves. We are standing near the outermost end. Five lines in the water. Two are Bill Loon's. One is mine. One is Bill Loon's sister, Mary Ann who hates to fish and never comes because she never catches anything good. But her girlfriend had to go somewhere, so she came. The fifth line belongs to Junior Malstrom who is Bill Loon's best friend. There are some on-lookers. A group that varies, but normally includes the Blue Hollar boy and a couple of younger Indian kids who are allowed to come and watch if they behave themselves, which they seem to do amazingly well considering Junior Malstrom is setting a bad example by jumping and cavorting around the dock as usual. Finally Bill Loon tells him to sit down. But Junior reminds everyone that it's his uncle's dock and he can do what he wants. So Bill Loon, who is the same age and twice as big, tells him to sit down or he will throw Junior into the water and tell his uncle much later after the sharks have invited him home for dinner and an octopus family is using his bones for toothpicks.

So Junior Malstrom sits down.

And then Bill Loon's sister had to go to the bathroom, but there is no bathroom on Humboldt Bay that we know about. Which is fine, if you are a boy. You can just go off the dock, next to a piling, holding your pole close. We all know that trick. But if you're a girl, it's a whole different card game according to Junior Malstrom who claims to know more about girls than most scientists. Time and again he informed us that there was no foolproof way for a girl to fish and pee from a dock at the same time. Too many things could go wrong. To hear his descriptions, I was sure he had seen it tried a lot of different ways. I don't know what dock he was on, but I was pretty sure it wasn't this one. Bill Loon called it Junior's dream dock.

Today Junior is silent on the subject and Bill Loon watches three poles while his worried looking sister skip hops off the dock and into the lupines and walks back two minutes later, smiling, freckles dancing, ready to fish again.

She takes her line and tells everyone she will go back to the house in a while and make sandwiches, if we think we might be hungry later. Later? We tell her to go ahead right now, but Bill Loon looks straight at the sun and says it's only about 9:20 and not time for lunch. So we try to relax and fish.

Junior Malstrom catches a perch and tries to shake it off his hook. It's an embarrassment. And I get two crabs, which is worse. But then Bill Loon gets a medium size mud shark so we get our lines out of the water right away so we won't get tangled and watch as he expertly gets him nearer the dock and then works him around the outside and finally pulls him into the soft sand on the shore. It's the first catch of the day.

Duck Fred pays thirty cents for mud sharks; fifty cents for stingrays. He feeds them to his ducks and geese, he says. A movie costs us twenty cents. The ferry to Eureka is five cents each way. A shark a piece will get us there and back. Two sharks means popcorn and a candy bar. Anymore than that and we are into funny books.

It's about ten o'clock. We walk out on the dock and put our lines in the water again. It's quiet for a while so Junior Malstrom starts reciting dirty poems, which he always does to pass the time and Bill Loon tells him to shut up, because his sister's there. But his sister says it's okay. We laugh as Junior starts right up again. It's obvious she never heard them or she wouldn't say okay so Bill repeats it's not okay and Junior says he doesn't remember any more anyway. And we laugh some more because he is lying. And another crab gets my bait.

Then Bill's sister says, "I've got something," and she looks like she'd be happy no matter what it was. She stands up and shows us the bend in her pole. "See," and she smiles. It kind of reminds me of family fishing in Oregon.

"Open the star drag," her brother tells her. "Just so you get in the habit."

"I don't care if it's just a crab," she says. "I'll make crab salad sandwiches!"

I still remember exactly what I am doing, when I hear her say those words, "crab salad sandwiches."

I am looking up at the clean, blue sky. The morning fog has gone by then, not the gradual way it disappears in other towns, but blown about a hundred miles down the coast somewhere. I realize that I am right in the middle of the few jewel precious minutes of sunny, calm weather we get each year, a time when the name "Fairhaven" no longer seems like the punchline to some long forgotten sailor's story. Fairhaven: a spit in the wind; short on manners, but long on huckleberry grit; on the ground and in the air.

My daydream is cut short by Mary Ann's loud, hellish wail that shoots a spray of panic over the end of the dock and time, as I know it, simply disappears for the rest of the day—creating a deep memory inside, undisturbed and fairy tale perfect.

The first thing I remember was Mary Ann, Bill Loon's sister, who made great sandwiches and hated to fish, running sideways across Junior's uncle's dock, trying to hold onto her fishing pole and stay on her feet at the same time. When she reached the end, where the Jack Salmon II was usually tied, she tried to grab a loose rope that wound around a piling, but as she reached for it, the pole jerked and she spun in a half circle, lost her balance and fell backwards off the docks still holding the pole. She clawed at the rope and her fingers squeezed a spot above a knot and somehow, she held on, to everything.

Unable to even adjust her grip, she was hanging by an arm, facing the dock with one leg straight out, barely touching timber, and the other one dangling twenty feet above the water. One hand had the rope and piling and the other one gripped the fishing pole like it was the Holy Grail.

Bill Loon reached her first. His big hands gripped her ankle. We all came running close behind, but no one else could figure what to do next. Bill Loon could. He started right away to talk her up. "You'll be okay. Drop the pole. Grab the rope with both hands," he said in an almost too quiet voice, as though something too loud might shatter the piling like fine crystal. "Do it without thinking. Right now. Then we can pull you up." No one moved or took a breath. We waited for Mary Ann to drop the pole. But she wouldn't drop it.

"Sis, drop the pole," Bill Loon said.

"I can't," she said, and her dancing freckles froze as she stared at us. She was more of a real fisherman than any of us thought possible. But, after all, she was Bill Loon's sister. Maybe it was passed along in the family bones. "Take it, Bill. I can hold on until you take it. I will. I promise."

"Drop it before you go off!" Bill Loon shouted.

"Help me catch it. I never catch anything good. I want to catch this one," she said.

"Go! Mary Ann!" Junior Malstrom yelled to the sea gulls as he leaped into the air. "We'll help you!" I didn't know what to do. Bill Loon whistled and we all jumped to his side. So many hands grabbed her ankle, we were clear to her knee. As I watched him stand and stretch, I realized that Bill Loon had a body that was designed for some sport that hadn't been invented yet. He reached over and around the piling, grabbed onto something I couldn't see and swung forward, suddenly leaping right onto the top of it, spread eagle, piling to belly button. With one hand he managed to reach down to where Mary Ann was hanging and grasp the pole exactly in the middle so it balanced perfectly as she released it to him. But he was in trouble right away. Trying to get leverage with one foot to get back to the dock, he was almost pulled into the water when the pole started twisting like taffy. He reached with his other hand and opened the star drag. The pole stopped bending, but the cutty hunk line began ripping through the tightened fist of his bare hand.

Even I could feel it burning into his flesh. There was blood already. He pulled himself to one side of the piling and leaped, awkwardly, but accurately back to the dock and splinters went into his back as he hit wood. He scrambled to his feet and tried to take control of the wild pole.

Mary Ann had two hands gripping the rope now, so we all kept grabbing further until we had her jacket and found that with enough slow tugging and shifting of our weight, we could get her closer until we finally rolled her right up and onto the dock. She jumped up faster than a sand crab and followed her brother cross the dock as he ran sideways.

Bill Loon stayed far from the edge of the dock. For a moment he stood completely motionless. Maybe he was trying to figure what it was. Not even his wide eyes moved. Maybe he thought the fish was gone. It happened that way sometimes. Mary Ann came up next to him. "You're not mad at me, are you?" Still he didn't move. That meant he wasn't mad. It took an awful lot to get Bill Loon mad and it was impossible before noon. He started reeling in very slowly with his bleeding right hand. He was dripping on the dock.

"Is he gone?" Mary Ann asked. We waited.

"No," Bill Loon said. "Bring something for my hand. The reel's getting sticky."

And then like a reverse bolt of lightning had suddenly shot through the dock end of the pole, down the other end went, nearly bending in two, pointing, straight at the bay and nearly causing Bill Loon to bend in after it. But Bill Loon was fourteen and he was big and he could fish. I don't mean which hook, what bait and where to stand. I mean he could really fish. Like Lash LaRue or Mighty Marvel.

Leaning back, he slackened the tension on the drag and wrapped his leg around a piling, just in case, and he started winding again. Mary Ann brought a piece of T-shirt and covered the inside of his palm where the blood was coming in little spurts.

What was it? It went toward the middle of the bay like a ray, but it went in random patterns like a shark. No one knew. Finally Junior Malstrom broke the tension with a couple of theories. First he thought it was an electric Barracuda that had been in an A-Bomb blast. Nobody even paid attention to that comment. That was probably the movie we'd see if we could ever catch enough fish to go this afternoon. Then he said the only other thing it could be was a salt water crocodile. Evidently that made more sense. At least everyone looked over at him, which he interpreted as a standing ovation. Smiling, he began to elaborate.

Bill Loon never took his eyes off the water. That meant only one thing to me. Whatever was on the hook wasn't going home tonight.

Every once in a while, he let his sister hold the pole, when the line wasn't burning friction tails into the air or the rod wasn't nearly breaking in two or the reel wasn't whining out of control. He wanted her to get the experience, I guess. I was getting plenty from right where I was.

After alternating portions of strain, sweat, wonder, worry and enough layers of Junior's commentary to bury all of us standing, up, the mysterious thing we had been waiting for suddenly spiralled close enough to the surface for all of us to see from the dock.

Mary Ann shrieked. Louder than before. She was right next to me. It was so unexpected, I screamed too. I think I even went into the air an inch or so without bending my legs. I had never done that before. And my hat blew into the bay before I could catch it.

"Cut the line!" Junior cried. "It will tear the dock apart! My uncle will kill us!"

It was a seven and a half foot leopard shark and in spite of its long ordeal, it wasn't tired. It was chewing the piling directly under us. The dock was shaking.

"It's okay, Bill. You can cut him. He's too big for you. Let's catch something else,"

Mary Ann said.

His concentration was so strong, I don't think he heard her. "You and me, Sis. We're bringing this one in," he said.

Everyone shut up, closed their eyes and tried to imagine they were somewhere else. Anywhere. Junior Malstrom tried to turn Catholic. He started crossing his chest with his finger. He wasn't joking around either. He said he heard it was okay with the Pope as long as you really meant it. He was probably lying, but I didn't care. I did a few myself.

The leopard shark was throwing his body against the pilings and barnacles flew in all directions. He flipped his tall into the line and twice it looked like Bill Loon was going to buy the bay for his sister. I looked down at the churning water, up at the sky, into the wind and every once in a while I crossed myself again, just in case I didn't get another chance.

It worked. It was a miracle. Bill Loon didn't go in the drink and the dock didn't collapse. We finally got the shark on the sand, I say we, because by this time, anyone who stayed on the dock, felt like they part of the deal.

As it thrashed on the wet shore, none of us could believe how big the monster was. It flipped its tail and hit Poley, the Blue Hollar boy, right in the back and sent him face first into the sand. He got up and walked right back to it and said "Grrr" like he was a bear, but he wasn't hurt and he wasn't mad. He was just surprised. Bill motioned to us to keep back. The big leopard was still dangerous. He pointed where there was a bullet and some buckshot in him.

"Somebody knows who this guy is," he said.

We were so tired we just sank quietly in the sand around the beast and waited while it died. Afterward, when it didn't move anymore, Poley leaned over close to it. "I say you were a good fish," he said.

It sounded funny the way he said it, but it was true. Bill Loon stood and took off his hat. So did Junior. So did Mary Ann. Everyone did. My hat was in the bay. I rubbed my hair and halfheartedly crossed myself again. Together, we rolled the shark over on its back while Junior who had been jumping and holding himself ran to the nearest log.

Bill Loon took his huge hunting knife and sliced the animal open all the way down the middle in order to clean him. That's the way Duck Fred wanted his fish. On the last swipe, we jumped back because ten or so little sharks flew out and flipped around in the sand. We thought the big leopard had eaten them for breakfast. Out of courtesy to Mary Ann and respect for the present direction of the wind, Junior was facing away, softly singing yes, yes, yes to himself. He turned his head when he heard the commotion and suddenly shouted, "That leopard shark is a cannibal!" not realizing he had turned too far. Everyone caught quick glimpse of something that was better left unseen. It happened so fast, to be truthful, I don't know what I saw, but it was connected to Junior Malstrom and I swear a river ran through it.

He finished his private moment with his back to us. But that didn't stop him from shouting over his shoulder, "Cannibal! Cannibal!"

"No! No!" Mary Ann yelled. "He's wrong. These are babies. She's a mother. This is her family." She quickly begin to carry the first of the newborn sharks, to the water. We lined up like a bucket brigade and began passing, each of the remaining ones to her while she stood knee deep in the rolling waves and eased each one of them for the very first time into their real world of salt water. At first, they went in circles, showing off their shiny new fins in a little shark show. Then two bumped into each other, turned upside down and died. When the rest of them saw that, they decided the show was over and disappeared.

We were tired and out of the mood for any more fishing. Except for Bill Loon with his mud shark and whatever Duck Fred would give him for the monster shark, none of us had caught anything to sell so we wouldn't be able to take the ferry to Eureka and go to the movies.

I looked at the huge leopard shark upright again like it was still alive. I had an idea. What if we covered it, and wheeled it house to house and charged twenty-five cents if anyone wanted to see it. Maybe we could go to the movies after all.

Bill Loon smiled slowly and over to one side. He sensed there was something basically wrong with the idea. He looked at Junior, then his sister, then the rest of us. "We can put it on a couple of wagons," I said. "It can't hurt anything," Junior said. "What can go wrong?" Bill Loon nodded and we cheered. "But don't get your hopes up. This is a fishing town. People may not want to pay to see a fish," he said.

It took all of us to lift and roll the big leopard onto the wagons. We covered everything except the wheels with an old green tarp and started down the road, taking turns pushing, pulling and walking along side like an honor guard.

At the very first house we knocked at, the woman yelled out the window, "Don't bury that bastard here!" She had been drinking and thought it was a funeral for an army deserter. She said she knew there was a body under there and if she had a phone, she would call the police. Junior Malstrom smiled and asked her if she would come to the door for just a second so we could explain quietly what we were doing. He was very comfortable talking with adults, even if they were upset, so he was our spokesman. The woman saw his smile and then realized how young we were, so she opened the door. He thanked her for hearing us out and then told her that if she tried to tell the police, there would be two bodies under the tarp. Before she had a chance to jump away, he whispered something to her. I don't know what he was saying, but her eyes got smaller and smaller. Then she said, "Okay," and threw us twenty-five cents to keep it covered and go away.

A few people paid, some weren't home then one man, a big lumber worker, said he didn't have twenty-five cents, but he wouldn't mind taking a look for free. Then he laughed and started coming out the door. He was a bully. Junior didn't mind. He was comfortable talking to lumberjacks. He stood in front of him and said, "You don't really think there is a fish under there do you? You think it's a trick to get your money."

"That's exactly what I think, Short Stuff," he said and laughed again like it was Jack and the Beanstalk and Junior had his goose.

"Okay. You can look for free," Junior said.

"Why, thank you," the man said.

"Don't thank us yet," Junior said. "Because there's one condition. If it is a leopard shark like we say and you don't pay, we get to put a curse on your house. Okay?"

"Okay," the man said. "This house is pretty much cursed anyway." And he laughed again.

"You just think it's cursed," Junior said. "Wait 'til you hear our curse. If you don't pay by thirty seconds after we show you, and I'll be counting, at the next high tide in a rainstorm, fifteen of these air-breathing maneaters are going to come crashing through your windows while you and your dog are asleep and have their way with both of you from all sides!"

We jerked the tarp off. The man shot backwards into the house and slammed the door. Junior motioned for us to wait while he counted very loud, "One thousand eight, one thousand nine . . ."

The man opened the door just a crack. "Do you have change for a dollar?" he asked.

"No," Junior Malstrom said with a big smile. "One thousand twenty-eight . . ." The door closed again and a dollar bill floated to the ground in front of us.

"Lumberjacks don't know nothin' about ocean fish," Junior said as we started off for the next house.

We weren't having much luck, then one lady seemed absolutely delighted that we were there on her doorstep. She even told Junior he gave a nice presentation about why we had come. Afterward we realized that for some reason, she completely missed the word "shark." She was so thrilled that we kids were participating in what she called "a neighborhood enrichment project" together, instead of running the sand dunes, getting into dangerous trouble and becoming juvenile delinquents. She said she was on a blue ribbon committee to improve children, but maybe she could learn some things from us. "You never know," Junior said, smiling like Mona Lisa.

She said she was more than glad to give us twenty-five cents to see our little travelling education project, as she called it. She waited. Junior held out his hand. "Oh, of course," she said. "Here's a quarter. Now what is it you *really* have under there?"

"You got wax in your ears, lady? We got exactly what we said. A giant leopard shark!" And the tarp came off.

She could scream louder than Mary Ann. "That's a nasty trick. You could stop somebody's circulation with that thing! Shame! Shame! How did you catch that? Not on somebody's dock I hope. Do your parents know about this?"

Junior Malstrom loved it. He was comfortable talking to club women. "Of course, they do, ma'am. There were ten adults supervising the whole time. It was sponsored by the Sea Scouts. Everyone had to wear two life jackets just to get on the dock. The Coast Guard, even the Mayor was there."

"What Mayor? We don't even have a mayor," she said.

"Not anymore we don't. He blew right off the dock. Everybody did. Except us. We are the only survivors."

"You are a little fibber. Soap's not good enough for your mouth. Shame! Shame! I want my twenty-five cents back," she said. "Right now."

"I wish I could do that, but my hands are tied," Junior said. "We are a no-profit enriching group. Libraries, museums, art places, movies, funny books . . ."

"You are nothing but a bunch of outlaw hooligans, charging money for heart attacks. Your parents are going to hear from my committee. So is the PTA and the sheriff!"

After that encounter, Bill Loon said to leave the tarp off. He decided it wasn't good morals to charge people money to see a dead animal, once we had enough for everyone to go to the movies. Besides he said he was getting a headache listening to Junior Malstrom talk to the neighbors; giving them malarkey, scaring them half to death and then taking their money. "This is how lynch mobs get started," he told us. Junior disagreed. He said that in order to get a lynch mob going, you need a horse or a woman that doesn't belong to you. Bill told him not to count on it.

It worked out a lot better when we left if uncovered. People were friendlier when they could see it coming. They acted a lot more normal. Just about everyone smiled and wanted to know which one of us had actually caught it. Without hesitating, Bill Loon said it was Mary Ann's catch, but her freckles started dancing and she turned red and said Bill helped her more than just a lot. But he said he talked her through a couple of tough spots. That was all. Did we shoot it for her? No, that was done some time ago. It was her catch all the way. Line catch. No guns. Look close, see? Old wounds. So by that afternoon, and in the days that followed, it was generally known and accepted that Mary Ann Loon had caught the biggest shark from a line on a dock that anyone could remember on Humboldt Bay. Later on, she got her picture in the paper and the cannery, whose workers had been constantly terrorized by it and had tried to shoot it, were giving her a hundred-dollar reward until they found out she had put ten more of them back in the bay.

For some reason, Junior Malstrom was angry at Bill Loon for letting Mary Ann take all the credit. Bill said that's the way he wanted it. He said it was a present to her. Just like a birthday or Christmas, only instead of giving her something he bought or made, he gave her something that happened. "You can't give something that happened to somebody else. It's again the laws of nature," Junior said.

"There will be years and years and plenty of chances for me to catch all the fish I want," Bill said. "It may not be that way for Mary Ann."

"Not the crazy ass way she fishes, it won't," Junior said.

The three of us were walking back to the Loon house to celebrate. Junior and I were invited to dinner. The sun was setting over the sand dunes. How could it be getting dark? I was thinking it's still morning when I was looking at the peaceful sky, and heard "Crab salad sandwiches!" Time is so funny.

I realize Junior is still arguing and Bill is tired. But Junior keeps it up and Bill decides to grab Junior's wool shirt, lift him up and start screaming in his eyes. "I want you to see this picture, Junior. Mary Ann is willing to go in the bay so she can catch a good fish. And she gets lucky. Now, while I am gutting it and you are pissing over your shoulder yelling 'Cannibal,' Mary Ann is putting more baby leopard sharks back in the bay than most people are going to see in their whole life. That's why she deserves it. And if you ever mention it again, you are going to be stuffed and mounted right here on the front of my house, next to my Dad's moose you broke the antler off of. That way I can talk to you every day without you yapping about who caught the leopard shark. Mary Ann caught the leopard shark!" Bill puts him down. "Okay?" Bill asks in a quieter voice.

"It's not okay." Junior is madder than a half-boiled lobster and almost as red. He swings at Bill Loon, but Bill jumps back and I almost get it in the face. Their words and actions are all mixed up, like seeing a book right in front of me without having to read. Junior is on Bill Loon's back hitting his ears. Bill spins around to throw Junior off and his engineer boots almost take off my head. I'm too small for these guys. I realize that words come to me sometimes out of books I never read. That's why I'm mixed up. Now I'm seeing a book and nobody even wrote it.

I jump away to find some tall grass on solid ground where I can feel safe until it's over. But in Fairhaven, grass is scarce and the only solid ground is sand, the oldest servant to the wind. It has been sifted and scattered side-angle through so many centuries of constant orders, all that's left is a shadow of something solid. A deserted drifter. Spread too thin for tenure. I dig my heels into the softness of the servant and wait. No wonder I don't feel safe around here most of the time. Three of the things of life, air and sand and water have no tolerance for fire. Even a flame as small as mine. I see they are laughing and shaking hands at last. I come of out of the lupines. They want to know if I ran away because I got scared or if I went to take a pee. I don't answer.

They laugh and tell me they're sorry. They say I almost got clobbered a couple of times. Probably almost killed, Junior has to add, nodding his head way up and down. I know they don't play with ten year olds. They are so old they probably don't even call it play anymore. I don't even know what they do call it. I know they don't call it work. I tell them that I'm kind of tired after everything, today. Maybe I better come to dinner some other time. They tell me no, no, no. They want me, Mary Ann wants me, his mother wants me, his dad, everybody. They do? I don't understand. I'm glad everybody wants me to eat, but I don't understand.

"You must be one of those guys who are so smart, they are stupid," Junior says. "I read about them."

"Where? In *Classics Illustrated*?" Bill Loon says and hits his knee. "You came up with the idea to take the shark around. That's why. It's turned out to be the biggest thing around here in a couple of months. Somebody called. They want to put Mary Ann's picture in the paper."

"Besides, you're funny and you don't eat much," Junior says and we all laugh.

I'm glad everything is quiet and stupid again. No more shark fights tonight, I hope. As we are sitting on the front porch of the Loon house, smells of steaming food are coming out of the screen door. Candles are burning brightly on the dining table. I feel safe. Bill's sister and mother are making dinner and laughing, freckles of two generations dancing all over the kitchen.

| Frederick Barthelme | *Torch Street* |

VICKY AND ROSWELL were in his stepfather's living room in the house on Torch Street in Bay St. Louis, Mississippi, three blocks from the water. If they went out into the street and leaned over and looked real hard, they could see a little thumbnail of Gulf under the heavy arch of the trees. Vicky had just come in. Roswell was stretched out on the shiny green velour sofa.

"What are you watching?" she said.

"I'm not watching anything," he said.

"You appear to be watching this television over here," she said.

"Be that as it may," he said. He had on jeans, rubber sandals, a white T-shirt, and was on his stomach on the couch. She had come home on her motorbike and looked a little windblown. She wore a seersucker shirt and carried a comically big crash helmet covered with gaudy purple graphics. She stood inside the front door, the helmet dangling from her hand, and stared at the television which was showing a picture of some airplanes, some old passenger airplanes, with an inset picture of some furry animal crawling around the rocks near a stream. Roswell was clicking up still pictures from the other channels on two sides of the screen.

"How many eyes you got?" she said.

"Forty," he said. His voice was muffled—he was talking into the pillow.

"Where's Jack, anyway?" she said. She took a couple of steps and sat down on the arm of the sofa. Roswell jerked his feet out of her way.

"Went for chicken," Roswell said.

"Great," Vicky said. "It's going to rain."

It was dark in the living room. The blinds were three-quarters closed and the skies outside were overcast, so there wasn't much light. The TV color looked aggravated by having all the stills frozen on the screen. There were pictures of police, weather maps, people hunting for something in a field, an irate short man with bristly hair, a Senator from somewhere. The window air conditioner rattled and hummed, stuffing the bungalow with damp, cool air.

Jack was the stepfather. The three of them had lived in the house on Torch Street for six months. Before that, Jack was there alone. Roswell had an apartment in a scummy complex down by the fishery where everything smelled of bad shrimp. He'd run out of money and asked if he could stay at the house. Jack agreed—he was happy to have the company. Then Jack met Vicky and brought her home from the casino where they both worked. It was a date for them, a little barbecue, but it went wrong right away. Roswell and Vicky hit it off, and Jack *was* older, was dreaming, and he knew it.

"You're a void," Vicky said, spinning the helmet into the air as if it were a football. She caught it heading for the kitchen.

"Throw me some chips or something," Roswell said. He was flicking the picture-in-picture back and forth, so he was picking up sound from different shows. On the mammal show he caught somebody saying, "Beaver lodge, my home . . . not only my home, but the home of my beaver people . . ."

He repeated that a couple times.

"What?" Vicky said from the kitchen. "No chips."

"What've you got?" he said.

She stood in front of the cabinet, one hand on each of the cabinet door knobs. "Oreos, gum, animal crackers—*the endangered collection*—Crazy Dough, Twizzlers."

"Oreos," he said. The air conditioner, a fat old brown Fedders with a dusty grille in the dining room window, did a triple clunk and cut off with a hissing sound. Vicky half-shut one of the doors and looked into the dining room at the air conditioner.

"Is that thing okay?" she said.

"It's older than you are," Roswell said.

"Got gas," she said. She grabbed the crackley bag of Oreos, stripped off the rubber band, took a cookie out and ate it as she carried the bag back to Roswell. "I think we ought to get married maybe. Move out of here."

"Too young," he said.

"Who?" she said.

"All of us," he said.

The room was dark and cluttered. Big furniture and heavy drapes, green to match the couch. Heavy chairs and a big sideboard and a couple of dark mahogany dining chairs put in the corner to keep them out of the way. The carpet was thick and musty and old. When you walked on it, you could hear the aching floor underneath. A thin stream of light cut in between the blinds of one of the windows, suddenly brightening the room. Gritty little dust circled in the light.

"This room is glowing," Vicky said. "Like those paintings where the guy has the candle, you know? Like the picture is glowing from inside?"

"It's me," Roswell said.

"Give me another cookie," she said, reaching down to get one out of the bag. "I'm going to be twenty-two pretty soon."

"Yeah, and I'm going to be a hair technician for Al Sharpton," he said.

"It's not that far," she said. She swiveled toward the television set, sat down on the floor with her back against the sofa.

"In the way," he said.

"You weren't watching," she said.

"I started watching after you came," he said.

"Did not," she said.

He shoved her aside by the shoulder. Her hair was red, short, kind of hacked off on one side. The neck was pale and thin. She wore glasses with black rims.

"Is Jack going to support us forever?" she said. She was gnawing the icing off half an Oreo.

"If we're lucky," Roswell said.

"He loves me more than life itself," she said.

"Mean," Roswell said. "You're a fresh young thing. You've got the natural charm. Everybody loves you. I don't know anybody who doesn't love you."

"We could find somebody if we looked hard," she said. "Darrin." Darrin was her last boyfriend.

"He doesn't count," Roswell said. "He's the one before the present one, if you know what I mean."

"Lies," Vicky said.

Jack came in with a fifteen-piece box of Popeye's, a quart of mashed potatoes, a quart of coleslaw, a pint of gravy, and nine biscuits. He was a chunky guy, an ex-beat cop from Chicago who had moved to the coast years before when he had married Roswell's mother. The mother had inherited a gas station on the beach highway. She and Jack worked it day and night, made plenty. When the marriage blew up, she got everything. He had to start a new career, so he started dealing blackjack at the Grand Casino in Gulfport, for six dollars an hour and tips. He'd worked the graveyard shift for a year and a half, but now he was working swing. Usually eight to four. He was used to eating dinner early. Roswell's mother had moved to Arizona.

"How you doing, Vicky?" Jack said, dusting his fingers over her hair as he went into the dining room and put the food on the table.

"Never better," she said. She got up and followed him and started unpacking the dinner, setting the table with paper towels for place mats and other paper towels folded into napkins.

"How's young Lochinvar over there?" Jack said.

"He's great," Roswell said.

"He's watching the beaver show," Vicky said. "And fifteen others."

Roswell said, "Not only my home, but the home of my beaver people . . ."

"Beavers," his stepfather said. "Check."

He was already half in casino uniform-black slacks, black shoes, white tux shirt. He didn't have the suspenders or his red tie-he kept those in the car. Dealing wasn't bad, especially in Mississippi, where things didn't cost much. He'd bought the house after the divorce for under forty thousand, complete with furniture, and he hadn't touched a hair on its head. An old woman had died in the house. At first Jack acted as if that scared him, but he gave it up. He was a decent looking guy, a little haggard maybe, with black hair that stayed combed whether he liked it or not, ruddy complexion, rough skin, the smell of cologne. And good-looking hands—he had his hands done once a week at a salon. It wasn't required, but when he was in blackjack school, they'd given him a list of places.

He brought two bottles of beer out of the kitchen and put them alongside the paper-towel place mat Vicky had made for him at the head of the table.

"Well, come on," he said. "I'm not waiting all day."

She brought the strawberry preserves and sat down with him. Roswell didn't move much.

"I like it cold," Roswell said.

"He would, wouldn't he?" Jack said to Vicky.

"He loves you a lot," she said, patting Jack's forearm. She had one leg folded under her and she sat up a little bit and leaned over the table so she could see into the box of chicken. "You want breast or thigh?"

"One each," Jack said.

She fished chicken parts out of the box and dropped them on Jack's plate. They used high quality paper plates—Chinet brand.

"He's never getting off the couch, is he?" Jack said.

"Not since I got here," Vicky said.

"At least it's not MTV," Jack said.

"I'm going to watch that later," Roswell said. He groaned and rolled off the couch, landing on his knees by the coffee table. Then he came in and took a drumstick out of the box and began eating it as he stood by the table, looking at the big Fedders. "We may be getting married."

"Uh huh," Jack said.

"I'm sort of serious," Roswell said.

"You are?" Vicky asked.

"Yeah, kind of," he said.

"We've been thinking about it," she said to Jack.

"Fine with me," he said. "Where you all going to live?"

"Here, if it's okay," she said. She looked at Jack, then Roswell. "I don't think anything has to change. Do you, Roswell?"

"Don't know," Roswell said.

"I'm worried about change," Jack said. "I don't like it. And I like you here anyway. I want you to stay."

"It'll be fine," Roswell said.

"Are you going to have a baby?" Jack said.

She laughed and snapped his cuff down over his wrist. "Nope. No babies," she said. "Never a baby. There are enough already."

"Too many," Roswell said. "People buy and sell 'em."

"Oh, hush," Vicky said.

"It's in the papers all the time," he said.

"How would you know? You never read," she said.

"So maybe it's on television. I've *seen* it. Rich people want babies but they only buy this certain kind and they go black market in Atlanta or someplace."

"Lots of babies in orphanages," Vicky said.

"We could become big suppliers," Roswell said.

"Well, keep it down in there," Jack said. He had a little hooked piece of fried chicken skin caught on the side of his lip.

"I might want to get a dog," Vicky said.

"Oh yeah?" Jack said.

"Sure," she said. "A big dog, something you could play with and walk around with and do stuff. Labrador. Yellow."

"Cost you a couple hundred to get a good one," Roswell said.

After Jack left for work, Vicky and Roswell got on her scooter and rode out Menge Avenue to Lake Forgetful, a couple miles inland. It was a tiny pond, really, maybe three, four acres, with a trailer park built around one end. There was a visitors' parking area with room enough for six cars on the road leading up to the trailer park. That's where Roswell put the scooter. There were ducks on the water, and a few lights in the tall pine trees that surrounded the lake which, in the dark, looked bigger than it really was. They walked arm-in-arm around the water in one direction, then turned and walked around in the other direction. They were kids, young lovers, just happy to be touching each other, to have their bodies colliding, to have their hips bumping into each other. She flattened her hand into the back pocket of his jeans. He felt the curve of her waist beneath the thin seersucker shirt. She was wearing a burgundy bra underneath.

"Why do that? That shirt? that bra?" he asked.

"I'm not trying to hide anything," she said.

"I'll say," he said. "You don't think it's a little—obvious?"

"I'd have to wear it on my forehead," she said. "In the world today." She swung around in front of him, walked backward, matching her steps to his. She held her arms out as if to showcase the bra, then said, "You know, sometimes I just want to kiss you for ages. We could be joined at the mouth. Wouldn't that be great?"

"We'd get a workout," he said.

She stopped and waited for him to catch her, then put a finger on his chin. "Make your lips soft," she said. "I want to kiss you."

"They're already soft," he said.

A moon was sliding up behind the pines. It filled the clearing over the lake with vanilla light. Cars fizzed by on the highway. There was some dinky music coming from the trailer park. Pine needles everywhere.

"What if we lived up here?" Vicky said. "We could have a place of our own. I bet these things cost next to nothing."

"They cost plenty," he said.

"I wouldn't mind having a baby," she said. "It would be like having a talking dog."

"They're not as sturdy," Roswell said. "Two legs. And they got brains. Say the wrong thing it drives 'em crazy. They grow up maniacs."

An owl hooted in a tree somewhere. Leaves rustled. The water lapped uncertainly at the edge of the lake. Lights winked on and off in the trailer park. Somebody came out and a screen door slammed. People were laughing, coming toward them.

"Babies don't have much hair," Vicky said. "Wrong kind, too. There's somebody coming here." She pointed behind them, toward the trailer park. They stopped and turned around and looked toward the sounds. They were almost directly across the water from the trailers. Two figures came out of the pines, out of the darkness, and stood at the lake's edge, laughing.

One of them said, "Why is heroin better than a woman?"

The other one said, "Huh?"

"Why is heroin better than a woman?" the first one said.

The second one laughed. Then with a rush, they heard one of the men pissing into the water, then the other one started.

"So that's how they do it," Vicky said in a whisper.

"Shh," Roswell said.

"Well?" the first guy said.

"I don't know. I give up," the second guy said.

They both laughed some more and finished up and started back for the trailers.

"Ah, you guys," Vicky whispered. "C'mon. What is it? What's the answer?"

When the men were gone, Vicky and Roswell skirted the end of the lake, crunching through the noisy grass. When they got to the parking spot, Vicky made an elaborate business of getting into her helmet-she smacked herself a couple of times in the head, readjusted the chin strap, grabbed the helmet with both hands and wiggled it until she was comfortable. She looked ready for space travel.

"I'm driving," she said, swinging a leg over the seat.

"Fine for me," Roswell said.

She kicked the scooter's engine to life and twisted the thing around, settling on the seat and bouncing. He got on the back and they shot out from under the high pines, away from Lake Forgetful. They went back into town and rode the beach highway toward home, Roswell with his arms around her tiny waist. She was singing as she drove. There was a lot of wind. Sleek and mysterious cars zoomed by them. Lights sparkled out over the Gulf. He kissed the back of her flashy helmet, sure that she would never know.

Micah Perks	*Anyone Is Possible*

HEAL ALL. Goldenseal. Blessed Thistle. Caroline is in the natural foods store in front of the long wall of herbs and spices. She is not shopping. This is her secret recipe for nerves: stand in front of the wall. Read the names off the clean glass jars in alphabetical rows. Angelica. Bee Pollen. Coltsfoot. She has no idea what any of them does except the easy ones—basil or thyme. But she imagines that every malady has its curative spice. Eyebright for myopia, intruders driven away with Blessed Thistle. Sometimes, when she is looking at the wall she has vague ideas of buying an herb book and filling her kitchen with row on row of small amber bottles, each with its own particular saving grace. Sometimes she unscrews the jars (she likes the sound) and takes a look in. Most of the jars are filled with small twigs. Most of them smell like hay.

Today her nerves are bad and the spices don't work completely; even sticking her nose over a curry smelling jar labeled Elder Flowers doesn't do the trick. She still feels it—a small round itch on the back of her hand, bug-bite sized, calling to be scratched. The nervous itch returned with the news of a murder in Boulder last night—a whole family of four shot in their heads, doused in gasoline and burned. Caroline thinks, there must be something else to think about, something besides these murdered strangers. Lemon Balm. Lobelia. Motherwort.

"Can I get something for you?"

Caroline is embarrassed—she wonders if the store people think she is weird—loitering in front of the spices. She opens a jar of Frankincense Tears and picks out a small, ginger-colored lump. "One of these, please."

"One?" the woman says. She is wearing a karate jacket and loose black pants.

Caroline nods. She follows the back of the karate jacket through the rows of over-priced, exotic vegetables. She gets misted by the continual spray of water that keeps the bok choy and Jerusalem artichokes glistening. At the check-out, Caroline says she doesn't need a bag. The clerk rings up three cents.

Caroline leaves the store. She drops the lump of Frankincense Tears into her breast pocket. She had been too embarrassed to ask the clerk what to do with it. Boulder has its usual sweet sky—high and blue and balmy, even in January. It's four in the afternoon and Arapahoe Avenue is empty. The spices were just a detour—she is on her way swimming. She takes the bike path to the university. She has a gym membership there. The path isn't beautiful and leafy yet, it is still under construction—it looks bare and urban.

All they know about the murders is that there was no forced entry. The smoke alarm alerted the neighbor. The mother and stepfather and six year old daughter were just charred bundles on the living room couch. The teen-age daughter was tied to a bed—shot and burned and never untied. Caroline realizes her hand is itching again. Suddenly, she does not feel safe on this path, the one she takes every day to the pool. Anyone could be anywhere—behind the piles of dirt or parked machinery. She turns around and starts back. She walks quickly, stiff-legged, out of breath. She glances over her shoulder. She feels adrenalin stinging through her arms and chest. She begins a stiff-legged run and makes it out onto Arapahoe Avenue. Boulder is ruined, she thinks, trying to regain her breath.

Between college and Colorado, Caroline waitressed in New York City. She hated everything about New York: the sinister looking bohemians dressed in black, the bad characters sprawled dangerously close to her on the subway or brushing against her on the street. She had never seen a rat or a cockroach before New York City. Most of all, she hated the crime. The possibility of it every time she fumbled for her keys in the vestibule of her apartment building, every time the grey doors of the service elevator opened to take her in. She longed for bars on her third story window. It was in New York that she had started her nervous itching. Scratching the back of her hand until it bled, scabbed and she could itch the scab off. She tried everything—wearing gloves, cutting her nails down, even steroid cremes. Still, she would feel a terrific urge to rake—all the time, in the middle of the night, on the subway, in front of a customer at the Mexican restaurant. It was impossible.

Her husband, Alan, then just her boyfriend and the cook in the restaurant, said her fears were irrational. "As long as you look tough, no one will bother you," he said. "You watch too much TV. The rash on your hand will go away when you want it to. But," he said, "if you really want a mellow place to live, Boulder is different. No way you could itch in Boulder." And when they moved there it seemed he was perfectly right.

People were friendly. They all wore bright, fleecy sports clothes and smiled and said, "Hey!" when you passed them on the street. They struck up conversations about skiing conditions on the check-out line. The air seemed thinner and dryer, and at first she had gotten dizzy whenever she moved quickly. Alan said her blood had to change, acclimate to the altitude. She liked that. She was even acquiring new, clean blood.

Almost as soon as she moved the itch disappeared, her hand healed over and she met her best friend, Avril. Later, she told Avril about her nervous itch and her fear of crime in New York. Caroline said she had decided that the frequency of violent crime was a myth propagated by the media to keep women from venturing out into the world. When she told Avril this they were sitting on Caroline's veranda drinking yellow Mexican beer. Caroline had stretched out her arms and felt her blood, full of strength and clarity, running down her arms. "Just think of all those New Yorkers," she said, "hiding in their apartments watching murders on television and scratching themselves." She had laughed, free of fear, surrounded by Colorado.

But Avril had not laughed. She had asked what kind of locks Caroline and Alan had on their door. Yesterday, Avril dropped off a sweet grass smudge stick. "If you burn this in the house, you'll purify it," she said, "drive away an evil fate." It bothers Caroline—the way Avril takes her fear seriously. She almost feels like blaming Avril instead of the murders for this new case of nerves.

She has walked the long way round to the pool. Swimming calms her almost as well as the spice wall does. She shows the cage attendant her card, puts on her black cap and goggles and submerges. But some annoying person in a purple suit keeps passing her, slapping her toes to tell her to move aside. Ruining her concentration. The woman careens through the pool in a breathless churning of water, then stands gasping at the shallow end for a few minutes. Then she does it again. Suddenly Caroline realizes that the woman in the purple suit is Avril. The next time Avril takes her gasping break, Caroline pulls up too.

"Caroline!" Avril says, "I didn't realize that was you. God! You're probably ready to kill me for mowing you down." Avril's voice echoes off the walls.

"No, I didn't even notice." Caroline yanks her goggles off. "You got a new suit." Avril and Caroline often meet at the pool, but they usually swim in adjoining lanes so they can kick board and talk. Now, they wade to the edge of the pool to avoid the lap swimmers. "How are you?"

Avril laughs in that bursting way she has. "Lovely."

Caroline laughs too. "What's going on with which man?"

Avril laughs again. "Don't ask. The same dilemma."

It's hard to hear Avril over the splash and echo of the pool, but Caroline knows the story by heart. Avril has been breaking up and getting back together with Leon for the two years that Caroline and Avril have been friends. Then Caroline introduced her to Rich, and for the last three months she has been breaking up and getting back together with both of them at the same time.

"There's just this tremendous spiritual connection," Avril says now.

"With Leon."

"Yeah—it's like we're telepathic. It's crazy—ever since I first saw Leon with his sensitive Elvis smirk—it was immediate." Avril loves Elvis. She has a shrine to Elvis in her frame shop: a plaster bust of him on a Greek column. She hangs trashy articles on the shrine—"Elvis seen in K-Mart" and "On the Moon" and "Lizard Man Walks Hand in Hand with Elvis." The customers love it. Avril even has two pit bulls, one named Elvis, the other Presley. She always ends her stories about men by saying, "Whatever happened to those sensitive, misunderstood rebels like Elvis?"

That was why Caroline introduced her to Rich. She thought he fit the bill. Rich works in the Mexican health food restaurant that she and Alan own. Rich's mother is Mexican, and he has that burnt sienna skin. He has muscles. He has two gold hoops in his ear and pouting lips. Mostly he has this rip in his white t-shirt: a narrow triangle that begins under his arm and ends across his right nipple. There is something outrageous about his clean, dark skin and that white, ripped cloth and then the darker nipple. Plus he told Caroline right away that he taught Tai Chi so Caroline thought he was perfect—sensitive (Tai Chi) and rebel (t-shirt rip). On their first date Rich and Avril had gone rock climbing, and then meditated afterwards. They had sex on the cliff and during and after meditation. Avril said it was the most AMAZING sex she ever had, but she just didn't feel a Spiritual Connection. Rich fell in love.

"Leon's the mind, Rich is the body—tragically separated," Avril says.

"But what a body," Caroline says, embarrassing herself with the catch in her voice.

"But what a mind," Avril says. "Leon's an incredible painter. We can talk about art for hours." Caroline and Avril climb out of the pool, pull off their goggles, collect their small white towels.

"So what's the problem?" Caroline already knows the problem, but she likes Avril to tell it this way, like a soap opera: going back to the beginning before adding the new installment. It's exciting and soothing at the same time. Caroline's own story is simple—there is no intrigue, no building tension. Caroline loves Alan, but it's not the kind of love that makes a good story. They have been together for five years and sex has always been comforting. Her favorite part is afterwards: she and Alan curled around each other under the quilt, her blood like whisked egg white, everything soft—Alan's skin, the pillow, the muslin curtain at the window. Sustained happiness isn't that interesting, Caroline says when Avril asks how she is. Still, it bothers her that she may have lost something, some opportunity given up—and that this lost thing is amazing.

Under the spray of hot water and the smell of Caroline's peach shampoo, Avril continues her story. "I haven't been physically attracted to Leon in a long time—years. Meanwhile, Rich hardly communicates, but he's so incredibly sexy. It's a wordless communication. And it's so easy to think words don't matter but then when I'm with Leon—we have this mind connection—"

—Caroline interrupts her. "I think you're creating this."

"You do?" Avril's heard this part before too.

"You're creating this mind/body split that isn't really there." They leave the showers and move over to the green lockers. Caroline has to try her combination lock three times. Avril is weighing herself, clicking her tongue at the scale. "I don't believe in extremes—good and evil, mind and body—you're pushing these guys into corners. Rich isn't dumb and you used to think Leon was sexy, right?"

"You could be right. But I'm still going to wait for the Third Man. The one who knows how to screw and make conversation at the same time."

"There is no third man, except in television commercials. And Elvis movies." Caroline enjoys dishing out truth like this—no frills, no nonsense. Personally, Caroline thinks Leon is a loser. He has totally sold out to the current Southwestern craze. All he paints now are Native Americans and lizards and howling wolves in desert colors. Plus she can't even look at Leon. He has a disturbing tattoo on his face—three baby blue tear drops dripping out the corner of his left eye. He's handsome in a Boulder, blond pony-tailed way, but there is something unbearable about those tears. And Rich. That tear in his t-shirt. Caroline imagines putting her fingers in the tear, widening it.

As they walk out of the gym, Caroline's long hair, not completely dry, tingles at the scalp. It is dusk, chilly. "Where's your jeep?" Caroline asks Avril.

"It's broken again, as usual."

"How are you going to get home?"

"Hitch."

"Are you joking? Nobody hitches. It's dark out."

"It's not far. I know almost everybody that drives up that road anyway." Avril lives ten miles up Boulder Canyon, in a cabin with her two dogs.

"No way are you hitching, Avril," Caroline says. "We'll walk to my house, and I'll drive you home." Caroline likes this idea: she will have company on the trek home.

"Okay," Avril says. They walk arm in arm through the cold city. The street lights are humming, the cars are switching on their headlights. They walk down the bike path and the murdered family land like a heavy arm on Caroline's shoulder. "How is your self-defense class?" she asks Avril.

"I don't think I could do any damage, yet. I don't go enough." They walk past the food co-op, all lit up, green and glittery as Eden. "Dusk is a lonely time," Caroline says. Avril squeezes her arm and agrees.

Finally they arrive at Caroline's Toyota. They climb in and Caroline tells Avril to buckle up. She checks the gas. She locks her door. It will be scary, she thinks, driving home in the dark down the canyon, alone. What if the car breaks down? She turns on her lights and pulls out. They drive out of Boulder onto the steep winding road towards Nederland and Avril's cabin. People have seen mountain lions on this road. The rock walls rise above them on either side. A truck rattles past. Bruce Coburn's angry voice rises out of the speakers, wishing for a rocket launcher.

Because she can think of nothing else, Caroline finally says, a little embarrassed, as if her obsession will show in her voice, "Did you hear about those murders?"

"Yes," Avril says. "It was eerie."

"Eerie in what way?"

"In—" Avril looks out her window. "In the way it echoed something that happened to me."

Caroline doesn't say anything at first. What Avril says shocks her. They are best friends. Avril has told Caroline her whole life in meticulous, sometimes exhilarating, sometimes tedious, detail. She has never told her about anything remotely like these murders. Finally Caroline says, as if she cannot back away from what is expected of her, "What do you mean?"

"When I lived in Aspen. That's why Leon and I moved here. We couldn't deal with Aspen after what happened."

"But you never told me this," Caroline says, almost as if that proves it isn't true. "What happened?"

"Someone broke into our house." Avril's voice fills the little car so full, Caroline has the urge to open the window to let some of it out. "He broke in through the basement. Around three in the morning."

"Who broke in?" Caroline has the absurd feeling that Avril is making this up.

"I don't know, they never caught him. He had on a mask. One of those ski things."

"What did he do?"

"He came into our bedroom. We were asleep, naked, in the bed. It's a little confusing because I, you know, was woken from sleep."

Caroline can't figure out Avril's voice. It seems so calm, like a recording.

"Does it upset you to talk about it?" Caroline says.

"No, I've been through it a thousand times, you know, with the police and in therapy and whatever."

"So he woke you in your bed?"

"At first we fought him, Leon and me. He tried to throw a blanket over our heads, but Leon punched him I think, and then all of a sudden Leon said, 'Stop fighting.' I didn't know it then but the guy had cut Leon across the chest."

"What? What? But, how could he? Leon is fine."

"Yeah, it was just a shallow cut. The man had a very sharp butcher's knife, luckily."

"Then what did he do?" Caroline asks.

"Then he cut the telephone cord and a lamp cord and tied us up to chairs in the dining room. He wanted money. Probably for drugs. But of course we didn't have any money, only like twenty dollars. He kept thinking we were hiding it. He stayed for about an hour and a half, then he left."

"But why? What did he do for an hour and a half?"

"He was freaked-out. He paced around a lot. Leon didn't say a single word. He was bleeding. Although at the time I didn't know it. We were blind-folded."

"You didn't say that before," Caroline says. She realizes she sounds like a prosecuting attorney. "It must have been terrible," she adds quickly.

"I tried to reason with the guy and he got crazed. I said, you know, 'Just leave, we don't have any money.' I remember saying, 'Don't you realize you're scaring us?' I was naked, and he tried to pry my legs apart. He threatened me. He said if I didn't shut up he would have to kill us both. His voice was weird—high and nasal. He shoved his fingers into my vagina."

Avril takes a breath. "You know, at first I thought he just wanted to rob us. But then I realized there was a good chance he was going to kill us. So I shut up."

Caroline sees Avril's house and turns in the driveway. Immediately there is a rush of barking, and the two dogs attack the car. Caroline switches the engine off. They sit there, staring into the few feet of frosted dirt lit by the headlights. She wishes Avril's voice would stop, but it doesn't.

"Afterwards, Leon and I were kind-of glued together by the experience. He was the only person who understood. But I didn't want to have sex with him anymore. And I still don't. I try to break up all the time, but, see, the week after it happened he came home with those tears tattooed on his face. And we both knew why they were there. We've never mentioned them though, neither of us. How could I leave him?"

Caroline opens the window a crack and breathes in the cold air. A pit bull growls into the opening. Slobber rolls down the glass. Avril says, "Presley! Down boy!"

"Aren't you scared to live alone?" Caroline's voice is hoarse.

"No, it's okay. I have the dogs. The thing that bothered me the most about those murders last night was that the guy killed their dog—a German shepherd."

Caroline doesn't know what to say. She remembers the hard lump in her breast pocket. "Here," she says to Avril. "It's Frankincense Tears. It does something good. I'm not sure what."

Avril licks it with her tongue. "Yuck. It doesn't taste good. Anyway, you don't believe in things like this."

"Things like what?"

Avril drops the Frankincense Tears on top of a pile of change in the ash tray. "You know, third men and herbal crap."

"Avril, can I ask you something?"

"Sure. What?"

"Well, you know how you always imagine these kinds of things and see it on TV or whatever. And it's almost unbearable, imagining it. Sometimes I've thought it would be a relief if it really happened, like the real thing would be better than always waiting for it and thinking about it. I guess I'm asking, is it really as bad as you imagine?"

"It's worse. I better go in Caroline. The dogs are going crazy."

They hug each other. Caroline says, "I'm glad you told me, but, I mean, this kind of thing is so rare, like a freak accident or something."

"It happens to a lot of women, more than you know. But. Life goes on. I'll call you tomorrow." Avril opens the door and pats her dogs. She whistles for them to follow her. Caroline watches her enter her cabin. A light comes on. Quickly, Caroline smashes the lock down on Avril's side of the car. She yanks the Toyota out of the drive-way and starts back down the mountain, fast. She forces herself to slow down. What if she had an accident now? She keeps going over the story that Avril told her, imagining it. She shuts off the music. The whining is driving her crazy. She turns a curve and sees the lights of Boulder, all pretty below her. She drives into town. According to the neon sign at the bank it is only seven at night.

She pulls into her driveway and doesn't stop to lock the car door. She runs into the house, double bolts it. She switches on every light on the first floor. She looks at the dark stairway leading upstairs. She doesn't have the courage to climb up. She calls Alan at the restaurant. "Alan, it's me. I'm really upset. I need you."

"Honey, my shift just started. I'm the only cook on. What's wrong?"

"Avril told me a terrible story."

"Don't listen to Avril. Her life is a two-ring circus. She's not normal."

"Alan, please. I'm not joking."

"Hold on."

She hears the metal scrape of cooking in the background and the voice of one of the waitresses: "There's no way he's going to eat this. I told you he was a macro."

Alan comes back on. "Listen, I can get off a couple hours early, so I'll be home by nine. If you don't want to be alone, why don't you call a friend? Okay? I've got to go, we're really busy."

"What are you cooking?" Caroline asks.

"What am I cooking? Ah. I don't know. Enchiladas, no they've already gone out. Look, I've got to go. I'll be home soon."

Caroline hangs up the phone. She stands in the middle of the house. What could Alan do for her anyway? She pictures Leon, bleeding, blind-folded in a chair. Those useless blue tear drops dripping down his cheek. She can't get herself to move. She notices she is scratching the back of her hand. She stops. She thinks, I cannot bare the possibility that my Third Man will enter through the basement, carrying a butcher's knife. She sees the sweet grass smudge that Avril gave her. She grabs it. Green dust falls onto the wooden floor. Caroline forces herself to walk into the kitchen for a match. She holds the match to the end of the sweet grass. The smudge glows, turns black and begins to smoke. It smells like marijuana. She inches through the house, waving the bundle of dried grasses in front of her, the slim thread of sweet smoke trailing behind her.

Mark
Wisniewski | *Pocket*

To BE HONEST, I don't know exactly when Pocket moved in here. All I remember is waking up one Saturday and going downstairs to take a piss and seeing a flat-headed dude with his jacket still on passed out face-down on our living room couch. His one arm hung over the side of the couch and his fingers were so close to a pair of them aviator glasses on the floor that you could hardly have slid a razor blade in between there. I was walking past the couch when he took a deep breath through his nose and lifted that flat-backed head and saw me, the skin on his forehead looking like a waffle from the upholstery on the couch. We both pretended he didn't see me. He went back to sleep and I went to take the piss.

When I got up for good that afternoon, I'd forgotten all about him, I didn't remember him until the next afternoon when a phone rang in our basement. Which at first I thought was from the TV, because we didn't have a phone. Then it rang again and Konat told me that there was a dude named Pocket living in the basement who put a phone in, paid all those deposits and hookup fees and everything. Only we couldn't use it unless we asked him.

I asked Konat why they called this guy Pocket. He said Pocket wouldn't say. I asked why Pocket was living in the basement when there was an empty room upstairs. He said something about Pocket wanting privacy, and right away I figured Pocket gay. The way he looked at me the morning before that fit right in with that, plus he had them aviator glasses.

But then Konat told me a story I sometimes like to remember.

He says that Pocket used to go to college. Says Pocket was taking this test and has some formulas written on the palm of his hand but ends up not needing them and forgets they are there and can't read a test question, so he raises his hand and the professor sees the formulas. Professor says, Let's see that. Pocket clenches his fist. Professor grabs Pocket's wrist and says, Let's see. Pocket says, right in front of the whole college class, You're not seeing anything inside this fist, just stars inside your head if you don't let go my goddamn arm. Professor says, Let's go visit the Dean. Pocket says, Let go. Professor doesn't let go, so Pocket makes a fist with his clean hand and lets the professor have one on the jaw, the professor's lit pipe flies across the room and lands in some smart fat girl's lap. Right on the crotch. Next day Pocket gets kicked out of college for hitting a professor in front of a whole college class, and for cheating.

Now for that first couple weeks there, neither Konat or me hardly heard or saw a sign of Pocket. Just his phone ringing and the bright yellow piss he left in the can. Then just like that Konat up and went to Minnesota, where I later heard he married a dancer with a snake tattooed on her neck.

For a week or so after Konat left I felt pretty alone here, even though that basement phone always rang at dinnertime and Pocket was always down there to answer it.

Then one night I was sitting on the living room couch and there was this bang on the door. I turned around and looked and Pocket exploded in, red-faced drunk. His eyebrows were black as charcoal and thick as my thumb and slanted down toward his nose, which was shaped like a baby's. I never saw a nose like that on anyone that big, Pocket probably went six-four, two-thirty. I guess our conversation got rolling after I asked him why they called him Pocket which made his face scrunch drunker.

Because that's what I was, he finally said.

I felt so stupid for not knowing what he meant that I couldn't look him in the eye.

Used to bet pro football in college, he finally said again. Big. Through a book and everything. Always won, too. So when my buddies lost and doubled up and lost again and needed money to keep the book from playing wishbone with their legs, I'd have it.

So *Pocket*, I thought.

Had so much dough one night after squareup I rolled a joint with a dime bag of sense and a hundred-dollar bill, Pocket said. Smoked it down to right between Ben Franklin's eyes and gave the rest to my buddies.

I started loading my ceramic Buddha-shaped bong but Pocket took off his aviator glasses and laid face-down on the floor, so I just sat there looking at his flat-backed head, to let him crash. But he kept talking.

Finally lost big one night, he said into the floor. Betting hoops. Took the points against Army and some bowlegged jarhead prayed in a buzzer jumper to bump the lead from eighteen to twenty, with the line at eighteen and a hook.

Shit, I said, even though I didn't know how point-spreads worked back then.

Two grand plus grease, Pocket said. So then I double up on a West Coast pro game and watch the Sonics cream me on cable. After that I quit.

Quit, I said. Betting's nothing I ever did enough to not do and call it quitting, I said.

Yeah, quit, Pocket said. Worked a night watchman job at that Josslyn Art Museum to pay it off. Was four grand plus change in debt but they trusted me with all those expensive paintings because I was in college. A year later I bet once more. Just twenty bucks. Another game right on the number the whole fourth quarter, just like that Army game. Lost by a free throw.

Sonofabitch, I said.

Decided at the buzzer that gambling is either real stupid or real smart, depending on which side you're on.

Got a point there.

And since every bettor ends up dumping sooner or later, the smart side is booking. So I start keeping my buddies' bets rather than calling them in for them. Took a lot of money from them that way, cause if they ever won big I'd just tell them I didn't get a hold of the book. Still lent them ammo when they were down, though. Cause they were friends.

Ammo? I said.

Green, Pocket said. *Cash.*

So they still called you Pocket, I said.

Until one of them found my tally sheet, Pocket said. Fell out of my pocket in the dorm shitter. After that they called me lots of things. Cause they weren't friends anymore. Just bettors.

Pretty soon every night round supper time Pocket and I would be in his basement bedroom, him running his business from his kid-sized desk, me laying on his bed listening.

Don't have the numbers yet, Pocket would say if anyone called before five. What's your figure, I got plus two ten. Two *sixteen*? You're wrong, pal. Add again, call me later.

Bang, the phone would go.

Cockeater can't even add right, Pocket would say to the wall.

Ring.

Yeah, Pocket would say. Theresa. Let me call you later. Yeah. *Bang.*

Theresa was one of Pocket's women, which he had lots of. Never got those women mixed up, though. Not even on the phone.

Learn voices real quick in this business, he once told me. *Have* to.

So all his women, Jane and Val and Theresa and Sue and the rest, used to think they were his girlfriends. Just like Pocket hoped he was Jane's boyfriend. Which he wasn't. Which he knew. Jane's boyfriend was some businessman who was always out of town on weekdays.

With women, Pocket always said, you don't wanna be the fave. Too easy to get upset. You wanna be the dog.

Said that one night just before the phone rang.

Yeah, Pocket said into the phone, I was laying on his fixed up bed with my hands under my head and my elbows sticking out, thinking about who I'd bet. Until Pocket started yelling.

I got sixty-odd college tilts, he yelled at the bettor, nine pro with over-unders, a caller on each ear, and you want me to repeat a Murray *State* spread? You better not be middlin' me, pal. It's six. No. Five. It's five. And put a hook on everything. *Bang.*

Sonofabitch drilled me a new asshole last week, Pocket said to the wall. Took me for two grand. You just know he's middlin' me.

You don't have no caller on each ear, I said.

I know, Pocket said.

Then why you say you do?

So they think I'm big. They think I'm big and they bet big. They bet big and they lose big.

And if they win big?

These stiffs won't. Not for very long, at least. And if they do, I've got the kitty pretty well built up.

Kitty, I said.

A safety deposit box down at that savings and loan on Farnham, Pocket said. Keep everything I make in there except for what I need to live on. You know. Beer. And food.

You mean them eggs and that orange flavored water you keep in the fridge?

Yeah. Beer and that. And vitamins.

Ring.

Yeah, Pocket said into the phone. Yeah. That's four *forty*. Say 'em with the grease figured in. Three and a *hook*. Anything else? *Bang*.

What was I saying? Pocket said to me.

Something about vitamins.

Vitamins? Oh yeah. My kitty.

Pocket leaned his chair back to get something from his front pants pocket.

See this? he said.

Do I look like Helen Keller? I said.

Want me to answer that like an honest man? he said smiling, and then he leaned toward me. He held a tiny copper-colored key between his finger and thumb.

To the kitty? I said.

Yeah, Pocket said. I wanted you to know in case I ever get busted and need bail money. Someone'll have to run to the Savings and Loan, and I'd rather not have it be some lawyer.

Why no lawyer?

Can't trust those bastards. A lot of my college buddies were studying to be mouth-pieces.

How am I supposed to get bail when the kitty key's in jail with you? I said.

It won't *be* in jail with me, Pocket said. It'll be here, he said. And he put the key under the left back leg of his kid-sized desk. I only have it on me around squareup, he said.

And if you get busted on squareup?

I'll call you, Pocket said.

With your one phone call.

Yeah. And don't try anything smart, cause we're the only two that know about that kitty and I keep track of the total. And you know what I did to that professor.

Pocket smiled, and I did too.

How much is in there? I said.

Never enough, Pocket said. But getting there. Maybe ten grand. He held his thumb real close to his dialing finger. That's only this much in hundreds, he said.

Then he got up and walked over to the busted wash machine and reached in and pulled out one of them big yellow envelopes.

See *this*? he said.

Yeah, I said.

Now this is sealed, so don't go looking in it, but I want you to give this to the old boy if anything ever happens to me.

I was ready to ask him what he meant by that when I figured it out.

What's in it? I said instead.

A few things I wrote, Pocket said. To the old boy. See the old boy used to play nosetackle for Iowa.

A Hawkeye, I said.

And he wanted me to play college ball like him.

You never played?

In high school I did. But not in college. Too slow, the scouts said. Won all these trophies, had my name in the paper a thousand times for high school, but I was too slow for college.

So you never played.

Not in college. They can fix too small in the weight room, but there's nothing they can do about too slow.

Plain bad luck, I said.

You got it. Went to college anyway, though. On the old boy's savings.

And then you got thrown out for hitting that professor.

And the old boy hasn't talked to me since.

So you got the last word in. In that envelope.

I wouldn't call it that.

You got one of them kitty keys in there?

No. Can't duplicate those keys.

You got a note telling him what to do with the kitty key?

Why you asking all these questions? Pocket said. He smiled, and I did too. The only way you're getting ammo from that kitty is if it's my bail money, Pocket said. Or if you bet lucky. You still like the Sixers tonight?

How many you giving? I said.

Got them at a pick, Pocket said, and he looked at me real serious.

The *Trib* had them getting three, I said.

Ring.

Yeah, Pocket said into the phone, and when he got to yelling at the bettor I got to staring at the pipes on our basement ceiling, thinking about the Sixers at a pick.

Put twenty on the Sixers that night. They dumped by one, which meant that if Pocket had gave me the newspaper line I would've hit. A forty-dollar swing, plus grease.

Next night I was kinda mad at Pocket for dicking with the line, but we still talked and joked like friends. I doubled up on the Sixers and they dumped again, which I couldn't believe, and which put me down forty-four.

Next day I didn't bet. Or eat. The only cash I had was thirty-some dollars, with squareup coming up a good week and a half before my next unemployment check.

Next night the Sixers played the Celtics, this time I bet against the Sixers cause it was at the Garden. Got so nervous before the news came on that night I couldn't eat, which was good because the Sixers beat Boston on the board, and which put me down eighty-eight.

I don't even want to think about the next two days, all I have to say is that when you bet on a road team playing on cable it's like eleven thousand idiots are in your living room cheering for you to lose money. And also that after them two days I was minus two hundred some.

Next day I rode it all on the Lakers. They were ten point faves and not on cable so after a hit off my Buddha bong I fell asleep on the couch until someone knocked on the door, I thought for sure it was Pocket coming home to get scores from the news.

But instead it was this red-haired Val chick I never seen before but who Pocket once told me how she looked naked, which he said was not as good as a black-haired girl.

Where's John? she said, which was Pocket's birth certificate name. He and I are supposed to go out tonight.

I don't know, I said, even though I knew he was out with Jane cause it was a weeknight and Jane's boyfriend the businessman was out of town.

You don't have to lie for him, she said. I know he's a book and that he's probably out collecting.

You're right, I said, which was another lie because squareup was the next day, I knew that because if the Lakers didn't cover that night I'd have to pay up somehow.

Could I come in from the cold and have a cigarette and wait for him? Val said. We had a fight last night and I have to see him.

Yeah, I said, even before I meant it.

Someone hit a parlay for twelve grand on John last night, she said. I just want to make sure that's why he was pissed.

Probably why, I said, even though I hadn't heard about no twelve grand. I figured the reason Pocket fought with Val was because Jane had just told him she wasn't sure she wanted to have a second boyfriend because she wanted to marry the businessman who was never in town.

Val sat on the chair across from me. She had a pretty face for cigarette smoking and after she shook out her match I turned on the TV cause it was almost time for sports scores to come on.

John talks about you a lot, she said when I sat back on the couch. I didn't like hearing her say John instead of Pocket. The only other time anyone called him John was his phone bill when I brought in the mail.

If it's good stuff it's lies, I said.

Val didn't smile, she just kept looking at me and smoking, and right then I remembered Pocket saying how it's best to be the dog with women.

The weather part of the news was on the TV and I started getting nervous about my Lakers bet. Val and I watched TV without talking and a commercial came on. Val crossed her one leg over the other and it started bouncing up and down real fast. You want a beer? I finally said.

Sure, she said. She smiled, and I did too.

I never drank Pocket's beer but Val wasn't my woman and I figured what the hell, if I can't think of anything to say, the least I can do is give her a beer. Only there were no Buds in the fridge, just Pocket's gallon of orange flavored water and eggs. I found a couple clean glasses and poured the orange flavored water and Val watched me bring hers to her. There was a car commercial on TV. Sports was next.

All we got to drink is this, I said.

Looks like a winner, she said, with her leg still bouncing. She smiled again, and I did too.

I sat down and pretended to watch the commercial and knew that she had it bad for Pocket and that she probably felt like a dog around him because he liked Jane, and that this meant that she wanted me, Konat once said that's the way women are and I could just feel him being right again.

I tried not to think about that but there was nothing else to think about except that the orange flavored water tasted like the fridge smelled, and that I'd be seeing my Lakers score any minute.

Then the scores started rolling and I subtracted mine out in my head. I thought the Lakers covered by a free throw, but then I subtracted on a piece of paper and they'd only won by nine, not the eleven I'd thought, so instead I *lost* by the free throw, which put me down over four hundred.

Sonofabitch, I said, and I remembered how Konat used to say that the problem with unemployment is that you can't work it for overtime. I also remembered the time Pocket told me to never double up when you're down big.

The thing was, Pocket knew I was down and booked me anyway.

I couldn't think of anything but the minus four hundred some, I didn't have the exact figure but I didn't want to pencil it out because I didn't have the money anyway.

Val asked when Pocket would be back from squareup and I felt so sorry for her that I lied again, I said, Not for a while, he went out with a buddy after squareup.

Does this buddy have a woman's name? Val said, her leg still bouncing.

I looked at her eyes and right then got real tired of lying for Pocket, so I said, Yeah. Jane.

Val's leg started bouncing faster, and then she asked where the bathroom was.

I took a hit off the Buddha bong while she was gone. When she came back she sat on the couch next to me and did a bong hit herself. I thought about what Pocket said about the way she looked naked and everything got real quiet. And then I felt her looking at me, so I looked at her. And then it happened. So quick I never even took my glasses off.

After we finished, when she was putting her one leg into her panties, she said, It's fine with me if tonight stays our little secret.

Right then I knew what Pocket meant about being a dog with women.

I was thinking of that when Val said, Well?

She looked so stupid without her cigarette or anything, her legs bent out like a frog's when she snapped her panty elastic onto her waist, and even though it felt better than I thought it would, now I had to think about getting some kind of infection, maybe the one Konat had the time I walked into our bathroom and he was taking that syringe to himself.

Well I don't know, I said. If you don't mind I think you should leave. Or did you want to stay for another one of them orange drinks.

You're *mad*? Val said.

Of course not, I said. Just tired.

You seemed a little nervous, she said. What, don't you screw very often?

I screw when I want, I said, which was a lie cause I hadn't done it for years before that, plus I'd just done it without really wanting to.

So are you gonna tell him? she said.

I guess you'll find out, I said.

You're mad, she said.

Maybe you should just leave, I said.

Maybe, she said, and she lit another cigarette and left.

When Pocket came back that night red-faced drunk we did a few hits off the Buddha and then he took off his glasses and put them and his change and wallet and stuff on the Salvation Army coffee table, which he always did before he laid down drunk on the wood floor to bullshit with me.

As soon as he laid down there I said, Guess what.

What, Pocket said.

Guess, I said.

I don't know, Pocket said. The Lakers covered and you're back to even?

No, I said. The Lakers dumped. I owe you four something.

Why you sound like you're smiling then? Pocket said.

Cause it's kinda funny, I said. You know that redhead Val that's got it for you?

Yeah.

I made love on her.

You *what*? Pocket said, and he sat up and looked at me.

I made love on her.

Pocket's face turned redder. What you go and do something like that for? he said. I oughta beat the cream corn shit out of you, glasses and all.

What you so mad about? I said.

YOU FUCKED MY WOMAN! Pocket yelled, and he stood up and stared at me with those slanted eyebrows and his eyes misaligned like some kinda crazy goofcock.

Pocket

She's not your woman, I said. You don't even like her.

I like her, Pocket said. I spend *money* on her.

You don't even like the way she looks naked, I said.

I think she looks *great* naked, Pocket said, kicking the coffee table so hard that a leg went flying under the TV and the Buddha did a swan dive into the floor, smashing into a million pieces that spread out like marbles from a busted bag.

I stared at the one piece of the Buddha next to my little toe while Pocket picked up his glasses and wallet and change from in between the other pieces, and then I said to him, You're just pissed cause you lost twelve grand on that parlay last night. And tomorrow's squareup.

What are you talking about? Pocket said. I didn't lose no twelve grand. Where'd you get an idea like that?

Val, I said.

So you went ahead and plugged her, he said. He walked to the door and left without even closing it, and when he didn't come back I felt more alone than ever.

Next day was squareup, so I went downtown and pawned my clock radio for ten bucks so I could at least put a dent in what I owed Pocket. But Pocket didn't come home that day, or the next day or the day after that.

The day after *that* was Saturday. I was watching a Nebraska hoops game and was pissed because according to the Gold Sheet the Huskers were tough dogs and I wanted to pile on them and win back my money, and now they were winning the game outright, but Pocket still wasn't home.

Right after halftime there was this knock on the door, I thought it was Pocket without his keys or something.

I opened the door and it was Val, her nose was red and running and blowing white cigarette smoke into the cold.

Where's John, she said.

He's out, I said.

When's the last time you saw him? she said.

Few days ago, I said.

He say where he was going? she said. And then I saw the newspaper under her arm and that she was shivering and that her eyes were red, too, not just her nose.

No, I said.

She took the newspaper from under her arm and started unfolding it with her cigarette between her fingers. You see this? she said.

She was unfolding the section with the weather map on it, and I only read the Sports, so I said, No.

And then she held it in front of my face and pointed to this article about this guy's body they found in a hefty bag in the trunk of a car after a police wrecker had taken it to one of them impounding lots. The guy's head had a bullet in it and the cops didn't know who he was.

I think this might be John, Val said, real nervous like.

You're crazy, I said.

He owed a lot of money, she said. For a long time. He told me that.

He never told me that, I said.

You never slept with him, she said.

He's my best friend, I said.

He's your only friend, she said.

You're crazy, I said. You just want me to make love on you again. Why don't you just leave?

I'm being serious here, Val said, and her eyes almost looked like it but not enough for me to believe her. I really think it was John, she said.

Then do the cops a favor and identify him.

I can't. I have a boyfriend and everything. I thought you might identify him. You being his roommate and all.

I don't think that was him in the hefty bag, I said. I think he's gone cause he's pissed at me for making love on you.

It says here, Val said, that the victim was twenty-five to thirty years old and was dead for a little over forty-eight hours. That sounds too much like John for me to ignore it.

Right then I remembered hearing about a girl they found naked and dead in Kearney but they couldn't identify her or tell if she was raped because buzzards had got to her before the search party did. And suddenly everything felt real different. Then I remembered Konat telling me that women will do just about anything to sleep with a guy if they have their mind set on it, so I said to Val, You just want me to make love on you again. And that's the reason he's gone in the first place.

Why would I want to do that again? she said.

Cause you're crazy, I said, and Val left crying.

Next Tuesday I was sure Pocket would be back any day and I was leaving the house to go to the Seven Eleven when this Buick pulled up, with Iowa plates. An old man and an old lady got out, and just when I reached the sidewalk the old lady said to me, Is this where John Tilleson lived?

I looked at her real close and she had that same baby's nose that Pocket had, so I said, Yes, ma'am. You're his mother?

She looked me in the eye when she nodded and she wasn't crying or anything, in fact she looked kinda mad, so I told myself that Val was paranoid about that hefty bag deal and that Pocket had just gone home to his parents.

We came to get his stuff, she said. If you don't mind.

Not at all, I said. And then I thought, She's so calm, Pocket can't be dead. And that made me shiver.

Pocket's dad looked at the yard and wobbled from side to side as we walked up the porch stairs, he didn't have very broad shoulders for a Big Ten nosetackle but then again, guys his age don't lift weights and he was probably a quick sonofabitch when he played for Iowa. From the way things looked, if Pocket got his size from anyone, it was his ma.

We walked through the living room right past the coffee table Pocket kicked the last time I saw him, it was wobbly even though I used Superglue to put that leg back on.

I led them into the basement and when we were all down there, Pocket's ma started taking the sheets off his bed as if she did that kinda thing every day. I watched her the whole time and she never looked ready to cry, not even once.

Then she went to the cardboard closet Pocket brought down from Konat's room after Konat left here, and took all his pants and shirts and things and hung them on Pocket's dad's arm, which he held straight out. With all them clothes on there, Pocket's dad looked a lot stronger than I first thought.

Then Pocket's ma pulled a big baggie from her purse and stuffed all of Pocket's underwear and socks in it, and when she was done with that I was staring at the storm window Pocket fixed when he moved in, and I felt sad, not because I thought Pocket was dead, but because living with his parents in Iowa might be worse than dead, with the same chance of him ever coming back.

I was looking at that window when Pocket's dad started making these crying sounds.

I told myself that he was crying because Pocket had been busted, not because he was the guy in the hefty bag. But then Pocket's dad said, with his voice real high, Do you have any idea why? And he was looking at me.

It wasn't easy watching that old Hawkeye wipe his red face with his handkerchief, so I looked back at the storm window and shook my head no, and everything felt real different all of a sudden, like midnight on New Year's Eve, but backwards. And worse. Everything even *looked* different.

When Pocket's ma and dad started walking to the stairs, I said, Wait.

I went to the busted wash machine and got the yellow envelope and gave it to Pocket's dad, in his free hand.

John told me to give this to you, I said, and I probably would've started crying right then if I'd have called him Pocket.

What is it? Pocket's ma said.

Pocket's dad managed to open the envelope, and he started reading a letter in Pocket's handwriting, which was all that was in there. Right then I remembered the kitty key and the ten grand and I thought, Maybe they killed him cause he refused to pay. I wanted Pocket's ma and dad to leave so I could see if the key was under the desk leg, which made me feel guilty.

He just told me to give that to his dad, I said to Pocket's ma. If something happened.

Then Pocket's clothes slid off Pocket's dad's arm and Pocket's dad hunched over and pulled his handkerchief back out and started crying even louder.

Let's go, honey, Pocket's ma said. Honey. She looked at me and I picked up the clothes and she led Pocket's dad by the hand up the stairs and out of the house. She said goodbye for both of them as I put the clothes in the back seat of the Buick, which Pocket's ma drove as they took off.

As soon as those Iowa plates disappeared around the corner I ran back inside and down the basement stairs and looked under that left back desk leg for the kitty key, feeling guilty and lucky at the same time. Only it wasn't there. I looked under all the desk legs to make sure and it wasn't under any of them or anywhere else around there. Then I thought it out. What made the most sense was that Pocket used the kitty key to pay off his bettors that squareup day after I last saw him, but the ten grand wasn't enough for someone not to shoot him.

Now everything felt even more different so I went upstairs and smoked a joint and a half of sense and laid down on the couch with my hands under my head and my elbows sticking out, like I used to on Pocket's bed while he took calls. I thought about the four hundred some I owed him and how that bullet in his head brought me back to even, which again made me feel guilty and lucky at the same time, and then I fell asleep.

When I opened my eyes I was face-down against the couch's damn upholstery, my arm hanging over the side, my fingers almost touching a piece of the Buddha bong I must have missed when I swept up the day after Pocket left.

That piece of the Buddha made me remember how Pocket kicked the table right before I saw his flat-backed head leave here for the last time, which made me remember why he kicked the table, which made me remember making love on that stupid redhead Val, which happened just because someone missed a free throw in that damn Lakers game.

When my eyes focused better, I saw that the piece of the Buddha was part of a pile of stuff you always see under couches, it looked like dust and some hair and a penny. A penny from Pocket's change he kicked off the coffee table, I thought, and I stretched my arm to pick it up. Like him having this penny in his pocket would have kept that bullet from his head when his kitty wasn't enough, I thought.

Only when I picked it up it wasn't a penny. It was a key, tiny and copper-colored, and pretty soon warm and sweaty, cause I was holding it between my finger and thumb like Pocket used to, back when he did the booking and I was broke and stupid about point-spreads.

| Arin | *The Dead Fly on the Dashboard* |
| Hailey | |

I HAVE AN EARLY MEMORY of standing in line at a Tas-T-Freez behind a group of nuns. That summer I was eleven and my dad had decided that we would all pile into our station wagon and road trip from where we lived in Baltimore to Mt. Rushmore. We were driving through the armpit of America in ninety-degree heat in the dead of August, 1976. That year being the bicentennial, and my dad being the usual corny dad-type, we laid down a soundtrack of our country's greatest patriotic anthems, family sing along style, as the station wagon windows featured a moving picture of amber waves of grain that went on and on and on. Dad begrudgingly agreed to stop the car somewhere in Ohio for a rest. He insisted that up until that point we were making "damn good time."

The summer sun in the Heartland of America burns through the sky and chars your skin like the fires of hell. My skin was wet with sweat and my stomach was wrung into knots as it had been since we pulled onto the turnpike and left Baltimore. As I shielded my eyes and wiped the moisture from my forehead, I took little comfort in dreaming of the strawberry malt oasis that I had been anticipating. I felt like I was going to sweat and faint and cry and I just wanted to break down and tell those nuns everything.

Most of my friends back in Baltimore were Catholic and they all said that you could tell a priest or nun anything and they would never tell a soul, even if what you did was so bad that you were going to hell for sure. I wondered though, as I took the first sip of my strawberry malt, that those priests and nuns would probably have to tell God about what you did if it was so bad you were going to hell, otherwise, how would he know to turn you away if you tried to sneak into heaven? I had tried just forgetting about the whole thing. I thought maybe if I could practice forgetting and fill my knotted stomach up with strawberry malts, I could make it so that the whole thing never happened. But there's nothing like sitting in the back of a hot crowded station wagon with your mom, your retarded little sister and your dad belting out their rendition of "Home On the Range" to make you tune out and sink into the quicksand of your own thoughts.

My sister really is retarded. I don't just hurl that word at her because she's my bratty little sister or anything. Believe me, the kids in our neighborhood would never let me forget that my sister's a "'tard." Ever since she was born I have heard the

237

names like bricks being thrown at the back of my head as I walked through our neighborhood, and when she started getting old enough to play with the rest of us, things only got worse. It's no secret that kids are just about the meanest little creatures of any species on the planet. Well, the king of the demons himself lived in my neighborhood and he went by the name of Billy Westin.

Every year when it got to be warm and the sun wouldn't go down until way after dinnertime, most of the kids in my neighborhood played kickball in the street until the street lights came on, at which point every kid in America would groan and start dragging their feet back home. Billy Westin was always one of the team captains and he would pick all the same kids, all boys, every time we played, for his team while the rest of us just prayed that we wouldn't be the last to get picked, which was probably one of the worst curses of suburban childhood.

"I'm takin' Sam, Bobby, Josh, Jason, and Alex," declared Billy, flashing a grin of gapped, buck teeth at Scott, the other captain.

"All right, I'll have Jimmy, Paula, Michelle and Miranda, I guess," offered Scott. It wasn't bad enough that my name was last, but did he have to add the "I guess?" I pretended not to notice or care and ran towards the team huddle like all the other kids. You couldn't cry. That was the worst possible thing you could do in my neighborhood.

As I squirmed my way into the group and craned my neck to hear Scott whisper the game plan, I heard my sister, running across the street and calling my name the whole way.

"Miranda, Miranda, Mom says to let me play, Miranda. Can I play, Miranda?"

My sister jumped onto my back and wrapped her arms around my neck before I could do anything, say anything to make it so that this wasn't happening to me. Scott looked up from the huddle as did all the other kids to look up at Miranda, Amazing Nerdgirl, last to be picked for kickball and a retard's sister.

"Scott, let's let her play," I attempted, "She kinda knows how and she won't mess anything up, okay, I promise."

"I don't know, Miranda, I mean . . ."

Billy came stomping over to our group like an angry umpire.

"What's this? No way, no retard's gonna play with us!"

"Shut up, Billy," Even I was surprised by my guts. "This isn't your team, so just shut up!" By now I didn't care that the kids always said getting on Billy Westin's bad side was like digging your own grave.

A resonant "Oooooooooh" rose from the group of kids, who had now gathered in one big circle around Billy, my sister and me.

"What did you say? What did you say to me Miranda, retard lover? Come on, say it to my face!"

"I said, shut up, Westin! Julie can't help it, she was born that way, okay?"

"Oh, she was born that way! Looks like it runs in the family, so why don't both of you go home and practice for the Special Olympics or something?" Billy's mouth exploded open in a cackle of laughter. I wished the gap between his front teeth was a fissure in the Earth that would swallow him up forever. My face turned red and my eyes started to burn. I was going to cry. I could feel it. So I knew what I had to do. I grabbed Julie by the wrist and pushed our way through the group. As I dragged her towards home, I heard Billy chanting "Tardo's going home! Tardo's going home!" Some of the kids laughed along, but most of them were silent.

That night I suffered through my parents' interrogation regarding the day's events as we sat at the Formica-covered kitchen table, silverware clinking against plates in an uncomfortable rhythm.

"So I heard that some of the children were making rude comments about your sister today?"

"Yeah."

"And so what did you say back?"

"I told them to shut up and then we left."

"And did you tell them, Julie can't help it, she was born this way?"

"Yeah, mom."

"Good girl, Miranda. See Julie, what a great sister you've got?"

Julie smiled and laughed, letting meatloaf fall out of her mouth and onto the heap of mashed potatoes on her plate. I looked outside. It was dark and the air had an orangeish glow that made everything look like it was in a dream. The streetlights were on.

"Mom, can I be excused? I wanna say bye to some of the kids since we're leaving tomorrow."

"Sure, sweetie, fine. Don't stay out too long, it's dark out."

"Yeah, mom," I called as I let the front screen door slam behind me. I walked out to the sidewalk and looked up the street. Sure enough, all the kids were heading home, moving down the street like a big black storm cloud. Kids dropped like raindrops from the group as they went to their houses to the sounds of "Bye, Sam, Bye Paula, Bye Alex! See ya tomorrow!" I sat myself down on the front lawn and waited. I knew that by the time the cloud reached my end of the street, Billy Westin would be the last little raindrop to come falling down.

"Hey, Billy, come here," I called, not too loud so that my mom wouldn't come out of the house to teach Billy the proper way to address my sister.

"Hey Miranda, how's the 'tard?" Billy's lips parted to display his usual diabolic smile.

"Cut it out, Westin. I've got something really cool to show you, but if you're gonna be like that, then just forget it. Do you wanna see it or not?"

"What is it? Did Julie learn some new 'tard tricks?"

"Billy, if you don't knock it off, I'm not gonna show you the snake I found in my dad's shed. If my dad sees it, he'll kill it, but if you want you can take it home as a pet. If you want."

"What kinda snake?"

"I don't know, I'm not a zookeeper. Come back to the shed and you can see it yourself."

"Okay, but make it quick. The streetlights are on, you know."

I led Billy around to the side gate of our house and let him in to the backyard. My dad had constructed a tool shed out of pine boards three summers ago. He said the pre-built aluminum sheds from Sears just couldn't compare to "good sweat and craftsmanship, damn it." So the shed sat against the backyard fence like a little miniature house. I unlocked the door to the shed. It was darker than the night air outside in there. It smelled musty and when we walked in together, cobwebs streamed across our face like sticky curtains.

"So where's the snake?"

"I don't know. I usually see it over there, in the back corner."

Billy walked over towards the pile of fertilizer sacks and yard tools that sat in the back corner of the shed and disappeared into the darkness.

"Well, how are you gonna see the snake Westin, it's too dark. Wait here, I'm gonna go get a flashlight."

I turned around and walked out of the shed. From outside I could see into the darkness. Billy crouched in the corner, searching for a snake that he wouldn't be able to see even if it had been there. I turned the key in the doorknob slowly and quietly until I heard a quiet "click" that sliced through the dark silence in my mind. Then I slammed the door shut with a loud "CRACK" that sliced through Billy's. I heard him jump to his feet and scuffle across the floor in the shed.

"What are you doing? Miranda? You closed the door, 'tardo. It's locked! Come on, let me out!"

I stood with my arms folded across my chest and listened for awhile. Billy's cries weren't very audible through the thick boards of the shed. At first, I could hear the shouts easily, but they soon subsided to whines and finally I had to press my ear to the door to hear Billy fall to the floor and start to whimper. My lips parted in a satisfied smile and I realized how good Billy must have felt tormenting all the kids. I had planned to let Billy out in the morning, just so he'd learn that he couldn't mess with me anymore and he'd get in big trouble with his parents. When the morning sun came breaking into my bedroom window, I was going to go out to the backyard and let Billy out, telling him he'd better keep quiet or I'd tell all the kids that I heard him crying because he was afraid of the dark.

When my mom came into my room, it was still dark. "Miranda, wake up, honey. We're going to get an early start this morning. Get up and get dressed, brush your teeth, your dad wants to be on the turnpike by 6:00 a.m."

I got out of bed, still in sleep, and mechanically performed my morning routine. By the time I sleepily put my toothbrush back into its cup on the counter, my mom was herding my sister and I out the door and into the car. My dad turned around in the front seat.

"Bright and early, little pumpkins," he breathed coffee breath into our drowsy faces. "Nothing like getting on the road before the mornin' can catch up with you."

The station wagon started with a jolt and a rumble and we rolled out of the driveway and away from our house. I sat with my eyes half open as we drove through our neighborhood with its familiar houses and the shopping center with its familiar grocery store and signs, still lit as if it were the dead of night. We pulled onto the turnpike and I felt the car accelerate to the speed it would carry until our first stop of the trip. My dad pulled back his sleeve and examined his watch.

"6:00 a.m. exactly. We should be in Akron by noon at least. Ah, if there's no goddamn traffic, we'll make fine time, fine time," my dad smiled, a serious road tripper, he was more than satisfied with his military-like time synchronization.

As the sights at the side of the turnpike turned unfamiliar, my eyes and mind finally came out of sleep and the world began to exist again. I realized we were on the road, it was morning, I was hungry. The thought came to me like someone shaking me out of sleep: I had forgotten to let Billy Westin out of my dad's shed.

The tingle of adrenaline came gushing out of my stomach, leaving it in a hard knot, and rushed out to my fingertips, where it butted itself against the skin, trying to escape in a mad rush. I had forgotten to let Billy Westin out of the shed. The thought repeated itself in my mind like a skipping record album. I had forgotten to let Billy Westin out of my dad's shed.

"Dad, I need to go back. I forgot something really important." I closed my eyes as I said the words, picturing Billy Westin curled in the corner of the shed like a medieval prisoner, sweating, thirsty, hungry and hallucinating images of the fictional snake.

"I'm sorry pumpkin. We're on the road now, on the road and making fine time. There's nothing important enough to go back and ruin our pace. There are stores in South Dakota, fine stores all across this fine country to get anything you need, God bless America. Don't you worry that pretty head of yours, angel."

My mom and sister heard their cue and broke into their first official anthem of the trip, my dad joining in soon after. Oh my God, I thought, 6:00 a.m. on the first day of our trip and my family is already singing "God Bless America" at full volume. And I forgot to let Billy Westin out of the shed.

He could be dead by now, I thought. Sure Billy's a jerk, but I just wanted to scare him, show him that the neighborhood kids weren't such babies after all, especially not me. What if I killed Billy Westin? My picture of the neighborhood kids carrying me off the asphalt kickball field high on their shoulders faded into one of them hissing at me, throwing rocks and calling me "Bully Killer."

All I could think of was getting back home, letting Billy out and begging him not to tell his parents a word about it. I'd promise to buy him a real snake, whatever kind he wanted. I thought about this and I thought about how much better a strawberry malt could make me feel.

"Dad, I wanna stop. I'm thirsty. I want a strawberry malt," I again closed my eyes as I pleaded my dad to make the impossible true, hoping that when I opened my eyes my dad would be handsome and charming like those on TV and would say, "Sure, honey. Was there something you wanted to go back for? We're only an hour and a half out of town. . . ."

"You and your strawberry malts, sweet cheeks. By God, I tell you one day this girl's gonna just balloon up like a fat red strawberry. Sure, we'll get you a malt, pumpkin. The best the Heartland can make. Only four and a half hours to Akron."

It was obvious that trying to convince my dad to stop or even slow down below the speed limit before the first designated stop of the trip was futile. I slumped down in the seat and looked out the window. The hills were turning brown under the summer sun, and autumn was coming. Autumn meant school and school meant another year of teasing from all the kids, especially Billy Westin. Without their leader, would the other kids be so bold and outspoken? I felt a flash of hope, wondering if everything could change, if I could be a new kid next year, having conquered the ringleader of all school bullies. Then I remembered. I forgot to let Billy out of the shed. Billy could be dead.

The morning sun came beating into the car. The air outside was already a scorching eighty-five degrees. I closed my eyes and thought of a strawberry malt. Slowly, the knot in my stomach began to relax, just a little.

"Honey, it's awfully hot in here. Let's roll down the windows. I'm practically suffocating," my mom turned to my dad, her voice sweet and singing. My mom was the TV mom.

As my dad obliged her simple request, which of course did not require any sort of break in pace, Julie straightened up in her seat, her mouth open, but no words coming out. She leaned forward, her arms on the back of the front seat and her head tilted towards my mom.

"Mom, what's suffocating?"

"Well, Julie honey, it's like when you're really hot and there is no air and you can't breathe."

"Could you die if you were suffocating?"

"Well, I suppose you could, honey."

My sister turned to face me. "Miranda, do you think Billy Westin is suffocating?"

I looked up, still slumping, my sweaty eyelids stickily folding back into my forehead. I looked at my sister. Was it possible that she could have seen everything? Moreover, was it possible that this trip could get any worse? I sat in disbelief, saying nothing. I wished it was all a bad dream and I'd wake up in my bedroom, sweating from the morning sun coming through my window and shining on me under the quilt. I wished that I'd get up to let Billy out of the shed and he would never have been there.

"Hmm . . . sweetie? Did you have a question about something?" My mom sang, turning around halfway in her seat to face Julie, who still leaned forward in her seat towards my parents even though she had presumably been talking to me.

"Yeah, mama, I was asking Miranda if Billy was suffocating in dad's shed, but she didn't answer me . . ."

"What? What would Billy Westin be doing in your father's shed? Miranda?"

I wanted to tell them. Maybe my dad would have actually gone back if I had told them the truth about me. I could have been a murderer. I looked up and saw a fly twitching on the dashboard. I watched its body pulse and listened to it buzz rhythmically as it fried to death, trapped under the windshield and grilled by the shiny black dashboard. That could be Billy Westin right now, I thought. That could be me in hell for all eternity.

"What? Huh?"

"You heard your mother, young lady. Why on God's green Earth would Billy Westin be in my tool shed? We expect an answer, and we want it now, Miranda Jean." My dad was capable of making the most serious of fatherly threats while occupied by a myriad of different tasks at once. As his voice raised to a higher and higher volume with each syllable, I stared at the speedometer. The red needle never sank below fifty-five.

"What? I don't know what she's talking about."

"Julie, honey, did you not just say that Billy Westin is in daddy's shed?"

"Yeah I saw Miranda and Billy in the backyard . . ."

"We were playing," I interrupted, "We were just playing in the backyard."

"Nah-uh, Nah-uh, you shoved Billy in dad's shed and shut the door and Billy was yelling," my sister shouted at the top of her lungs in the hot, crowded car. She looked triumphantly at my parents and then at me. Before I knew it, six pairs of eyes were staring me down like a murderer in a precinct lineup.

"I have no idea what you're talking about. We were just playing."

"Miranda Jean," my dad enunciated, "Now your sister has just given us an account of a scene in which you have pushed one Billy Westin into the backyard shed. Now I for one would like to know the truth, and I'd like to hear it from you, now."

"I told you, Dad . . ."

"Miranda Jean Bogg . . ."

I was pressed to the wall. I wanted to tell them all about it, after all I hadn't meant to do it and I did it because I had had enough of Billy Westin picking on my little sister. Which is why what I said next seemed to just fly out of my mouth like words from someone else's mind intended for some other conversation someplace else. "I can't believe you're taking her word over mine. She's *retarded*, for Pete's sake. She doesn't even know how to tie her shoes. She can't even play kickball. And you believe *her*?"

Time seemed to stop at that moment, though the car kept barreling along the stretch of highway, never slowing, never stopping. The six eyes again focused on me, the pressure of their collective stare squeezing me into a tiny ball on the backseat. No one said anything. The air inside the car was hot and thick with silence, and a cloud of guilt surrounded me. Not only was I a liar and a possible murderer, I had just sold out my poor retarded little sister, whom I had spent my whole life up to that point protecting and sticking up for.

The car moved steadily. The sun beat down relentlessly onto the top of the station wagon, but it didn't stop there. It burned its way through the windows, frying the poor fly on the black dashboard and subtly reminding me of the kind of climate I had to look forward to for all eternity. I was going to hell for what I had done, that was all there was to it. I told myself that I had to accept that I was a murderer, I was a liar, I was going to hell and maybe even prison for the grisly torture of Billy Westin. Nothing or no one could help me. When I am on death row, walking the long walk to the chair, no one will be able to help me. Not even the priest they make go with you in case you decide you want to be good after all. I will tell the priest, "there is nothing you can do. I know I am going to hell, I accepted this when I was eleven, when I committed this crime. I know you won't tell anyone what I have told you, but don't sweat it. I'm sure God already knows what I did and that's why I'm going to hell. Besides, I wouldn't want you to risk your job lying to God for me or anything."

"Half hour to Akron!" my father trumpeted as if the conversation that transpired earlier had indeed never taken place. My mom smiled into the visor mirror at me.

"And we'll get you your strawberry malt, hon." That was my mom. Ready to send me off to Antarctica and forget she ever had a daughter one minute and treating me like her own perfect TV kid the next. It seemed like I should be the one treating her like the domestic sitcom queen that she was. It seemed like I should be the one begging for forgiveness. I was a murderer and I was totally resigned to it. Maybe she didn't know it yet, maybe God hadn't even found out yet. I knew, though, just as sure as I knew that there was no way my dad was going back to Baltimore. I knew I was lost forever. I knew I was no longer just Miranda Jean Bogg, a kid from Baltimore who liked to play kickball and was basically a good kid because she always did her homework and chores and always defended her little retarded sister. I was going to hell.

I had to make my peace with God. He had to know what I had done. But if the priests and nuns are the ones who talk to God about what's going on in the world and they're not allowed to tell anyone what people do, then how was I going to let him know? How could I tell him what I did? I was sure with all the priests and nuns in the world plus all of the people whose prayers he has to listen to, it's got to be really hard to get through to him. But I had to tell him. I had to tell someone about it and at the moment, God was the only one I could think of who I could tell that would believe me and that wouldn't yell at me or ground me for the rest of the summer for ruining the family trip.

"Mom, who can talk to God? I mean who can get through to him best?" I asked the only person I had known in all my eleven years to have an answer for every question.

"What? What brought this on, sweetie?"

"I don't know, just thinking."

My mom looked out the window. "Well, when I was a girl your Grandma sent us kids to a Catholic school for a few terms. Lets see. Honey, I would say that the nuns and the priests talk to God just about every day. Yes, that's right. See, with nuns sweetie, it's like they're married to God. And when you're married, you tell each other absolutely everything. No secrets. Isn't that right, Stan, honey?" My mom reached over and smoothed the back of my dad's hair.

"Yep, baby, you said it right there. You know, Miranda, pumpkin, someday when you make a man a good little wife. . . ."

The Dead Fly on the Dashboard

I tuned out right there. I couldn't think about all of this. I was eleven years old and going to hell for lying and torturing and making fun of my own sister and I didn't need to think about marrying or even kissing a boy someday. I just needed to find some nuns fast, before my little secret worked its way out, like a worm peeking out of an apple or exploded me into a million pieces all together.

We pulled into the Tas-T-Freeze on the outskirts of Akron. My sister was guffawing with joy as she jumped out of the car and ran towards the building with the giant Fiberglass ice cream cone perched on top, like a holy shrine to the god of American summer. I climbed over the front seat and looked at the fly on the dashboard. It was long dead now, and it lay on its back on top of its fried wings, its legs in the air.

"Come on, sweet pumpkin, I thought you just couldn't wait for that strawberry malt." I looked out the window to see my dad, mom and sister standing as if they were posing for the first family portrait of the vacation. They looked like a perfect American family, without me. I got out of the car and headed towards them. As we walked toward the line of wrinkled road-tripping families, teenage couples french kissing and neighborhood kids with their allowance grasped in their sweaty hands, I saw them. A group of nuns stood off to the side, under the shadow of the giant ice cream cone. One of them was sipping through a straw what appeared to be a strawberry malt. As I approached her, my stomach in knots and sweat seeping out of every pore on my body, I thought of how much better I would feel after a strawberry malt. But that would have to wait. I had to tell God about me, about what I had done.

"Excuse me ma'am, but I understand that you're God's wife and that you tell him everything, no secrets. Well, okay I'm gonna tell you something and you have to promise to tell him, because it's real important and maybe he can do something about it or maybe not but he has to know. Okay here goes. I locked Billy Westin in my dad's shed. He's a real bad kid but he doesn't deserve to die and he could be dead right now. Plus I lied to my mom and dad and I sold out my little sister, who is retarded. Anyways I know I'm going to hell and everything, but can you please tell him because I want to start being good and I don't want to tell any more lies. Okay? Thanks."

By now the entire group of nuns stood staring at me, their faces blank. Being the ones that could get through to God best, I'm sure they heard some real wild stories, but none as sordid as this. It seemed forever that they looked at me, saying nothing. I was getting used to the pressure of staring and silence. This will come in handy, I thought, when I'm walking down the long hall to the chair.

"Oh dear," the nun with the strawberry malt finally spoke up, "my goodness."

"What?" I searched the nuns' faces. It couldn't be that bad. It couldn't be worse than hell. "What? What?"

"Well, my child, you seem to have a dead fly stuck in your hair. There," the nun said as she reached her fingers into the stringy clumps at the side of my head and pulled out the fly, the fly that fried to death on the dashboard of my family's station wagon. "There," she said as she laid its dead body gently into the bushes. "There, child."

Tina
Wiatrak

Heroes

MY DAD used to tell us these stories about World War II. He never called it The Big One or anything. I'd get him to haul out these photos crammed into the top shelf of my grandmother's closet. She lived with him and his new wife Sandy, which didn't thrill Sandy or my grandmother. He'd dig through a pile of baseball caps from past Teamster Local 285 Labor Day parades. Behind these was the bag, soft as flannel, of photographs from the war.

He told us how in England the girls in pubs called him Monty. We thought this was pretty funny since his name was Marv. We would point to the frayed photographs of him and a buddy in front of a B-17 bomber, their arms hanging in a cocky way over the shoulders of two English girls.

"Who's that, Dad?" one of us would ask.

"Oh Christ," he'd say and earnestly try to recall her name for a good minute. "I think her name was Lucy. Her friend, the one with Ernie, her name was Ethel."

"Very funny," my older brother Gregory would say. That's not what you told us last time.

"I made a mistake last time, smart ass."

We were sitting on the front porch eating ice cream, French Vanilla, and my brothers and I got him started. "Tell about the time you stole the plane and flew to France from England."

"Commandeered," he corrected and then told us the story like we hadn't heard it fifty times before. Like we were strangers. "I was a Sergeant in charge of eight—ten guys. We did maintenance on army planes. They flew us to different airfields, wherever they needed us. Hell, sometimes not even an airfield. We'd go to wherever a plane crashed and try to patch it up. We worked on the skin, the sheet metal on the outside of the plane. B-17s, P-51 Mustangs, but bombers mostly. If it was too far gone, we salvaged parts."

"What about the boots," said Kel, my middle brother. He was letting the ice cream drip through a hole in the bottom of his cone onto some ants.

"Don't," I begged my dad. "Not the boots."

246

"Sometimes, if we got there soon enough . . ."

I stuck my fingers in my ears and started to hum.

" . . . we would come across a boot. Some GI's boot and it wasn't empty all the time. Sometimes there was a foot in it."

A large truck roared past with half a dozen license plates on its rear doors. Some leaves from the elm tree rustled and then surrendered, floating onto the thick green lawn. "Christ, did you feel that breeze." We held our faces up to the autumn sun like it was water and we were on fire. We all three of us knew that he would give anything to be in that truck going somewhere exotic like Texas or California.

"The foot," reminded Kel, his palm spread flat against the warm pavement, impatient with an ant for not crawling onto it.

"Don't," I pleaded.

"Hey sweetie, I can't change the facts. War is a dirty place." He put his arm around me. "We were a pretty tight group of guys, Red and Morty, he's gone now and Tony. He was a crazy one. Italian guy, carried pictures of his wife and his girl-friend in his wallet. He used to say when his kids grew up and got married, the girlfriend was going to be at the wedding. 'They know my situation,' he'd say. 'Look at me. You can see I'm too much man for just one woman.' God, he was somethin' else."

He took a cigarette from his shirt pocket and tapped it on the back of his hand. "It was a Friday night and we finished early on this bomber. We had two days leave comin' and we were bored with. . . ."

"Fred and Ethel," Gregory interrupted.

"Am I telling the story or am I telling the story?"

We all laughed. "Go ahead," said Kel, pulling leaves off of the lilac bush, using them to bomb the ants. His knee vibrating up and down. His foot tapping on top of my dad's. Dad put his hand on Kel's knee.

"So we were bored, da-da-da and three days leave and right, we commandeered this aircraft along with a pilot pal of ours. Officially we were taking the plane for a test flight across the channel to make sure everything was acey ducey."

We groaned when he said old sounding stuff like that. "Acey ducey," repeated Kel.

"So me and my crew took off for Marseilles for a few days of R and R."

"Rest and relaxation," Gregory informed us.

"No kidding," said Kel, his knee pumping away again, mumbling something at Gregory. He thought he was safe because dad was right there. Gregory swatted him, my dad swatted Gregory. I smiled.

Dad took out his lighter and handed it to me. It was gold and smooth, almost oily feeling. With two hands I ignited it. Sizzling, I held it up to his cigarette. I could feel my brothers' eyes glaring, trying to burn holes through my shoulder blades. I felt pretty icy so it didn't hurt. He inhaled and exhaled real deeply and the three of us watched the smoke jet from his mouth in a steady stream which seemed to last longer than it actually could have.

"We had a surprise waiting for us in Marseilles. No sooner do we land than boom, the shit hits the proverbial fan."

"Shit," repeated Kel like he was memorizing it.

"We got Kraut planes like bees."

"Krauts," mumbled Kel picking at a scab on his arm.

"Germans," explained my dad,"and they're strafin' us. So we jump under the wings and duck our asses. Behinds," he corrected himself. "It's dark out and they only see our headlight and the headlight of the plane across the runway that's about to take off. So they think we're one larger plane with two lights and blow the hell out of the runway between us."

"How come you didn't jump into the gun turret and blow 'em away?" Gregory's face was turning kind of red.

"That's movies. In real life you don't do that shit. You want to play baseball with your buddies. You want to kiss a girl." Kel groaned and gagged as he strangled himself.

"I woulda' shot somebody," said Gregory.

"You're talking out of your ass," said my dad. He flicked his cigarette into the grass.

"I just know what I woulda' done."

"You're young," said dad, like that explained it.

"I woulda' ducked my behind," I added, really thinking ass. Both boys swatted me in the head.

"Not in the head," warned my dad as he rubbed my hair.

"It's too late," said Kel.

"She already has brain damage," Gregory finished it for him. I didn't care what they said since it was my head resting on my dad's lap.

"Gregory, an ethical question here. Say you're in a concentration camp. You're pulled out of line. The line of people headed for the gas chamber."

"Yuck," I said not knowing exactly what a gas chamber was. I reasoned out that it had something to do with gas and gas had to do with gas stations which smelled bad and were not places I wanted to be waiting in line to go.

"It's hypothetical," my dad said. I shook my head yes like I understood. Pulling his hand down the length of my braid he stroked it like a cat's tail. Kel glared at me until I met his eyes. He knew I had no idea what hypothetical meant. He shook his head like he was the most disgusted he'd ever been. Even more disgusted than the time I got my foot mangled up in the spokes of his new bicycle and he had to get it out. There was blood splattered on the tire, spokes, seat. Blood everywhere.

"You're given the choice of being put to death or becoming one of the prisoners who does maintenance on the gas chamber. Filling it up. Cleaning it out and so on. Which would you choose?"

"Dad," whined Gregory.

"Think about it. Which would you choose?"

"Neither."

"You have to choose one," said Kel.

"Shut up gonad."

"If he can't, he can't." My dad lit another cigarette.

We watched the cars drive by. Kel and I counted Mustangs. We all waved to Rita next door as her screen door squeaked open and she sat in her lawn chair pretending to read *The Detroit News*. Rita once worked as a receptionist in a dentist's office and loved to pull out the loose teeth of any kid in the neighborhood who would let her. She tied a string, one end to a doorknob, the other end to the loose tooth and slammed. We three pulled our own loose teeth.

"Die," blurted out Gregory. "Otherwise you'd be yellow and a traitor. Ethically speaking."

"Wrong. In my opinion, you would choose to live. Hey we are all animals after all and it's against our nature to choose to die. When the time comes you choose to live." He got this charitable grin on his face like the Jehovah's Witnesses do when they come to your door. Like he felt sorry for him for being so ignorant and not even realizing it.

Gregory got broody after that. Dad threw the football around. Gregory didn't try to trip Kel or tackle me once from behind. Finally he said, "What about heroes? They choose to die sometimes." He placed his fingers on the laces of the football and threw a perfect spiral to dad.

"I don't know whether heroes choose to die. I think most of them don't have time to think. Like that time, I'm out on my route and I'm passing by this house. There's this lady out front screaming and pointing to the roof. 'My baby,' she's screaming. I jump out of the truck and sure enough there's this kid up on the roof. He's a little younger than you Rae, maybe four or five. He's got on this Superman cape and it looks to me like he's thinking maybe he can fly. So I hustle up there bip, bip, bip. I talk to him real gently and get him to take my hand. I tell him the wind isn't good for flying. I throw up a leaf or something to show him the wind is no good. In a way I guess you could say I risked my life to save his."

"No you didn't," said Gregory. "Climbing a roof isn't that big a deal."

"Jesus, Gregory you're not getting my point. The point is people who do heroic things don't think about them. They just do them. If they had time to think. . . ."

"No," said Gregory cutting him off. "Some people are heroes." He threw the ball hard, back at dad.

"Cut the crap Greg." You could tell he was getting pissed by the way he was smiling, his teeth all clenched.

"You're not a hero. So just don't say that, okay." Gregory was clenching his teeth too. He walked toward my dad.

"Don't. Just stop."

Kel took my hand and pulled me up onto the porch. He had tears in his eyes which always made me feel like a tornado was coming. My heart pounded too fast when stuff like this happened. I looked around to see who was outside. Rita next door. She wasn't even pretending to read anymore. She sat with the paper falling off her lap, staring. I didn't look anywhere else.

The look on their faces before, that's what scared me. Before anything happened. The hairs in my nose started to sting and I started to pray, in my head so I wouldn't cry. I didn't know how to pray right so I made it up. "Dear President Kennedy who art in heaven, thy kingdom come. Please make them stop. A bolt of lightning. Not to kill them. Just to knock them out. It doesn't matter just stop them, stop them, stop them, please, please, please."

My father and Gregory looked the same. Jaws twitching, necks red, fists, eyes looking into each other like they were staring into a mirror. "Heroes don't hit women." Gregory said this hard so spit flew out of his mouth and his chest heaved.

Kel said, "Jesus." The tears were welling up on the edges of his eyelashes.

It's hard to say who threw the first one because it happened real fast and I was crying. I remember little things. Rita coming over and yelling, "A son shouldn't hit a father." She was all hysterical and I hated her for ever being born. Kel tried to get in the middle and got punched in the eye like usual. He laid on the sidewalk crying. Sandy, my dad's new wife, yelled, "No Marv!" from inside the screen door for a while before she called the police. I remember thinking Mom would have jumped right in. My grandmother yelled, "Shit!" and turned up the volume of the Tigers game on the radio.

By the time the police came, my dad had Gregory pinned. There was blood on their shirts but you couldn't tell who it came from. It might not be anything, anyway. Sometimes you bleed a lot from a very small cut. Especially on the face.

Inside the kitchen Sandy gave lemonade to the policeman, my dad and Gregory. It was the seventh inning stretch, so my grandmother brought Kel ice for his eye. She rushed back to her room holding her hand over her mouth having forgotten to put in her dentures. She left her door open a crack so we would think she was listening.

Kel locked himself in the bathroom and wouldn't let me in so I stood with Sandy. She wouldn't fight with anyone. That's why my dad loved her. She smoked a cigarette and blew the smoke out of the kitchen window. Her fingers were tickling my arm. She kept checking to see if I was smiling. It made me want to smile for her but I couldn't. The policeman took over and they talked about different things. My mom and dad's divorce. How Gregory wanted to live with my dad full time not just on weekends like we were now. How he was tired of being, "The little man," in my mother's house. The policeman said stuff about Gregory and hormones and what a tough time it was for a kid his age. My dad was saying how he knew all this. That Gregory had to try to understand and be mature. Gregory knocked over the chair on that one. His glass of lemonade went flying. Sandy started to cry and wipe it up. "You see," she told the policeman, "It's an impossible situation." Sandy didn't have any kids of her own.

Then the policeman said something strange. "Son," he said, "when you see red, you just take this football and you go across the street to the park and you throw it against the ground as hard as you can as many times as you need, until you don't see red anymore." We all looked at each other kind of puzzled. It was then that I realized just because someone was a policeman and believed he knew what he was talking about, didn't mean that he did. "Son, you should never take out your anger in a violent way against another person. So will you promise me you'll use that football instead of your fists the next time you get pissed off." He hesitated when he said pissed off like it wasn't natural to him.

"I'll try."

"Don't try," said the policeman, "Do it."

"Okay," agreed Gregory.

"Now go and take care of that lip."

"Yes sir."

The policeman shook his hand. "You're a good kid. You just got to get a handle on things."

I hated the policeman as much as I hated Rita. I hated him knowing anything about us. My dad was outside talking to him, leaning against his patrol car. They were both smoking cigarettes. The policeman was laughing. Gregory was pounding on the bathroom door. Kel was yelling at him. I wanted to run outside but I didn't want anyone looking at me. Sandy was heading for the front door to get my dad. I wanted to run so fast I couldn't be seen by the human eye. Run to a place where no one knew me. Where I'd have to learn a new language and people would believe me when I told them I was normal. That I had no cavities, no scars, no recollections of that sound you get inside your head as it smacks up against the red of a cold brick wall. A place where my memories were filled with stories read to me at bedtime. Where quiet doors opened into quiet rooms, where tornados never came.

The Woman Who Lives in the Avocado Grove

JACQUELINE LIVES IN A HOUSE in the middle of an avocado grove. Her husband, Frank, and her daughter, Pauli, used to live there too, in this house surrounded by the trees with the low and reaching branches, but now Jacqueline stays alone.

This morning Jacqueline wakes up with tears streaming down her cheeks. It is appropriate. She sits bolt upright in bed and sees herself in the mirror above the dark wood dresser. It is Pauli's twenty-first birthday today. Jacqueline says, "Maybe Pauli will call," but Jacqueline knows this will not happen.

She finds her own voice comforting, almost like hearing another person. Right after Frank left, hearing herself speak in the silent house startled Jacqueline, but she has grown quite used to it.

As Jacqueline sits on the end of the bed and pulls on the faded jeans and t-shirt she wore yesterday, she looks at the picture of her mother on the dresser, the one in the silver frame.

Frank, who will soon want to discuss their divorce, called last night. He is coming by for lunch today because it is Pauli's birthday.

"Pauli'll come back." "She's just being a teenager." "They all do crazy stuff sometimes." The other parents had tried to console Jacqueline and Frank after Pauli disappeared one day. Sixteen years old. The police insisted on calling her a run-away, one of thousands. The policeman said, "You don't know teenagers."

"But I do," Jacqueline insisted.

And that is what scared her. Jacqueline had taught history at Valley Center High, a school just six miles from the avocado grove, for fourteen years.

She knows teenagers. She knows how they can turn on you, like snakes. "Pauli gives great head." She found it scrawled on her blackboard one day in pink chalk. And Jacqueline was a favorite teacher among the students.

Jacqueline begins to wander through the house, not to visit its rooms, but to look out in each direction into the grove that contains her. She sees Miguel out by the tool shed. He is repairing a section of the drip system. It needs constant attention. The water comes from the Colorado River—dirty water. If Frank lived here, he would spend half of every day checking the nipples under each tree, making sure grime had not clogged the inner workings. But Frank no longer lives on the land and so now bigger sections of the system break down more frequently.

Frank believed Pauli ran away, too. Jacqueline couldn't stand it that he thought this. Jacqueline knew someone had kidnapped Pauli, someone had stolen her.

Pauli learned to walk while Frank and Jacqueline learned to graft one kind of avocado onto another's root system, turning trees that produced watery Zutanos into ones covered with creamy Fuentes, large, roundish Bacons, pebbly skinned Haases. It was spring, a Saturday, when Pauli took her first steps. The family had gone down to the trees growing along the river. Frank prepared the understock, splitting it several inches through the smooth, straight-grained section. Jacqueline, having shaped two of the scions into long and gradually tapering wedges, was easing them into position in the understock when she looked up and saw Pauli with her tiny hands wrapped around the edge of the wheelbarrow, pulling herself up into a standing position. Jacqueline had seen this maneuver hundreds of times before, but on this day her daughter's eyes caught hers. In them was a glimmer, a wonderment, the primitive awareness of a moment when the impossible is transformed and becomes, suddenly, reachable.

Jacqueline whispered to Frank, "Look," as Pauli's little fingers loosened their grip. They both watched as their daughter stepped out into the unknown. Back then that had seemed so exciting.

The screen door slams closed behind Jacqueline as she walks out into the August heat. At the sound, Miguel faces her. He takes a step back, says, "Good morning."

Jacqueline can only nod. On her way over to the sprinkler spigot she feels the blades of grass between her bare toes. Miguel's son is Pauli's age. He works summers at the nursery in town. Frank works there now, too, but he comes to the grove to talk to Miguel. Frank worked these fifteen acres too hard and for too long to simply walk away, or go very far. He lives in an apartment above a t-shirt store in town. It was supposed to be temporary, but it didn't turn out that way. He moved in there three years ago. When Jacqueline thinks of his apartment, she imagines the old one where he lived when they were students. She will not go to the new one.

Jacqueline met Frank at the Mediterranean coffee house on Telegraph Avenue in Berkeley in 1964. They were both freshmen, but Frank was older; he had been in the army for four years. At the time a lot of boys had stopped shaving, or had never started, and peach fuzz covered their rosy cheeks, but Frank had a real beard, and his black eyebrow hairs met in the middle of his forehead.

Frank had seen Jacqueline on campus, in Murphy Hall. Jacqueline knew because this was Frank's opening line: "Aren't you in Mueller's history class?"

To Jacqueline, Frank seemed mature, sophisticated. He found Mueller's historical perspective "narrow and simplistic." Frank had a room of his own, off campus. Jacqueline had seen the place, a big, old, Spanish-style house with a painting of Castro on the front gate. Some of the people who lived there called it a commune. Frank called it a place to crash.

Frank took her there that afternoon, to his room with the Indian bedspreads billowing down from the ceiling and the candles lining the window sills. A flag hung across the opening to the closet. A water pipe occupied the desk, and books on Buddhism, nihilism, and existentialism covered the floor beside the mattress with the grayish, crumpled sheets.

Frank eased Jacqueline in through the door and asked, "Want a bowl?" as he walked over to the water pipe and picked up one of its octopus arms.

Jacqueline had smoked pot before, but always discreetly, in thin joints, or in the shells of emptied cigarettes—never in a hookah pipe.

"Come on, let's get high," Frank said.

Jacqueline turned around on the heel of one foot. By the time she had completed her circle, Frank was breaking the buds.

Pauli was smoking pot at twelve. Jacqueline caught her doing it in her room, alone, and had a different reaction than she ever would have expected. She pretended she didn't see it or smell it. She pretended she didn't notice her daughter's glazed eyes. Pauli used a bong pipe. Jacqueline found it the next day while Pauli was at school, hidden inside a roller skate. Jacqueline never told Frank because she knew Frank would want the three of them to *discuss* it.

Jacqueline hasn't taken any illegal drugs in almost fifteen years. The only buds she worries about these days are the ones on the avocado trees. If blooms come too early, a frost might take a whole crop. But it is summer now, the fruit is set, the avocados are on their way. In six weeks it will be time to pick the majority of the Haases. She finally manages to say "Good Morning" to Miguel.

Jacqueline inherited the land from an uncle, her mother's brother, a man she hardly knew. He had bought the place years before as an investment. Jacqueline had never even been there, to that valley sixty miles north of San Diego and thirty miles inland from the Pacific Ocean. She knew three things about the area: it had mild winters, hot summers, and soil that avocado trees loved. Soon after the title papers arrived, she and Frank drove down to see what an avocado grove actually looked like.

As the probate lawyer drove around the perimeter of the property, all the green seduced Jacqueline. She barely heard him, the pluses and minuses: six of the fifteen rolling acres covered in producing trees, flood damage from the heavy rains in '63. Then the lawyer took them down to the end of the dirt drive, to the buildings. When Jacqueline saw these, when she stepped out of the car and stood in front of them, a calm came over her, something captivating. Unlike the other ranches in the valley, the house and the work shed on this property sat in the middle of the grove. Avocado trees enveloped them.

Jacqueline and Frank spent the next five days working their way through the old house, poking into the attic, the basement, the closets, making love on the sun porch. They found magazines from the forties, and a drawer full of crocheted antimacassars. And in the heat of the afternoons, they would go out to the grove, to one of the trees near the house, and they would each grab hold of one of those low, horizontal limbs and pull themselves up onto it. They would each straddle a branch and talk.

Jacqueline gave birth to Pauli the first summer they spent in the valley and Jacqueline fell in love with her new baby, and Frank and Jacqueline fell in love with each other all over again.

Jacqueline's own mother had died when Jacqueline was six years old, of a brain tumor. Two weeks after the funeral, Jacqueline's father gave her the framed picture that stands on her dresser today. In the picture Jacqueline's mother, at twenty-one or twenty-two, leans against the Chrysler Building in New York City. She is smiling. She has on a fashionable forties dress and her eyes look clear and bright. The same day that Jacqueline's father gave Jacqueline the picture, he put all the rest of his wife's personal belongings into the car and drove them down to the Goodwill. The photograph in the silver frame was all Jacqueline had left of her mother. She turns from Miguel and walks toward her house.

In Berkeley, in the house with Castro on the wall, Jacqueline and Frank found out all sorts of things about each other. They spent afternoons, whole weekends, in that bed with the crumpled sheets. Jacqueline loved the sex of it, the sensuality—the smells, the tastes, the sounds. She also dreamed of a little girl, but still she was careful, for Jacqueline also knew how she wanted it to be—for them to have a real house and real jobs, to be a real family.

Frank was spiritual, back then. Jacqueline's soul intrigued him. He found it mysterious, as curious as the night sky, he used to say. He described it as something dark that lurked inside of Jacqueline, between the practical part, the way she alphabetized the books on the shelves under the window, and the secret part, the way she, each night, placed her brush and hand cream and the silver-framed photograph of her mother on the thrift-shop dresser they had bought the week Jacqueline moved in. It would be years before Frank actually understood he would never be allowed to see into the dark, that Jacqueline would keep him out forever.

Jacqueline and Frank smoked the hookah pipe a lot when they lived in that house. They dropped magic mushrooms, hitched into San Francisco to the Filmore to hear Hendrix and Joplin. They marched against the war, threw water balloons at policemen in riot gear, took bad acid and ended up at the Free Clinic begging for hits of Thorazine. Frank practiced Buddhism for a couple of years—he ate nothing but whole grains and lentil beans and he always smelled like incense. Jacqueline was more focused. She spent most of her free time concentrating on classes—Social and Intellectual History of Europe to 1815, History of War in the Modern World, Comparative Socialism. The subject intrigued her.

Pauli hated history. Pauli hated science, English, art history. Pauli hated school, period. Nor did she like baseball, or after-school ballet lessons. She didn't want to play with any of her classmates, whom Jacqueline would have happily had over any afternoon. To witness her daughter choosing this isolation pained Jacqueline in places she hadn't known before. Jacqueline ended up screaming at her little girl, "Talk to me." Pauli glared at her and turned around and walked away. Frank tried to help. He read books, he talked about boundaries and respect. Jacqueline screamed at him, "Don't interfere." Frank screamed back, "We're talking about our Pauli."

Jacqueline knew exactly how she and Pauli should be together. She had known this since she was eight or nine years old. It was supposed to be like it would have been with her mother—them in harmony with each other and with the world. Jacqueline experienced the need for this primitively, like hunger, like desire. And when it didn't happen she felt senselessly terrorized.

But that can only last for so long. In time, Jacqueline stopped feeling anything.

Frank cried in Jacqueline's arms one night after he tried to make love to her. He wanted back into his wife's heart. Jacqueline could only see Pauli, ten years old now, standing in the schoolyard, her mouth filled with grass, dirty tears streaking her cheeks, three of her classmates around her, jeering, and Pauli yelling back at them, "Sons of bitches."

Standing at the kitchen sink, Jacqueline watches through the window. The rainbird spits water out over the small patch of lawn by the back door of the house. Miguel works at the bench in front of the shed, cutting a piece of plastic pipe with a hack saw. Jacqueline says, "I should help him." But she doesn't move, for she knows she can no longer cooperate. Jacqueline tried to get Pauli's picture onto the milk cartons in L.A. county. Mr. Morley, the man in charge, said, "Sounds like a runaway to me."

The last fun Jacqueline had was on the night in 1985 when the Rolling Stones played the Los Angeles Coliseum. Frank and Jacqueline's best friend from Berkeley, Ted, was visiting. He had arrived that Friday morning. He had been down in Baja, Mexico, fishing, and when he and Frank walked in through the screen door, Ted looking so big and tan and relaxed, his blond hair gleaming, Jacqueline started to look forward to the weekend, to the three of them spending some quiet time together. Pauli, now a surly fifteen, was going to ride up to Los Angeles with a group of friends for the concert and then spend the night at an aunt's house. Frank had called the aunt to confirm Pauli's plans. Jacqueline had been against the trip. "I don't trust her," she had said to Frank. Frank's attitude was more accepting. "She's a teenager, Jacqueline. Cool down." To Jacqueline, Frank sounded like some new-age guru. He didn't understand how wrong it all felt to her—their lives, everything that happened in the house. Pauli had shaved her hair off above her right ear. Jacqueline could hardly bear to look at her. She dreaded being around her own daughter, yet was anxious when Pauli left the house. Still, part of Jacqueline felt relieved that Friday afternoon when Pauli got into the car with her friends and they all drove away.

She breathed the relief out in a sigh as she finished washing the home-grown lettuce she had traded for avocados earlier in the day. Ted was sitting at the breakfast table, a bottle of tequila and a bottle mescal in front of him. He had bought them before crossing back over the border. Ted said, "It's just a haircut, Jacqueline."

By the time they finished dinner Jacqueline and Frank and Ted had worked their way through half the bottle of mescal. Frank and Ted had been at the Stones' Altamont concert in 1969. Drinking shots made the remembering all the more vivid. While Jacqueline and Ted did the dishes, Frank dug out all his old Stones albums from 1966 and '67 and '68. Pretty soon "My Sweet Lady Jane" and "Back Door Girl" and

"Ruby Tuesday" blared out from the living room speakers. Shot glasses in hand, the three of them sang along with Mick Jagger. They sang at the top of their lungs. For the first time in years, Jacqueline actually lived for a few hours without Pauli haunting her. She looked at Frank and felt turned on. She started twirling around the room. Frank and Ted followed her—the three of them dervishes spinning toward some moment of clarity. They emptied the bottle of mescal and ended up dividing the worm three ways, each eating their piece solemnly, like a sacrament.

Just before dawn Frank led them to the highest point on the property, up to where the trees that made the best avocados stood. Ted picked a tree (he said the tree picked him) and they all climbed up into it. Jacqueline, the lightest, stood on the highest and thinnest branch. She hadn't, in years, looked beyond, hadn't really seen a whole landscape. She felt herself open up inside, hard crusts peeling away, as the three of them, there in the branches, watched the sun rise up over the valley.

After Jacqueline turns the rainbird off, she decides to take a shower, wash her hair before Frank comes over for lunch. She looks at herself in the mirror. With the end of a finger, she smooths out the skin around her eyes. She notices that her lips are getting thinner, her nose broader. In the bedroom, after pulling a comb through her wet hair, Jacqueline finds a pair of clean jeans in the dresser, and a blouse, an ironed one, in the closet. She looks out the window, into the avocado trees, as she dresses.

Jacqueline used to love the trees with their hearty leaves, their long, elegant limbs, and that fruit, tender and seamless. And she used to love the house too. In the summer there was no better place to be in the valley than in this house, cooled by the air under that canopy of green. A little breeze would blow through and the house would swell with the sweetest scents—just hints of earth and trunk, and sometimes, late in the afternoon, a trace of alfalfa, especially if Old Man Walker had watered recently. And Pauli was growing tall and strong. Her kindergarten teacher called her a rebellious child, but this didn't worry Jacqueline. A little rebellion never hurt anyone.

By the time Pauli was seven years old, Jacqueline was driving one hundred miles a day to a special private school for difficult children in Escondido. The counselor at the local grammar school had recommended the institution. Pauli simply made no effort to get along with her peers, her teachers, with anyone. And at home, Jacqueline knew, Pauli refused to participate. At meal-times she wouldn't eat if Jacqueline or Frank insisted she use a fork or spoon or knife, and she could go without food longer than either of her parents could refuse her. And sometimes a day or two would pass when Pauli wouldn't utter a word. Jacqueline's feelings started wrapping around themselves, becoming tangled. Every time she tried to think about Pauli, every time she tried to plan a talk with her, she found herself helplessly confused, up against some wall inside herself that she could not get over. Frank wanted to help Jacqueline; he insisted that somehow the two of them could survive anything—that nothing could stop them as long as they were together. But part of Jacqueline lived behind a barrier, in the dark, with her mother, in the cloudy childhood corners, in the time before the tumor slowly compressed her mother's brain and turned her wicked. Jacqueline would not discuss this though, not with Frank, not with a psychiatrist, not with anyone.

Pauli came home from The Rolling Stones concert with a tattoo on her arm—a large rose with "I love Mick" in script beneath it. Jacqueline went crazy when she first saw it, some three weeks after the concert. She happened to walk into Pauli's room one afternoon while Pauli was changing her clothes. Pauli tried to hide the scabby mess on her arm. She said, "You didn't knock." When Jacqueline started screaming and hitting Pauli, Pauli laughed at her. By the time Pauli disappeared she had two more tattoos: a snake around her ankle, and a tear rolling down her cheek.

Jacqueline hears Frank's truck rattling its way up the drive. By the time she gets back to the kitchen, Frank, tall and as thin as he was in Berkeley, is standing in front of the work bench talking to Miguel. When Jacqueline opens the back door, Frank turns, as if sensing her. He waves. "I'll be right in."

Today is Pauli's twenty-first birthday. It is the fifth time Jacqueline and Frank have celebrated the day alone. Yesterday Jacqueline picked up a cake at the bakery, a small one. Frank will come inside in a few minutes. They will make tuna fish sandwiches and share a beer as they eat them. Then they will have the cake. Together, they will cry. Frank will hold Jacqueline and kiss her hair and they will feel themselves break again.

This is the last birthday Frank wants to celebrate. He will tell Jacqueline this as he gives her a present, a picture of Pauli in a silver frame. Pauli will be fourteen years old in the photograph. She will not be smiling, but will look beautiful.

Frank and Jacqueline will sit together, without speaking, for a little while, and then Frank will leave and as he leaves Frank will take the rest of the birthday cake out to Miguel and Miguel will eat it in the shade behind the shed. Later, Jacqueline will take the picture in the silver frame to her bedroom. She will stand it next to the one of her mother.

That night, in a dream, Jacqueline will find herself in a fantastic palace. She will be the tattooed woman, every inch of her body covered in an exotic design. When she looks out the leaded windows, she will see her trees, their trunks covered with tattoos like her own. She will walk out to them and stand, like a goddess, arms raised, chin high. When the wind blows, the grove will swell with the sweetest smells.

For years people in the valley will whisper about the woman who lives in the avocado grove.

Contributors' Notes

FREDERICK BARTHELME is author of nine books including *Moon Deluxe*, *Second Marriage*, *Tracer*, *Two Against One*, *Natural Selection*, *The Brothers*, and *Painted Desert*. He is an occasional contributor to *The New Yorker* and has published in *GQ*, *Kansas Quarterly*, *Epoch*, *Playboy*, *Esquire*, *TriQuarterly*, *North American Review*, *Frank*, etc. He teaches writing at the University of Southern Mississippi, where he also edits the *Mississippi Review*.

CHARLES BAXTER is the author of three books of stories, most recently *A Relative Stranger*, and two novels, most recently *Shadow Play*. In spring of 1997, Pantheon will publish a new book of his fiction consisting of six stories and a novella, titled *Believers*. Also in spring of 1997 Graywolf will publish a book of his essays on fiction, titled *Burning Down the House*. He lives in Ann Arbor, Michigan, with his wife and son, and he teaches in the University of Michigan M.F.A. program for writers.

MARK BLICKLEY is a playwright with seven New York production credits. His short stories and essays have appeared in books, magazines and journals from across the country. He currently teaches writing at Brooklyn College where he received a MacArthur Foundation Scholarship Award for Drama.

KIKA BOMER has a Ph.D. from the University of Washington in Comparative Literature. She has poetry published in the journals *Between the Lines*, *The Howling Mantra*, *The Eclectic Muse*, *Spindrift*, *Space and Time*, among others. Currently she is working on a collection of flash fiction based on Mother Goose rhymes, two of which are in this collection. She also works as a freelance editor of novels and teaches research composition at Front Range Community College in Westminister, Colorado. Kika resides in Lyons next to a river in a house with a huge yellow tabby named Bruno.

GREG BOYD is the author of two collections of short fiction, *Water & Power* and *Carnival Aptitude*. His most recent book is the novel *Sacred Hearts*.

MARK CULL has had fiction published in *Webgeist* and *Texture*. He is the editor of Red Hen Press.

STEPHEN DIXON—born, raised, reared, kicked around and schooled and worked and worked and worked in New York City. Did work other places: Columbus, D.C., L.A., San Francisco, Paris, Redondo Beach, points east, points west, racking up no points tho, all kinds of jobs, finally landed on his head in Baltimore, where he teaches, and has been teaching, in the Writing Seminars at Johns Hopkins University since 1980. He has published nineteen books of fiction. The last two, *Man on Stage: Playstories,* from Hi Jinx Press (Davis, CA) in late 1996, and *Gould: A Novel in Two Novels,* from Henry Holt, early 1997. All the books he has published are fiction: twelve story collections and seven novels. About four hundred and twenty-four short stories have been published too and one poem and two nonfiction articles, the first and last of which was "WHY I DON'T WRITE NON-FICTION" (he can't).

JOHN DOMINI is the author of the collections *Bedlam* and the forthcoming *Highway Trade,* from Red Hen Press. His stories have appeared in *Paris Review, Ploughshares,* and have made Honorable Mention in *Pushcart.*

CAMERON FASE is a student at Moorpark College, California. "Some Kind of Smorgasbord" is his first published work of fiction.

RANDALL FORSYTH was born in a very large small city: Hollywood. Since an earlier brother had been born dead, Randall was a particular joy to his parents. Since he survived birth, he thought he might become an artist too. Recent credits include works in: *Poetry/LA, Blue Satellite, Bakunin, Paragraph, Fiction International, Asylum* and *Beet.* His education includes an MFA from CSULB in Painting and Drawing. He teaches Art in southern California.

KATE GALE has two books of poetry published, *Blue Air* and *Where Crows and Men Collide,* also a novel, *Water Moccasins.* She teaches at California State University Northridge and California State University Los Angeles.

LEONARD GRAY is a former government employee and former non-fiction writer who now writes short stories, novels and plays. "It's for You" is his first published work of fiction.

RICHARD GRAYSON is the author of the story collections *With Hitler in New York* (Taplinger, 1979), *Lincoln's Doctor's Dog* (White Ewe, 1982), *I Brake for Delmore Schwartz* (Zephyr, 1983), and *I Survived Caracas Traffic* (Avisson, 1996). He is a staff attorney at the Center for Governmental Responsibility at the University of Florida.

Contributers' Notes

ARIN HAILEY is a student at the University of California, Berkeley. "The Dead Fly on the Dashboard" is her first published work of fiction.

MARY HAZZARD, a graduate of the Yale School of Drama, is the author of three published novels and several plays. She has been writer-in-residence at the College of William and Mary and has received Yaddo and MacDowell fellowships, as well as an NEA playwriting grant. She lives in Waban, Massachusetts, where she is working on a novel, *Voices of Children*.

TRAVIS HODGKINS is a student of film and philosophy. "75 MPH" is his first published work of fiction. At 16 he started writing for the local daily and at 17 was promoted to an editor position which he quit a year later for an opportunity to live in New York. Now 19, he lives in Southern California and boasts of being the only person he knows who has ever caught twenty-eight lobsters in a single dive.

MONA HOUGHTON (B.A./M.A. CSUN, MFA Vermont College) has had stories in *Carolina Quarterly*, *Crosscurrents*, *Bluff City*, *West Branch* and *The Northridge Review*. A half hour script she wrote, "Leave of Absence," won The Best American Short Film award at the Houston Film Festival in 1988. In 1995 she wrote a script from her short story "The Striptease" for Aronson Films Inc. She teaches creative writing and composition at California State University, Northridge and Pasadena Art Center College of Design.

JORDAN JONES is the author of *Sand & Coal: Poems* (Futharc Press) and the translator of *The Anti-Heaven* by René Daumal (in MS). He recently moved from the shadow of the Reagan Library to the even more haunted penumbra of the Nixon.

NANCY KRUSOE is an L.A. writer most recently published in *Unnatural Disasters*, an anthology of recent California writing, *The Northridge Review*, *13th Moon* (excerpts from a collaborative novel written with Jan Ramjerdi), and *The Best American Short Stories, 1994*. She is currently teaching and working on a novel.

DOUG LAWSON'S work has recently appeared in *Glimmer Train Stories*, *The Sycamore Review*, *The Mississippi Review-Web* and other places. He received the Transatlantic Review Award for Fiction in 1995, was a Henry Hoyns Fellow in Fiction at the University of Virginia, and his collection of short stories will also appear from Red Hen Press in 1997. He founded and edited *The Blue Penny Quarterly* from 1994-1996, and currently edits *The Blue Moon Review*.

JOE MALONE is professor of linguistics and department chair at Barnard College, Columbia University. His stories, poems, translations, and essays have appeared widely; he is the author of *The Science of Linguistics in the Art of Translation* (SUNY Press, Albany, 1988). The story "Now, Now" is from the Park Slope (Brooklyn) cycle

Above The Salty Bay, of which another story, "Ninth Street", was a winner in the 1986 PEN Syndicated Fiction Competition.

ROCHELLE NATT is a reviewer for *American Book Review* and *ACM*. She has published fiction and poetry in *Negative Capability, Colorado Review, The MacGuffin*, and many anthologies. She was a finalist in the Judah Magnes Award and Eve of St. Agnes Award.

LANCE OLSEN, Idaho Writer-in-Residence and Finalist for the 1995 Philip K. Dick Award, is author, most recently, of the novels *Burnt* (Wordcraft of Oregon, 1996) and *Time Famine* (Permeable Press, 1996).

MARLENE JOYCE PEARSON has one book of poetry published, *A Fine Day for a Middle-Class Marriage* (Red Hen Press 1996). She teaches writing and literature at California State University, Northridge and California State University, Los Angeles. She has won the Academy of American Poets Award and twice won the Rachael Sherwood Poetry Prize. She writes poetry, fiction, and is constantly at work on a variety of photographic projects.

GARY JOHN PERCESEPE is a former fiction editor at the *Antioch Review*. A native New Yorker, he was a student of T. Coraghessan Boyle (back when he was just Tom) in high school, and has studied with William H. Gass and Mary Grimm. The author of four books in philosophy, he has a novel in progress as well as a new book on postmodern theory, *Beyond Suspicion*. His fiction, essays, and poems have appeared in the *Mississippi Review Web Edition*, *Enterzone*, and other places. He teaches at Wittenberg University and has a bird named Romeo and a cat named That Baby.

MICAH PERKS' stories have been published in *The Southwest Review, Epoch, American Voice* and others. One of her stories has been nominated for a Pushcart Prize, and she has recently been awarded a Saltonstall Foundation for the Arts grant. Her first novel, *We Are Gathered Here*, was published in 1996. She lives with her family in Ithaca, New York, where she is at work on a memoir.

ROBERT REID has published short stories, essays and plays in *The Prague Revue*, The *Annual Czech Language Anthology of the Jama Cultural Foundation*, *Poems and Plays*, *The International Third World Studies Journal & Review*, *American Culture and Literature* (Haceteppe University: Ankara, Turkey), *Confrontation* and *Fiction and Drama: The Literary Magazine of the National Cheng Kung University*. He has worked at Bilkent University in Ankara, Turkey, King Saud University in Riyadh, Saudi Arabia, The University of Kentucky in Cumberland, Kentucky and Tennessee Wesleyan College in Athens, Tennessee. He teaches Writing, Native American Literature and Asian Literature at the University of Guam.

NORA RUTH ROBERTS is a teacher at Michigan State University and a writer who has published stories and poetry in *Playgirl, Wastelands Review, The Minnesota Review, The Bridge*, and many other places; she started her career with a travel memoir, *The Voyage of Nora's Ark*, published by Funk and Wagnall's. She has published numerous academic articles and presented papers at over a score of academic conferences. The award of a Danforth Fellowship, Helena Rubinstein Fellowship, and grant from the Jewish League for the Education of Women has enabled her to pursue doctoral studies in English at City University of New York, where her dissertation—on three radical women writers of the thirties—won the Carolyn Heilbrun Award and has recently been published by Garland. In addition to writing more stories and poems, Roberts is now working on a new book for Garland: *Ideology and Discourse in Contemporary Working Class Culture.*

FERNAND ROQUEPLAN is a graduate of the Iowa Writers Workshop. XIB Publications recently released his first chapbook, *No Stopping Anytime.* He has other work with *Paris Transcontinental, Xib Review, Indiana Review, The Laurel Review, Greensboro Review, Florida Review, Fiction & Drama* (Taiwan) and *Prism International.*

HELEN SALTZBERG SALTMAN has published essays on John Adams, Ann Bradstreet, and Classroom Research. After retiring from teaching writing and American Literature at California State Northridge, she is writing short stories and has recently completed an adolescent novel. She lives with her husband in cool Kensington, California.

LESLIE STAHLHUT received her MFA in creative writing from Warren Wilson College. She has published fiction in *Bakunin.* She lives in Northern California with her husband, the ceramic artist Mark Gordon, and her two sons.

BRAD WETHERN is a Realtor from the Inland Empire of San Bernardino County. He likes antique cars, beautiful women, fast horses and big fish. "But not all on the same day." This Berkeley graduate is a southern California native and has lived in New York, Chicago, Toronto and as the story included in this anthology reveals—the north spit of Humboldt bay. His most recently published work is "The Eyes of Texas," which appeared as the feature story in *The Animals Voice Magazine.* He is currently working on a collection of his short stories, a novel *Spit in the Wind* and a screenplay *Stewball.*

TINA WIATRAK lives in Santa Monica, California with her husband and five year old son. She loves her family and her friends. She loves to write.

GARY D. WILSON lives in Baltimore, Maryland, with his wife and two sons. He teaches fiction writing workshops for The Johns Hopkins University School of Continuing Studies and directs a writing center at a Baltimore City middle school. His fiction has appeared, among other places, in *Glimmer Train*, *Quarterly West*, *Witness*, *Street Songs: New Voices in Fiction*, *The Laurel Review*, *The William and Mary Review* and *Kansas Quarterly*.

MARK WISNIEWSKI'S novel, *Confessions of a Polish Used Car Salesman*, is published by Hi Jinx Press (Davis, CA). Over fifty of his short stories are published in magazines such as *American Short Fiction*, *Fiction International*, *The Missouri Review*, *Fiction*, and *Crazyhorse*. He teaches creative writing at CUNY and fiction writing correspondence courses for the UC-Berkeley Extension.